THE
CITY
BENEATH
THE
HIDDEN
STARS

SONYA KUDEI

THE
CITY
BENEATH
THE
HIDDEN
STARS

bhc
press™

Livonia, Michigan

Editor: Jamie Rich
Proofreader: Alexa Nichols

Map of The White City & the Realms illustrated by Sonya Kudei.
Copyright © 2022. Used with permission. All rights reserved.
Excerpt from *Det Norsk Bibelselskap* 1930. Public domain.

THE CITY BENEATH THE HIDDEN STARS

Published by BHC Press

Library of Congress Control Number: 2021944668

ISBN: 978-1-64397-310-4 (Hardcover)
ISBN: 978-1-64397-311-1 (Softcover)
ISBN: 978-1-64397-312-8 (Ebook)

For information, write:
BHC Press
885 Penniman #5505
Plymouth, MI 48170

Visit the publisher:
www.bhcpress.com

Dedicated to

Anne, Janet, Diana, Diana's mom, Amy, Alice, Ben, Val from downstairs (I've never actually seen you, but I'm sure you exist), the guy who brought the pound cake, the guy who made a hole in the ceiling, Moko the dog, Dietrich the dog, and all other past, present, and future residents of a certain Victorian conversion in North London (including casual visitors, resident dog-sitters, and repair persons of dubious skills and questionable qualifications).

The Celestial Realm

The Withdrawn Realm

The Threshold

Grič   Kaptol

The Underworld Realm

The White City
& the Realms
S.K. MMXXII

Legend

1. Bear Town Fortress
2. The Queen's Well
3. The Stone Gate
4. The White Tower
5. The Hidden Tower
6. Illyrian Square
7. Mirogoj Cemetery
8. The Little Brethren
9. Dolac Market
10. The Square
11. Manda's Well
12. The Cathedral
13. Stella's tram
14. East Central School

THE
CITY
BENEATH
THE
HIDDEN
STARS

THE STARMAN

A number seventeen tram sat silent and abandoned on the tracks of a turning circle on the outskirts of the city in the middle of the night. On a soft patch of grass inside the circle, a black cat with white paws sat licking its nether regions with meticulous care.

A cluster of anemic trees with limp branches that drooped almost all the way to the ground hovered awkwardly in the background. In the half gloom of a solitary lamp that only barely illuminated the station, the trees looked like some obscure breed of tram fairies that came quietly in the night to tend to trams injured during rush hour, soothing the bruises inflicted on them by jostling pensioners and healing the cuts scratched onto the backrests of the wooden seats by bored adolescents, before disappearing into the ether with the rising sun.

Of course, there are no such things as tram fairies.

This could have been a quiet, boring night like any other. But there was a faint vibration in the air, one with a certain quivering quality that would make the hairs at the back of one's neck stand on end. It was the kind of vibration that suggests that something at last is about to happen.

And sure enough, something did. First, a brilliant flash blazed in the sky, and then a thick beam of golden light zigzagged down toward the ground, spearing into the relatively narrow space between the trees and the tram. The beam soon condensed into a glowing semisphere of light that looked like a small dome tent inside of which someone just happened to have turned on a five-thousand watt lightbulb.

The glow faded, leaving in its wake the crouching form of a man who didn't look happy to be there. In fact, he looked as if he would have preferred to be in any other location in the universe.

This was, in his case, not a figure of speech but a perfectly plausible statement.

The man, who went by the name of Leo Solar, was not really a man, or at least not in the limited sense of the word. Pedestrian concepts such as fly-fishing, dental floss and death were alien to him. At the same time, he wasn't completely unlike a man. He had an almost paralyzing fear of hair loss, which in his case was completely unwarranted since, over the many millennia of his existence, he had never once lost a single hair, not even the time he accidentally slipped, tripped and fell onto a particularly aggressive neutron star whose strong magnetic field nearly bent his forelock out of shape.

Leo was what was in ancient times referred to as a "star daimon" and what is in modern times referred to as nothing in particular, since according to modern theories, the universe is nothing but a vast void characterized by enormous distances expressed by multidigit numbers to the power of other multidigit numbers, a void whose shape may or may not be reminiscent of a donut or a bagel or a Danish pastry.

Being a star daimon, Leo found it perfectly natural to come down from the stars, at least on those occasions when he was summoned, such as the present one. Occasions of this kind were extremely rare, but still not rare enough to his liking.

His name was not really Leo Solar—it was Regulus. He, however, only used the latter for formal occasions, such as the Star Council Assembly held annually at the Starboard Palace inside the right ear of the Horsehead Nebula. Otherwise he preferred the other name, since it had a more natural ring to it. Not to mention that someone once told him Regulus sounded like a digestion supplement.

Leo sighed and, as if making some sort of resolution, raised his head and put on a brave face. And what a face it was—with arched eyebrows, features that could only be described as chiseled and eyes whose pale irises were only slightly alarming. The whole thing was framed by a mane of somewhat frizzy blond hair that almost, but not quite, reached his shoulders. It was an impressive mass of hair that was all bushy assertiveness at the top but morphed into something rather tame and even a bit flat near the ends, as if it had gradually lost interest at some point below the ears. And if this style bore a passing resemblance to a mullet, this was only because where Leo came from, which was space, they didn't know any better.

Leo rose to his feet, looking strong and determined, as if the brief moment of low motivation had never happened. It was the sort of attitude that personal development coaches the world over would have approved of. Unfortunately, there were no personal development coaches around to see it.

Leo's outfit was an elaborate electric-blue affair adorned at the front with three pairs of intricately wrought silver-and-gold clasps. He also had a silver belt with a gold buckle shaped like a delicate eight-pointed star, and there was a long, hooded cape of the same shade of blue as the outfit slung over his shoulders. Both suit and cape were made of the finest artisan fabric such as cannot be obtained anywhere on Earth, except maybe Etsy, and parts of the outfit—strategically placed ones—were interwoven with delicate golden thread.

The area in the direct vicinity of Leo had not remained unaffected by the unorthodox method (at least unorthodox by local standards) of his arrival. The side of the tram that had been in the way of the scorching light now had a wide gash that stretched from the roof all the way down to the ground. And at the spot where the beam had struck, there was now a shallow, round pit. Leo barely gave the whole thing a passing glance.

The cat, seemingly dismayed by the series of untypical events that had just transpired, sprang to its feet and wandered off into the night, its tolerance for inexplicable phenomena having apparently reached its limit.

With a dramatic sweep of his cloak, Leo turned to face the direction where a few faint lights of the sleeping city twinkled sluggishly. Somewhere in the distance, a melancholy dog let out a single feeble bark. The dog was probably the only creature still awake at this hour apart from the white-pawed cat (although the cat might well have gone to sleep by now).

Leo tightened his jaw and began to stride purposefully toward the city lights. He had barely taken a few steps when he was stopped in his tracks by a sudden screeching sound. Leo realized two things at the same time—first, he was standing in the middle of a road, and second, a car had ground to a halt less than a hand's breadth away from him.

The car in question looked as if a group of blind, sentient aardvarks had come together in a scrapyard to assemble a tub out of scavenged bits of metal but in the end changed their minds and decided to use it as a trolley instead.

An old man with thick glasses held together with black duct tape stuck his head out of the window on the driver's side.

"Careful, young man!" he shouted with the too-loud voice of the near-deaf. "I nearly hit you with my car. If someone less eagle-eyed than myself had been behind the wheel, you'd be lying dead on the side of the road now."

"I should thank my lucky stars then," said Leo.

"Where are you off to on foot this time of night? Don't you know there are no trams at this hour?"

"I was just taking in a bit of air."

"If the city is where you're going, I'd be happy to give you a ride."

"No, thank you," said Leo.

"Are you sure? I was on my way there myself, going to the market a bit early to beat the morning rush."

Leo considered the situation. On the one hand, the car was a death trap. On the other hand, he was immortal. "Go on then," he said and got into the car.

THE WHITE CITY

I n a hidden corner of the eastern flank of Central Europe (or the western flank of Eastern Europe, depending on your point of view), in a green valley of a winding river, there is a city that certain locals, in those rare moments of inspiration, refer to as the White City, although the less poetically inclined, as well as those who don't know anything about the place other than that it exists, call it Zagreb.

This is not the kind of noisy, hectic city that makes people stressed, obese, prone to rants about the accelerating pace of modern life, and likely to have a midcareer breakdown followed by an extensive backpacking trip to a remote country. If anything, the place is fairly sober and subdued. If the White City were a character in a Regency novel, it would be one of those comely, levelheaded types that ends up marrying the parson.

The city has a sprawling east-west axis and a somewhat stunted north-south one, formed by a moderately high mountain on one end and a river on the other. It is between these two natural landmarks that the city proper has evolved like a bacterial culture in a large petri dish. The center of this coordinate system is the main square, known simply as the Square. This is a proper city center if there ever was one. If you happen to be at the Square, you can be sure that you are at the very heart of the city, like a yolk in the center of a fried egg or a circle in the center of a mandala.

Towering above the northern end of the Square is the medieval core of the city built on two hills, Grič and Kaptol, although the height difference between the two is so pronounced that Grič has earned itself the nickname Upper Town,

whereas Kaptol…well, it hardly looks like a hill at all. The less altitudinally endowed of the two hills boasts only a gentle slope going from the northeast corner
of the Square up to the cathedral.

If you were a bird surveying the architectural features of the two hills from
the air, this would be, first of all, pointless, since birds are terrible at architectural
surveying, and second, somewhat bizarre because, providing that you managed
to overcome your severe avian disadvantages, you would notice that the two hills,
when seen from above, bear a striking resemblance to a pair of lungs. This, as
previously stated, is quite bizarre. It is also completely irrelevant. Therefore, you
would soon turn your attention to other things.

As you soar higher into the air (moving ever northward, of course, since
there would be no point flying over the boring south), you would notice the trees
becoming even wilder, taller and more all-over-the-place the closer you get to the
unchanging background presence of Bear Mountain.

Sprawled on top of one of its upper slopes in an ominous way are the ruins
of Bear Town Fortress, the bane of the White City.

Well, one of its banes. The city has had, since its dubious founding during
the murkiest pseudohistorical quagmires of the Dark Ages, more than its fair
share of banes. And, according to an unverified source discovered in an illuminated manuscript by a Benedictine monk who subsequently set it on fire while
attempting to use it as a hair straightener over a tallow candle, a fair share of
banes for a city of Zagreb's size is about three per 732 years.

Since, however, it is a well-known fact that the White City has had on average five banes per 258 years, it follows that the city's share of banes indisputably
exceeds the fair level.

The design of Bear Town Fortress is extraordinarily simple. Someone, possibly Einstein, once said that things should be made as simple as possible, but
not simpler. Bear Town Fortress is simpler. It does what it says on the tin, namely fortification, and is not bothered about anything else. One would not gain
much architectural satisfaction by inspecting the edifice at close quarters. Indeed,
to appreciate the fortress aesthetically, it is advisable to be as far away from it as
possible.

Although the rulers of Bear Town Fortress were many, few have earned a
special place in the locals' hearts for their acts of kindness. Nobody can say for
certain how many masters Bear Town Fortress once had or even who all of them

were, but one thing is sure—whoever they were, they were up to no good. Their universal favorite pastime seemed to have been finding different ways to oppress the residents of the city below by using a varied repertoire of feudal methods ranging from tried-and-tested ones such as pillaging and taxation to novelty ones such as mutilation by trained birds.

The most notorious resident of Bear Town Fortress was undoubtedly Barbara Cilli, a fifteenth-century despot whose penchant for black clothing inspired the local citizenry (and peasantry) to give her the epithet "Black Queen."

According to the many local legends that have sprung up since the Black Queen's death in 1451, black clothing was not Barbara's only major interest. She also liked to convene with demons, bathe in blood and abuse servant girls, and she maintained a personal guard of giant snakes and a pet raven whom she occasionally sent after peasants who displeased her, so that it might gouge out their eyes. All in all, hers was not the behavior of someone brought up on Aristotle's *Ethics*.

What a relief it is, then, that the Black Queen is now long gone and Bear Town Fortress nothing more than a harmless ruin.

PART ONE

LATE SEPTEMBER

1

BLACK QUEEN ONE-TWO-THREE

Aband of shabby pigeons was assembled in the northeast corner of the Square. This particular corner seemed to be a perpetual source of attraction to this type of bird, and it was seldom unoccupied by at least a few dozen members of the species. The number of pigeons congregated at this spot on this particular late September day was somewhere in the upper margins of the lower-than-average range.

The pigeons currently perambulating the area lingered in the vicinity of Manda's Well, a round stone fountain built on the site of a well that was said to be the mystical point of origin of the city. Not that this piece of information made any difference to the birds, whose attention was entirely focused on plucking at the discarded cigarette butts, lumps of dried chewing gum and other random objects lying on the ground.

At the foot of the nearby Upper Town, the Dolac Farmers Market was in session, its tightly packed wooden stands and red parasols hidden just behind a row of buildings that delineated the northern edge of the Square. Many shoppers, most of them matronly women of an imperious disposition, bustled to and fro across the Square on their way to the market. The bustling was purposeful and more than a little self-satisfied; it was exactly the kind of activity the word "bustling" was invented for.

Not everyone, however, was bustling. Some of the people present at the Square were stationary objects. Whether these individuals were clustered in groups or standing on their own, they were united by a single purpose—waiting for a tram.

Presently a blue number seventeen tram entered the scene, gliding calmly on its tracks before the eyes of the expectant crowd. It pulled to a stop and opened its six sets of two-winged doors. Like a giant magnet, it instantly drew people from every direction, not only from the immediate vicinity of the stop but from other parts of the Square as well, even as far as Dolac Market itself. This was the fate of the Square, to be used as a glorified tram stop, but it bore its burden gracefully.

A few of the pigeons fluttered their wings nervously, disturbed by all the tram-related commotion. Any increase in the fluctuation of passersby was likely to trigger alarms in the pigeons' overstimulated, city-addled brains.

A plump matron with an enormous bun tied at the back of her neck waited for a tram a safe distance away from the pigeons. A number of leafy greens protruded from the large wicker basket she clutched in her hand. These were collectively referred to on the Zagreb farmers' market scene as *grincek*. The woman glanced at the pigeons with a sour look, unaware that the name of the soup vegetables in her basket was a bastardized form of the German word *Grünzeug*, a compound noun meaning "green stuff."

A loud trilling sound, similar to the ringing of an old-fashioned telephone, resonated throughout the Square. A young man in a denim jacket had dashed across the tracks directly in front of the tram as the latter started moving, causing it to let out its familiar noise of electric annoyance.

"Idiot," muttered the matron with the basket full of *grincek*.

One of the pigeons paused in the middle of its random pacing and then did that thing birds sometimes do where they tilt their head to one side and stare into space as if suddenly faced with a realization of grave importance. The bird seemed to be genuinely perplexed by something. It flapped its wings as if shaking off loose feathers and then inexplicably soared into the air, leaving the rest of its flock behind.

It flew above the now-packed number seventeen as the tram entered a funnel of buildings where the Square gave way to a busy street that extended eastward. The bird continued following the tram tracks farther down southeast, leaving the number seventeen behind.

When the main road became leafier and quieter, the pigeon tilted its wings to the south and flew over a patchwork of parks, two-story houses, apartment buildings and a cluster of high-rises that jutted out of their surroundings like rockets on a launchpad.

Farther ahead, beyond a two-lane road whose name was either nonexistent or too unremarkable to be committed to memory, a vast gray school building loomed over the neighborhood and its assortment of greenery like a castle in the midst of some medieval fiefdom.

The school, which was in fact two schools in one—the East Central Primary School (ground floor and first floor) and the East Central Secondary School (second and third floor)—was a grim concrete edifice that looked like a combination of military barracks, a Gothic castle and an insane asylum. The building had a long nave-like body with an imposing stone staircase in the middle and a pair of sturdy turret-shaped towers, one at the southern end and the other at the northern one.

The most interesting part of the school grounds, at least to the pigeon, was the enormous playground that sprawled like a small independent country to the west of the main building. It was made up of various types of playing fields padded by patches of poorly tended grass that brought the whole thing together like a green carpet. Among other things, it contained a cluster of red gravel tennis courts, an athletic track and a football pitch. On the other side of the athletic track, directly next to the school, there was an asphalt-covered basketball court. At the far end of the court, the flank of the school formed a corner with the hangar-like gymnasium that jutted out of its side.

In this corner, several tall trees rose out of a small patch of dry ground that had escaped the asphalt. Beneath them, four children aged about eleven were playing a game of elastics. A rounded boy with dark hair and a girl with lots of frizzy auburn hair stood about eight feet apart, facing one another like a pair of bookends, except instead of books, they supported a bright orange elastic loop, which was currently strung around their waists. A girl with a ponytail skipped tirelessly from one side of the elastic loop to the other, while another girl watched the game with eyes that sparkled with anticipation.

The pigeon lit upon a branch of the tallest tree and promptly relieved itself, as birds do.

"Did you know," said Tin from his end of the elastic band apropos nothing, "that the school was once a prison?"

"I don't believe you," said Rea without delay from the other end.

Ida, who was performing an elaborate elastics combination, was oblivious to their chatter, while Stella, who was waiting for her turn at the sideline with her back against the gymnasium wall, had the focused look of a sumo wrestler about to enter the ring. The wall was nicknamed "the squash wall" because middle-aged men with sweatbands and receding hairlines were often seen playing squash against its concrete surface on weekend afternoons. But that particular day was a Tuesday and the men were in their offices, wearing suits and staring at computer screens, leaving the entire squash area free for elastics.

"Yes, it was. During the war."

"My uncle went to our school during the war and he says it was just an ordinary school," said Rea.

"Not that war."

It was then that a small white missile shot out of the ash tree towering over them and landed on the asphalt next to Tin with a loud splat.

"Did you see that? It nearly hit me!" Tin half turned and pointed at the wet white spot on the ground just a few paces away from him.

"Careful," said Ida midjump. Her statement was not an expression of concern but an admonition against Tin's inadvertent tugging of the elastic band.

Tin looked up at the tree. Not a single living creature could be discerned among its leafy branches. Although, to be fair, the trees did sport a lot of leaves at that time of year, and any perched bird smaller than an albatross was bound to remain hidden from view.

"I heard it was a dungeon," said Stella. "During the Middle Ages."

Rea huffed. "That's impossible. The building is not that old."

"But some parts of it could be old. Like the cellar." The last word made Stella shudder.

The school basement was a perpetually dark and abandoned space contained under the semicircular stone steps that led up to the north tower. No one knew what was in the cellar because no one was allowed to go in. A small metal grating at the top of the steps was the only thing that offered a glimpse at what lay beneath, and the view was never anything other than pitch darkness.

"Exactly," said Tin. "You have to wonder why no one's allowed to go down there. I bet it's full of torture devices and stuff."

Ida executed her final move, and then it was Stella's turn. They were now moving on to the challenging shoulder-high elastic band level, which required all her concentration, and the topic of the cellar was quickly abandoned.

The first four steps were straightforward, even with the ends held at shoulder-level. But the fifth was the stage when it became difficult.

Stella took a deep breath and began. "One." She stood with feet on either side of the front elastic. "Two." From her current position, she jumped high in the air, swinging her feet over the back elastic and landing with feet on either side of it.

Tin made a low whistling sound. "Well done."

"Three." Stella jumped back to the front elastic. Her feet landed on either side of it, which was exactly where they were supposed to be.

"Excellent," said Tin. He was a subpar elastics player himself, one who hardly ever managed to advance beyond waist level, but despite his shortcomings, he was an invaluable observer and commentator, gifted with the ability to appreciate the various nuances of the game.

"Four," said Stella as she stepped with both feet inside of the loop. This was an easy step, nothing more than a preparation for step five, which was the hardest of all. Its objective was to jump up and land with legs straddling the elastic band.

"Five," Stella said, and jumped. But when she landed, her right foot was still inside the loop. Tin let out a huff of disappointment. This was the end of the current round for Stella. It was also time for them to switch places and allow Tin and Rea to take a turn. But since they had already been playing for over two hours and as neither member of the latter pair was particularly prone to physical exertion, everyone agreed that now was a good time to take a break.

They went over to the other side of the gymnasium building. Their destination was a secluded spot they called the Dead Zone because of the strange stillness that always seemed to permeate the area. The only sound that could ever be heard there was the noise of passing cars from the unseen road beyond the playground fence (a rare occurrence, since it was an obscure road used only by locals trying to get to a less obscure road).

The Dead Zone was a patch of land covered in thick, matted grass that showed no evidence of ever having been cut. In the middle of this space there was a neglected athletic sandpit that was in the process of being reclaimed by the wild. The sand, always damp and cold, was partly covered with a carpet of mud-green moss. The concrete edge around the pit was falling apart, and weeds had sprouted out of the many cracks that lined its surface. The red earth of the runway that led up to the sandpit had turned olive brown, its surface dotted with tufts of grass. Beyond the sandpit, spiky bushes bearing tiny red berries rumored to be poisonous mingled with a group of tall trees whose long leafy branches formed a canopy over the Dead Zone, making it perpetually cool and shadowy.

Behind the row of trees stood a high concrete wall that separated the playground from the outside world. The part of the wall that formed a corner with the Dead Zone side of the gymnasium was strangely old and dilapidated. Pieces of it were crumbling off, and large parts of it were covered in ivy. It looked like a fragment of an ancient temple, the kind whose resident deity had either been too irrelevant or too depraved to be included in the polite society of conventional mythological pantheons. It was either that or just a very poorly maintained wall.

Stella sat down on the crumbling edge of the sandpit, and the other three, perhaps driven by some primal herding instinct, followed.

"Watch out, you're sitting on a crack," said Ida to Stella, who immediately shifted to the side.

"I don't get it," said Tin.

"If you sit on a crack, you're going to die."

"I thought it was if you step on a crack, you're going to die," said Tin.

"You can never be too careful." Stella was not sure whether to believe the many superstitions that circulated the school playground or not but decided it was best to err on the side of caution.

For a while they sat with their feet buried in the damp sand like holiday-makers dipping their feet in a swimming pool. The sky was beginning to get less luminous, the air more still. Not that the air ever appeared to be anything other than still in the Dead Zone. The area had a deadening effect on all the elements.

Rea kicked the sand lazily with the heel of her trainer. "What are we going to do now?"

"We don't have time for anything interesting," said Stella. "It will be dark soon." She looked at the western horizon, which was starting to turn a deep red.

"We could do some *playding*," said Tin, taking a bunch of small pictures held together by a rubber band out of his pocket.

Playding was an important term for the East Central Primary School pupil population. It denoted a kind of game whose objective was the trading of a number of small collectable pictures that came inside bite-sized chocolate bars which could be purchased in any corner shop. Each picture showed a representative of a particular species of the animal kingdom.

The game itself involved a minimum of two players, who typically sat cross-legged on the ground facing one another with a number of Animal Kingdom picture cards placed facedown between them. Each player attempted to turn over as many cards as possible by forming a sort of upside-down cup with their hands, which was then placed over the back of each picture before being swiftly lifted up. The abrupt motion created a vacuum that sometimes made the picture flip over and sometimes didn't. Whoever managed to turn a card over by applying this method got to keep it.

Tin shuffled through his cards, oblivious to the fact that he was the only individual present with a pack of Animal Kingdom cards on his person.

"Look, I have the bowhead whale." He held up a picture of a strange cetacean apparently in the process of swimming upside down while sporting an enormous scary grin, like a killer clown's, on its face.

Stella cleared her throat. "I haven't got my Animal Kingdom cards with me," she said. The others said the same thing but with fewer words.

Tin looked shocked. "What's wrong with you people?" He shoved his cards back into his pocket. "One doesn't just...leave the house without one's Animal Kingdom cards. That's just..." he sputtered, unable to finish the sentence.

The others made some perfunctory excuses. Then a strange, ominous look suddenly appeared on Ida's usually serene face. When she spoke, her voice was barely audible. "We could play Black Queen One-Two-Three."

There was a breathless silence, the kind that follows statements full of heavy foreboding.

The Black Queen One-Two-Three game was known to the greater part of the city's school-aged population, although no one really knew what precisely the game was about or even what exactly you were supposed to do with it. These were the main reasons why the game was rarely played. Not as rarely as, for example, dodgeball (since very few people, even those of primary school age, like being hit in the face with a heavy spherical object) but certainly less often than elastics, hopscotch, hide-and-seek, catch-me-if-you-can, roller skating or *playding*. There seemed to be a tacit understanding that the Black Queen One-Two-Three game was somehow special and that it was best not to overuse it.

"Sure, why not?" said Stella. "We haven't played it for a long time."

"We've *never* played it," said Tin.

"There you go."

"I wanna go first!" cried Rea.

The space before the crumbling, ivy-covered wall of the Dead Zone was the ideal setting for the Black Queen game. The shadows there were deep and the smell damp and musty, reminiscent of buried things. The most prominent part of the wall was a kind of crude alcove in the middle, created over time by the gradual erosion of the surface material. The shadows inside the alcove were almost black, and the ivy formed a curious gate-shaped arc over it.

Rea climbed on top of a small mound of rubble heaped at the foot of the alcove while the rest of them shuffled awkwardly before her. None of them were sure how to proceed, since the rules of the game were sketchy at best. The only thing that was clear was that participants took turns being the Black Queen, and whoever chanced to take on this role was expected to command other participants to transform into something. Everything else was open to debate.

"Black Queen One-Two-Three," began Rea. This was the standard opening chant. The rest of it contained a variable element.

"I see…" Rea paused. "Mushrooms," she continued, "and mushrooms are ye."

Having uttered the spell, she closed her eyes, turning away and facing the wall. The three players behind her were now left alone to go through with the motions, whatever that meant in this case.

Stella fumbled with her hands, unable to decide what to do. She had to be quick—if Rea saw her moving when she turned around, Stella would be the next Black Queen. Those were the rules.

She looked up. Rea was still turned away from them, her shape framed by the dark outline of the alcove. Stella tried to will her arms to move, but they were numb, and her hands felt as cold as ice. All she managed was a feeble twitch of the forearm. It just so happened that at that very moment, Rea turned around and saw her.

"Ha! Stella is the next Black Queen," cried Rea, and then hopped off her improvised pedestal, rushing to join the rest of the players.

With an oddly heavy heart, Stella dragged herself over to the wall to take Rea's place on the earthy mound.

"I think we should be going home soon," she said.

"Come on, just one more."

Slowly, she climbed onto the pile of debris that served as the Black Queen's throne.

"Let's have some kind of animal this time," added Tin from his middle position on the grass below.

"Shhh, you are not supposed to talk to the Black Queen," hissed Rea, making up a new arbitrary rule to be added to the long list of existing arbitrary rules.

Stella closed her eyes and began to utter the chant.

"Black Queen One-Two-Three." The words were shockingly loud in the stillness of the dusk. The air felt charged with a magnetic force that smelled faintly metallic.

"I see—" Stella realized she had no idea what she wanted to say next. Her mind helpfully suggested the word "porridge," which, on second thought, wasn't helpful at all.

For a brief moment, she opened her eyes again, as if searching for a clue. The other three players looked remote and unreachable from where she stood on the rubble pedestal. Above her, in the branches of one of the tall trees, there was a flash of something that looked like a black wing.

"—ravens," she said, "and ravens are ye."

Then she turned around, letting the darkness of the alcove swallow her.

At first there was no sound. Within a few seconds, a hollow hum, like the faint white noise echoing inside a conch shell, emerged out of the silence. At the same time, the air inside the alcove became even stuffier. Then, inexplicably, she felt a gust of cold wind brush against her face. She opened her eyes.

What should have been nothing but the playground wall had now become an open doorway leading into a moonlit courtyard. High walls made of rough stone enclosed the courtyard on all sides. A small chapel loomed out of the darkness in the background. From the peak of its steep roof, a stone cross reached up to the black sky, its four arms quartering the white orb of the full Moon that seemed to hover directly behind it.

In the center of the courtyard, halfway between the chapel and where Stella stood, there was an ancient stone well. Thick white mist covered the ground, making the well look as if it were floating on a cloud. A stocky, balding man dressed in the tattered clothing of an anachronistic peasant knelt beside it, his feet and shins buried in the mist. The peasant had taken off his simple hat, which he now wrung with both hands as he stared all around him with mute terror on his face. He did not appear to be able to see Stella though.

A sparkle of red light flickered into existence inside the chapel. Soon the eerie glow expanded and grew brighter, spilling out of the narrow windows like the beacon of some hellish lighthouse.

Then the chapel door burst open. An imposing silhouette stood in the doorway, framed by the hot red light glowing from the inside.

The kneeling peasant went into hysterics, stammering out a torrent of pleading words.

The figure in black slowly descended the chapel steps. The peasant instinctively lurched backward, his back bumping into the side of the well. He reached behind him clumsily, clutching the stone edge with shaking hands.

As the mysterious form emerged into the moonlight, Stella could see that it was a woman in a long black dress with a tight, stiff bodice that looked almost like armor. She had a flowing, inky cape with a strange collar that stood rigid behind her head like a fan. Her face was as pale as the Moon, and her hair, pulled up high in a severe bun, was jet black with a liquid-blue reflection. A large black raven perched on her shoulder.

There was something familiar about the figure. The sternness, the blackness, the raven-on-the-shoulderness of her. Stella couldn't quite put her finger on it. Then it hit her—*the Black Queen*. Yes, the Black Queen of Bear Town Fortress. The evil one who had done…Stella was not quite sure what, but she knew that the Black Queen was meant to be scary. And evidently she was.

Seemingly unaware of Stella's presence, the Black Queen took another step toward the peasant, who was now pleading in earnest. But the Black Queen seemed to suddenly lose interest in him. Instead, she turned to her raven and rubbed her cheek fondly against its face. The bird responded in kind, edging closer to her. The whole scene would have been rather touching if it hadn't been for all the desperate pleading.

For a moment the peasant looked ready to bolt, but then six growling, halberd-carrying guards in full armor emerged from the shadows and promptly formed a threatening semicircle behind the well. The peasant froze and looked up at the Black Queen again. She was still caressing her raven, affecting lack of interest.

Then she abruptly turned her head, shot the peasant a nasty glare, and released the raven. The black bird swept across the courtyard like the shadow of some prehistoric flying reptile and descended upon the peasant's head. There was a flapping of great black wings, followed by a sickening shriek as the raven started pecking at the peasant's face.

Deciding she had had enough of feudal antics for one day, Stella squeezed her eyes shut.

After a while, the screams died down, and then there was only chilling silence. Stella opened her eyes to see the peasant's lifeless body slouched limply on the ground with its back against the side of the well, the head slumped against the chest.

It was then that she noticed three grotesque dark shapes lurking in the shadows behind the Black Queen—monstrous beasts with glowing red eyes, one of them sporting long arachnid legs. Stella gasped.

The Black Queen shot a glare in her direction. Even from a distance, Stella could see that her eyes were as dark as black pits. The pale face contorted into a terrifying angry grimace. Then her arms formed a strange cruciform gesture. The raven fluttered into the air. The Black Queen brought both arms to the front, hands held out like spears pointed at Stella.

The gesture sent the raven flying toward her like a bullet, the red embers of its eyes brightening with a burning intensity.

The black bird approached with frightening speed. Less than three seconds later, it rushed past her, one of its spindly wings brushing her cheek.

The other three creatures followed, making for the open portal. Stella froze. The monsters were coming. She blinked. Not only were they coming, but they were also *shrinking*. They were changing shape right before her eyes, their size diminishing by the second.

She took an impulsive step back but lost her footing and barely managed to keep her balance. Another gust of wind made the door start swinging shut. Stella saw a furry thing scramble through, followed by something long, scaly and slippery. Then the door closed with a bang, its outline becoming immediately indistinguishable from the alcove. It was just an ordinary wall once again.

Vision blurring, Stella collapsed onto the grass, but not before she saw a big black spider emerge out of the alcove.

❧❦❧

When she opened her eyes, she was sitting on the grass with her back propped against the Dead Zone wall, Tin and the others crouching around her. The sky was turning indigo blue.

"Did you see them?" she said urgently. "Where did they go?"

"Where did who go?" asked Tin.

"The raven…and the others."

"There was a bird," said Ida. "It flew over the wall."

"It didn't fly over the wall," said Stella. "It flew *out* of the wall. Except it wasn't a wall. It was some kind of doorway, and the Black Queen's castle was on the other side."

Now everyone was looking at her as if what she was saying didn't make perfect sense.

"Stella," said Tin cautiously, "I think you should go home."

Somewhere above them, a raven cawed.

2

ETERNAL TORMENT OF HOARDERS

Dario Taubek dragged his feet up Fishpond Street, a dark canyon of neglected buildings just a few blocks north of Zagreb Cathedral. It was a cloudy night, and there was no sign of the Moon, which made the surrounding brown facades blend in with the black sky. The muddy yellow streetlamps and the trailing taillights of passing cars were the only source of light.

He had been out with a few friends and had perhaps had a beer too many, but under the circumstances, it was permitted. After all, it wasn't every day that you decided to drop out of your fruitless university course in order to dedicate yourself fully to the pursuit of…Dario wasn't quite sure what, but he was confident that he would find out. Eventually.

He paused for a moment to breathe in the refreshing night air, letting out a little cough when a small insect recklessly hurled itself up his nose and tickled the back of his throat only to die a pointless and completely avoidable death therein.

His head was starting to throb, but at least he was still able to walk, and would probably have been able to drive too, had he had a car and, more importantly, a driving licence. All he wanted to do now was go up to his room without encountering Madam Mina, his live-in landlady, and then go to sleep for at least fourteen hours—an unlikely scenario, since he had to go to work in less than nine, but he was determined to do his best.

Dario stopped outside a nondescript three-story building, the same as all the others but for the familiar brown Škoda parked directly in front of the entrance. The sight was at once both a beacon of familiarity and the source of an automatic inward cringe. He looked up at the top right window. The lights were off. Good. That meant Madam Mina was almost certainly asleep.

He took his house keys out of his pocket, careful not to make any loud jingling noises, but the keys slipped through his fingers like tiny silver fish and landed on the pavement with an earsplitting crash. Cursing silently under his breath, Dario picked up the keys with one shaking hand, then unlocked the front door and went into the musty foyer.

Inside, the building was as quiet as a mausoleum on a desert island. The silence was not altogether strange, since the ground-floor apartment was unoccupied, and the one on the first floor had only one resident, Madam Tereza, a ninety-two-year-old near-deaf woman whose bedtime was around 8:00 p.m. As for the top floor, if he had been anticipating any strange noises from its direction—noises such as eerie meditation music that stimulated certain chakras or the low murmur of Madam Mina having an intimate conversation with her dog—there weren't any to be heard. That was good.

Dario went up the worn-out stairs as quietly as his heavy black boots would allow. The farther up he went, the narrower the stairs appeared to become. But this was only an optical illusion. Madam Mina was a hoarder with a penchant for old pottery and Persian carpets, and she kept an excess of these items on the stairs. Stacks of heavy earthenware pots, rolled-up carpets and other random items cluttered the side of the staircase that was nearer to the wall. The other side was dominated by smaller rugs which had been slung over the banister at random intervals. Dario had gotten used to this chaos once the initial shock, first experienced upon his moving in about two years before, had subsided.

He finally reached the top landing, which was also the epicenter of the hoard. If Hieronymus Bosch had depicted the setting for the eternal torment of hoarders in one of his paintings of the infernal regions, it would have looked like this. Hundreds of cans of dog food were piled on top of large linen sacks full of sand or artificial fertilizer or some other contextually incongruous substance. Stacked on top of all this, there were several levels of plywood, plastic crates and beige pillar candles. This central pile, the master pile, the sovereign of all piles, reached all the way to the ceiling and would probably have gone through the roof and beyond if only such things didn't require a planning permission. There were also a few smaller, localized piles mostly made up of various building materials. A large clay Buddha sitting cross-legged on top of a pile of roof shingles was a new addition, one that Dario hadn't noticed while leaving the house that morning.

Quietly, he unlocked a door that bore a crooked metal three near the top, and snuck into the apartment. A small lamp with a crimson shade illuminated the hallway with an ambient glow. He didn't see this as cause for alarm. Madam Mina always left the hall lamp on overnight. On the right, the door to her room was firmly shut, and no light could be seen coming through the crack at the bottom. Another good sign. Dario tiptoed down the corridor, past a mountain of kitten-heel shoes, past a wooden rack stuffed with half a dozen polka-dot umbrellas and other vertically placed objects, past an enormous wall-mounted mirror framed with a string of fairy lights, stopping only when he reached the door to his room.

The door was slightly ajar, which meant that Madam Mina had once again been inside his room for some reason unknown to him while he had been away, but at the moment he was too tired to be annoyed by this. He pushed the door open and was already starting to think that all would be well when the door at the other end of the hall suddenly burst open. The next instant, a grinning head with curly hair the color of high-fructose tomato juice popped out like a scary, middle-aged Muppet operated by a sadistic puppeteer.

"Dario dear!" cried Madam Mina in an affected, overly enthusiastic voice. "I thought it might be you!"

Dario's arm fell bonelessly to his side. Slowly, he turned around, his hazel eyes widening with a puppylike meekness. His nonconfrontational nature made him unable to be rude even when simultaneously tired and drunk. There was also the matter of Dario's tenancy. His room in Madam Mina's flat was not only unusually cheap but also ideally located just a ten minutes' walk from both the Square and the small publishing house where he worked on a part-time basis. It was certainly the best a penniless former Zagreb University student with no living relations other than an aging aunt could ever hope to find in the city center. He didn't know if this was because Madam Mina was a philanthropist or just severely out of touch with current market prices, but in either case, he didn't want to give her a reason to rethink her pricing policy. Therefore, it was best not to antagonize her.

"Good uh…evening, Madam Mina." If Dario felt awkward as he uttered his greeting, this was only because it was past 1:00 a.m.

"Dario dear!" repeated Madam Mina in the same annoying tone as before. Her red locks bobbed. "How convenient that we should bump into each other like this. I was just about to check on you to see if you're awake." She stepped into the hall. She wore a crimson dressing gown with magenta flowers, and there were two huge metal curlers on her head, one behind each ear, although it didn't look as if either supported much or any hair. Instead, they seemed to have been randomly attached with hairpins to nothing in particular for some reason. Dario didn't want to know what that reason might be.

An old, weary-looking dog, apparently a cross between a dachshund and a footstool, its gender indeterminate or nonexistent, doddered behind Madam Mina's heels on short, stubby legs. It looked up at Dario with sad, damp eyes that seemed to be saying, "Kill me...please kill me."

Dario released a tiny noncommittal sound through his nose. He stared at his landlady intently, blinking hard in an attempt to dispel the blurriness of his vision.

There was a moment's pause as Madam Mina arranged her face in a forced smile that always seemed to appear before she made an inappropriate request, which was often.

"I was wondering if you could give me a hand."

An unpleasant chill ran down Dario's spine. He had heard that sentence from his landlady countless times before, and it did not bode well.

"Uh, I was just about to turn in," he said, hovering in the limbo of the doorway, one foot inside his room and the other lingering in the hall.

"Oh, but this won't take a minute." Madam Mina's grin became even wider, showing two rows of yellowing teeth.

Dario swallowed audibly and waited for the other shoe to drop. Meanwhile, the dog tottered over to Dario's side and stood on the doorstep, gazing into the darkness of Dario's room while giving the air a faint, half-hearted sniff.

"Don't worry—Flo will not go into your room," said Madam Mina, at which point the dog promptly went into the room.

"Floki!" exclaimed the landlady in a resonant, drawn-out voice, unconcerned about the late hour of the night. The dog's nose poked out from behind the door, and then the animal came back into the hall, but not without some reluctance.

Madam Mina turned her attention back to Dario. "I just need you to help me carry a tiny little thing down to the car."

The next thing he knew, Dario was lugging a heavy rolled-up carpet down the stairs while Madam Mina and Floki followed close behind. He could barely see where he was going from the combination of drunken exhaustion and the burden of the huge, bulky object, as heavy as a dead body, hanging over his shoulder, but that was fine because Madam Mina was giving him helpful directions every step of the way.

"Watch out—there's a stair ahead of you. Wait, let me get these pots out of the way. OK, you can move on now, Dario dear. Oh, wait, there's a vase on the stairs. Don't knock over the vase."

By the time he staggered down to the first-floor landing, she was starting to sound grateful. "I really do appreciate your help, Dario dear. I wouldn't have asked you to do this, but I'm driving down to my sister's place tomorrow morning, and I promised I'd bring her the carpet. So I thought it would be best if we just got this over with tonight. And I couldn't really ask anyone else, Dario dear. You know how it is with people these days; you can never rely on anyone to help out when you need them."

Hauling the carpet down to the brown Škoda was not the end of his troubles, as Madam Mina also asked him to help her fit the carpet into the back seat of the car. When it became evident that the carpet did not in fact fit into the back seat, or any other seat or combination of seats, Madam Mina went back up to the apartment, returning a few minutes later with a considerable length of rope. Then she asked him to help her tie the carpet to the roof of the car, explaining that the likelihood of the carpet being stolen at this time of night was very low.

When he was finally back in his room, he was so exhausted that it took him a full five seconds to realize that his bookcase was in the wrong place. It was now by the window, whereas when he had last seen it earlier that day, it had been on the opposite side of the room, by the door. Madam Mina must have gone into his room while he was away specifically to move his bookcase for no particular reason and without any forewarning. None of it made any sense.

With that thought, he collapsed onto his bed and fell asleep in his clothes. Just before he drifted off, he briefly pondered on the randomness and the apparent meaninglessness of his life. *What is all this for?* said a tiny voice in his head, but Dario made it shut up, since it sounded too much like a line out of some cheesy 1980s movie uttered by some trailer-park-dwelling protagonist only minutes before being unexpectedly recruited by a spaceman to fight an evil invading armada with his latent shooting skills.

3

THE GHOST CANDLE OF STONE GATE

Leo was not happy. The person whom he was supposed to meet at St. Katherine's Square had not turned up. The person in question was an old grime-encrusted hermit who had alerted the Star Council to the latest Black Queen threat. The Star Council had promptly dispatched Leo to Earth, binding him to the city until his mission had been completed or until he was officially released, whichever came first. And Leo certainly hoped it was the latter, and preferably on that same night. But now the wretched hermit wasn't there.

Grunting with frustration, Leo kicked a metal beer cap that lay discarded on the ground. The cap bounced down the pavement with an effete tinny sound. Seconds later, a cat meowed. Then all was silent again.

He proceeded to stride impatiently up and down the deserted square, a pitiful provincial thing that looked as if it had once been a village market place. After about ten minutes of this, he turned left into Jesuit Square, which was marginally more interesting only because there was a fountain with a statue in it, not that it mattered much to Leo, since it was too dark to see the statue properly, and besides, he didn't care much for sculpture anyway.

Then he wandered off even farther into some grim, winding side street full of baroque buildings whose facades looked as if they hadn't been touched up since Louis XIV's favorite dog was a pup. Once he'd had enough of that, he marched fitfully back to Jesuit Square.

Something stirred in the shadows. A ripple of particles disturbed a handful of dry leaves lying scattered in a dark corner by a walled garden, making the leaves swirl around in a perfect geometric pattern, and for a moment, Leo was almost relieved, thinking it was the hermit. But this assumption was soon to be proved false.

The form that materialized before Leo was distinctly not that of a hermit with lax personal hygiene standards. Instead, it was that of another star daimon—one with a pale face, blue-black hair, a diabolical grin and a fashion sense that made him look like a cross between Edgar Allan Poe and a leather-clad biker.

"Algol," said Leo.

"Leo," said Algol, and flickered a bit, like a moving image projected off a film reel in which every third frame was blank.

Unlike other star daimons, who visited Earth only if they had a very good reason, and sometimes not even then if they could avoid it, Algol came and went whenever he pleased. And, unlike other star daimons, Algol was also a demon star. Therefore, it was generally not a good idea to talk to him in a way that could make him angry, as he could flip into demonic mode at the drop of a hat. In fact, it was best not to talk to Algol at all. Most other star daimons tended to avoid him on principle, but Leo was not disciplined enough to have principles. Also, Algol just kept appearing all the time.

"I hope you haven't come here to gloat," said Leo, "because I am too busy being bored out of my mind to care."

Algol looked curious. "Does this mean you haven't confronted any of the Black Queen's bloodthirsty subterranean creatures yet?"

Leo sighed. "I almost wish I had," he said despairingly, "because the alternative is being idle in the most uninteresting place in the universe."

"What, this?" Algol briefly disappeared and then reappeared on the roof of a nearby baroque building. Then he disappeared and reappeared on the far side of the square. Then on the bell tower of the Jesuit church. Then on a branch of a tree.

"It's not that bad," he finally said. After a pause, he added, "At least it's not the Middle Ages."

Leo squeezed his eyes shut, shuddering a bit. "Please, don't remind me."

Algol disappeared again and then reappeared in the middle of the fountain, standing by the statue.

"Look, this is pretty interesting."

What with the subtle icy glow cast by Algol's face, Leo could now see that the statue was that of a crouching man apparently in the process of strangling a snake. Leo still thought the statue was fairly boring and didn't hesitate to say so aloud.

"Is your aversion to boredom the reason why you've made Antares so frightfully furious?" asked Algol. Leo winced.

Antares was the leader of a belligerent group of star daimons who called themselves, pretentiously and (at least in Leo's opinion) hilariously, the Star Warriors. Antares was also, for some reason that Leo couldn't quite fathom, his sworn enemy. Not that Leo would ever have bothered with something as prosaic as having a sworn enemy. The swearing had all been done on Antares's part. Leo was not the type to waste his time or energy on long-term animosities or long-term anything.

Overall, the Star Warriors were a humorless and fairly tedious bunch, which was why every once in a while Leo had the urge to do something that would wipe the grim, self-righteous scowls off their faces. It just so happened that his most recent attempt at doing just that had entailed falsely reporting Antares to the Star Council for indecent interdimensional exposure. This had led to a needlessly drawn-out process against Antares and a temporary suspension of his stellar activities, since the Star Council was apparently just as humorless as the Star Warriors.

"That was just a harmless lark," said Leo casually. "Surely it's already blown over."

"It doesn't sound like it." Algol was viewing the snake's face critically from various angles. "Last I've heard, Antares has vowed to find you and exact some sort of revenge."

Leo waved the thought away. "That's just empty bragging. Nothing to worry about."

"His exact words were, 'I am going to track that scoundrel down even if I have to chase him to the darkest, most antimatter-infested corner of the universe, and then I am going to turn his insides into interstellar gas.'"

"A gross exaggeration, I'm sure," said Leo. "Besides, I'll be perfectly safe for as long as I'm being delayed in this burrow of boredom. I don't think Antares would follow me to this godforsaken armpit of the universe even if he could. No one would do that to himself."

"Is the Black Queen causing trouble again?"

"I don't see what else it could be."

"You really have to hand it to her for being a force to be reckoned with even after being literally *wiped off the face of the earth*." Algol's eyes sparked with demonic amusement, as if replaying some fond memory. "When was it? Five hundred years ago?"

Leo shrugged. "Who cares?"

"Did you ever stop to think that the reason you keep getting summoned to the White City to clean up the Black Queen's mess is that it was you who, back in those horrible medieval times when everyone was poor, illiterate and a peasant, gave the Black Queen the secret knowledge that ultimately turned her into the scourge of the city?"

Leo gave this some thought. "It sounds pretty bad when you put it that way."

"And you did all this out of sheer boredom!" Algol had now appeared in the middle of the square, just a few paces from Leo. "I sometimes think you're even more evil than I am." His image was now starting to disappear, but not in the usual on-and-off sort of way. This was the particle-swirling vacuum of imminent departure.

"You're leaving?" Leo didn't want to admit that even talking to Algol was better than being by himself in a benighted city that also happened to be his least favorite place on this side of the asteroid belt (for the record, Leo's least favorite place on the *other* side of the asteroid belt was Saturn—that place simply lacked cohesion).

"Leo," said Algol as if stating something unbearably obvious, "you should know better than anyone else that the only way to not perish of boredom in this city is to avoid being in it for more than ten minutes at a time."

"You don't have to rub it in," said Leo.

But Algol was already gone.

After another hour or so, Leo finally had to admit to himself that he had been stood up. Stood up by an old man whose mind had not entertained the thought of personal grooming since the invention of the ear pick. The indignity of it was maddening.

Frustrated and unable to decide what else to do, he marched off in the direction of the Stone Gate. This wasn't a very long march, since the Stone Gate was about twenty paces from him.

The Stone Gate was the oldest surviving city gate, the others having been torn down in a vain attempt to make Upper Town look less like a medieval witch-burning hub. For a city gate, the Stone Gate looked very much like a church. Notable among its features were wooden pews, a vaulted ceiling, and a shrine containing numerous items dedicated to the Virgin Mary, including paintings, statues, stone plates with inscriptions, and votive candles, many adorned with her picture.

It really was like a church in practically every respect apart from the presence of a winding cobbled road that just happened to run straight through it. There was also the matter of several massive iron doors that appeared to be sealed into the walls. This, however, did not stop them from looking as if at any moment an undead Knight Templar might burst out wielding a bloodied mace in one hand and a crucifix in the other while chanting "Mur-Tur-Mini-Mur-Tur-Mini" in a frantic, high-pitched voice. (While the fact of "Mur-Tur-Mini-Mur-Tur-Mini" being the chant Templar Knights used during their secret ceremonies is not widely known, it is nevertheless true.)

That night, the Stone Gate was predictably sepulchral, although a few church candles flickered feebly in the corner by the main shrine, their glow only barely managing to make the atmosphere more tolerable.

Among them, there was one special candle, one that at first looked ordinary apart from the fact that it was black whereas the others were white. Most Stone Gate visitors, however, did not possess the required powers of observation to be able to tell the difference. This candle had a special purpose that was known only to a select few. It was called "the ghost candle" because lighting it caused the inexplicable appearance of a ghost. The said ghost was that of a medieval goldsmith who, apart from being perplexingly insistent on appearing in ghost form when summoned, was otherwise fairly unremarkable. But Leo was getting desperate, and the ghost could occasionally be useful.

He went up to the candle tray, his impatient gaze flicking among the many half-burnt lumps of wax. Finally, he saw it. The ghost candle sat half-hidden at the back, near the wall, its base buried in a pool of melted wax.

Leo rifled through the debris lying around the tray until he found a usable match, which he lit with a flick of the wrist so swift it looked almost like magic.

The ghost candle began to glow with a transparent silver flame. Eerie shadows fluttered across the vaulted ceiling. A thin white mist, seemingly appearing out of nowhere (which is exactly where it had appeared from), entered the interior of the Stone Gate from the Upper Town side and proceeded to slowly ooze down the central aisle, curving with the bend of the road in the middle and trickling out through the other entryway.

A sudden gust of wind made the flame flicker. Somewhere in the distance, an empty beer can rattled ominously as it was tossed about by the breeze.

He rolled his eyes. Was the stupid ghost ever going to appear?

Leo's mental thread of impatience bordering on disgust was interrupted by a low murmur of someone talking to himself. Then a small fat man wearing absurd glasses with thick round lenses and a frame as complicated as a miniature steampunk crane strolled in from the Upper Town side. He wore dapper medieval garments—inasmuch as anything medieval could be said to be dapper—and on his head there was a curious hat that looked like a paper plane, except made of leather.

"…some steamed turnips and goulash," muttered the goldsmith to himself. "And cottage cheese too."

He stopped abruptly when he saw Leo.

"Why, hello there, young man," said the goldsmith cheerfully. "Taking a stroll through our charming city?"

Leo sighed. The ghost had the memory retention of a haddock, always acting as if he hadn't seen him before.

"Oh, you know," said Leo, "just doing a bit of the usual. Sightseeing, shopping, responding to badly articulated transcosmic summonings."

"You will see many wonderful sights in the White City. Although perhaps not in the dark." The goldsmith looked momentarily bashful. "And if it's shopping you are interested in, may I recommend my humble establishment, which is just round the corner?"

"I wouldn't miss it for the world."

"I sell all kinds of things. A much greater variety than you might expect. You know, everyone thinks I am just a goldsmith and clockmaker. But I am a lens-cutter too."

"Is that so?"

"See, I made these." The goldsmith took off his improbable glasses, presenting them to the disinterested Leo, then quickly rubbed the lenses with his handkerchief before putting them back on.

"I make the finest spectacles in town." The little man gave him a conspiratorial wink. "I could make you a fine piece too, if you wish."

"Thank you, that won't be necessary. I can see just fine."

"Are you sure? You have a bit of a squint."

"That's only because at the moment I'd rather not have the ability to see." Leo could practically feel his eyes shrinking into their sockets at the continued sight of the wretched city.

The goldsmith peered up at Leo quizzically, like a small rodent looking up at a curious nut dangling off a tree. His eyes looked tiny behind the inch-thick lenses.

"Do I know you?"

"Actually, we might have met a few times in passing, but it was quite a while ago. You might not recognize me, since I wore my other Earth outfit back then. The one with the beige cuffs."

The goldsmith slapped his forehead, as if suddenly remembering something important.

"Of course!" he said. "You're the one the hermit's told me about."

"Ah." Finally the silly clockmaker was starting to make sense. "So the old man has been here recently, has he?"

"Yes! Yes!" The goldsmith nodded emphatically. "He's left a message for you." He took a small rolled-up piece of parchment out of his pocket. Leo accepted the scroll and took a quick look at its contents. He was dismayed to see that the note was written in a geriatric scrawl that would have given a professional graphologist a run for their money. Leo thanked the goldsmith nevertheless, mainly as an attempt to make him stop talking.

"Well, I'll be off then," said the ghost. "Do let me know if you change your mind about those spectacles."

"Yes, I'll be sure to do that."

And the tiny goldsmith wandered off in the direction of the Radić Street end of the gate, his stocky figure becoming fainter and fainter as he neared the stone arch.

Leo snuffed out the candle, and the goldsmith vanished the same instant. The utterly pointless oozing mist disappeared with him. Leo brought his attention back to the abysmally illegible note. He looked with dismay at the length of the note and its erratic breeziness. This was going to be painful.

The note read, as far as Leo could tell:

Dear Leo,

Hello! As you know, I am a hermit. This means I'm not in the habit of writing notes, so I'll try to make this brief. Because I wouldn't want to waste your time. Not that it matters in your case, as you are immortal and therefore certain to have an unlimited amount of time at your disposal.

Where was I?

Ah yes—the meeting. As you can probably tell by now, I am not here. By "here," I mean here with you at the place where you are right now, not "here" where I am now, which is in a different place.

Where was I?

Ah yes—the meeting. Leo, as you can see, I haven't been able to meet you there at the arranged time. By "there," I mean the place where we would have met if things had gone according to plan, not the place where you are at now, because this is probably not the same place. Unless you have gone back to the original place to read the note. In which case, I apologize for my incorrect application of the principle of deixis.

Where was I?

Ah, yes—the meeting.

Leo, something terribly unexpected has happened. Or I should rather say "terrible and unexpected," since it is both terribly unexpected and terrible. Namely, I have left the stove on, and I must go home right away to turn it off. How could one possibly expect such unexpected things to happen? One could not go on for another day, not to mention nine hundred years, if one lived with such terrible expectations. And I should know, because I have lived for nine hundred years. And let me tell you, a positive outlook has been the key to my longevity. That and a high-fiber diet. Not that it matters to you either way, since you're immortal.

Where was I?

Ah, yes—the meeting.

I am not going to bother you with any further details at this point because I'd like to keep this note brief. I will tell you everything when we meet tomorrow. Until then, please feel free to make use of your former temporary lodgings in the Hidden Tower.

The tower is still unknown to most people, being hidden, and you should therefore not be disturbed. Please note, however, that the floors have not been swept for some two hundred years and the linen was last washed around the turn of the sixteenth century. It has, however, been aired recently, sometime around the year 1867, I believe, so you should not find it too disagreeable.

Yours,
The Hermit

PS Oh, yes! The meeting tomorrow. I've nearly forgot to tell you where to meet, which would have made it difficult for you to attend. Leo, could you meet me tomorrow at 4 p.m. in the botanical garden under the ginkgo tree.

Yours,
The Hermit
Oh, wait, I've already said this. Never mind; ignore the last two lines.

Leo crumpled the note and sighed with exasperation. Then he dragged his feet down Radić Street, turning left onto the Bloody Bridge and then into Tkalčić Street, where he peripherally noticed with a lack of interest that the Medveščak was now a street. Last time he was in Zagreb, it had been a stream. Leo went up Tkalčić Street until he found a secret door that led into a secret garden. At the bottom of the secret garden stood the Hidden Tower, so called because it had managed to exist for hundreds of years in the center of the city, in a leafy, overgrown area between Tkalčić Street and Opatovina Park, without anyone noticing that it was there.

With labored steps, he went up to the first floor. Inside, it smelled like mold and petrified mouse droppings. Leo was too tired and dejected to even care. Instead, he collapsed on a dusty pile of rags and went to sleep miserably.

4

THE BBP

Dario woke up to shafts of sunlight piercing his eyeballs and noises of a persistently banging typewriter assaulting his ears. He blinked a few times while staring at the ceiling, trying to pinpoint his exact location in the space-time continuum. It was tomorrow morning. The tomorrow of yesterday was now the today of today. Madam Mina was still there. She should have been gone, on her way to her sister's farmhouse on the other side of Bear Mountain. She should have been on her way with her abominable carpet in tow rather than making typing noises in her room at an ungodly hour of the morning. Dario slowly turned his aching head with its aching brain toward the digital alarm clock on the bedside table. 6:34 a.m.

Moaning feebly, he turned over to his side and buried his head under the pillow. Not his favorite sleeping position, but it would have to do. His shift began at noon, and he was not getting up before 11:30.

He promptly dozed off again and had a dream in which he wandered aimlessly around a green field while a black cow stood silently watching him from the side as it chewed some semi-digested cud ominously.

When he awoke for the second time, the apartment was blissfully quiet. Madam Mina must have left while he had been napping. Dario glanced at the clock. 11:17. He sighed contentedly.

The typing resumed—Madam Mina's typing, coming from the other room, this time with even more assertiveness than before.

In all honesty, Dario was not even surprised. These kinds of things, where he would assume one thing and then experience the exact opposite of that thing within a few seconds, tended to occur with striking regularity whenever Madam Mina was around. It was a kind of anti-synchronicity. Or perhaps it was just ordinary synchronicity operating under a twisted premise: namely, that the universe was a cruel, sardonic place that existed for the sole purpose of making him miserable.

There was, however, an element of uncertainty in this assumption. He still couldn't be a hundred percent sure that the typewriter noise was indeed being produced by Madam Mina. Its cause could just as easily have been an armed intruder who happened to be a vintage Olympia enthusiast. The said intruder could have broken into the apartment with the intention of burglary before getting distracted during his ransacking of the premises by the sight of Madam Mina's alluring Olympia SM4 sitting on her desk. Unable to resist the typewriter's charms, the miscreant may well have sat down before it, inserted a fresh piece of paper, and proceeded to type away noisily right there and then. It was a less probable scenario, to be sure, but one that was nevertheless worthy of some consideration.

There was only one way to find out which version was true. Turning onto his stomach, he propped himself on his elbows and then crawled across the vast expanse of the bed toward the window. He grabbed onto the window ledge like a drowning man gripping a raft and pulled himself up to peer out of the window. Madam Mina's car was still parked outside the building, the enormous rolled-up carpet lying on top of it like a giant slug from outer space trying to mate with a colossal beetle. The more probable scenario had been vindicated, and not for the first time either.

Dario slid out of bed, put on some presentable clothes, and hurried into the bathroom at the end of the hall. He urinated what seemed like 85 percent of his total liquid body mass, then carefully flushed. The cistern was mounted on the wall almost as high up as the ceiling, and the flushing mechanism was a rickety contraption with a chain that had to be handled with care to avoid death by accidentally detached ceramic lid.

Madam Mina's inevitable call came just as he was emerging from the bathroom, while the waning flush and the bubbling of the refilling cistern murmured like a gentle forest stream behind him.

"Dario dear!"

"Yes?" he called out from the hall in the hope that there was a way of getting out of this conversation without having to go into her room.

"Could you come here for a moment?"

Dario sighed. Then he obeyed. There was no avoiding this.

Unlike the staircase, Madam Mina's room did not contain any building materials. But it did contain everything else—books, clothes, mismatched shoes, creepy porcelain ballerina figurines, staplers, antique milk jugs, filing cabinets and uncut quartz crystals, among other things. Not for the first time, Dario had the feeling that Madam Mina's room was a depository of all objects that did not fit into any other part of the universe. In the center of it all, like a small island in a raging sea of random matter, stood a massive oak desk, its desktop dominated by Madam Mina's huge typewriter and stacks of A4 paper. His landlady had either not caught wind of the invention of the word processor yet or, if she had, she did not see in what way it could be used for typing.

Dario uttered a cautious good morning. "I'm surprised to see you here, Madam Mina. I thought you said you were going to your sister's place."

"Did I?" Madam Mina sounded genuinely surprised, as if the recent carpet maneuver was a long-forgotten event from a remote past that had survived only as an ambiguous myth transmitted through oral tradition. "Well, I didn't feel like going this morning, Dario dear, and besides, they say it's going to rain in the afternoon. There's no point driving all that way only to get rained on. You know how it is, Dario dear."

Dario tried to quell the surge of disappointment that welled up in his stomach like nausea. She went on, oblivious to Dario's internal anguish. "I'll go some other day. Maybe tomorrow or next weekend. The carpet can stay in the car. Oh, Dario, I woke up with such a big surge of inspiration. New ideas keep pouring out of me. I've been sitting here all morning, trying to write them all down."

Madam Mina wrote confessional romance stories under the pen name "Eulalia Bartok." These entirely fabricated, predictably mind-assaulting narratives were regularly published in a magazine called *Life and Destiny*. The intended readership, ladies of a certain age who talked to their cats, did not mind the poor quality of these verbal confections. On the contrary, they positively relished the tripe, and rushed to the nearest newsstand every twenty-fifth of the month, which was when each new issue came out.

"Isn't it wonderful when ideas are just pouring out of you?" Her voice took on an absent tone as she began typing again. Floki poked its nose from under the desk and then staggered out onto a nearby Persian carpet. The dog looked even more pitiful under the harsh light of day than the previous night. The sides of its face were covered in strange growths reminiscent of graying sideburns. Its midsection had a prominent bald patch, and there were no nocturnal shadows now to hide it. Dario felt itchy just looking at it. The dog's eyes were turned up at him in supplication, leaving thin white crescents exposed under dark irises. It was as if all the sorrows of the world had descended upon him. Or her—Dario could never quite remember which one it was.

"It sure is," he said, swaying back and forth on the balls of his feet. Then he clapped his hands with feigned nonchalance. "Okey dokey. Well, I think I'd better be—"

"Oh!" exclaimed Madam Mina just as Dario was making his retreat. "I've just remembered why I called you."

She rummaged through the piles of newspaper clippings, old opera programs and postcards lying on her desk and fished out a misshapen, jagged crystal the color of dry ice. She handed it over to Dario wordlessly, as if the gesture itself somehow made sense.

"Um, thank you," said Dario, taking the proffered object. "And this would be a…"

"The Tear of Manda, of course," said Madam Mina in a distracted tone, as if she had finished saying what she intended and was now being unnecessarily kept from getting back to her creative endeavors. "It's a magic protection stone. You have been slightly aimless lately, Dario dear, and such a state can make a person vulnerable. So you'd better make sure to have it on you all the time."

This wasn't too much out of the ordinary. Dario already had a few birthstones lying around in his room, as well as a tiny bottle of greenish ointment that was meant to do wonders for the occasionally dry skin around his toenails.

"Right." He slipped the crystal into his jeans pocket. "Um…thank you, Madam Mina."

But Madam Mina was once again banging away on her typewriter, having apparently forgotten that Dario was there.

He excused himself and left his landlady alone with her dog and the dubious contents of her room.

Ten minutes later, Dario was on his way to work, cutting across the sprawling Fishpond Park, whose many trees were slowly but surely starting to show reddish-yellow leaves and other russet-tinted signs of the coming autumn season. Above the treetops rose the two Gothic towers of the cathedral, which faced away from Fishpond Park, as if deliberately ignoring its autumnal charms.

He proceeded down Under the Wall, a street that followed the outline of the old city wall that no longer existed. He went up Tkalčić Street and turned left onto Bloody Bridge just as the cathedral bells were starting to toll noon.

Bloody Bridge was many things—charming, not too long, pedestrianized and conveniently located. What it wasn't was a bridge. Or at least it hadn't been a bridge lately. Nowadays it was just an ordinary street, albeit a picturesque one, its early baroque buildings and old-fashioned streetlamps like an illustration from a history textbook.

But Bloody Bridge was once a real bridge. This was back when Medveščak Stream, which runs from the Queen's Well on Bear Mountain down to Manda's Well at the Square, was still aboveground. In those days, Medveščak Stream separated Grič Hill, aka Upper Town, in the west from Kaptol in the east. These two hills, which were now two adjoining blocks in the center of the city, used to be two separate fortified towns for hundreds of years. The former was a town of craftsmen, merchants, common laborers and other medieval types, whereas the latter was the seat of the clergy, with the cathedral at its center. The relationship between the two was never the most amicable one. In fact, it was fairly fraught. Conflicts and disagreements were a common motif.

As the only link between the two antagonistic towns, Medveščak Stream Bridge, as Bloody Bridge was known back then, was often the site of territorial unpleasantries and even occasional full-fledged battles. Sadly, those battles were hardly the stuff of legend. The residents of the two towns, preferring roast meat, buttery pastries and other sources of saturated fat to close combat, were ever loath to engage in battles that even remotely approached epic proportions. Indeed, if the people of either burg had ever felt compelled to gather an army of thousands to march against the forces of the other, the records of that particular event are yet to be found. Nevertheless, these battles, such as they were, still managed to be enough of a nuisance to earn the Bridge the epithet "Bloody."

With time, the two warring hills merged into one city, and the existence of a dividing stream stopped being seen as something that was necessary or even practical. There was also the stream's pesky tendency to flood the city center every once in a while, causing all manner of material damage. And so it was decided to have the stream covered up. A road was built over it, and Bloody Bridge became just an ordinary road leading to the newly created Tkalčić Street.

Dario worked at the BBP (short for the Bloody Bridge Press), whose office was on the ground floor of an old yellow building on the corner where Bloody Bridge met Radić Street. On either side of the front door there was a window with blinds that were always drawn halfway, so that the whole building looked like a face with two sleepy eyes.

Reaching for the antique brass handle, Dario could already hear the agitated voice of his boss, Mr. Vinko, coming from inside.

"Yes…yes…" said Mr. Vinko's voice from the other room as Dario entered the office. "I'm sorry about that. Our freelancer…our freelancer has had some problems of a personal nature…an unexpected visit from her in-laws, you see, and she didn't have time to…"

The interior of the BBP headquarters was no bigger than a two-bedroom apartment. Mr. Vinko's tiny office was behind a perpetually closed door on the right, while the slightly more spacious main part of the office was on the left. A narrow corridor formed a buffer zone between the two areas. Its walls were lined with framed covers of the early issues of the *White City Chronicle*, the city's longest-running local monthly magazine and the BBP's flagship publication. Its audience was not huge—it consisted mainly of arty types, history buffs and old ladies who used its ad section as a kind of local Craigslist for tracking down missing cats—but it was loyal.

"I know that it isn't, and I'm sorry. We'll send…we'll send you the proofs by end of day tomorrow."

Mr. Vinko's voice had the kind of high-pitched, squeaky quality it always had a week before press day. As usual, he was hidden behind the closed door to his office, but Dario could imagine him sitting behind his cluttered desk, scalp sweating and eyes bulging as he clutched the telephone receiver with one pudgy little hand.

Dario went down the corridor and entered the cozy but perpetually murky production part of the office, which showed every sign of having been recently vacated by Luka, the only other permanent employee of the BBP. The two of them had to coordinate their work schedules in such a way as to ensure that each was at the office only at those times when the other was away, since they only had one computer between them.

Luka was the BBP's part-time graphic designer, and Dario was the part-time proofreader, subeditor and administrative assistant. The actual writing was done by a ragtag assortment of gallery owners, poets, urban artists, film academy students and other cultural types willing to write for free. There were also a handful of freelance contributors—professional journalists that actually expected to get paid, and some of them even did every once in a while. These were the more tenacious ones. Occasionally Mr. Vinko did some actual reporting himself for those events he deemed worthy, which were rare.

The only other person sporadically seen working at the BBP was Sandra, Mr. Vinko's part-time bookkeeper, whose hours averaged around twelve per month and were fitted around the gaps when neither Dario nor Luka was using the computer, a clunky machine with an old-fashioned monitor the size of a tumble dryer that the two of them referred to as "Mother."

There was a brief moment of silence as Mr. Vinko's conversation ended. Then the phone rang again, and the high-pitched tirade continued.

Dario sat down before Mother and quickly brushed aside the pens, scraps of yellow paper, balled-up pieces of adhesive tape, crumpled chewing gum wrappers, used cinema tickets and other typical Luka debris off the desk.

He unplugged Luka's medium-sized graphic tablet and pushed it to the side, replacing it with his mouse, which had somehow ended up entangled with the many cables behind the computer's tower. Then he went through his usual start-of-shift routine. He opened his email inbox and the files he was currently working on, then brought up his work Twitter feed.

Unsurprisingly, quite a few editorial tasks were queueing for his attention in his inbox, but before he had a chance to take a proper look, his eyes were drawn to a few peculiar tweets on the side of his screen.

Strange lights spotted in the sky over Prečko last night, said one of them. Its source was an obscure account called WWC (Weird White City) that few people followed and even fewer took seriously. It was accompanied by a blurry photo of a white flash against a murky background that could have been just about anything.

The second tweet was more revealing inasmuch as it contained a video, recorded by what appeared to be a personal development coach who happened to be in the vicinity at the time of the mysterious event. The video showed a bright white flash, followed by the appearance of a man dressed in a strange outfit. It was hard to see all the details because the video had been made with a shaky hand from behind what seemed to be a small copse of trees, but Dario thought he might have caught sight of a star-shaped belt buckle. The video had no text other than the hashtag #PrečkoStarman.

Dario searched the #PrečkoStarman tag and found a few more tweets with links to covertly taken nocturnal photos and videos, but all were accompanied by skeptical comments to the effect that this had to be the worst and most amateurishly Photoshopped hoax ever. Dario was nonetheless intrigued. He clicked on the link of the personal development coach's blog, which promised a full article on the subject. This, however, turned out to be little more than a short, incoherent blog post ending with the not particularly convincing closing line "Guys, this really happened." All in all, it didn't look as if the Prečko Starman was likely to make national news anytime soon.

Two things happened then, almost at the same time. First, Mr. Vinko burst out of his office. Second, what turned out to be a hidden audio ad in the blog's sidebar finished loading, unleashing a loud blare of inspirational music out of the speakers.

Dario scrambled for the "close" icon, shutting the whole window just as Mr. Vinko's small, agitated form entered the room.

"Luka, can you remind me if I asked you to do a proof for—" Mr. Vinko stopped midsentence when he saw a somewhat panicked-looking Dario sitting at the production desk.

"Oh." Like a bemused mouse, Mr. Vinko twitched his nose and blinked his beady little eyes, which looked even smaller behind his thick glasses. There was something of the rodent in his short stature and nervous disposition. His face was sweaty, just as Dario had imagined it, and his greasy hair was plastered across the bald patch at the top of his head. "Dario—it's you."

"Um…yes, it is." Dario shuffled his clunky mouse around as he closed all other potentially hazardous applications.

"Has Luka left?" asked Mr. Vinko, even though the answer to the question was obvious. If Luka had been in the office at that moment, he would have been in sight unless he had shrunk to the size of an ink cartridge and hidden inside the printer. But as the owner, CEO, CMO, COO, HR manager and sales director of the BBP and the editor of the *White City Chronicle*, Mr. Vinko always had a lot on his mind and did not always notice the obvious.

Mr. Vinko liked doing everything by himself partly because he was a great believer in the "if you want to do it right, you've got to do it yourself" adage, but mainly because he was cheap. As a result, he was loath to invest in things such as staff and more than the minimum amount of computer equipment. Dario had even heard from Luka that Mr. Vinko cleaned the office himself. He did not believe this rumor though. The office had clearly never been cleaned.

Dario confirmed that Luka had indeed left, and Mr. Vinko was just about to ask him something else when his phone started ringing once again in the other room. Mr. Vinko scurried back into his office. In a moment, the whole place was once again reverberating with the echo of his agitated voice.

He returned a few minutes later, stopping at the same spot as before, a flattened, worn-out patch on the coffee-stained maroon carpet. Mr. Vinko always tended to stand in the exact same spot whenever he talked to Dario, as if wary of crossing some invisible line. Dario had never seen him on the other side of the office.

Mr. Vinko resumed the conversation as if he had never left. "Did I mention anything about the Upper Town Poetry Society Festival quarter-page ad last week?"

"No, you didn't," said Dario. "This is the first time I've heard of it."

"Oh." Mr. Vinko stood at his familiar spot on the carpet, wringing his hands and looking like a schoolboy who had just been called out in front of the whole class. "I don't suppose you could do a proof this afternoon?" His forehead was getting sweaty. "I know graphic design isn't your area, Dario, but if you could come up with something—just anything that I could show them today, that would be…"

Dario said that he would try.

The front door crashed open and in walked Mr. Vinko's ten-year-old daughter Marica with her dog Snowball tugging frantically at the end of an orange leash. Snowball was a hyperactive fluffy little white thing that peed on every surface it came into contact with. Marica, on the other hand, was an insufferable brat, and Dario could only endure her sporadic visits by retreating into the innermost sanctum of his being.

As ever, Mr. Vinko was so delighted to see the brat that he immediately forgot all about his advertising woes.

"Sweetheart!" he exclaimed, while Marica, ignoring Dario completely, launched into an inane monologue about her extracurricular activities and her allowance and the film she was seeing in the cinema that evening, her reedy voice becoming whinier by the second.

In the meantime, Snowball scurried into Dario's part of the office as far as its expandable leash would allow, sniffing around the desk and peeing excitedly all over the place. The carpet owed much of its texture and patina to the dog.

"Snowball!" Marica finally shouted from the corridor, and the little dog retreated, leaving the scent of freshly released urine in its wake. Then the two of them were gone, followed by an energetic slam of the front door.

"Well, yes—if you could do that sometime this afternoon, that would be good," said Mr. Vinko, returning to their earlier conversation.

"Sure."

"Thank you, Dario."

There was a muffled thud as Mr. Vinko once again shuttered himself in his office.

⸙

Dario spent another half hour trawling the Internet in search of more information on the Starman, but there was none to be found. Apparently the Starman had disappeared into the night just as suddenly as he had appeared, and no one had seen him since. Dario was startled out of his thoughts by a kind, grandmotherly voice.

"Excuse me, young man."

He looked up to see a petite old lady standing in front of his desk. This happened a lot at the BBP—people were always popping in and out as if the office were a corner shop. Some of the unannounced visitors, such as freelancers who came in to demand payment of their latest invoice or people who wanted to post an advertisement in person, had a legitimate reason to be there. But every once in a while, a random rambling eccentric or cantankerous drunk would wander in from the street, assail Dario with some bizarre monologue, and then wander out.

This particular visitor looked as if she could easily slot into the latter category. The old lady wore a quaint black coat with lots of mismatched buttons, and a hat that had the appearance of a small fruit bowl. Pinned to her breast pocket was a tacky brooch with a handful of semiprecious stones arranged in the shape of something that could have been either a petunia or a shrunken pink trumpet. Despite this ambiguity, there was something inherently old-lady-like about that brooch. Which was only fitting, seeing as its owner was an old lady.

"Can I help you, madam?"

"Are you the *White City Chronicle*?"

"Yes," said Dario hesitantly. But just to make things perfectly clear, he added, "That is to say, I am not literally the *White City Chronicle*, but I do work for the company that publishes it." He immediately felt better. He had made a concentrated effort to make the universe a more orderly, rational place. It was a small contribution, to be sure, but one that undoubtedly had some impact in the grand scheme of things.

The old lady nodded in a quiet, self-assured way, as if the answer he had given her was exactly what she had expected. "I need you to put a story for me in the paper."

"Um. Right. We don't normally…"

The old lady looked at him with so much earnestness that Dario found himself at a loss as to how to phrase "no way" politely. "I think you'll have to talk to the editor. He's not here at the moment, but if you would like to leave a message…"

The old lady looked politely put out. "I'm afraid this is rather urgent," she said. "I have an important message for the people of the city, which I need you to write for me."

This was certainly not the direction Dario had expected the conversation to take.

"Um, all right. What is the message?"

"The Black Queen is coming."

"The Black Queen is coming," repeated Dario slowly. He knew, of course, who the Black Queen was. She was the quintessential archvillain from a semi-mythical past. In spite of this, the Black Queen did not get featured in the *White City Chronicle* all that often. This was mainly due to the fact that she was dead—very dead—some five hundred years dead, to be precise.

"Yes, the Black Queen of Bear Town Fortress," explained the old lady helpfully. "The witch from the mountain. The scourge of the White City. She is coming back from the other side. I have seen her."

At some point, possibly not long after the "scourge" reference, Dario had decided that what appeared to be a harmless old lady was in fact a dangerous lunatic, and that it was in his best interest to persuade her to leave the office as soon as possible, preferably before she started hearing voices in her head.

"Right," he said. "I'm afraid you've come to the wrong press office, madam. You see, we don't publish those kinds of stories here. It sounds to me as if you're looking for *Life and Destiny*. And their offices are in Savska, I believe. If you go and catch the number seventeen right now, you should be there in no time."

"Now listen to me, young man." The old lady's voice suddenly took on a steely, take-no-prisoners edge.

Dario gulped.

"I don't know what it is you're suggesting," she went on, "but I assure you that what I have to say is the absolute truth."

"I have no doubt that it is, but—"

"I have seen the Black Queen myself. I have seen her in my tea leaves. And the tea leaves don't lie."

The old lady looked at him with the fixed determination of someone who would not leave until other people's time and energy had been wasted to a satisfactory degree. Dario made a mental note to tell Mr. Vinko that having a proper front door, one that prevented people with too much time on their hands from wandering in from the street, might be a good idea. Maybe one of those things that could only be opened by keying in a numeric code or scanning a plastic card.

But for the time being, the best course of action was to stop disagreeing with the delusional old woman and act interested. So he picked up a pen, opened his tattered spiral-bound notebook, and encouraged her to tell the whole story.

The story went like this:

The old lady was the tea reader Vera Melada, who, though not a household name, was a well-known personage in certain circles. She had been doing daily tea readings for many years, using only the finest Chinese pu-erh leaves delivered to her directly from the Yunnan Province. It was she who had predicted the minor Bear Mountain earth tremors of 1997 and the delayed barn swallow migration of 2005.

Imagine her surprise, then, when she looked at the bottom of her reading cup the other day and saw the menacing figure of the Black Queen rising out of its round base, covering almost the whole side of the cup with her billowing black cape. Not surprisingly, the evil queen's black raven was at her side, but there were other things, very strange things, there besides.

"Something that looked like a piece of string, or perhaps it was a fire hose," said Vera Melada. "And then there was something that looked like a kind of hammock but with lots of ropes."

Dario scrawled in his notebook vigorously, nodding at all the right places, if such a thing was even applicable under the circumstances.

"And I saw one more thing, although its shape was very vague. But if I had to make a guess, I'd say it was a fox."

"A fox?"

"A fox." The old lady nodded.

Dario updated his notes with the fox detail.

"As you can see," said Vera Melada, "the matter is a serious one. The Black Queen is clearly planning some kind of attack. The people must be alerted."

"I agree," said Dario, getting to his feet. "And we will give the matter all the attention it deserves."

This seemed to appease Vera Melada. Dario escorted her out of the building, thanking her for the story and reassuring her that he would pass it on to the editor at the earliest opportune moment.

When Dario was finally left alone once again, he felt a vague sense of excitement. Vera Melada's story was no doubt nonsense, nothing more than the ramblings of a person whose connection to reality was fraying around the edges, but on the other hand, what was the likelihood of a story as absurd as Vera Melada's appearing on the same day as the alleged Starman sightings?

The most plausible explanation was that this was nothing but a bizarre coincidence. Perhaps there was something in the air that day—possibly a kind of radiation—that made people talk interesting nonsense. But there was also the infinitesimal chance that these two occurrences had actual meaning, and that they might even be somehow related. And for someone with a life as uneventful as Dario's, even an infinitesimal probability of something interesting finally happening was not a thing to be dismissed lightly.

He spent the next hour trying to put the Starman and Black Queen references together in a way that made sense, but when combined, those two terms yielded nothing more than something that sounded like a glam rock tribute band.

Then his phone pinged. It was a text from Martin, one of his friends from university. The text read:

gig tomorrow night
from 9pm @ the ditch
black metal
quite brutal
not your thing
be there

Without thinking, Dario texted back, *I'll be there.* (He was the kind of person who used proper punctuation even in text messages.)

For the time being, he put the whole matter of the Starman and the Black Queen out of his mind.

5

UNDER THE GINKGO

The botanical garden was a bit like the rest of the city—boring, neglected and barely noticeable from the outside. And all the trees looked the same. Leo had to ask the caretaker, an unwholesome, bloated middle-aged character with bloodshot eyes, to take him to the wretched ginkgo. The man, who had been hibernating by some shed in an alcoholic stupor, looked dumbly flabbergasted at being asked a botany-related question, or for that matter, *any* question, by a visitor.

Leo found the hermit sitting on a bench in his filthy hermit robe, feeding stale bread to pigeons and staring about him with an infuriatingly placid, childlike expression, which somehow managed to be visible even through the hideous beard that grew out of his face like some kind of hairy parasite.

He had encountered during his cosmic journeys a type of terrible alien parasite resembling a crawling long-haired wig with tiny sharp teeth that attaches itself to its victim's face, remaining there until the end of their days, feeding off them and making them look as if a cluster of long, bushy hair had sprouted out of their face. Leo often wondered whether what was referred to as a "beard" on the earthly plane was in fact a manifestation of that ghastly parasite. That interpretation at least offered some sort of logical explanation for the presence of hair on people's faces, i.e., that the beards were there because the parasites would kill the hosts in the event that any attempt of removal was made. But the idea that beards were something that people voluntarily chose to have—now *that* was a disturbing thought.

When the hermit noticed Leo, he pointed up at a sorry-looking tree standing all by itself in a neglected corner.

"Look, a ginkgo."

"Fascinating," snapped Leo.

"I'm so glad you could make it, Leo. I've been so looking forward to seeing you."

"I wish I could say the feeling was mutual."

The hermit offered Leo a seat on the other end of his birdshit-splattered bench, and Leo reluctantly obliged, making sure his pristine blue cloak didn't touch the hermit's grimy brown robe, which looked like the home of several thriving flea colonies.

Leo went straight to the point. "What exactly is it that I have to do? What are these renegade creatures of the Black Queen that I have to subdue before I am finally allowed to leave?"

The old man looked at Leo as if he had only just realized he was there. Then he seemed to pick up the thread of the conversation again.

"Oh, the creatures," he said, tossing a piece of bread crust to a particularly mangy-looking pigeon. Then he fell silent again. The silence dragged on for ages until Leo finally asked the hermit to continue.

"Where was I?" asked the hermit.

Leo pinched the bridge of his nose. "The creatures."

"Oh, yes, the creatures. To be honest, we are not quite sure what exactly happened. My sister, who is almost as old as I am and a great prophetess, saw a number of them in her tea leaves recently, but it is an uncertain number and the nature of the creatures themselves is quite uncertain too. There is a distinct element of uncertainty here! What is certain is that something bad is about to happen. Something very bad. Certainly. This is why we alerted the Star Council."

Leo took a shaky breath. "You do realize that I am not able to leave this place until I have done the thing I have been sent to do? That I am physically unable to leave? I'm stranded! And here you are, telling me that you don't even know what is going on."

The hermit made a cooing sound at one of the pigeons. Then he fell silent again.

Leo cleared his throat.

The hermit started. "Where was I? Oh, yes…yes, you're stranded." The old man stroked his beard wistfully before continuing. "I truly am sorry for your predicament, Leo. Believe me, I am. But we are unable to deal with this situation on our own. We simply don't have the…" He waved his hand around for a few moments, as if trying to remember the right word. "…the resources."

"What situation? There is no situation. Nothing has happened!"

"Oh, it will. Something is about to happen soon. Very soon. Something evil. The Black Queen is up to something. I can feel it in my bones. My bone, actually. My left femur. It always starts to ache when—"

"Listen, hermit, you've got to give me something to work with. At least a starting point. I can't be expected to hang around this abominable city indefinitely until Barbara decides to possess someone remotely via enchanted bottled water."

"Yes, you're right. You do need something to get you started. Let me think."

The hermit looked thoughtful for a long moment. Then he scratched his beard, which made a dry rustling sound that sent shudders of revulsion down Leo's spine.

"Well?" said Leo eventually.

The hermit blinked. "Ah, yes. Where was I?"

Leo hung his head dejectedly for a moment before saying, "You were going to give me something to work with."

"Oh, yes, that's right. Well, let's see. You could always start by talking to the Little Brethren. They always seem to be on top of all the latest goings-on."

"Never," said Leo curtly. "I'll never subject myself to the mental torture of talking to those little pests ever again. I'd rather cut my hair than go to them. I'd rather…" Leo briefly pondered over the worst possible thing that could ever happen to him. "I'd rather grow a beard."

The hermit didn't seem particularly affected by Leo's rant, or perhaps he just hadn't been listening.

He handed the last of his bread to the pigeons. "There, there, Leo. No reason to get excited. I'm sure something will turn up that will give us an idea—a clear idea, possibly even a direction. Have patience, Leo."

"Patience?" Leo sprang to his feet. "I won't have anyone telling me to be patient when I'm being made to suffer in this prison of a city!" And he stormed off in the direction of the gate, which turned out to be the wrong direction (his memory of the gate's exact location must have faded during the course of the conversation).

In the end, he had to ask the alcoholic caretaker for directions again, which was embarrassing, to say the least. All in all, it took him almost ten minutes to find the exit.

As soon as he was out in the street, it started to rain.

"God, I hate this city," said Leo miserably.

PART TWO

OCTOBER

6

THE FORBIDDEN CELLAR

Classroom 5B was suffused with a nervous murmur. There was a legitimate reason for this—the dreaded Professor Radovan was about to come in any moment.

When the door burst open and the towering figure walked in, the pupils promptly stood up in unison. The scrawny metal legs of thirty-seven chairs scraped against the worn-out parquet.

The teacher didn't even glance in the pupils' direction as she walked into the classroom. Instead, she headed straight for her desk, the rubber soles of her orthopedic wedge-heel shoes making squeaking noises against the floor. The beige fabric of the shoes was nearly bursting against the bulk of her swollen feet. Her stiff legs, jointless like lampposts, worked mechanically underneath the hem of her swamp-brown tweed skirt. Tucked safely under her right arm, the enormous blue class register book swung back and forth with her steps.

Professor Radovan tossed the heavy register book on her desk with a baneful thud and then eased herself into her creaky chair.

"Sit," she commanded through clenched teeth. They did.

As the teacher wrote the day's date in the register, Stella scribbled *Schoolwork* at the top of a new page in her notebook. She didn't want to look up from the page. If she couldn't see Professor Radovan, then perhaps Professor Radovan couldn't see her.

A tense silence had settled over the classroom, interrupted only by the occasional rustling of large sheets of paper. This could only mean one thing—Professor Radovan was going through the class register. The awful book contained all the information on the pupils of class 5B—their names, their grades, their sick days. Everything.

Professor Radovan's nerve-racking inspection of the register was a daily ritual. She would scrutinize the pages one by one until she selected one pupil who would then have to show his or her homework to the teacher or answer her revision questions.

Judging by the thickness of the pages on the teacher's left-hand side, she was now going through the critical part of the book, the first third, which contained all of the surnames from *A* to *F*. Stella's own surname, Fleger, was among them.

Professor Radovan suddenly paused, her brow furrowing. She peered at something on the page through her tiny reading glasses for a long time. Her chin was raised as she read, creating the impression of someone peering down from a great height.

The tension in the class had reached a nearly tangible level. Stella risked a glance in Professor Radovan's direction and noticed that the page she was inspecting was right at the end of the fateful first third of the register, which was exactly where the *F* surnames were. Stella's heart was hammering in her chest.

Professor Radovan suddenly lost interest in whatever it was she had been reading and started turning the pages again. She was now leafing through the relative safety of the first half of the second third. Stella let out a little sigh. Her heart began to slow down. But then, in the blink of an eye, Professor Radovan flipped the pages back to the first third again and uttered one sharp word.

"Flegar!"

The heads of the thirty-six pupils of class 5B who did not respond to the name Flegar turned toward Stella. To be fair, Stella didn't normally respond to Flegar either, but everyone knew that for all intents and purposes, Flegar meant her. Whenever Professor Radovan called out Stella's last name, she made a point of mispronouncing it in some way.

Stella picked up her notebook and set forth meekly through the labyrinth of desks leading up to the front of the class. The five years she had spent as Professor Radovan's pupil had conditioned her to be obedient, like a caged laboratory rodent trained to respond to a stimulus by moving in a specific direction. Thus, her demeanor showed no signs of resistance.

As soon as she reached the teacher's desk, Professor Radovan snatched the notebook impatiently out of Stella's hand, flinging it onto her desktop as if it were some unsanitary thing too repulsive to be handled. Then she started poring over the notebook's contents, suddenly breathing as loudly as a wild boar.

Her hand, red pen in its grip, hovered over Stella's most recent homework assignment in a strange state of suspended aggression, making tiny stabbing motions in the air. It was as if the teacher couldn't decide which parts to cross out first.

The moment of deliberation finally over, Professor Radovan tossed the notebook on the floor before Stella's feet.

"Your handwriting is terrible, Flailer," the teacher said. "Rewrite everything."

Stella picked up her notebook without uttering a single word and went back to her desk. She picked up her pen and promptly dropped it with a little gasp as a tiny black spider suddenly scampered across the open pages of her notebook. It disappeared over the edge of the desk just as abruptly as it had appeared.

She remembered the spider she had seen coming out of the wall in the Dead Zone and shuddered. What was it with these spiders? Why did they insist on inexplicably appearing all of a sudden? If only Zagreb were more like Australia, where they have those spider-eating birds. Or was it bird-eating spiders? Not that it mattered either way, since they were not allowed to keep birds in class.

Tin gave her a sympathetic look from where he sat two desks down to her right. Stella made what she hoped was a "did you just see a spider walk across my notebook?" face. Tin only shrugged innocently. Clearly he had no idea what she was trying to say.

Stella made a "never mind" gesture. There was no need to make a fuss over an irrelevant little spider.

The next class should have been a welcome relief, since it was biology with Professor Novak.

Mira Novak was not the kind of person who was ever likely to bother bragging about her personal philosophy, but this was only because she never bothered to do anything. Her personal motto could have been summed up as "live and let live, as long as this doesn't create any additional work for me." Because if there was one thing Professor Novak didn't like, it was work.

Take biology, for example. This was normally a rather hands-on subject, one in which the average student was expected to do a fair amount of practical work—growing potted plants to observe their development, dissecting worms to study their intestines, cutting up drugged toads to peer at their miniature gonads and other things of that nature. But who had any use for that? Certainly not Mira Novak. Besides, practical work was too much of a hassle, and it made your hands dirty.

So, to avoid doing any practical work whatsoever, Professor Novak had a modus operandi whereby she would tell the class at the beginning of each lesson to read a long passage on a particular topic from the textbook and then let the kids figure it out on their own while she did crossword puzzles for the next forty-five minutes.

On this day, the assignment was to read a chapter on the life cycle of moss, and most of the pupils looked bored out of their minds. The only one who did not look utterly bored was Stella, who still hadn't gotten over the spider sighting. She nearly jumped when she saw something move with the corner of her eye and was relieved when she realized it was only someone shaking a pen that had stopped working.

"Teacher," said a reedy little voice. It was Ivica, a scrawny boy who sat directly behind Stella.

"Yes," said Mira Novak in a drawn-out, nasal voice.

"Teacher, may I please go to the bathroom?"

Professor Novak sighed a jaded sigh. "Go—what do I care?"

Ivica scurried out of the classroom, his slippered feet brushing against the wooden floor with brisk sweeps that sounded like miniature brooms operated by trained hamsters.

Professor Novak blew out a bored, disdainful breath as she slowly filled in the solution to "12 Across."

A few moments later, a piercing scream resonated down the school corridor.

Professor Novak raised one disinterested eyebrow. "Now what?" she said without bothering to take her eyes off her crossword.

From the corridor there came a *pat-pat* of tiny running feet. Ivica burst into the classroom. He was panting excitedly, and his eyes were as big as saucers.

"Teacher!" he cried.

Mira Novak finally looked up from her crossword.

"What?"

"Teacher, I saw a big black spider going down the stairs to the Forbidden Cellar."

"Did you."

Ivica nodded vigorously. "I did! It was huge. The size of a dog. A big dog!"

"Sit down," said Professor Novak.

"But, Teacher—"

"Now."

Ivica got back to his seat.

Professor Novak sighed another weary sigh and went back to her crossword. No one noticed that Stella had gone as pale as a sheet.

"We have to go down to the cellar as soon as possible—maybe even today," she announced to Tin, Rea and Ida during their lunch break as the four of them nibbled on their packed sandwiches while sitting among the shrubbery at the top of a slope on the northern side of the playground, an area they had dubbed Lookout Hill. Stella had suggested that they go sit there, ostensibly because of the view, but actually because it was as far from the Dead Zone as you could get without crossing over to the football side of the playground, which all four of them avoided.

A handful of boys were currently playing football on that side. They looked so far away that they might have been in another country.

"You don't really believe what Ivica said is true?" asked Rea.

"Of course it's true," said Stella.

"I wouldn't believe everything he says," said Tin. "You know what his asthma medicine does to him."

"This was real. Can't you see? The spider is one of the creatures that got through when we played Black Queen One-Two-Three."

Rea rolled her eyes. "Nothing got through! Where would it come from? You imagined the whole thing."

"I don't know! And I didn't."

"Supposing it's all true," said Tin calmly. "That's all the more reason not to go down there. I mean, who would want to go into a cellar if you knew there was a dog-sized spider there?"

Before Stella could answer, a football came flying in their direction and landed in the bushes. In the distance, on the football pitch side of the playground, a small boy standing by the goal was waving at them with both arms. He had stripped to his waist, his skinny, pale chest like a gecko's. The tiny black hole that was his mouth kept opening and closing rapidly, but no coherent words reached them—there was only a distant squawking sound.

Rea grabbed the football and kicked it toward the boy with savage intensity.

"Watch out, you losers!" she shouted in the general direction of the pitch. The ball described a long curve through the air and landed on the far side of the pitch. The boy squawked once more and then turned away to attend to the goal.

"I don't care if no one believes me," said Stella. "I know what I saw. I let those things in, and I can't just sit back and pretend it never happened. If I can get rid of at least one of them, that'll make me feel better."

"How are you going to kill the spider?" asked Tin.

"I don't know—how do you usually kill spiders? I guess I'll stamp on it or something."

"You could use Raid," said Ida.

"You're all being ridiculous," said Rea. "I am going back in to revise my homework." She promptly marched back into the school building. Ida soon followed.

"How can you be sure the spider actually got into the cellar?" asked Tin. "Maybe it was just passing by."

"I know it went into the cellar because the cellar is the darkest part of the school. And the Black Queen's creatures are drawn to darkness." This wasn't really an established fact, but it did have a kind of evil logic to it.

"So where did the other creatures go? You said there were a few of them."

As if on cue, something that looked like a raven flew over the playground. On second glance, this turned out to be nothing more than a very dark pigeon.

"See? That might have been another one," said Stella.

Tin stared at the sky wistfully for a few moments after the bird had gone out of sight.

"What do you say? Are you in?"

Tin sighed. "All right, I'm in."

They waited for the rest of the kids to clear off at the end of the school day and then padded down the corridor toward the Forbidden Cellar. They had nearly made it halfway when the cleaning woman emerged from the boys' toilets on the left and stopped before them, barring their way.

A sturdy pylon-legged type that seemed to have been made from the same template as Professor Radovan, the cleaning woman was a textbook example of the socialist adage that could be paraphrased as "do only as little as you have to in order to keep your job until retirement, preferably less than that if you can get away with it, and make sure not to smile under any circumstances." And this was hardly surprising since, judging by the age of Professor Radovan and the cleaner, this was obviously the period that both women had spent their formative years in.

Clutched in each one of her hands like a weapon was a long wooden pole. Stella knew those poles. When a dirty rag was suspended between them, they formed an improvised sweeping apparatus, which the cleaner ran up and down the corridor twice a day. As far as the cleaner was concerned, this was what constituted cleaning. She wasn't paid much: therefore, she didn't do much. And if she ever saw so much as a slice of salami fall out of some hapless kid's sandwich and hit the floor, she would give him hell. *What did these damn kids expect her to do? Clean after them?* There was an almost 90 percent certainty that in a previous life the cleaning woman had been a hardened cowboy who chewed tobacco and spat it out through a gap in his teeth.

Stella knew that the cleaner was done with the sweeping apparatus for the day since she always finished cleaning before the end of the last lesson. This must have been why, at present, she looked content to do nothing other than stand before Stella and Tin like a scowling barricade.

"What are you kids doing here?"

Tin gulped.

"Uh, nothing, Madam Cleaner," said Stella. "We were just going to fetch our stuff from the other cupboard."

"Well, then get your damn stuff and get the hell outta here. And you'd better do it fast, cause I ain't gonna ask you again."

"Yes, Madam Cleaner," said Stella and Tin in unison.

The cleaner nodded grimly and retreated back into the shadows of the boys' toilets. The two of them continued down the corridor.

"Is it safe?" whispered Tin. "What if she follows us?"

"Are you crazy?" Stella whispered back. "She couldn't care less where we go. They don't pay her to police kids after hours."

They snuck to the northern end of the corridor, where it was always murky and dust motes hovered in the air like indoor smog. They stopped when they reached the top of the stairs that led to the Forbidden Cellar.

The stairs looked grimy and untrodden, as if no feet, particularly those of a cleaner, had touched them for a very long time. Farther down, there was a small landing, its surface covered in hardened dirt so thick it might have been petrified lava, while another shorter flight of stairs went down to the mysterious gloom of the lower ground floor, where the door to the Forbidden Cellar presumably was.

A distant clatter of a heavy door being shut disturbed the stillness, and they both started.

"It's fine; that was just someone on the second floor," whispered Stella. The second floor belonged to the secondary school, which was a separate universe entirely different from their own and thus had no bearing on the events that transpired on their level. Tin nodded, and then they began their descent.

The musty gloom that awaited them at the bottom concealed a graveyard of discarded school furniture that loomed threateningly over them out of the darkness like predatory man-eating trees in an enchanted forest. There were three distinct piles—one made up predominantly of tables, cupboards and wooden crates, another consisting of old TV screens, printers and keyboards, and one made up of broken wooden chairs stacked one on top of another, the legs sticking up like antennae. The floor was covered in flattened cardboard boxes that had been haphazardly strewn in the gaps between the stacked furniture. The one thing that was not accounted for in the mess was the cellar door.

"Can you see it?" said Tin in a barely audible whisper.

"Nope," said Stella. Then something caught her eye. "Wait a minute."

She went up to an enormous flattened box poking out from behind a broken cupboard that might have once belonged in a chemistry classroom. Moving the cardboard aside revealed a strange iron door with a covered-up opening near the top that looked like the sliding hatch on a prison cell door. There was no flashing neon sign that said "Forbidden Cellar" above it, but this had to be it.

There was one catch though—the door was secured with a padlock—a huge rusty one the size of a fat man's fist.

When he saw the padlock, Tin let out a low whistle of awe. Then he grabbed it, gave it a quick rattle, and looked at Stella compassionately, shaking his head like a TV doctor delivering bad news.

Then something unexpected happened. The chemistry cabinet, which had been leaning precariously to the side due to one of its legs being broken, suddenly tilted forward and crashed to the floor like a felled tree. The resulting noise pierced the cryptic quiet of the school like a needle bursting an overinflated balloon. The echo of the crash resonated down the empty corridors.

Seconds later, a feeble old man's voice said, "Who's there?"

Stella and Tin looked at one another with identical deer-in-the-headlights expressions and then bolted up the stairs.

A lanky old man in a dark blue janitor's uniform emerged from a small storage room by the stairs. "What are you doing here?" he called in a weak, dazed voice, but they just ran past him.

"It's the janitor!" yelled Stella.

"Never mind; just run!" cried Tin.

❧

"Did you see his face?" said Tin, panting.

They hadn't stopped running until they had reached a small park across the road from the school's northern tower. They had named it Dog Sitters' Park because it was frequented by people, mainly elderly ladies, who came there to walk their dogs but never bothered to do much walking. Instead, they would just lounge on the benches while their dogs, mainly pocket-sized terriers, did all the walking themselves. Fortunately, at that moment there were neither terriers nor elderly ladies around.

"Briefly," panted Stella.

"He looked as drunk as a skunk."

"You would be too if you had to spend all your time there." She gestured vaguely at the school. Stella had heard that Rudi the janitor lived in the school, and the thought made her shudder.

Tin clutched his spleen with a pained expression, as if trying to prevent it from bursting.

"Well, at least now you know about the cellar," he said.

Stella didn't look convinced.

"No giant spiders could have got in through that door," added Tin. "And if there were any creeping about, Rudi would have seen them."

"I don't know." Stella gazed wistfully at the northern tower, which loomed like the prow of an ocean liner across the road. "I still want to go in."

"There's no way to get into that cellar," said Tin. "And even if we found a way to break the lock, Rudi would hear it, and he'd find us before we got any further."

"Maybe."

As Tin walked home after he and Stella had parted ways in the park, he tried to talk himself into thinking that now that they knew the cellar was inaccessible, Stella was bound to finally get over her strange Black Queen fixation. Tin had known Stella for almost five whole years, and if there was one thing he had learned about her during that time, it was that she was nothing if not reasonable. Therefore, she was now bound to come to her senses and stop jumping at shadows.

He took a left turn into his street, colloquially known as the Village. At that moment the street was completely deserted apart from a few old cars parked along the sides, most of them looking as if they hadn't been driven for years. The Village extended before him like the setting of a showdown in a Western. One could easily imagine tumbleweed rolling across the road and disappearing behind the hulk of a rusty car.

On each side of the street, a row of mismatched houses stretched out in a neat line toward a vanishing point in the distance. Some of the houses sported yellowing shutters and paved yards that were used mainly for storing things that no longer fit indoors, while others had nicer, freshly painted woodwork and actual gardens. Tall evergreen trees and weathered lampposts lined the street at irregular intervals.

On Tin's right, a tiny red car without wheels sat mounted on a pile of bricks. It was a *Fićo*—a cheap Yugoslav version of a Fiat 600 from the '70s and '80s with a structure so simple that if anything was broken, it could be fixed with duct tape or WD-40.

A stray ginger cat was occasionally known to lounge on the car's cramped back seat. Tin paused and glanced at the back window. There was no cat inside, only a discarded beer can.

Then he heard voices coming from farther down the street. Rough, wavering, undeveloped voices. The voices of academic underachievers and potential vandals. With a sigh, Tin got going again. There was no point postponing the inevitable.

Farther down the road, just behind a cluster of lanky trees, there was Borna, a thin, pimply seventh grader with mean, squinty eyes and a ratty ponytail, and Alen, a sullen kid with a shaved head who should have been in high school but was still in the eighth grade of primary school. The reason for this was that he had failed all subjects other than art and music, but this was only because those two subjects were something that practically everyone passed almost as a default. He had even failed physical education due to nonattendance.

As usual, Borna was standing astride a gray BMX bike with blue padding around the horizontal bar. Tin had never seen Borna standing without the support of the BMX. There were football-themed patches and badges all over Borna's denim jacket. Alen was wearing a khaki bomber jacket and the black Doc Martens boots that he was never seen out of. He gave Tin a moronically insolent look, as if challenging Tin to draw something more dangerous than a pencil sharpener out of his school bag.

"Hey, fatso," said Borna when he saw Tin. "Do you have a smoke?"

"No," said Tin, slowing down his pace without stopping.

"Give us some cash then."

"I don't have any money," said Tin and went on his way.

"Fine," said Borna after him. "If you *say so.*"

When Tin reached a low wooden fence that had a blue metal plate with a white "27" painted on it, he opened the gate and proceeded toward a yellow bungalow that was barely visible behind the clutter of discarded weather-eaten household objects that had grown into a sizable heap over time in the garden. He could hear the TV even before he had finished opening the front door. Fast, excited, high-pitched chatter, like the yapping of an agitated handbag dog; the sound of many throats cheering and booing at the same time; the piercing sound of a whistle.

Football.

It was dark in the hall, and he had to be careful not to trip over the litter of shoes lying scattered on the floor. He tossed his slipper bag in the corner and peeled the straps of his perpetually overloaded school rucksack off his shoulders. He parked the bag in its temporary space against the wall, where it would remain for a few hours until it was time to worry about doing his homework for the following day.

"Hello, Dad," said Tin as he passed by the open door to the living room. All he could see from where he stood was the back of an old brown armchair and a shiny bald scalp poking out at the top. An answering grunt came from its direction. At the far end of the living room, directly in front of the armchair, towered the TV, its big screen filled from edge to edge with the bright green of a football pitch. Milling around the green field like ants were many tiny X-shaped homunculi pushing around a tiny white dot.

Tin was already bored. If random shots of sheep placidly grazing grass in a meadow had been inserted at random intervals into the footage, he wouldn't have noticed the difference. He did not understand how anyone could subject himself to ninety minutes of such mind-numbing boredom.

On the TV, there was a close-up of one of the football players, who was just in the middle of spitting out what looked like half a pint of phlegm onto the field. The player had a bony, equine face, a pale, sickly complexion, thin mousy hair on the shorter end of the mullet spectrum and large, bulging eyes that were continuously darting this way and that, as if unable to take in the horror of it all.

Better you than me, thought Tin.

A gaunt shadow crept down the school's deserted corridors. It went from door to door, opening one, peeking inside, and moving on to another. It was getting dark, and the hour was late, or perhaps it was early. It didn't matter either way. Once everyone had gone home, every hour felt the same.

Rudi opened the last door at the end of the second-floor corridor with shaky hands. Having taken a quick look at the black silhouettes of the unoccupied desks and chairs, he banged the door closed behind him. Its impact against the frame resonated down the corridor with a shockingly loud echo that seemed to fill all the empty spaces left behind by the schoolchildren. It was an uncanny sound, one that belonged in the same liminal category as the sound of one hand clapping or the crash of a single tree falling down unobserved in a forest.

It was a strange way to live, one man alone in a vast building, but it was the only life he knew. There had been a time, long ago, when he had lived with other people, long-gone days when he'd had no reason to think that the future would be any different. He had tried to find his place in the outside world, and for a while it looked as if he were on the verge of succeeding. He even had a steady job once as a printmaker's assistant. And then *it* happened.

Rudi stopped in his tracks. His hands trembled. In his mind, he heard a distant metallic groan, the sound of something big and heavy skidding against a metal surface. He gasped and clutched his head. He stood like that for a few minutes, waiting for it to end. This was how it went every night, and Rudi had found that there was nothing he could do about it. Best to just let it happen.

With the corner of his eye, he could see a large black shadow moving erratically on the ceiling above him. When he looked up, it was gone. It had been there though. He knew it. He could feel its invisible threads hanging everywhere. His mind might have been slow, but he was still able to sense things that nobody else could. He didn't know what it was. This wasn't another echo from the past coming back to haunt him. This was something else.

Whatever it was, he didn't like it. It seemed to feed on secret fears and traumas. It kept trying to make him remember.

But he was not going to let it.

Rudi staggered to the stairwell at the end of the corridor. The last traces of gray dusk were coming in from the outside. The night was descending fast. There was now just enough light left to see the outline of the corridor. That was good enough. He didn't need light anyway. He knew the layout of the school by heart.

It used to frighten him at first, the idea of living in the school building by himself. But when he was offered to live there for free in exchange for looking after the premises, he accepted without hesitation. He already knew he was no longer fit to live in the outside world. Gradually, he got used to the nocturnal emptiness of the school. He even found comfort in the quiet of the corridors and the stillness of the shadows. And with time, he had become one of the shadows.

A cold draughty tendril swept past him as he staggered down the stairs. He shivered. Nearly tumbling off the last step, he headed toward the main entrance. An orange glow streamed in through the glass panes from the streetlamp outside, and it made him squint. He closed the heavy double door with a noisy clang. With a trembling hand, he took a bunch of keys out of his pocket. He selected a large corroded key dangling in the middle and locked the door, giving it a little push, as he always did.

Satisfied that the school and all its secrets were securely locked inside, he retreated back into the shadows.

7

A NIGHT AT THE DITCH

The Ditch looked like the remains of a car wash that had been converted into a makeshift hideout by a mutant motorcycle gang in a postapocalyptic wasteland. But while its appearance left a lot to be desired, the darkness that accompanied its usual opening hours (rarely before 9:00 p.m.) did a lot to disguise any imperfections and arguably even managed to transform them into a kind of anti-chic. By day, the Ditch had the eerie, desolate air of a place that is only used for nocturnal gatherings. At night, it was one of the few focal points of activity by the flat, grassy and generally unremarkable bank of the river Sava.

Dario trudged down a footpath without end. He had been treading the same path since disembarking at the number fourteen tram stop what seemed like hours before, but there was still no end in sight. The faint outline of the path in the moonlight was like the last remaining thread of civilization in some benighted limbo.

When the sinister Ditch finally emerged out of the darkness, Dario almost longed for the return of his erstwhile desolation. The place was like the mouth of Hell. First, there was the skeletal pillar constructed out of metal bars that towered over the main building like the remains of a wicker man left in the aftermath of some unspeakable pagan rite. Then there was the sound. Muffled buzzing of violent music leaked out of the venue, making the ground vibrate under his feet. It sounded as if the place were being besieged by a giant angry queen bee armed with chain saws. A huge black raven swept down through the night air, circling over the Ditch like a vulture.

A few long-haired, black-leather-clad people with spike-covered wristbands were standing outside smoking. As Dario passed them by, they gave him suspicious looks. He smiled and nodded at them awkwardly. This was not his scene, but he was making an effort to maintain friendships with his former colleagues from the University of Zagreb's Philosophy Department, a handful of whom he immediately spotted loitering a bit farther down the path.

There was Martin, with unkempt hair and a fashion sense heavily inclined toward khaki hues. Standing next to him was Bruno, who had a lot of unbrushed blond hair pulled back in a ponytail and whose wardrobe consisted of a faded black T-shirt and khakis.

Both of them were students of what was sometimes referred to, always in hushed tones, as Pure Philosophy. This was a course of study in which one studied philosophy and nothing but philosophy for four years. It was a challenging course that made students question the very purpose and foundation of existence. They questioned the purpose of everything—everything, that is, apart from the purpose of their course.

Martin saw him and waved. "Old man!" This was a popular term of address among non-old persons, and Martin used it liberally.

"Great timing, old man," he said as Dario approached them. "We've just had to suffer through a whole hour of the supporting band. What were they called?" He looked at Bruno. "Demonic...Dysentery?"

"Demonic Dismemberment," said Bruno.

"But the headliners, Crepuscular Immolation, are said to be pretty good. I mean, good in a black metal sort of way."

"Their singer, Nidhogg," added Bruno by way of explanation, "is said to occasionally eat raw pigs' heads on stage."

"Sounds awesome," Dario lied.

The noise coming from inside the Ditch suddenly rose to earsplitting levels, announcing the start of the Crepuscular Immolation set. The long-haired smokers duly flicked away their half-smoked cigarettes and proceeded inside. Dario looked at Bruno and Martin. The latter shrugged as if to say "why not?" and the three of them followed the smokers into the cavernous interior of the Ditch.

The moment he set foot inside the venue, Dario was treated to a barrage of demonic shrieking, spasmodic drumming and frenzied screeching of electric guitars, all of which, when piled one on top of another, sounded oddly a lot like

sizzling oil gushing out of a giant shower in Hell. And that was only the foyer. Dario could feel his eardrums shrinking, like tiny crustaceans retreating into
their shells in the face of imminent danger.

They walked past an improvised stand where a number of Crepuscular Immolation T-shirts and other merchandise were on display. The band logo was a
barely legible scrawl with the *t* in "Immolation" drawn as an upside-down cross.
Most of the T-shirts featured the cover image taken from their latest album,
Death Throes in Arboreal Hollows.

Inside the dedicated gig area, Crepuscular Immolation was a larger-than-
life presence on the tiny stage. The four band members were so long-haired and
long-strided that the room could barely contain them. The two guitarists on either ends of the stage wore tight black leather outfits and wielded special black
guitars shaped like battle-axes. The drum kit behind them, embellished at the
front with the band logo, had enough snares and cymbals to equip fourteen
marching bands.

The singer, Nidhogg, prowled the vapor-covered stage like a ghost in the
fog at a church graveyard. His long black hair was impeccably groomed, his
black leather trousers very tight and his transparent black top like a screen that
showed piercings in various uncomfortable-looking places. On his forearms, he
wore leather gauntlets with enormous spikes. His face, frozen in a diabolical grin
as he shrieked out what must have been a song, was painted a chalky white. The
black smears painted around his eyes made them look like pits. Although his vocal style was too distorted to allow for even a basic comprehension of the lyrics,
one could easily infer from the context that the words were not something that
was likely to be uttered during a Sunday church service.

"Blargh!" shrieked Nidhogg over the thick wall of furious background music. "Blarghwadda largh of Satan!"

Dario, Martin and Bruno lingered at the back, partly in order to get a
big-picture view of the scene but mainly to avoid the space directly before the
stage, which was a chaos of jumping, jostling, devil's horns flashing and moshing.
Dario scanned the stage for signs of pigs' heads, but there were none to be seen.
Perhaps the singer had already had supper.

The current song ended abruptly, leaving Dario with a ringing afternoise in
his ears. The roof of his skull felt strangely floaty and weightless.

"We are Crepuscular Immolation," proclaimed Nidhogg in his banshee voice, "and this is…" He ended the sentence with a bloodcurdling shriek that may or may not have contained a verbal element. The band promptly launched into a new aural onslaught even more aggressive than the previous one, thereby all but drowning out the cheering of the crowd.

Bruno and Martin exchanged ironic nods of approval. Then Martin gave Dario a friendly pat on the arm, as if to check that his former philosophy colleague was all right. Dario grinned and gave him a thumbs-up. This was just an act, of course, for on the inside, his entire nervous system was cringing, while his eyes desperately roamed the room, as if looking for an escape hatch.

He paused when his gaze landed on a man who stood in a relatively nonturbulent spot in a corner, looking even more out of place than Dario felt.

The man in question was tall, trim and outfitted in a spectacular electric-blue costume that included a dramatic full-length cape. He had a full head of blond hair that looked as if it had come out of an early Duran Duran video. His facial expression was a curious mixture of alertness, annoyance and amusement.

Suddenly Dario had a nagging feeling that he knew this person. He desperately tried to put a mental finger on it. His brain scrabbled frantically for a suitable memory but came up empty.

He gave up when Nidhogg's high-pitched screech turned into a strange throaty wheeze, like the sound of someone trying to cough out a hair ball while reciting the opening lines of Milton's *Paradise Lost*.

Then the singer abruptly fell silent and remained standing in the middle of the stage as still as a statue. His eyes were huge and glassy. He started chanting something unintelligible in a breathy, husky voice.

"*Og den* åpnet *avgrunnens brønn, og en røk steg op av brønnen som røken av en stor ovn, og solen og luften blev formørket av røken fra brønnen.*"

Dario turned to Bruno with a quizzical look.

"I think it's part of the song," said Bruno uncertainly.

Soon the rhythm section of the band started faltering, apparently unable to keep up with the unexpected new lyrical direction Nidhogg was taking.

Dario glanced in the direction of the unknown man again, as if the sight of a calm, mature figure in the midst of mass lunacy would assure him that everything was all right with the world after all, but the man was gone. Dario gazed around the room. He couldn't see him anywhere.

Meanwhile, things were getting progressively more bizarre up on the stage. Nidhogg's oratory was turning more and more forceful, the words rapidly turning into snarls. Spit sprayed out of his grimacing mouth with each word he uttered.

Finally, he flung his microphone onto the floor, threw his head back, and let out an inhuman growl that seemed to come out of the bottom of his duodenum. Amps screeched. The music stopped, but the gurgling growl that remained in Nidhogg's throat was loud enough to fill the whole venue. Two meaty men with shaved heads, apparently the security guards, jumped onto the stage, but Nidhogg grabbed them, one with each hand, and threw them across the room with the ease of a child tossing unwanted toys out of his playpen.

"Whoa!" cried Martin, taking a picture with his phone.

A few people in the audience cheered, possibly mistaking the singer's surreal tantrum for a standard set piece.

On the stage, Nidhogg's body was contorting in a most peculiar way, the muscles in his arms stretched like violin strings and his hands twisted into claws. Having reached a critical, ligament-tearing point, he threw his head back again and let out an even louder growl.

Something rather unusual—that is, unusual in terms of the newly revised standards of reality—happened next. First, a sprinkle of dust crumbled off the ceiling directly above Nidhogg's head. For a moment, Dario thought this was fake snow, the kind they used in Muppet Show Christmas specials, not that this would have made any sense in a black metal gig context. Then he realized that the ceiling was caving in.

"What the hell?" said Martin beside him.

Nidhogg remained frozen in his spasm as a shower of debris collapsed all around him. Dario barely had time to register that the starry night sky was showing through the hole in the ceiling before the stars vanished from view behind an ambiguous black shape that had appeared from above.

A big black raven burst in through the opening and swept over the room. Its wings had the span of a Cessna, and its eyes were two burning red points of light.

Had this been a normal event, this would have been the point when people started stampeding in the direction of the exit. However, this being a black metal gig, people not only stayed but actually cheered.

But the raven started spiraling over the room like a vulture circling a carcass, and suddenly the mood of the crowd visibly deflated. First, the cheering died down, then the clapping, and then the people just stood there, looking lost and dejected. Dario felt it too. It was like a sudden surge of utter hopelessness that made him want to curl up somewhere and indulge in self-pity.

"Dude, what's going on?" said a despondent Martin next to him. He might have been addressing Bruno, but Bruno looked too depressed to respond.

"I can't take it," said an edgy male voice. Dario followed the source of the sound and saw a biker with a receding hairline, a ZZ Top beard and tattoos all over his beefy arms standing on the opposite side of the venue. "I can't go on like this," continued the biker. "It's all too much to bear." He broke down and burst into a near-hysterical fit of sobbing.

The circling raven promptly dived down at him, claws out and red eyes flashing. The biker cowered helplessly. But before the raven had a chance to reach him and presumably scratch his bald scalp off, the blue-cloaked stranger with the New Romantic hair emerged from the crowd and placed himself in the path of the approaching raven like a traffic policeman stopping a car.

He whipped out a black leather-bound book from the folds of his cloak and held it up like an exorcist brandishing a Bible. Except, instead of some Latin incantation, he said, "Get lost!"

The raven hissed as if burned, and shot up.

The mystery man moved quickly, clearly anticipating another attack. Dario saw a flash of gold, followed by the sight of a star-shaped buckle, and it finally hit him.

"Starman!" he gasped. "The Starman!"

"What?" asked Martin distractedly. Bruno only stared at the spectacle with his mouth hanging open. In the background, Nidhogg, recently untangled from his contortionist pose, staggered around on the stage in a swoon.

The raven soared up to the ceiling. It made one counterclockwise turn in the air and then plummeted toward the Starman in a most threatening way.

The Starman stood his ground. "I said, get lost!" he shouted and opened the book.

A pillar of white light shot out of the open pages of the book. It was as if a crack had opened on the surface of the world, showing a glimpse of another dimension that was pure light. The raven tried to skirt away from the terrible brightness but only got entangled in it. The light held the raven in place, and all the bird could do was shriek and flap its giant wings uselessly. Then, with a powerful magnetic thrum, the light beam pulled the raven down until it was sucked into the bright white abyss of the open book.

When the last of the raven had been absorbed, the Starman snapped the book closed, and the light disappeared. The next moment, he was gone, making a dash for the exit through the confused crowd.

"Wait!" said Dario and made as if to go after him, but then he tripped on a discarded beer bottle in a way that would have produced a slapstick result if Martin hadn't grabbed the back of his shirt.

"Easy, old man," said Martin.

On the other side of the room, Nidhogg jumped clumsily off the stage. "Fuck," he said to no one in particular, and threw up on the floor.

Contrary to popular wisdom, after Crepuscular Immolation's abortive set, the show did not go on. Dario tried to find the Starman after the beer bottle debacle, but it was no use—as soon as the raven was out of the picture, the Starman had vanished, and no one had seen which direction he had gone.

Nidhogg was driven off in a white ambulance van despite his protests and various proclamations to the effect that he was perfectly capable of going back onstage; the two security guards were medically examined and judged to be unharmed; the floor was swept and the disaster area cordoned off.

Afterward, the club manager, a nondescript balding man who looked like a bartender, and who might have in fact been the bartender, got onto the stage and announced that what had just happened had been a bizarre display of hooliganism and that everything was now under control. He was promptly booed off the stage, because nobody liked being told fabricated explanations of an event they had personally witnessed, least of all a black metal crowd, who knew a creature of darkness when they saw one. After that, the event turned into an improvised black metal club night, giving Dario ample opportunity to reinforce his previously established conclusion that the genre was simply not his cup of tea.

"What the hell happened there?" asked Bruno as the three of them walked back to the number fourteen tram station sometime after 1:00 a.m.

"I don't know," said Martin while tapping the screen of his phone, "but all the pictures I took are shit. Look!" He held up the phone so that both Bruno and Dario could see the dark, blurred photos he had taken of the Starman vs. raven scene. Most of them looked like a vague black shadow flitting across the room while someone in a blue coat repeatedly attempted to photobomb every single shot for no apparent reason.

"Mine are just as crap," said Dario. "And I blew the only opportunity I'll ever get to talk to the Starman." He had to explain what he meant, because apparently he was the only one who followed the obscure WWC blog.

"So you think this is the same dude?" asked Bruno.

"Well, it had to be," said Dario, blinking bemusedly in the manner of someone who had just witnessed an inexplicable banishing of a demonic raven. "How many people could there possibly be in this city who go around town exorcising ravens with glowing red eyes while wearing an outfit with stars on it?" He suddenly remembered what the old lady had said earlier that day about the Black Queen with the raven by her side, and he felt himself getting light-headed.

"No way that raven was real," said Martin. "It was just some kind of...very sophisticated puppet show."

"A puppet show?" asked Bruno. "Who's ever heard of a puppet show at a black metal gig?"

"I don't know."

"And why would those guys do it?"

"Because their stuff is shit. Hey, Dario old man, what's the matter? You look a little woozy."

Dario shook his head, grinning sheepishly. "It's nothing. It's just that this is the second weird thing that's happened to me today."

"What was the first?"

"There was this nutty old lady at the BBP." Dario sighed and shook his head. He could not bring himself to relive that particular episode before he'd had a chance to sleep on everything, preferably for a very long time.

"See, this is the problem with your living and working near Upper Town," said Martin. "You only get to see old people. You should start hanging out at Lower Town, where the under-70s live."

"Yeah, come back to the Department of Philosophy," said Bruno.

They all laughed at that one.

About an hour later, after Martin and Bruno had alighted at their respective stops, Dario found himself alone in the back carriage of a night tram the three of them had boarded despite its indeterminate number. However, judging by the direction in which it was heading, the ill-defined tram appeared to be a fourteen, or at least the closest nighttime equivalent of it. The characteristic external features were certainly there, as were the overheated, butt-cradling seats, and so, as he sat warm and snug in a red seat at the back, Dario found himself being gently lulled to sleep.

"Tickets, please," said an unpleasant nasal voice, startling Dario awake. Dario cracked open an eye. A short, dumpy moustached man in a black conductor's uniform was towering over him.

Dario blinked owlishly. There couldn't possibly be a tram conductor standing before him demanding to see a ticket on a night tram at 1:00 a.m. on a Saturday. He blinked again. The conductor was still there. The man persistently continued to exist.

This couldn't be real. Dario knew how to dodge tram conductors. Every self-respecting Zagreb resident knew how to dodge tram conductors. Only pensioners didn't know how to dodge conductors, but they didn't have to, since they got to ride for free.

Dodging conductors was fairly easy. All one had to do was stand by the door and keep an eye out for dejected-looking people in black conductors' uniforms, then make a quick exit if necessary. Alternatively, one could stand close to the ticket machine with an unused tram ticket kept at the ready. Then, if a conductor started making an inspection, all one had to do was pop the ticket into the machine before the conductor came their way. But even the most vigilant tram conductor-dodger let his guard down after 7:00 p.m., especially on weekends. There was no way a tram conductor would ever go out tram conducting at such a late, blatantly off-peak hour. Not a single record of that kind existed in the collective unconscious of tram conductor-dodgers. And there was a simple reason for this—no such thing had ever happened. It couldn't possibly happen. And yet, here was evidence to the contrary, standing before him and staring at him with a judgmental expression while wearing a big gray moustache under his nose.

It was a very expressive moustache. Unlike the man himself, the moustache had character. It looked almost like the hindquarters of a specially trained tap-dancing mouse, and it kept twitching, as if itching to hop off and perform a musical number on the tram floor.

"May I see your ticket, please," repeated the conductor in his monotonous voice.

"But…you can't possibly be the conductor," said Dario, more to himself, not realizing that he would soon regret this ill-advised retort.

"Oh really?" said the conductor. "Is that because you thought that us tram conductors were never out this late at night?"

"No, I—"

"Is that because you weren't expecting to see a tram conductor at all?" The conductor's voice had become even more nasal. Dario briefly wondered whether the pronounced nasal quality of the man's voice might have been due to the moustache obstructing normal airflow in and out of his nose cavity.

"No, I—"

"Is that because you don't have a valid ticket, conductor-dodger?"

The last bit was like a slap in the face. Dario had no choice other than to admit that he did not in fact have a valid ticket, or any ticket. Then he had to give the conductor his ID while the conductor issued him a fine on a nondescript slip of grayish-blue paper.

Once the conductor was finally gone, Dario pocketed the fine and leaned back in the seat that continued to overheat his backside with wild abandon. His head lolled to one side, banging heavily against the windowpane.

"Ow," he said, blinking groggily. He peered out of the window. The tram had stopped at the north end of Frankopan Street. The stop looked desolate in the darkness. The brightly lit windows of the deserted shops made the whole scene look even bleaker. An arched gate between two shops that led into a hidden courtyard looked like the opening of some black tunnel.

Dario's mouth fell open. There was a figure standing in the darkness of the gate. He couldn't see anything other than its eyes. The eyes were unblinking, their gaze fixed on him. They had a reddish glow, but this might have been a reflection of the streetlight. There was something else about the eyes too—at first, he couldn't tell what it was, but as he stared at them, transfixed and unable to look away, he realized what it was. They had vertical reptilian pupils.

He blinked and shook his head. When he looked up again, the figure with the reptile eyes was gone.

8

THE SUPERNOVA

The Diadem was one of the most popular spots in the Boötes-Virgo corner of the universe, a favorite rest stop for passing star daimons who needed a place to rest and stop. One could lounge in one of the Diadem's jewel-shaped platforms indefinitely, drinking in the stillness of the cosmos undisturbed. Otherwise, there wasn't really that much to see there, unless there was someone nearby blowing up a sun.

Coincidentally, that was exactly what Leo was about to do.

While star daimons did not have jobs in the everyday sense of the word, they did have certain innate talents and abilities—one might call them powers—which they were expected to employ in such a way as to ensure the smooth and unimpeded running of the universe.

Also, to fight barnacles. Every star daimon was required to take part, each in their own fashion, in the perpetual struggle against that loathsome species of space predators whenever the need arose.

Barnacles were hideous, bloodthirsty creatures from the dark underbelly of the universe. Although vaguely man-shaped and man-sized, there was something crab-like about their appearance, not least the large shells on their backs. Their nature was part parasite, part predator. Whenever a barnacle was in need of nourishment, it would attach itself belly-first to the surface of a planet, hibernating under its shell while it fed on the host planet's energy. This was the barnacles' parasite mode.

Since barnacles moved in droves, whole planets had been reduced to little more than lumps of dead rock by the preying of these leeches. As for their predatory mode, barnacles were in the habit of attacking and killing anyone they came across, just to pass the time.

Leo liked to stay out of the whole star daimons vs. barnacles saga as much as possible. In his opinion, his powers were wasted on something as pedestrian as a cosmic fight against evil. The collectivism of it was distasteful. After all, he was an *individual*. One with an innate ability to control fire.

He could literally do whatever he wanted with fire—breathe it, walk through it, fly across space inside a ball of it or shoot it out of the palms of his hands, among other things. He could walk on the surface of the hottest sun in the universe without so much as breaking a sweat. And he liked to use his talents to create spectacular cosmic events—solar flares, sunspots, shooting stars and the like—not chase after a bunch of misshapen space crustaceans.

His powers were, of course, not entirely unique to him. Several other star daimons, most notably Rukbat and Ankaa, could also control fire, each in their own way. But Leo had an additional skill, a rather specialist one—he could reignite suns. Whenever there was a faltering sun, one that needed a bit of a leg up to bring out its full sheen, it was always Leo the Star Queen turned to.

But that was not all. The same power that Leo used to revive suns could also be used to destroy them. This was why, in the event that some weary old sun needed to be put out of its misery, Leo was the Star Queen's go-to star daimon for the job.

Leo had no preference in this matter—he enjoyed blowing up suns as much as he liked lighting them up. And so, when the Star Council summoned him to inform him that the Star Queen wanted him to decommission an aging sun near the Diadem complex, Leo wholeheartedly accepted the job, heading out on his mission with a spring in his step and a whistle on his lips.

When he arrived at the Diadem by way of a speed-of-light blaze of golden fire, Leo couldn't help noticing that there was one other star daimon already hanging out in the neighborhood. This lifted his already high spirits even higher. The one thing he liked even more than being able to use his unique powers was being able to use his unique powers in front of a live audience.

Fomalhaut was a shy, quiet star daimon who liked nothing better than to go to the farthest corners of the universe all by himself in order to sit there writing terrible brooding poetry on scraps of paper. This was exactly what he had been doing, curled up on one of the Diadem's smallest, most secluded platforms, when Leo turned up for the demolition job.

"Leo," said Fomalhaut, getting awkwardly to his feet and stuffing a piece of paper guiltily into the pocket of his floaty greenish robe.

"Fomalhaut!" cried Leo cheerfully.

"What brings you here?"

Leo briefly explained to him the nature of the day's mission. "But you're welcome to watch," he added quickly.

"So…you're basically going to blow up the sun?" asked Fomalhaut.

"Precisely," said Leo, taking off his blue-gold cloak and folding it neatly before placing it onto the platform. "But you needn't move—you're not in the way at all."

"You're sure? I could always move to another platform."

"Nonsense. Just stay where you are. Besides, this won't take a minute. You'll barely notice anything's happened."

"Oh. All right." Fomalhaut hovered uncertainly on the edge of the Diadem.

"Maybe if you just take a step back," said Leo. "And another."

Fomalhaut was now cowering at the very back of the platform.

"Perfect," said Leo. "Now." His face and hands were already glowing with an inner fire, while the gold strands on his outfit melted and blended, so that it looked as if he was made from head to toe of burning gold. "Watch this."

He leaped off the platform and plunged toward the red sun that glimmered lazily like a dying ember beneath him. The fire that enveloped him grew brighter and brighter, dissolving his features, until he was a blazing comet.

The impact was the most peaceful part. This was the moment of stillness before the storm. It was only when the star's core collapsed at a quarter of the speed of light, followed by the inevitable all-out particle outburst, that the real action began. Leo hovered inside the core of the exploding giant, arms out, letting the flaming shower of fragmented matter burn through him. It was pure bliss. He only stopped when an internal alarm reminded him that any further exposure to the center of the blast would make his hair go static for days.

He whizzed back up to the Diadem, where Fomalhaut half sagged against the back of the platform, looking mildly shell-shocked.

"Woo-hooo!" Leo's voice was ecstatic. "Did you see those neutrinos go?"

Despite his elation, Leo was still observant enough to notice that something was out of the ordinary, and it wasn't just the supernova.

He followed the direction of Fomalhaut's nervous gaze and saw Altair, a fearsome star daimon with pristine white eagle wings and sculpted white hair, levitating in the particle-soaked ether behind him. The aftershock of the blast hadn't ruffled a single one of his feathers.

Leo greeted him warmly, but a sliver of wariness was creeping through his unrestrained joy. Altair was one of the Star Force Seven, elite servants of the Star Council and a sort of informal police force that kept the other star daimons in line, ensuring that no one abused his or her powers. And while their role may have been an informal one, they were nevertheless feared. It had been Altair who had apprehended Leo in the aftermath of his foolish misconduct in the White City all those years before.

Altair apologized for interrupting Leo but didn't sound apologetic at all. He sounded as stern and unflinching as usual. But that was just Altair. Leo didn't let this worry him, not on a day like this.

"What can I do for you, Altair?" he asked amicably.

"The Star Council has asked me to summon you. Leo, you must come with me immediately. The matter is rather urgent."

Leo's stomach sank. "What is it?"

"The Black Queen of the White City is back."

"No," said Leo, reeling with horror and disbelief. "It cannot be."

"I assure you, it's the truth," continued Altair in the same merciless tone. "And in all likelihood, you will once again be sent earthward."

"No." Leo clutched his head. "Nooooooo!"

"Noooooooo!" He woke up screaming. It took him a while to remember where he was. He was still in the White City, in the Hidden Tower, and he was still no closer to being released from his bondage. Leo nearly wept when he realized that the dream he'd had wasn't fantasy. If only he had known back then what awaited him upon his return to the Diadem, he would have stayed inside the exploding star forever, hair be damned. No one would have found him there.

But, as they say in the outer Omega Centauri provinces, it's no use crying over spilled Milky.

9

CHESTNUTOPIA

"Isn't it a lovely day for a walk?" Madam Mina sounded out of breath. Floki padded behind her as quickly as the dog's short legs would allow, its paws making soft sticky sounds against the pavement.

"It's delightful," said the formidable boulder of a woman on her right. Madam Rosanda was a heavy six-foot-two matron who, despite her floral-patterned dress, tiny sky-blue heart-shaped purse that she clutched to her ample bosom and a hairstyle that could only be described as a beehive, had the air of a battle troll.

Dario followed them miserably a few steps behind, wheeling behind him Madam Mina's old-lady shopping trolley, a mortifyingly undignified task in an already embarrassing context.

The three of them and their canine appendage strolled down Opatovina, a picturesque old street running along the eastern edge of Upper Town. They were on their way to Dolac Market. Madam Mina had eventually gone to her sister's place in the country, leaving Dario in blissful peace and solitude, free to commandeer the apartment whichever way he wished, but her absence had been all too brief, and she had come back after only four days. And, as if to make up for any freedom she might have inadvertently granted to Dario by being gone, she had mobilized him immediately upon her return as her trolley porter.

"And there's nothing better than a nice walk before lunch. It really helps with the digestion afterward," said Madam Mina.

"Absolutely," proclaimed Madam Rosanda with her chesty, resonant voice. "My Branko and I always used to go for a walk before lunch when he was alive, God rest his soul."

Madam Rosanda was a part-time activist with the Save the Chickens Agency, an organization that raised public awareness of the plight of egg-laying hens. She had zeal and energy, and she strode with the vigorous tempo and relentless determination of a Spartan marching toward the pass of Thermopylae.

Dario and Madam Mina were barely able to keep up with her. The hapless Floki was practically running behind them. Its tiny legs worked tirelessly under its pathetic, sausage-shaped body like the mechanism of some grotesque clock that was spinning out of control.

If Dario had been asked to reconstruct the chain of events that resulted in his being on his way to Dolac Market with Madam Mina and a tough-as-nails Save the Chickens activist on that particular morning, his mind would have probably broken down like the overheated engine of a car doing 90 miles per hour in a desert in order to escape from a mysterious truck intent on pushing it down a ravine. All he remembered doing was going innocently into the kitchen to get his breakfast cereal only to be immediately appointed Madam Mina's temporary trolley-puller.

Madam Mina considered herself a socialite of sorts, and liked to cultivate contacts with people from all walks of life, particularly bohemian poets, crystal healers, members of the Hare Krishna, painters who had made a name for themselves by painting monochrome blotches, failed musicians and animal welfare activists. But above all, she valued her friendships with other Upper Town ladies, her friendship with Madam Rosanda being one of her longest-standing ones. Fishpond Street was not exactly Upper Town proper, but Madam Mina considered herself an Upper Town resident nevertheless.

There was an unwritten rule that every Upper Town lady knew every other Upper Town lady, the corollary being that the said ladies regularly met to exchange the latest gossip. This was like an Upper Town internet of sorts, or rather an intranet. Even before the invention of the World Wide Web, the ladies of Upper Town had their own network, one that was as reactionary and saturated with vicious comments as its contemporary equivalent. And Madam Mina certainly played her part, perhaps even too eagerly, possibly as a compensation for the fact that she didn't actually live in Upper Town but merely near it.

"Exercise is the best medicine," continued Madam Rosanda. "That is what I always used to say whenever Branko, God rest his soul, complained about his chronic pain. 'It will do you good,' I always used to say. And it did. Well, at least it did until he died, God rest his soul."

"True, very true." Madam Mina nodded vigorously. "It's very good for a person to be active. I personally always like to stay busy, and I always aim to encourage others to do the same. For instance, I keep telling Maja from Radić Street to go out once in a while. Maybe take up Pilates or something of the sort. Because, you know..." Madam Mina lowered her voice to a hissing whisper. "...she has really let herself go. Ever since her husband left her for that little floozy from Remete."

Madam Rosanda let out a shocked gasp. "It's an outrage!" she cried. "An absolute outrage! I felt so sorry for the poor thing when I heard. Can you believe it? Men these days are nothing but degenerate, no-good trash. Why, if I had my way with them, I would—"

At that moment, one of the wheels of the trolley Dario was pulling hit a chestnut lying on the road. This made the trolley swerve a bit to the side, bumping into Floki's rump. The dog let out an offended whine.

Madam Mina tsked and cooed at the dog, giving Dario a reproving sideways glare.

Madam Rosanda whipped round to face Dario. "And who are you exactly?" she hooted at him fiercely, knitting her brow.

Dario opened his mouth to reply, but Madam Mina cut in. "He's just my lodger. I've asked him to come with us to help me with my trolley. Dario is a student, aren't you?"

"Former student," said Dario, grinning at Madam Rosanda sheepishly. Madam Mina had a distinct lack of interest in Dario's personal life, as it was outside the Upper Town ladies' network's catchment area. This was why she had not bothered to register his dropping out of university yet. According to Dario's estimate, it was going to take at least a year for her to process the new information and for it to be added to the intranet database.

"Dario studies philosophy, don't you?" said Madam Mina in a sickeningly patronising tone, as if speaking to a four-year-old. "He reads all kinds of books."

Madam Rosanda looked Dario up and down with a contemptuous gaze. "These young people," she harrumphed. "Always wasting their time on trifles." Then she turned away and plowed on down the street, continuing with her narrative about the unfortunate Maja from Radić Street, briefly touching upon the importance of vigilance in the face of potential chicken oppression.

It was not long before they reached a small square at the end of Opatovina Street, which was packed with flower stalls stocked full of seasonal, autumn-themed arrangements that looked more like the props of some ancient pagan harvest ritual than floral displays. The chestnut and the gourd were the most common motifs, but there were considerable amounts of apples and walnuts as well. Another feature of the square was a bronze statue of Petrica Kerempuh, a local literary minstrel character who had once provided a cynical commentary on grim historical events through the medium of the folk ballad. The figure held a guitar and leaned against a pillar against which two emaciated bronze peasants slumped despairingly. His debonair pose conveyed a sense of ironic detachment.

Madam Mina and Madam Rosanda made a round of the stalls, expressing vociferous admiration for the autumnal arrangements, but neither of them purchased so much as a prune. Within a few minutes, the two noisy women turned and headed for the steps that led down to the main Dolac Market, leaving a trail of inane chatter behind. Dario followed at a discrete distance, the rusty wheels of the trolley squeaking behind him like two frightened mice.

Dolac Farmers Market was a sea of traditional red parasols and stands piled with seasonal produce, including alarmingly large quantities of the city's favorite autumn staple—the sweet chestnut. There were small mountains of freshly picked chestnuts from Bear Mountain, as well as roast chestnuts, boiled chestnuts, chocolate-covered chestnut truffles, chestnut slices and even pots of chestnut puree served with whipped cream. It was a chestnut-lover's idea of Chestnutopia.

The variety of produce provided Floki with an olfactory extravaganza that seemed to be driving the poor beast mad. The dog sniffed around the discarded roast chestnut shells and rotting bits of fruit lying on the ground with frenzied interest, its damp nose darting from one odorous object to another, apparently unable to focus on any one thing at a time. A few pigeons browsed among the scraps too, but their enthusiasm was somewhat curbed, as if their long-time residence at the place had desensitized them to the various stimuli it had to offer.

Madam Mina stopped by a vegetable stand to buy a cauliflower, a kilo of yellow peppers and a generic bundle of *grincek*, all of which she immediately handed over to Dario to put into the trolley, while Madam Rosanda bartered with a nearby fruit seller over a punnet of pears.

They eventually made their way to a building at the back of the market, which was reserved for more pungent wares such as fish and cottage cheese, when all of a sudden Madam Rosanda inhaled sharply, like someone who had just seen something shocking.

She stopped short in a wide stance, her arms stretched out dramatically. When Dario got closer, he saw that she was planted before a stand where an elderly peasant woman wearing a traditional local peasant costume, red with white, sat behind a tall stack of egg crates.

"What is this?" hissed Madam Rosanda at the egg seller.

"Eggs, ma'am," mumbled the apparently toothless seller.

"These eggs come from caged chickens. I can tell," said Madam Rosanda.

"Aye, probably," said the egg seller, nodding wisely. The corners of her eyes were turned down in an amused squint.

"Probably?" Madam Rosanda was the image of stunned outrage. "Probably? Jesus and Mary, you don't even know where your eggs come from?"

"These ain't my eggs," said the seller. "I just sell 'em."

Despite himself, Dario snorted. Madam Rosanda turned to him with a look of wild fury. "What are you snickering at, little one?"

"Nothing, I was just—"

"Quiet!" she bellowed, taking a swing with her right arm. Dario, sensing that he was about to be cuffed, immediately fell into a passive and perversely fascinated daze. He saw an enormous meaty hand gliding through the air in slow motion. The sensation was akin to what he imagined it must be like to be confronted by a bear. He knew that the right thing to do was to crouch and make yourself look as small and harmless a prey as possible, but he felt frozen with terror. It was only when Madam Rosanda's heavy, calloused palm connected with his cheek with a loud smack that his cognitive activities were once again set in motion. But then it was already too late. There was nothing left to do in the aftermath of the bear slap other than reel from the blow as stars danced before his eyes.

"Cheeky little snotface!" yelled Madam Rosanda. "You know nothing about the plight of the common chicken."

Dario rubbed his ear, feeling like a chastised five-year-old.

"Good heavens," said Madam Mina, although she sounded more intrigued than outraged.

Madam Rosanda turned once again toward the egg stand. "People of the White City!" she belted theatrically for all market-goers to hear. "Behold the sad, pale eggs of caged chickens deprived of fresh air and daylight. Chickens that are locked up in tiny cages where there is barely enough space for them to spread their wings! Chickens that are oppressed!"

"Calm down now, ma'am," muttered the egg seller from her relatively safe position behind the stand. "If you don't want the eggs, leave 'em."

Madam Rosanda gasped. "Whom are you telling to calm down? I will not calm down until these eggs are removed. Clear them all out!" Fiercely, she stabbed her right index finger through the air in a direction that presumably signified "out."

Her patience visibly waning, the egg seller rose to her feet. Upright, she looked almost as formidable as Madam Rosanda. "And 'oo do you think you are to be orderin' me around?" she sputtered, suddenly indignant.

"I am the vice-secretary of the Save the Chickens Agency," said Madam Rosanda imperiously, "and I am ordering you to take these eggs away from here."

To accentuate her order, she grabbed one small, pale egg from the top crate and flung it in the general direction of the egg seller's person. The egg flew past the peasant woman's left ear and landed on the ground behind her with a soft crunch.

"That's it!" shouted the egg seller and sprang around to stand before Madam Rosanda in a belligerent stance.

An improvised ring of spectators formed around them in an instant. The farmers from surrounding produce stands gathered in a loose semicircle behind the egg seller, while curious market-goers and other passers-by hovered near Madam Rosanda's side. Madam Mina, naturally, pushed her way to the front. Presently, the butcher and the fishmonger emerged from their shops and joined the now cheering crowd. Noisy fights involving overconfident peasant women had been a staple of this particular market since early medieval times, and each new iteration of the theme was welcomed with at least a moderate degree of interest.

Madam Rosanda and the egg seller glared at one another while shouts of encouragement echoed from various directions. Dario tried to gravitate to the background. Behind Madam Mina, Floki was whining quietly. A few pigeons watched the proceedings from the sideline.

"I'll get you for destroying my eggs!" yelled the egg seller, shaking her fist.

Madam Rosanda's eyes bulged dangerously. "I'll destroy every last one of them, you chicken-oppressor!"

Half a second later, the egg seller rushed at Madam Rosanda ferociously, going straight for her beehive hair. A shower of hairpins fell upon the ground.

"Jesus and Mary!" gasped one of the spectators.

Madam Rosanda let out a terrifying battle cry and smacked the peasant woman on the head with her sky-blue purse. Dario noticed that the front was embroidered with the emblem of the Sacred Heart. The peasant retaliated by stamping on Madam Rosanda's foot.

The fight, although a vicious one, remained in a stalemate until two policemen with an average body mass index of over twenty-seven arrived a few minutes later and separated the warring parties. This was no mean feat either. Madam Rosanda, too immersed in the fight to notice that she was dealing with the law, struggled fiercely, spitting out "You snotface!" and "How very dare you!" Only when the older of the two officers gave her a strongly worded reprimand did she become moderately pacified. It subsequently turned out that Madam Rosanda was no stranger to the two police officers. In fact, she seemed to have acquired a substantial record of public disorder offenses, whereas the egg seller turned out to have been operating without a valid license. In the end, both women were escorted to the police station amidst enthusiastic cheers from the crowd.

And so it was that Dario, Madam Mina and Floki found themselves making their return journey from Dolac without their outspoken companion.

"Appalling scene, absolutely appalling," muttered Madam Mina as they made their way up steep, cobbled Skalin Street toward Kaptol.

"I have known Rosanda for years, and I never would have dreamed that she'd be capable of something like this," she continued in a morally superior tone, even though she had enjoyed every second of the fight. "You just can't tell with people, Dario dear. You never can tell." Then she tutted a bit.

Dario stared at the ground before him, his feet on autopilot. His right hand had become numb from dragging the now-overloaded trolley, but he didn't mind—at least the numbness helped him forget that he was dragging a trolley.

His train of thought suddenly stopped with a screech. A figure clad in a blue cloak with a hood that entirely obscured the face slunk past him from the opposite direction. The solitary shape was as quiet as a shadow, its motions as fluid as blue ink. As Dario turned, he caught sight of a single trailing edge of the cloak as the figure turned the corner into Tkalčić Street and disappeared from view.

Floki barked sharply, once, and then proceeded to whine in a pitiful small-dog way.

Dario faltered. Madam Mina didn't even notice. "What is it, Floki?" she asked the whining dog in an annoying nursery voice.

The mystery figure was the Starman—it had to be. Dario was not quite sure, but he thought that in the fraction of a second when he had seen the figure from the front, he might have caught a glimpse of a star-shaped belt buckle. But even if he had imagined the buckle, how many people went around town wearing a hooded electric-blue cloak?

"Dario dear, are you all right?" asked Madam Mina, turning around when she realized he had fallen behind. Floki regarded him suspiciously from behind her ankles.

"Uh, yes," he said. "Madam Mina, I'm afraid I'll have to leave this with you." He wheeled the trolley over to her side. "There's a place I urgently need to go to."

"Oh, Dario," said his landlady. "Can't you hang on for just one more minute, until we're back at the flat? That would be so much better than using some unsanitary public place."

Dario felt his face going red. "Not that place. Some other place."

"Oh." Madam Mina made a displeased "how inconvenient that tenants should have a life that extends beyond helping me out with random everyday tasks" face, but made no further comment.

Dario excused himself, turned on his heel, and hurried down the street.

10

HOW TO KILL TWENTY MINUTES

When he got down to Tkalčić Street, there was no sign of the Starman. All there was to see was a lot of people drinking coffee in outdoor cafés or milling about aimlessly while gazing at shop windows. For a moment, Dario regretted incurring the inevitable passive-aggressive wrath of Madam Mina for no reason, but then he saw a flash of blue ahead of him.

The Starman had emerged from a group of slow-moving tourists in which he had apparently become entrapped like a fish in a tangle of seaweed. He was forced to slow down once again as he went past a noisy crowd pouring out of a pub at the entrance to Opatovina Park. He went neither into the pub nor to the park, but continued down Tkalčić Street. Dario followed.

As he found himself catching up with the Starman, he realized that he had no idea what he intended to do. He couldn't continue shadowing the Starman indefinitely. That would be pointless at best, in addition to being somewhat creepy. Which meant that he would have to at some point walk up to the Starman and ask him…what? Whether he really had come down from the sky? Whether he knew something about the Black Queen?

He had no time to brainstorm possible scenarios because the Starman, who was now only twenty paces ahead of him, suddenly took a sharp right turn, opened an antique metal gate of an old three-story building and went inside, shutting the gate behind him.

Dario strolled up to the building, acting casual and doing his best not to look like a stalker. The massive iron gate looked like a relic from a medieval past when every building in Tkalčić Street had been a fortress. It looked like something that couldn't be torn down with a battering ram the size of a bullet train.

And yet, when Dario pushed the heavy gate, it opened easily.

He found himself peering into a narrow alley wedged between the side of a building and a crumbling gray wall. There was no one in sight.

Cautiously, Dario stepped into the alley and closed the gate behind him. The murmur of the Tkalčić Street crowds immediately faded out, leaving him in eerie silence.

He took a tentative step forward. Then another. He had a strange feeling that every step he took carried him at least a mile away from the outside world.

At the end of the alley there was a spacious garden enclosed inside a circular wall of rough stone that looked as if it were at least a thousand years old. At the back of the garden there stood an ancient watchtower made of the same type of crumbling stone. It was a crude structure with a square base and a primitive wooden roof, like a barn's, with a small terrace wedged inside the gable. Many rickety wooden platforms projected from the sides of the tower at odd intervals. These were connected to one another with a bizarre network of rudimentary wooden stairs that zigzagged all over the outside of the tower like a surrealist scaffolding, forming an erratic pattern that looked like the background of an obsolete arcade game. Several mismatched, ancient-looking doors were arranged at irregular intervals across all levels, the scaffolding serving as a kind of external staircase.

The only thing more baffling than the bizarre design of the tower was the fact that the structure even existed—there, at the very center of the city—without anyone being aware of it. Or at least Dario hadn't been aware of it. And if everyone else had known about it all along, then they were doing a remarkably good job of never talking, writing or tweeting about it, or otherwise referring to it in any other conceivable way.

A murmur of voices was coming from inside the tower. As Dario crept closer, his ear noted that it was actually only one voice—a man's voice, presumably the Starman's. He was either talking to the most unresponsive person in the world or to himself. Dario dismissed the possibility of him talking on the phone, as it felt un-Starman-like.

"This is outrageous," said the voice. "I've eliminated the Black Queen's raven. Without any help from the hermit, I might add. Not to mention the rest of that useless lot. It was through idle chatter with some tattooed, leather-clad time-wasters who wanted to know where I'd bought my coat that I accidentally found out about the event in the first place. As soon as one of the wastrels mentioned 'evil vibes,' I knew this would be fertile hunting ground for Barbara's creatures. I was right. And I was lucky to have been there. Well, sort of lucky…the raven nearly scratched my face off as I fussed with that wretched banishing book. You know, things would be almost tolerable if I could at least use my powers while on Earth instead of having to rely on whatever crude, ineffectual weapons I can find in this dead end of the universe."

Dario reeled from all the information that had just entered his brain. So it was true—the Starman was somehow connected to the Black Queen, whoever it was that the name actually referred to.

"But anyway," continued the Starman, "I could have just as easily not been there if I hadn't run into those losers in the street. But that's beside the point. The point is that I have completed my mission, and there is nothing else for me to do here. There is not a sign of a single other thing, being or abstract entity that might have been unleashed by the Black Queen upon the unsuspecting city. The threat, such as it was, has been defused. The Star Council has been duly notified. And yet…and yet they still haven't given me the all-clear. Why is that?"

There was a pause. Then a sharp, frustrated exhalation. "Why can't you ever appear when you're needed?"

A narrow staircase led from the ground floor to a platform that began at one side of the first floor and extended about two-thirds to the other side, so that it looked like a poorly aligned balcony. A massive iron door stood ajar at the far end of this structure. This was where the voice was coming from.

Dario treaded up the stairs with soft steps as measured as a ballerina's. When he got onto the platform, he leaned against the wall by the side of the half-open door and listened.

An angry growl came from the inside. "When will someone finally tell me what I have to do to get out of here?" This was followed by a loud crash of a solid object, like a piece of furniture, being kicked. Then there was a soft thump of a body landing on a padded chair. "God, I'm so bored."

There was another pause. Then the voice spoke, more loudly this time. "Oh, for God's sake, will you show yourself already? Or just go away."

Dario froze.

"Yes, you," said the voice. "How many invisible beings do you think I'm talking to right now?"

Inside of Dario's internal systems, a battle between the fight and flight modes was in progress. In the end, a third mode, the "fail to do anything other than look stupid" one, won.

"Unbelievable," said the Starman as Dario shuffled up to the doorway and lingered awkwardly just outside the threshold.

The Starman was sprawled in an antique throne-shaped armchair, which might have been a real throne once, in a spacious room that looked like a derelict medieval hall. His elbow was propped against a massive oak table that looked as heavy as an Arctic icebreaker. An ancient, cobweb-covered chandelier was suspended on a thick chain, its ring-shaped frame dotted with many half-burnt candles. Several swords, two crossed axes and a mace, as well as a large but unidentifiable coat of arms, were mounted on the bare stone walls. And if that wasn't medieval enough, there was also a trapdoor with a rusty metal ring in one corner.

"I'm sorry," said Dario. "I didn't mean to—"

"How on earth did you get in?" asked the Starman. To Dario's relief, he didn't sound angry but merely curious.

"Uh…through the gate."

"That's impossible. The gate is supposed to be invisible."

"It looked…fairly visible when I saw it."

"Or perhaps it was rather that the secret gate only appears to those who are…what was it? Brave? Confident? Incontinent? Something to that effect. Anyway, did you need anything in particular or were you just stopping by to say hello?"

Being confronted like that made Dario fully realize the absurdity of his situation. But since he was already in over his head, he couldn't think of any option other than being blunt.

"Are you the Starman?" he blurted.

"The who?"

Dario took out his phone and brought up a picture of the Starman standing by a scorched Prečko tram. "Is that you?"

"What is that?" The Starman looked as if he had never seen a phone before.

"Someone took a picture of you last week, after they saw flashing lights in the sky."

"Oh, so you're able to do that these days? How progressive. Does my hair really look that flat under artificial lighting?"

"So you did land from the sky in a blaze of fire?"

"It was just a routine landing." The Starman waved the whole matter away, as if discussing an everyday triviality. "Barely more than a flash."

Dario felt the Starman's attention slipping before he'd had a chance to find out even the most fundamental things about him. In order not to lose momentum, he said, "Do you know anything about the Black Queen?"

The Starman threw his head back and laughed. He continued laughing until tears welled up in his eyes.

"What makes you think," he said eventually while wiping his eyes with his sleeve, "that I know anything about that particular subject?"

"Um…I saw what you did at the Ditch the other night. That seemed to have something to do with the Black Queen. At least, that's the impression I got."

The Starman had another, briefer, laughing fit, like an aftershock of the first one.

"You know…" He looked up at Dario with a "your name?" expression.

"Dario."

"You know, Dario, I've no idea who you are or what you're doing here, but I haven't laughed this much since I arrived in the city. And laughter, under the circumstances, is a welcome distraction. So if information on the Black Queen is what you're after, I'd be more than happy to provide. I'm pretty sure this is something I am not supposed to do, but I'll do it anyway because, first, I don't care, and second, I am terribly bored."

❧

"The White City," began the Starman (whose real name turned out to be Leo Solar), "although boring and pedestrian in every possible way, is not exactly an ordinary place. You see, the city is poised on the threshold between the ordinary, everyday world and a sort of…well, there's no other way of putting it— magic realm."

"Magic…realm?" said Dario as he sat down on a stool on the opposite side of the table.

"I'll explain. Or maybe I won't—it's all a bit tedious. Just be quiet and listen and try not to interrupt too much. I get distracted easily. Anyway, this threshold is referred to by those in the know as—you'd never guess this—the Threshold, while the magic realm is somewhat less intuitively called the Withdrawn Realm.

"The two realms used to coexist for many centuries without much friction. The people of the city were aware of the Withdrawn Realm folk—the tree spirits, river gods, mountain elves, hearth gnomes and the like—but they did their best to stay out of their way, since the magic folk are overall annoying and treacherous. And the magic folk themselves never had much interest in the ordinary world, preferring instead to stay on their own side of the Threshold unless they had some business to do in the city. And this business wasn't always honest. As I've already mentioned, these Withdrawn Realm bastards—I mean folk—are treacherous.

"But then Barbara moved into Bear Town Fortress sometime during that intolerable quagmire of superstition and lack of indoor plumbing that was the fifteenth century, and from that point on, it didn't take long for the delicate balance of the realms to be disrupted.

"At first, no one thought her in any way remarkable. She was the wife of some king or other, and on the surface, she didn't appear more threatening than any other fifteenth-century housewife. Besides, the townspeople were already so up to their necks in the combined wretchedness of poverty, pestilence and gratuitous violence that they no doubt thought that another potential cause of misery on top of the various existing ones would hardly make much of a difference. But they were wrong.

"To the discerning minority—and rest assured that this was a very small minority—it was obvious from the start that Barbara liked to dabble with sorcery. That she had, in fact, more than a passing interest in the dark arts. Her husband didn't approve of her hobby, but she didn't let this deter her. Instead, she worked in secrecy, secluded in her tower.

"Soon Barbara became a widow, and this was when she showed her true face. Without so much as a symbolic sniffle of sorrow, she promptly set to work taking control of Bear Town Fortress with the use of dubious black magic, wasting no time in setting her secret plans in motion. It was during this period that she started wearing only black as a mockery of her, as some have suggested, *intentionally* caused widowhood. Soon she became known as the Black Queen.

"She quickly came to realize that the White City, with its easy access to the Withdrawn Realm, was the ideal playground for her schemes. The place was clearly the perfect means to achieve her dark ambition. And her ambition was no less than to rule the world, starting with the White City. If she could harness the innate powers of the Withdrawn Realm and make the magic folk do her will, then her evil influence would increase a thousandfold.

"At first, her efforts yielded modest results. The best she could do was poison wells and cause minor localized outbreaks of the plague. But then she unexpectedly got some external help."

Dario had been listening with dumb awe, his consciousness completely absorbed in Leo's story, but the last remark made him speak up. "What kind of help?"

Leo cleared his throat. "Expert help. She managed to summon a sort of... hmm...demon."

"You mean like a demon from Hell?"

"No!" Leo sounded affronted. "Not one of those common earthly demons! He was a...different kind of demon. At the same time, he wasn't a demon at all. It's a matter of semantics, really—historically, the word 'demon' has been used to indicate a variety of different things, and its real meaning has become muddled. In the original Greek, it didn't mean 'demon' at all."

"So was it a—"

"May I go on? Thank you. Anyway, this demon or whatever, having underestimated her intentions and abilities, made her privy to certain...er, secret information."

Before Dario was able to ask another question, Leo quickly added, "But the demon didn't mean anything by it! He never thought that giving the Black Queen this secret knowledge would make any difference. I mean, this sort of thing happens all the time...well, maybe not all the time, but at least some of the time, and nothing ever really comes of it because the majority of people are too dim to do anything with even the most exclusive kind of knowledge. And there was no reason to think that Barbara was any different. Well, I suppose that her single-minded dedication to the dark arts, combined with her distinct fashion style, could have been an indication, but this demon was too bored to notice such details, and anyway, it was the Middle Ages."

"So this demon basically made the Black Queen what she is?"

Leo winced, looking for a moment as if he were about to say something caustic. Then he sighed, nodding grimly, and continued:

"It soon turned out that the Black Queen had not only readily absorbed the secret knowledge but also applied it in practice in a most spectacular way. Little by little, she poisoned the Withdrawn Realm with her newfound powers, turning water spirits of the mountain's hidden streams into her agents and enchanting the animals from the mountain's slopes to make them do her bidding. And her bidding always involved preying on the population of the city.

"But the Black Queen's rise was checked when she encountered an unexpected obstacle along the way. The people of the White City—well, some of them, at least—started offering resistance to her forces, and some of them soon became proficient in fighting off whichever animal abominations she set upon them. They were aided in their efforts by Nestis, the ruler of the Withdrawn Realm, who had become virtually banished from her own domain thanks to the Black Queen's evil magic.

"The Black Queen was so outraged that mere citizenry should attempt to thwart her evil master plan that she soon started to hate the White City with the irrational hatred of the deranged. She no longer wanted to merely subdue it—now she wanted to destroy it, along with every living creature in it. The conflicts between her forces and the city became increasingly heated, finally culminating in a big clash between the Black Queen and Nestis on the slopes of Bear Mountain."

"But…wait a minute," said Dario. "Why is none of this mentioned in the history textbooks?"

Leo waved the question away. "Those things are useless. They never cover anything truly important."

"Oh…" Dario's head was swimming. "So what happened then?"

"Nestis did her best to try to destroy her enemy once and for all, but the Black Queen had become so powerful that she could no longer be killed. In the end, Nestis had no choice other than to find a way to confine the Black Queen. So she created a big vortex that sucked the Black Queen and all of her creatures through the Queen's Well into the caves beneath the mountain, where Nestis sealed her in."

"How?" asked Dario.

"What?"

"Um…you said that Nestis sealed the Black Queen in. How did she do this?"

"Oh. She cast some sort of spell." Leo waved his hand dismissively. "A special enchantment that created a magic barrier between the Black Queen and the outside world. Apparently, the effort of doing this was so great that Nestis perished in the process. Needless to say, with her demise, the Withdrawn Realm's days were numbered, and the whole place gradually diminished.

"The Black Queen has remained in her underground prison ever since, seething with fury and plotting to break out and destroy the city. Every once in a while, a crack appears on the surface of the barrier and something slips through. And it looks as if something of that nature might have happened again recently. If I knew for certain what was going on, I'd tell you more, but as it is, there's nothing more to tell. Either way, I wouldn't worry about it. The Black Queen has been buried alive under the mountain for such a long time that she's probably lost all her powers. There is something about centuries-long subterranean confinement that dampens even the most zealous of black magicians."

There was a long moment of silence as Leo rested his vocal cords and Dario tried to process everything he had just heard.

"So…you're basically saying that the Black Queen still exists?" he finally said. "Somewhere under Bear Mountain? And some of her creatures have escaped and you're chasing them?"

"Yes, that pretty much sums it up."

"And this place? This sort of hidden tower? What is it?"

"This hidden tower is called…the Hidden Tower. Honestly, this is getting so predictable it isn't even funny," Leo said, sounding almost apologetic.

"Oh." Dario was too bemused to be let down by the name's underwhelmingness.

"It is one of the few remnants of the White City as it once was, before it was turned into the grimy, dishwater-stained tub of mediocrity that it is now."

Somewhere outside, a sparrow burst into a short-lived barrage of agitated chirping as the combined weight of all the new information slowly began to sink into Dario's brain.

"Is…is any of this actually true?"

"Of course not," said Leo, laughing airily. "But we did just kill at least twenty minutes."

Dario felt a strange mixture of uncertainty and disappointment. He had encountered in his time quite a few nutcases—the BBP office certainly provided him with ample opportunity to do just that—and he had become skilled in identifying them with a reasonable level of accuracy. He was fairly certain that

Leo did not belong in this category. In fact, far from being a nutcase, Leo looked like the embodiment of rational thought—or at least he did in every respect other than his willful choice of a mullet.

And yet, the story he had just narrated couldn't possibly be true. This in turn was disappointing because the idea of Leo's story being true was far more interesting than it not being true. And this, in essence, was the cause of Dario's conflicting emotions.

"It just…" Dario began. "I just have this feeling that there's something going on. I don't mean just here. I mean throughout the city."

"Of course! There is always something going on, even in this city, but this something probably isn't an undead queen lurking under a mountain. Perhaps there is an old people's convention going on. Old people are the one thing this city is never in short supply of."

Then Dario remembered Vera Melada and promptly told Leo about the old woman's tea-based prophecy concerning the imminent comeback of the Black Queen.

"This must be the same hag the old man was talking about," said Leo to himself. "And did she give you any further details?"

"No, she didn't have any."

"Of course!" Leo banged his fist against the table. "They never do."

"So there is something going on then?"

Leo briskly got to his feet. "Listen, Dario, I've really enjoyed this little chat, but it's getting late now, and you'd better be off. But do drop by again if you ever happen to be around." He escorted Dario to the gate.

"But you are the Starman?" asked Dario as he was being ushered out.

Leo snorted. "Certainly not," he said haughtily. "I am a star *daimon*." And he slammed the gate shut before Dario could say another word.

☙◦❧

A flash of light shot through the great hall, a gust of wind rippled through the musty air, and Leo rolled his eyes.

"Well, that was interesting," said Algol. His image was flickering on and off at such an annoyingly irregular rate that it might have given anyone who wasn't a star daimon an epileptic seizure. His grin, however, was oddly fixed.

"Have you been eavesdropping?" asked Leo.

"Maybe a little."

"Then you know what a terrible predicament I'm in."

"Your predicament is not that terrible. Look, you have a minibar." Algol pointed at some antique, dust-covered bottles that sat on the table. The unidentifiable brown liquid contained inside was almost certainly out-of-date.

"Please, Algol." Leo no longer cared about concealing his despair. "Do you know anything, anything at all, that might help me figure out what I need to do to get out of here?"

"You could always try the Secret Library of the Little Brethren."

Leo shuddered. "Never," he said through clenched teeth. "I am never subjecting myself to the mental anguish of having to deal with those little bastards ever again. Even being in the same room with them is mental hell." He paused, suddenly uncertain. "Besides, it's not as if they have anything useful."

"You never know. Rumor has it that their collection has grown substantially."

For a moment, Leo's forehead wrinkled in thought. Then, as if deliberately destroying some mental bubble, he cried, "Out of the question!" He started pacing the room again. "There has to be another way. A saner way. One that doesn't involve the Little Brethren."

"In that case, I've run out of ideas." Algol sighed with mock regret. "The White City is as much a mystery to me as it is to you."

"I should have known you wouldn't tell me anything useful. You enjoy seeing me squirm."

"You'll be fine—you have a sidekick now." Algol smirked demonically, which, for a demon star, was the only possible way to smirk.

Leo snorted. "Hardly."

"Do you think he has any idea that everything you've told him is true?"

"Who cares? It's not as if there are going to be any more sightings of Barbara's stray menagerie. And, once it becomes perfectly obvious that *nothing is happening...*" The last part of Leo's utterance was loud enough for all the Celestial Realm to hear. "...he'll forget everything I said."

11

A BAD DAY FOR TRAM-SPOTTING

The trams of Zagreb were stealthy beasts, inaudible and, on some occasions, invisible. With their unassuming blue hues, they blended in with the dull gray streets like those moths that have, through mimicry, made themselves indistinguishable against tree bark. The trams lurked silently, always just on the outside of one's field of vision, waiting for the most opportune moment to pounce.

This was typically not a problem for Stella, who lived with her mother in a small house overlooking a busy road, where trams zoomed back and forth day and night. Living in such close proximity to the tram tracks had provided Stella with the experience that enabled her to dodge the trams' stealth attacks without effort. It also turned her into a tram-spotter. She knew all types of trams in the Electric Tramway Company network and was an expert on their individual temperaments.

There was the boxy, unstable number one, the rounded, fiery number nine and her favorite, the calm and dignified number seventeen, which she thought of as "her" tram, with its archaic shape reminiscent of nineteenth-century horse-drawn trams, except without the horses, and a single round headlight that reminded her of miners' helmets. She could tell each type from miles away. But even tram-spotters have their bad days.

It had been a day like any other, though perhaps a bit cloudier than most, and Stella was crossing the road on her way to school. She was still a first grader back then, and as such no stranger to being told repeatedly by practically every adult she knew to make sure to look first to her left and then to her right before crossing the road. But on this particular day, she wasn't her usual alert self. She didn't check if there were any trams approaching from either direction. There was no need—it was so quiet.

As she was about to step onto the tracks, something tugged her collar from behind, and she found herself being pulled back. At the same time, a fast-moving blue blur invaded her line of sight from the left, from where it had apparently been approaching silently the whole time without her being the least bit aware of it.

The tram in question was one of the short, stubby compact types with a boxy body and an accordion middle, the kind of model that was typically assigned to the number one route. It was not Stella's favorite type of tram. In fact, it was her least favorite type. There was too much of it in terms of height and too little in terms of length. As a result, the tram was unpleasantly wobbly. Whenever she had to travel on the number one, the constant swaying inevitably made her feel almost seasick. To add insult to injury, this type of tram also had a tendency to go too fast whenever there was a long straight portion of tracks ahead and then to stop abruptly without any particular reason, making anyone unfortunate enough to be on board clutch the nearest handle to avoid falling over. The number one tram was a menace to society.

With a gust of wind, the offending tram rushed past her like a blue torpedo. Naturally, it swayed from side to side as it dashed by, its two vaguely eye-shaped taillights making the whole thing look like a huge bobbing head. Its electric bell rang out in passing, but only feebly, as if the tram couldn't even deign to make a proper noise to alert just one single pedestrian.

Once the boxy monstrosity had finally passed and started to recede in the distance in the vertiginous manner typical for that model, Stella could see a yellow number thirteen printed on the square black plate at the back. That was unusual. The number thirteen didn't normally operate on that road, although, every once in a while, it was possible to spot an errant one that had taken a detour due to some obstruction elsewhere on the tram network. Apparently that day had been one such day.

Leaning against the back window of the receding tram, a middle-aged man reading a folded newspaper briefly looked down at Stella over the top of his tiny half-moon glasses, his face bearing an expression of world-weary indifference. Evidently a minor everyday incident such as the one that had just transpired barely had a fighting chance of penetrating his deep-set boredom with life in general and the Zagreb transportation system in particular. The man had no way of knowing that if someone hadn't pulled Stella back at the last moment, the tram would almost certainly have hit her, and even if he had known, he probably would have been just as indifferent.

Stella remained standing on the edge of the tram tracks for another few seconds as another tram coming from the opposite direction passed by. Before she was finally able to cross the tracks, she turned and looked behind her for the briefest of moments, stealing one hesitant glance.

Three unknown men stood behind her, all of them tall, composed and somewhat gloomy. Two of them were generic men of unspecified age with neat short haircuts like Ken dolls, and the third one was an older man with tired eyes. None of them were looking at her. None of them gave any indication that they might have just saved her life.

Stella said a silent thank-you to whomever it may have concerned and crossed the road.

The school is looking festive. Its walls are bedecked with bloodred autumn leaves. Kids in fancy dress and scary masks are going up to the main auditorium. But down beneath, in the darkness of the school's hidden cellar, a black shadow is rising like a sea at high tide. Its dark tendrils crawl up the walls like a giant squid climbing out of a black abyss. Soon the shadow engulfs the whole school.

The building shudders with a sudden tremor. Its walls start twisting and turning, moving slowly upward as if pushed by the very foundations of the building. Blood oozes down the walls. The two towers become even higher, their roofs steeper. Battlements spring up along the top of the building. The rose garden at the front sinks into the earth to be replaced with a moat. Once the tremors have settled, the building looks utterly transformed.

And on top of the northern tower, the Black Queen stands triumphant, as solid and unmoving as a statue.

Stella awoke with a gasp.

Afterward, she was too shaken to go back to sleep and felt groggy in the morning. She was almost late for school and made it to the classroom only seconds before the bell rang. It was only after the bell announced the much-awaited midday break, when they were let out to roam free around the playground, that she felt lucid enough to tell Tin, Ida and Rea about the disturbing dream.

As she narrated her morbid vision, Ida looked mildly curious, Rea indifferent, while Tin looked increasingly alarmed.

"I had a similar dream once," said Ida after Stella was done. "Except it was about Gollum and there were bats in it."

Tin had gone sickly pale. "I…I think I might have had a similar dream last night," he said. "At first, I didn't remember what it was, but now it's coming back to me."

"I didn't have any dreams," said Rea with an air of accomplishment.

"This must mean something," said Stella, ignoring the final remark.

All four of them burst out into excited chatter, everyone offering their opinion, until Rea finally said, "I don't think we should take any of this seriously. It's not as if this event where everyone wears masks is ever going to happen."

"Maybe the masks were symbolic," said Stella.

"What do you mean?" asked Tin.

"Maybe the masks represent some hidden parts of ourselves or our spirit animals or something."

"I once had a dream," said Ida, "that my uncle's dog was run over by a car, and it didn't mean anything."

"How do you know it didn't mean anything?"

"Because the car was a *Fićo*, and *Fićos* never mean anything. Also, my uncle doesn't have a dog."

"Maybe Ida is right," said Tin. "Even if we both had it, it's still just a dream."

Stella shook her head. "This was no ordinary dream. It felt real. It was as if I were there. I can still hear the walls bursting to pieces. But the worst thing was the black stuff in the cellar."

"Not the cellar again," said Rea.

"There's something down there!" Stella paused, startled by the forcefulness of her own voice. "There is something down there that belongs to the Black Queen. Maybe it's the spider or maybe it's something else. Whatever it is, I know it will try to break out somehow."

"How? When?" asked Tin.

"No idea."

Rea rolled her eyes. "Unbelievable."

"What I do know," continued Stella, undeterred, "is that we are the ones who let it in. Therefore, we have to do the right thing."

There was a brief argument as to what "the right thing" might be under the circumstances. They kept coming back to the same thing, namely the necessity of going down into the Forbidden Cellar.

"There has to be another way in," said Stella. "What could it be? Think!"

"They say," said Tin, "that there are secret passages all over the school."

"Who says?"

"Older kids. But they probably mean the dungeons."

Rea slapped her forehead.

"My uncle," said Ida, "says that someone from his class once found a hidden chamber. It was very dark and he had to go back and get a flashlight. But when he came back, the chamber was gone."

"Where was the chamber?"

"In the library."

"Of course!" Stella's face brightened. "This could be it."

"This could be what?" asked Tin.

"Can't you see?" said Stella. "The library is in the northern tower, on the first floor. That's the same side as the cellar."

"And?" asked Rea.

"And if there's a secret passage going into the cellar, the library might be where it begins."

The others looked torn between a childlike eagerness to believe that exciting things could exist in their midst and a proto-adult skepticism that suggested they couldn't.

Stella turned to Ida. "Did your uncle tell you which part of the library the hidden chamber was in?"

"The front," said Ida. "Or maybe the back."

"Doesn't matter. I'll check everything." Stella turned to go. "I'm going there right now."

"You can't," said Tin. "The library closes at 1:00 p.m."

"Fine. Then I'll go tomorrow morning."

"I can come with you, if you like," said Tin.

"No," said Stella with steely determination. "Who's ever heard of so many kids wanting to use the library at the same time? It'll look much more realistic if I go there by myself."

As Stella walked home after school, a number seventeen tram glided calmly down the tracks beside her. The tram paused for a few moments at the nearby stop like a perambulating philosopher stopping in his tracks at the arrival a sudden thought. It opened its doors, and a few people got off. No one got on. The tram closed its doors and was on its way again, heading westward with the same laid-back pace as before, apparently not bothered by the possibility that some more recent model might be making better time. Stella knew there was a good reason for that. A lot of power lay hidden beneath the quiet, clunky exterior of the old number seventeen tram. There was an inner core that could make the blue machine go faster than any new model when and if it wished to.

Stella had had firsthand experience of this phenomenon, having once been on a number seventeen that suddenly went into hyperspeed. It was on the other side of town, near the bridge where the number six and fourteen trams cross the bridge over the river Sava into New Zagreb. Stella's tram had just taken a right turn before the bridge, heading west down a particularly long and straight stretch of tracks that ran along the edge of the university campus, a park, a field and other areas of little interest. About halfway down the road, the tram seemed to buck before proceeding to speed down the remaining segment of the tracks like a DeLorean doing 88 miles per hour, only without the special effects. The force of the surge had Stella plastered against the back window of the first carriage as the tram bolted with vertiginous velocity all the way to the next station. When the tram finally stopped, it was with remarkable ease, as if it did this sort of thing all the time. Stella couldn't see if the tracks behind it were on fire, but she imagined that they must have been.

Presently she turned into a tiny concrete-paved garden that looked like an extension of the street. She cast one final glance at the receding blue form of the tram and closed the gate behind her.

12

NOTHING BUT POTTERY

In the aftermath of the revelation in the Hidden Tower, Dario had found himself hovering in a state which, for want of a more adequate term, he thought of as the "willing suspension of belief." He hadn't shared what he had learned with anyone. And he hadn't tried to seek out Leo Solar again. He didn't want himself to be influenced by the opinions of others until he had made up his own mind. He had to decide for himself what the truth was before committing to any particular course of action.

For the time being, the only action he could commit to was the routine drudgery of the BBP. Disappointingly, there had been no insight to be gleaned from the *White City Chronicle's* online comments section. Dario had already suspected that few black metal fans read the *White City Chronicle*, and their complete lack of effort to contact the WCC team with any information, views or even rumors concerning the events at the Ditch had confirmed his suspicions. But apparently this reluctance to share information on what happened the other night extended to the rest of the Internet too, seeing that he couldn't find a single reference to the doomed Crepuscular Immolation gig on any other website either.

He briefly considered pitching Mr. Vinko an article about the Ditch fiasco himself, but just as he was getting ready to put the idea into words, Mr. Vinko, looking even more stressed than usual, burst out of his office like a mechanical bird out of a cuckoo clock, planted himself at the usual spot on the carpet, and said:

"This is a complete madhouse. I am being bombarded from all sides with features on amateur kayaking for the spring special issue. But I still haven't even got the main coverage from the Regional Pottery Exhibition for the winter issue. And now I have to take Snowball to the vet because she is having bouts of explosive diarrhea, poor thing. I wouldn't abandon you at such a critical time, Dario, but you have to understand that Marica is devastated."

"Um...okay."

"So would you please, while I'm away, take all my calls and tell everyone that, for this issue, we're accepting articles on pottery and nothing but pottery."

"Sure."

"Nothing but pottery will do," added Mr. Vinko, blinking mousily.

"Okay."

After a short pause, Mr. Vinko clarified, "The only kind of articles to be featured in the coming issue are those pertaining to pottery."

Dario confirmed, in no uncertain terms, that he fully understood Mr. Vinko's point about pottery. This made Mr. Vinko's anxiety finally come down a notch. At the same time, Dario's idea for an article about Leo's battle with a demonic raven died a quiet, unmourned death.

As he weathered the rest of his shift, Dario almost wished some nutcase would barge in with another half-baked prophecy about the Black Queen, or at least a tale of the city's long-lost magic realm, or pretty much anything that wasn't pottery (which, on that day, Dario came very close to developing a lifelong aversion to). Sadly, however, there were no nutcases to be seen that day— not even a passing cantankerous drunk.

13

CONFESSIONS OF BROTHER BENEDICT

L eo sat in a café in a busy Lower Town street on a Friday afternoon. That he should surrender himself this way to an everyday ritual of the city was his ultimate show of defeat. He had even ordered a cup of coffee. It tasted like wet mud and made him sick, but everyone around him was drinking the stuff as if they actually enjoyed the revolting thing.

Everywhere he looked, there were men with hair in all the wrong places and not enough hair in the right places. *How did the world come to this?* he thought. At least back in the Black Queen's day, men had the sense to grow hair on their heads, if not necessarily to shave it off their faces.

At some point, a scruffy middle-aged man with a bald patch sat down at Leo's table and started talking to him as if they knew one another. Ignoring the man would have been easy, yet Leo's mind kept itself tuned in, at least sporadically, out of sheer boredom. The man had some sort of theory about life and was not shy about communicating it.

"It's…it's like a game," the man was saying. "Like…like a computer game. Or maybe…maybe not a computer game but more like a video game, you know? Like…like one of those consoles. Like one of those Game Boys. Did you ever own a Game Boy?"

Leo nodded vaguely.

"Or maybe not like a Game Boy but…"

Outside in the street, not far from where Leo sat, there was a statue of Nikola Tesla, who crouched on top of a large stone block, looking as dejected as Leo felt. At first, Leo had found comfort in the presence of a fellow sufferer, but as he sat there inhaling the combined fumes of espresso, secondhand cigarette smoke and pistachio-flavored ice cream, whatever was left of his spirit started to crumble. As much as Leo hated to admit it, Algol was sometimes right. Not often and certainly not always, but sometimes. And after searching under every rock, tree and park bench in the city and finding no clue to tell him what he had to do next, Leo had to admit to himself that in this case, Algol might have had a point. Maybe he really should pay the Little Brethren a visit.

Leo had told himself many times that he would never subject himself to their jarring presence again and that he would only suffer himself to be in the same room with them as a last resort, but as far as he could see, this *was* the last resort. That is, unless he suddenly decided he no longer craved to be back in the infinite reaches of space, free to roam wherever he pleased, and that he would instead prefer to settle down in the city, perhaps in a modest one-bedroom apartment in New Zagreb with a small balcony and central heating. The very thought made him shudder.

"I had one that was like a football and it had…it had one red button on the left and another button on the right. And…the other button was red too. Did you have one of those?"

Leo nodded.

Talking to the hermit again would be futile. The man was old, senile and overall useless. As for the goldsmith of Stone Gate, Leo was sure the little man knew more than he was telling. But whatever it was that he was keeping from him, Leo knew that he wouldn't be able to tease the information out of the minuscule craftsman by any ordinary means, not even force. The goldsmith was as obstinate as he was short.

And as for trying to track down any possible remnants of the Withdrawn Realm, if there were any to be found at all, this would have been ill-advised at best. Leo knew that the few remaining denizens of the Realm hated him because they blamed him for the near extinction of their world.

This was partly because beings of the Withdrawn Realm were easily excitable, irrational and prone to rash judgment. For the most part, however, it was because it was true. Yes, it had been the Black Queen and not himself who had taken over the Withdrawn Realm, thus ultimately leading to its destruction, but she never would have been able to do this if Leo hadn't given her the knowledge that enabled her to wield immense power.

Needless to say, Leo had learned his lesson, i.e., that sharing forbidden knowledge indiscriminately and with no consideration for the potential consequences was bad, very bad, and he was, of course, very sorry. But he was also very eager to leave the sorry place called Zagreb behind. What all this came down to was that Leo was left with only one option.

"...or maybe like a pinball machine," the man was saying.

"If you'll excuse me," said Leo, rising from his chair.

The scruffy man continued expounding his theories undeterred, speaking to the vacant seat as if it were still occupied.

Leo was one of those individuals endowed with the ability to avoid being detected whenever he wished, blending into any surroundings as effortlessly as a stick insect against a stick. This invaluable skill functioned flawlessly in all types of environments but one—the kind where everyone other than himself was three feet tall. Incidentally, the monastery of the Order of the Little Brethren was just such a place.

And so, as he lurked behind a tree in the courtyard of the Kaptol monastery, watching the little hooded figures waddling in and out of the main building, Leo decided that in terms of his ability to execute his freshly minted plan without being seen, timing was of the essence. Leo had been to the Secret Library before and knew how laughable the security was—the miniature monks collectively abandoned their posts whenever food was being served in the nearby refectory building.

As he had anticipated, he didn't have to wait long. This was because the Little Brethren were fed approximately every forty-five minutes. He had barely been standing by the tree for a quarter of an hour when the monastery bell rang, its sound launching a horde of pint-sized friars in the direction of the refectory and the prospect of an early supper.

The puny monks had greedy round faces with beady eyes, and their matching hooded robes were all done in dreary dirt-brown hues. Or at least the robes appeared to be brown. Leo could never quite tell whether the dirt-brown was the color of the fabric or whether the robes actually were dirty. Oh, how he would have loved to see those annoying little pests being rolled in dirt.

But now was not the time for violent fantasies. He had a job to do. And so, as the last of the tiny robed creatures entered the refectory, Leo dashed out of his hiding place, racing up the stone steps of the main monastery building and then up a narrow spiral staircase all the way to the top floor.

The library was predictably deserted. The monks had left all of their current study materials, most of them books that had been out of print since the early 1700s, lying open on the desks. A murky, semicircular, secluded spot at the back, like an apse, housed the Secret Library section. It was so called because it contained the remaining books from the Old Era, when the Withdrawn Realm still existed.

The Little Brethren, however, were merely the keepers of the secret books, and reluctant ones at that. They didn't study them or try to decipher their many secrets in any way, and generally wanted nothing to do with the things. They only kept the secret books to make sure they remained secret. The townspeople knew nothing of the old magic realm or the real history of the city. Whatever knowledge had survived about the ancient White City had first turned into rumor, then into lurid tale, then into legend, until it finally completely faded from the collective unconscious of the region and its inhabitants.

But the books could not simply be destroyed—the magic contained within their pages was too powerful, and any such attempt would have been reckless. The only other available option was to get them out of sight, to keep them hidden lest they end up in the wrong hands. And it had been the Little Brethren who volunteered for the job themselves—ostensibly because of a sense of duty but mainly because this gave them an excuse for their passive-aggressive self-righteousness.

As soon as Leo stepped into the musty-smelling gloom of the Secret Library, he regretted it. The shelves that lined the wall of the apse were stuffed with so many books that even if one of them did contain the information Leo needed to figure out what the Black Queen was up to, it would have taken him a giant turtle's lifetime to find it.

Irritated by his own powerlessness, Leo began to pick up random volumes off the shelf, quickly browsing each one before shoving it back onto the shelf once he ascertained that it was useless. This didn't take long, since useless was what they all were.

Then he saw it—a battered leather volume with the words *Confessions of Brother Benedict* printed pretentiously on its spine in a barely legible Gothic script. Leo would have rolled his eyes if they hadn't already been engaged in scanning his environs for incoming minuscule monks.

Brother Benedict had been a Withdrawn Realm enthusiast back in those days when such predilections were still not considered a delusional eccentricity. His interest, however, had been more than merely academic. After studying the Withdrawn Realm from a distance for many years—by reading whichever books on the subject he could get his hands on and befriending whichever errant magic beings from the other side that he could find in the city—Brother Benedict decided to study the magic world firsthand. To this end, he made it his mission to venture into the Withdrawn Realm himself. This was considered a dangerously foolhardy undertaking at the time because a person could easily get lost in the ever-shifting, illusory magic world, never to find their way back again. But the valiant monk went and ended up having a number of adventures. After his return, he compiled his reminiscences of the journey in his *Confessions*, which had subsequently become an unofficial compendium of all things Withdrawn Realm.

Leo had never met Brother Benedict, but if there was one thing he knew about monks, it was that they were all oversharers. This was why when he opened the dusty manuscript, it was with a certain amount of reluctant interest.

He leafed mechanically through the many pages of illegible calligraphic script peppered with margin drawings of small frolicking animals in suggestive poses until a grotesque drawing in frantic black lines and red highlights made him stop.

Although the drawing was poorly executed, one couldn't help noticing that it depicted a black snake, a raven, a giant fox and a spider with what looked like a thousand legs. All four of the creatures had red dots for eyes.

The spider made him shudder. Leo hated spiders. One of his favorite things about living in outer space was that there were no spiders in it. But it was the raven that filled him with a cold certainty that he had found what he was looking for. There was no doubt that this was the demonic bird he had fought at the Ditch.

The text underneath the drawing read:

I will now call to mind a past foulness, the most terrible corruptions of the Realm, not because I love them, but that I may review their wicked ways in the bit-

terness of my remembrance of the time when I was nearly torn piecemeal while being
lost among a multiplicity of things, the multiplicity being the fearsome Four.

Whence is this monstrousness? And to what end?

These things I then knew not, nor observed; they struck me on all sides, and I
saw them not. Yet many truths concerning these creatures retained I from this encoun-
ter: the truth that the Four are known in the Realm as the Fox of Destruction, the
Raven of Despair, the Snake of Seduction and the Spider of Illusion; the truth that
they have appeared suddenly and no one knows whence; the truth that their powers
are great and that they answer to the Black Queen alone; the truth that the Four are
the menace of the Withdrawn Realm.

And that sums up the truths I discovered during my brief encounter with the
Four. (What dost thou mean, God, it is not much? I barely made it out of there alive.)

Whence is this monstrousness? And to what end? These things I knew not then
and I know not now.

The problem with being earthed—well, one of them, at least—is that one's
mind becomes somewhat sluggish. In the Celestial Realm, Leo's thoughts flowed
freely, like data flowing down a fast broadband connection. But in the horren-
dously oppressive realm of Earth, his thoughts were gagged, hobbled prisoners.

And so Leo was unable to immediately pinpoint why exactly this idea of the
Four felt so disturbingly familiar. Brother Benedict's rambling monkish language
didn't help either. Leo's instincts, however, immediately responded by unleashing
a chilling sense of rising dread.

So absorbed was he in this sense of dread that he didn't notice the murmur
of the monks returning from the refectory and resuming their work in the main
part of the library. There is no way of knowing how long he would have remained
there staring at the terrifying page, oblivious to the outside world, had a high-
pitched voice not suddenly cried out from behind him:

"What is this? Who are you?"

Leo let out a slow, heavy sigh. It was the sigh of helpless resignation. He put
the book back on the shelf—he had seen enough. Then he turned around.

A pint-sized monk in a brown robe was standing before him, his fat-cheeked
face turned up at him with the vigilant look of an overzealous terrier.

"What are you doing here?" yelped the creature.

"Nothing," said Leo quietly, trying not to draw any more attention to himself. "I was just browsing."

"Keep your voice down!" cried the monk. "Can't you see we're in a library?"

"I *am* keeping my voice down." Leo glanced around nervously. Some of the other monks were starting to look up from their books.

"Will you stop shouting?" shouted the monk. "This is study hour, and the Brethren are engaged in serious study."

"I am not shouting—*you're* shouting."

"No, *you're* shouting!" shouted the monk.

"No, *you're* shouting."

"No, *you're* shouting!"

The other monks had by now abandoned their posts and were looking with interest at what their fellow Little Brother was shouting about.

Suddenly the monk's eyes caught sight of Leo's star belt, and the little creature gasped with shock. "The demon!"

Leo rolled his eyes. "Not demon—*daimon*."

"How did you get here?"

"Like everyone else, through the front door," said Leo. "I thought it was allowed. Isn't today your open day? I thought I heard something about it on the radio."

"There is no such thing!"

"Oh, I'm sorry. They must have been talking about some other monastery then. In that case, I'd better be off before they close."

But before Leo was able to slip away, another, more senior-looking miniature monk materialized before them.

"What is all this about, Brother Gregor?" asked the other monk.

"Prior Dominik," said Brother Gregor, "this is the stray demon that brought so much suffering to the city all those years ago. He has come to sow discord again."

"Is that so?" said the prior before Leo had time to protest. The little friar looked him up and down, as if he were the one who had the vertical advantage over Leo rather than the other way around. His face and his whole posture were brimming with attitude.

"I have not come here out of mere idleness," said Leo, realizing that there would be no easy way out. "I have been sent to the city on an important mission."

"And what mission would that be?" asked the prior haughtily.

"To save the city from certain destruction by the forces of the Black Queen."

A strange thing happened then—all the little friars covered their ears with the palms of their hands and started shaking their heads with matching expressions of intense denial. Leo blinked like a confused ostrich until the bizarre spectacle was finally over.

"We will not have this kind of talk in our library," said Prior Dominik eventually.

"What do you mean? This kind of talk *is* your library." Leo gestured to the apse behind him.

"No one is allowed to read or even look at those books, not to mention talk about their contents."

"Well, that's not very helpful, seeing as the Black Queen is about to break out of her underground prison and the city has got practically no one capable of stopping her."

"No! Noooo!" said the prior, and the whole collective head-shaking began all over again.

"Pretending the problem doesn't exist won't make it go away," said Leo.

"The Black Queen no longer exists," said Prior Dominik. "The witch of Bear Town is gone—gone forever. And all these tales about her are nothing more than superstitious nonsense."

"Well, in that case, my work here is done," said Leo in a casual tone, strolling toward the exit. "Oh, and by the way, you might want to be on the lookout for the Fox of Destruction."

"No! Noooo!"

Leo didn't stay for the head-shaking.

The disturbing revelation he had gleaned from *Confessions* left Leo feeling like one of those lobsters kept alive in a pot of water in a seafood restaurant until it was ready to be cooked. And so he did the only thing he could think of other than getting drunk on cheap supermarket beer and passing out in a ditch. He waited until nightfall and then headed for the Stone Gate. The place was deserted as usual. He quickly lit the ghost candle and averted his eyes to avoid having to look at the annoying oozing mist shtick. The goldsmith made an appearance a few uneventful minutes later.

"Why, hello there, young man," said the little craftsman airily. "Back again for another tour of our great city?"

"Enough with the theatrics," snapped Leo. "You know very well who I am and why I'm here."

The goldsmith sighed. He took off his glasses, rubbed one of the lenses with a handkerchief, and then put them back on.

"I'm sorry, Leo," he said. "I wish things were less complicated."

"Did you know?" asked Leo. "Did you know from the start that this wasn't just another breach of the barrier? That this was something huge and terrible? That there might not even be a way to destroy those creatures? That I'd be stuck here the whole time until I figured out the solution to an impossible problem?"

"We couldn't be sure until at least one of the creatures made itself known. All we had to go by was a vision from one of our seers, and this vision was blurry at best."

"And are you sure now? You've heard about what happened with that infernal raven, I'm sure."

The goldsmith nodded grimly.

"Does this mean that the remaining creatures are also members of the Four?"

"Considering the contents of the vision, that seems highly probable."

"How did the damn spider and the rest of them even end up with the Black Queen?" Leo started pacing from wall to wall. "Aren't they supposed to be gone forever...faded away or whatever...with the rest of the Withdrawn Realm?"

"It appears..." The goldsmith made a quick adjustment to his glasses. "It appears that while she still ruled Bear Town Fortress, the Black Queen somehow managed to win the Four over to her side. And in her final hour, she took them to the Underworld with her."

"Well, that's great. I'm really happy for her." Leo's pacing had become so hectic that it looked like some kind of novelty cardio workout. "So what am I supposed to do now? How do I track down the rest of them? Why are they hiding anyway?"

"It appears that they are waiting for something."

"What?"

"The Night of the Witches."

Leo looked blank at the mention of the vernacular name for Halloween.

"October 31," explained the goldsmith. "The time of year when the boundary between the ordinary world and the Withdrawn Realm is thinner than usual."

"So what if it's thinner? There is nothing left of the Withdrawn Realm other than the Threshold."

"Sadly, there is one more thing left—the Underworld."

Leo suddenly felt sick. It must have been the coffee.

"It might be out of sight, beneath the surface," continued the goldsmith, "but it's still a part of the Withdrawn Realm. Nestis put the Black Queen under the mountain, and it is Nestis's spell that is keeping the Black Queen imprisoned. If the spell breaks, then so will the boundary that is keeping the witch from the city.

"And since this year's Night of the Witches will coincide with this unfortunate hour when the Black Queen's most dangerous creatures are out on the loose, there is no doubt that she will use it as a once-in-a-lifetime opportunity to break out into the city. She will make sure that whatever is left of the Four sees that this happens."

"So basically I have less than two weeks to find the rest of them?"

The goldsmith nodded regretfully.

"You do realize," said Leo, "that even if I do find them in time, trying to fight them with the meager weapons I've got would be absurd? Need I remind you that the Star Council has banned me from using my powers while on Earth?" Leo nearly staggered at the unbearableness of that thought. "I can only use such magic tools and weapons as are available to me in the city. What this comes down to are primarily spellbooks and self-combusting carved sticks. How would I fight that abominable spider with any of those things? The most I'd be able to do with a magic combustible stick is light the spider's cigarette while it slowly devours me."

"I know, Leo, I know." The goldsmith nodded sadly. "That is one of the reasons we didn't tell you about the spider from the outset."

Leo stopped pacing. "What do you mean?"

The goldsmith looked troubled. "Trying to confront the Spider of Illusion, with or without your magic weapons, would be madness."

"Why?"

"The Spider of Illusion can see the inside of everyone who tries to approach it, and it always retaliates accordingly. If it saw what you really are, it would fight back with such force that it would destroy the whole city, if not all of Earth."

"Well, then what am I supposed to do? I can neither squeeze nor fart." This was a local saying that Leo had picked up during his time in the city but had never had a chance to use in context. Despite the circumstances, he was pleased that he had now finally been given the opportunity to do so.

"There might be another way to stop the Black Queen before she tries to cross over into the city. Something other than waiting for her remaining servants to make a move."

"And what might that be?" Leo had a peculiar sinking feeling, the kind that comes just before you hear something you really don't want to hear.

The goldsmith shuffled his feet awkwardly. "You could try stopping her from the other side." When he saw Leo's gaping expression, he added, "From her side."

"You're not…" Leo's mouth had gone dry. "You're not actually suggesting that I…go there? To the Underworld? To Barbara's lair? To the dark, musty basement of the White City?" He stopped only because he couldn't think of another metaphor.

"No, no, of course not." The little goldsmith held up his hands defensively. "I am only saying that this, too, is a possible course of action, one that should not be discarded without a second thought."

"That would be suicide. No one in their right mind would even think of it, let alone do it."

"Yes, admittedly, the option does contain a certain degree of risk," said the goldsmith. "But it could also potentially pave the way for complete success. Think about it: on the one hand, you could wait for all three of the remaining creatures to show themselves on the Night of the Witches. Then you would have to somehow fight them all at the same time. And if you failed in any way, allowing even one of them to slip out of your grasp and help the Black Queen into the city, it would be all over for everyone. But if you nipped her evil plan in the bud at its source, you would have achieved success with one stroke."

Leo shook his head in disbelief. "This is madness. Even if I went to the Underworld, how would I ever 'nip her evil plan in the bud?'"

"You would find a way, Leo. Even in your fallen state, you are still the most powerful being on Earth."

Leo did his best not to show that he was flattered. Then an unpleasant thought put a damper on his pride.

"But...the spider," he said, his voice filled with exasperation. "Even if I somehow stopped the Black Queen from the inside, the goddamn Spider of Illusion would still be out there in the city. As well as the other two creatures."

"You can deal with the rest of them when the time comes. As for the spider, there is someone else who might be able to help."

"That sounds very reassuring." Leo's dismissive tone was carefully calibrated to convey the idea that sparing so much as a single thought for "someone else" was beneath him. Within three seconds, however, his curiosity got the better of him. "Who?"

"Oh, no one you've met before." The goldsmith's tone was casual, but the twinkle in his eye was unusually sly. "One of the locals. A young person—young but precocious. One with certain nascent talents."

The little goldsmith's deliberate reticence annoyed Leo to no end, and he would have loved to put a stop to this particular conversational thread with a snarky comment, but the opportunity to learn about the existence of a potentially less than typically useless local was simply too intriguing for him to pass up. "Really," he said.

"In fact, dear Leo, you might be interested in meeting this gifted child." The goldsmith's expression was now positively wily.

"And why would I wish to do that?" Leo tried to make his voice icy and aloof, but it came out sounding unfashionably nagging.

The goldsmith opened his mouth to utter what must have been meant to be an enthusiastic, uplifting retort only to snap it shut all of a sudden. For a moment, the goldsmith frowned, blinking and looking uncertain, like an esteemed university professor that had just been asked in class the one question he did not know the answer to.

"Because," he began, folding his hands together, "it would be a good teaching opportunity." As the goldsmith finished uttering the sentence, his face at once regained its familiar positive glow. He appeared not to have noticed Leo wince.

"And why should I care about such fluff as 'teaching opportunities?'"

"Why not, dear friend? We all need some relaxing diversions every once in a while. I thought that the opportunity to offer guidance to a promising child would be something you would, if not exactly accept with open arms, at least consider doing. After all, er…" He fidgeted with his pocket watch before clearing his throat politely. "You have reached a certain age—"

"What!"

"—the sort of age when it is natural for a person, star daimon or any other sentient entity, to consider sharing some of the vast knowledge and experience acquired throughout their long and no doubt eventful existence."

Leo was aghast. The insolence of the little man! He primed himself for an outburst of celestial fury but then shrugged, deciding that taking the present conversation any further would be a waste of intelligence and oxygen. "All right." He exhaled with the shakiness of a punctured tire. "Where and how do I meet this youngling?"

"Fear not, my friend." The goldsmith made a calming yet excited gesture with his hands. "An opportunity will present itself when the time is right. All you have to do is be at the right place." The goldsmith knitted his brow in contemplation. "At the right time," he added as an afterthought.

Leo squeezed his eyes shut and pinched the bridge of his nose. "All right, never mind. Can you please just let me know what I need to do in the meantime to get this whole Barbara business wrapped up?"

"Oh!" The goldsmith blinked owlishly. "Well, that much is clear. All you have to do is go to the Underworld and stop the Black Queen before she is ushered into the city by one of her creatures."

"I thought it would be that easy."

"I know this sounds like a daunting challenge, dear Leo. But if you do decide to pursue the course of action we've discussed, you already know how to get to the Threshold. From there, follow the path until you meet the one who will show you the way to the secret door under the mountain." The goldsmith put his hands behind his back, radiating once again his relaxed, professorial air. Then his hand shot up, as if grasping a stray thought. "And make sure to set out on your journey well ahead of All Hallows' Eve." The hand quickly retreated behind his back, as if embarrassed by its own impulsive outburst. "The Underworld is a dark and treacherous place, and it might take you a while to find the seat of the Black Queen's domain."

"Thanks for the useful advice," said Leo. "I won't be needing it."

"I hope you're right," said the goldsmith.

14

THE ATTACK OF THE GIANT WEREFOX

The colors of the Electric Tramway Company headquarters were gray, muddy brown, rusty brown and gray. The building was a grim concrete affair shaped like a rudimentary box, with only a few peremptory decorative elements to break the monotony, and even they looked like something out of a cubist's nightmare.

The place was tucked away in the shadows behind some trees at the end of the number twelve line like an abandoned bunker. Its two stories were defined by rows of weathered, urine-yellow shutters that looked like bad teeth. Some of them had ribs that had partly broken off and now sagged pitifully over the bottom edge of the window frames.

Dario went inside.

The interior was even worse, if for no other reason than the fact that in order to see it, one had to be inside. The building was a maze of gray corridors as intricate as the labyrinth of Minos and just as poorly lit. The light that came in through the shutters seemed to refract in such a way as to make it imperceptible to the human eye, and the halogen tube lights that lined the ceiling like the wiring of a doomed spaceship emitted muddy light, as if stuffed with the contents of a vacuum cleaner bag. The reception desk stood deserted, a silent foreshadowing of the sort of customer service that the visitor was about to be subjected to.

As there were no signs to point Dario in the right, or indeed any, direction, he picked a random corridor and started walking, the soles of his boots squeaking against the floor, until he found himself in the heart of the labyrinth. This turned out to be a murky little office with extensive wood paneling and no windows.

Instead of the minotaur, what awaited therein was a small, ill-tempered woman lurking behind a long green-topped counter. She looked up at Dario with a slow, disdainful upward roll of the eyeballs. Her eyes crawled over his too-comfortable blue jeans, his much-worn leather jacket, his doe-eyed, boyish face and his overgrown brown curls with an expression of utmost distaste, and suddenly Dario felt self-conscious. Had he been a potted plant, he would have withered right there and then; had he been a pot of milk, he would have churned.

"Yes." The woman's tone was too disinterested to even attempt a rising intonation.

Dario cleared his throat and explained what had happened with the tram conductor the other night.

"Name," said the woman.

"Dario Taubek."

She got to her feet with obvious reluctance and went to the back of the office without another word. She opened one of the many filing cabinets stacked against the back wall and proceeded to shuffle through what sounded like twenty thousand cardboard folders. She came back to the desk a few minutes later with a piece of paper. She was squinting at it.

"You have been issued a fine," she said without looking up.

Dario explained, as coherently as he could, that he had until recently been a student, a card-carrying one with his own student season ticket, and that he had not had the time to properly familiarize himself with nonstudent fares. "So would it be possible to waive the fine?"

"No."

"But can I at least appeal?" Dario hoped he didn't sound too desperate. But then again, the fine was equivalent to a week's worth of BBP wages.

The woman raised a cynical-bordering-on-nihilistic eyebrow and reached for something under the counter.

"You can try," she said. She laid out three different forms before him—a blue one, a green one and a beige one. Each contained large chunks of single-spaced print so tiny that it looked like solid blocks of black ink. The fine print was broken up only by a number of empty lines that needed to be filled in.

"How long would it take for the appeal to be processed?" Dario asked.

The woman gazed into the mid-distance. This went on for what seemed like a full minute, and for a moment, Dario wondered whether she had forgotten that he was in the room or was perhaps experiencing some kind of blackout.

"Twelve weeks or so," she finally said in a bored, nasal tone. Her manner carried the implication that "twelve" in this case meant "forty-seven if you're lucky."

So Dario paid the fine after all and collected his ticket, which he put into his back pocket with the trembling hand of a man who knows he will have to cut meat out of his diet for at least two months to make up for his financial loss.

The ETC ordeal over, he hopped on a number twelve tram at the Remiza turning circle. Even though this was the first stop, the tram was already full. Luckily, there was one last remaining seat in the carriage, and he promptly parked his behind on it with a little sigh of relief. Normally he would have gone to stand by the window, which was his favorite tram conductor lookout spot, as well as being well out of the way of any seat-grabbing pensioners, but at the moment, he was too mentally exhausted to care.

It wouldn't be a long ride anyway. Fifteen minutes, twenty at the most. However, no sooner had the tram gone past the first intersection than he was startled by a sound like a cross between a growl and a murmur.

Dario looked up to see a fearsome old woman towering over him, glaring down at him with unchecked disapproval. She had tiny, sharp eyes, white close-cropped hair that almost looked like a crew cut and a wrinkled, bony face like a mummy's. She wore a beige coat that was cut like a uniform and a brown beret that was skewed to one side. A foldable umbrella the size of a baseball bat was stuffed under her armpit.

"What is it, young man?" said the old lady in a way that suggested she was used to putting young men in their place, possibly on a daily basis, and that she had put in place men bigger and older than him. "Do your legs hurt from too much standing?"

Dario blinked a few times in quick succession. He sat up straight and clutched the metal bar of the seat in front of him. "No," he said. His tongue suddenly felt thick and sluggish. "Not at all."

"In that case, would you mind giving up your seat to an old woman with aching bones?"

A muscle in Dario's cheek twitched at the memory of Madam Rosanda's bear slap. "Certainly." He sprang to his feet immediately. "Here you are, madam."

The old lady sat down with an angry grunt. There was no thank-you forthcoming. Their conversation had come to an end. Dario went to stand by the window.

It wasn't long before the tram reached the Cibona Tower stop, with the familiar sight of the Hole looming on the other side of the road. The Hole was a term of endearment for the dingy little café disguised as an Irish pub that had become an unofficial meeting place for the Pure Philosophy contingent over the years. This was where he had hung out with Martin and Bruno when he was a student; it was a place Dario could go whenever he felt like it and be certain that there would be at least one philosopher there. He hopped off the tram when it stopped by the Technical Museum, a sullen brown building that huddled behind a shrubbery-lined fence like a highway bandit behind a bush. Then he crossed the road and went into the Hole.

Inside, the place was filled with the comforting murmur of multiple laid-back conversations accentuated with the occasional soft clink of glassware. The low-key lighting was about halfway between intimate and too dark to see where you're going. Dario headed straight down to the back of the pub, where the smoking section was.

The smoking section consisted of three tables on the left side of the premises. These were located directly next to the nonsmoking section, which comprised three tables on the right side. The two sections were separated from one another by precisely nothing. There was no cleverly designed invisible barrier that could not be breached by cigarette smoke. Nor was the nonsmoking section fitted with a special kind of air vent that extracted smoke particles and immediately transformed them into fresh, lavender-scented air. In fact, the entire interior of the pub was suffused with the thick miasma of cigarette smoke.

He saw Martin and Bruno right away. The two of them sat immersed in a philosophical discussion at a small table on the far left of the smoking section.

There was a third person with them, whom he recognized as Boris, a sort of unofficial mascot of the Philosophy Department. Boris had thick glasses, shoulder-length hair that was beginning to turn gray around the temples and a posture that conveyed a sense of intellectual ennui.

"Old man!" cried Martin when he noticed Dario's presence in the dimness of the pub.

Dario exchanged ironic handshakes with all three of them before joining them at the table.

"A grave injustice," said Martin, shaking his head with mock compassion after Dario had narrated his earlier experience at the ETC office. "What with you being such a dedicated tram user and all."

The waiter came to take Dario's order. He was about to order a large Guinness but then remembered that he was now poor, reduced to near penury by the unfair tram fine. So he ordered a cup of chamomile tea.

"Did you hear anything else about that night at the Ditch?" asked Martin after Dario's steaming cup of herbal tea had arrived.

"Um…no." Now that he was among his peers in the familiar surroundings of the Hole, Dario no longer felt like sharing what Leo had told him. A sudden pang in his gut made him feel that bringing his still unverified knowledge into the light of day would extinguish the last glint of hope that it might be true.

If revealed, the story would be promptly put under the spotlight of Pure Philosophy, where it would surely perish, smothered by the merciless hand of logic.

"So have we reached any kind of consensus as to what actually happened?" asked Bruno. "Because I still have no idea."

"I think it was just a bird," blurted Dario.

Martin and Bruno gave him identical comically startled looks, while Boris continued with his silent meditation as the smoke from his cigarette rose languidly in a column beside his right ear. He had the air of someone who knew everything.

Boris was what was commonly known as an eternal student, i.e., a person who pursues a particular course of study over a period of time much longer than the conventional four-year duration of a typical Zagreb University course. Examples of eternal students engaged in a (typically leisurely) study of their chosen field for up to ten years were not unusual, and even fifteen was not unheard of. In Boris's case, however, the figure was rumored to be more like twenty. So it was quite possible that he did know everything.

"You know," continued Dario, "like, um…a pigeon or something. It must have got in during the day and then…nested somewhere in a corner. But then the noise agitated it, and it had a sort of fit. And in the dark it only looked like a raven. It was probably just a black pigeon."

"Nice theory, old man." Martin's eyes twinkled with amusement. "Solid reasoning."

But poor earnest Bruno was actually considering Dario's argument as if it were something that was supposed to make sense.

"So you think," said Bruno, "that the bird was just sitting there for the first few hours, tolerating the noise, but then it just sort of blew a fuse all of a sudden?"

"Well, maybe it was freaking out the whole time but we only noticed it at the end. Or maybe it was…hibernating at first."

"Was there birdshit?" asked Martin. "Surely if it had been a frenzied bird, there would have been birdshit all over the place."

"I don't remember seeing any birdshit," said Bruno.

"I think I saw some," said Dario.

Boris turned to them with a look that suggested he was about to announce to the world an idea of great importance. He looked up at the column of smoke rising from the end of his cigarette and said, "A bird of ill omen never shits on the same fence twice."

There was a short stunned silence as the rest of them tried, and failed, to process what Boris had said.

"Any word from the BBP nutcase brigade?" asked Martin eventually.

"No, not recently. They—"

"What the—" Bruno was staring at the TV screen mounted behind the bar.

The caption on the screen said *Breaking News*, and the footage being shown featured a bizarre creature that looked like a bristly black fox the size of a small car. The giant fox was thrashing around the city center, menacing the pedestrians, overturning news kiosks and tearing out tram cables.

The bartender turned up the volume.

"*…is yet to be identified, although some zoologists believe it to be a member of the Pseudalopex genus. The creature was last seen on the corner of Ilica and Franko-pan Street. Residents are advised to stay away from the city center until further notice.*"

"What the hell?" said Martin.

"It's probably a boar," said Bruno.

As Martin and Bruno began to argue about the probability of a wild boar roaming through the city in the twenty-first century, Dario was struck by the certainty that what he was seeing on the screen was the clue he had been looking for—definitive proof that would tip the balance of his internal decision-making mechanism toward accepting that Leo's story was true. The rampaging monster on the TV screen had to be another one of the Black Queen's creatures—one of the group that both Leo and Vera Melada had mentioned. In the murky confusion of the Ditch, it had been possible to doubt one's senses and attempt to rationalize the raven away. But in the light of day, faced with the objective footage shown on the screen, there was no room for doubt. What he was seeing was real.

Just like that, Dario suddenly knew that it was all true—everything Leo had told him. And that he was perhaps the only other person who knew it. Therefore, he had to act. But he had no idea how.

Reflexively, he took his phone out of his pocket. His Twitter feed was predictably inundated with references to the fox monster. But there was something else too: a text message. It read:

Might need help with this one.

Meet me in the woods north of Illyrian Square if you can.

Pls get my banishing book from the tower on your way, if poss.

Dario blinked. This had to be a message from Leo. He was certain, however, that he had never given him his phone number. Leo had never asked, nor did he seem to have a phone of his own.

Nevertheless, if Dario needed an incentive to act, which he did, then this was it.

He pocketed his phone and excused himself, rising from his chair. "I need to be somewhere. It's, uh…work-related." And he was off.

"Jesus, old man, what's the rush?" said Martin after him and then took a big gulp of beer.

"He's abandoning us," said Bruno after Dario had gone. He didn't look the least bit serious. "It had to happen sooner or later."

"He's changed." Martin shook his head regretfully. "Ever since he threw his hard-earned student status to the wind and went on this…this…employment rampage."

"He's being reckless," said Bruno.

"This is just a phase," said Martin. "It'll pass. Sooner or later, he'll come to his senses, and then he'll come back to us. And when that happens, we shall be magnanimous."

"Yes, we shall be magnanimous."

☙◦❧

As soon as he was out of the Hole, it became obvious that taking the tram was out of the question. The city center was in a standstill—trams sat motionless on the road, police cars were everywhere, and sirens wailed in the distance. One of the trams, an old number seventeen, had a deep gash running down its side, as if it had been torn open by a gigantic claw. Dario decided that his best bet would be to go on foot and stay off the main roads.

This was a sensible method, albeit a time-consuming one, and it took Dario over half an hour to get to the Square and then up to the Hidden Tower.

Although the great hall looked even more unsettling without Leo in it, Dario had no trouble finding the banishing book. He saw the slim black volume resting on the table right away.

Feeling elated to have successfully accomplished the task he had been given, Dario tucked the book into the inner pocket of his jacket and headed out in the direction of Illyrian Square.

☙◦❧

The woods to the north of Illyrian Square were much more than a token green space for dog walkers. They were like a miniature forest that just happened to be in the middle of the city. In fact, it was one of the many fringes of verdure that extended from the slopes of Bear Mountain in the north, covering that whole side of the city in a patchy toupee of trees. As such, it was not the most convenient place to track down a lightning-fast man and a rampaging fox monster, which was why Dario soon found himself lost in the woods, with no Leo or any other person or monster in sight.

A helpful hint came to him by way of a savage snarl from the top of a thicket-covered hill just off the path. Dario followed the direction of the sound.

When he reached the hilltop, which he did not achieve without a fair amount of swatting at the various branches and bushes that tried to scratch his face off, he saw Leo battling something that looked like a cross between a werewolf and a giant fox with a T. rex's tail. In short, it was a werefox. The monster's fur was spiky, more thorns than hair, and if its snout resembled a fox's, this was only in passing, the way a Venus flytrap resembled a flower. Its clawed front limbs looked almost as atrophied as a T. rex's, but this didn't prevent the monster from trying to slash at Leo's face with terrible ferocity. Its back limbs were as thick as tree trunks. Its bulky head would have been almost featureless if it hadn't been for its two beady eyes and a huge slobbering mouth full of teeth.

But it was the tail that seemed to be its most dangerous weapon. The were-fox kept lashing the hideous appendage like a whip, making Leo jump this way and that (with an acrobat's skill, Dario noted) to dodge it. All trees within a twenty-foot radius lay in ruins around them, cut down by the lashings of the werefox's tail.

Another notable detail was the fact that Leo was fighting the monster with a sort of wooden sword-shaped stick that sprayed fire out of its tip. The were-fox, however, didn't look too impressed. It kept snarling like a rabid dog, snapping at him with its jaws and lashing at him with its tail, but Leo warded off each blow with superquick wooden sword strokes. This went on like a superbly choreographed fight sequence on fast-forward until the werefox finally decided it had had enough and charged at Leo like a battering ram, headbutting him in the chest.

The force of the impact sent Leo flying back ten feet through the air. He crashed into the trunk of a tall chestnut tree that had remained standing just outside the disaster area, landing heavily on a knot of gnarled roots. He was back on his feet in the blink of an eye, fiery stick poised and ready to deflect another werefox attack.

"Leo!" shouted Dario.

Leo shot him a surprised glance.

"What are you doing here?" he asked tetchily.

"Um…you asked me to meet you here."

"No, I didn't."

"Yes, you did. You asked me to bring you your banishing book. And I did."

Dario tossed the banishing book to Leo. He caught it deftly with one hand while sparring with the werefox with the other, took a quick glance at it, and tossed it back to Dario.

"That's not my banishing book."

"What?" Dario felt numb.

There was a pause as Leo wrestled with the werefox.

"I've got my banishing book with me, and it's useless against this cursed creature. The book that you've brought is a special leather-bound edition of *The Hobbit*."

"Oh." Dario opened the book. The title page did indeed say *The Hobbit*. There was even a stylized drawing of the dragon Smaug underneath the title.

"Please tell me you've at least brought a spare Stick of Sylvicolus."

"A what?"

Leo growled with frustration. "Why are you here? You're useless!"

"Um…"

"Haven't you taken anything with you besides the book?" The motions of his swordlike wand were becoming impatient. He was clearly fed up with the werefox and wanted to finish it off.

"I haven't."

"Well, have you got any sort of weapon at all?"

"Um…no?"

"You NEVER come to fight a creature of darkness without a weapon. You ALWAYS carry a weapon with you. You never—" Leo lashed impatiently at the monster with his stick. "…leave…" *Lash.* "…the house…" *Lash.* "…without it!"

"But I thought the book was a weapon!"

"Never"—Leo took an exceptionally big swing with his sword—"mind!" And he hit the werefox squarely in the forehead.

The monster blinked once, slowly and stupidly, but it recovered almost immediately and was upon Leo once again.

"You ugly, annoying thing! Just die already!" Leo sounded like a man on the edge.

In the meantime, Dario had wandered off in search of something, anything, that could be used as an additional weapon. He came back with a sturdy branch the size of a champagne bottle just as the werefox struck Leo down again. As Leo hit the ground, he lost his grip on his weapon. The fiery stick fell to the ground halfway between him and the monster, and the werefox promptly stamped on it with one elephantine foot.

The situation was clearly critical. Leo lay semiconscious where he had fallen, the werefox advancing upon him with a menacing gait that foreshadowed what might happen to Leo's skull if he didn't move.

This was why Dario didn't hesitate to sneak up behind the werefox and smash the branch against the back of its head. The impact was so hard that the branch cracked in two.

But the werefox barely flinched. Instead, it swerved, nearly knocking Dario off his feet with the sweep of its tail, and sized him up with its evil eyes (which, from up close, looked as if they were lit by a red glow from within). The monster snarled, its hairy nose twitching.

In the background, Leo had just managed to raise himself to one elbow. His eyes were glazed at first, but when he saw what was about to happen, his gaze quickly regained focus.

"Mario!" he shouted.

"Um…it's Dario," said Dario.

"Sorry, I meant—*Dario!*"

Leo was up on his feet in an instant, but the monster was even quicker. It sprang at Dario, teeth bared and claws ready to rip off his face.

Almost without thinking, Dario stuffed his hand into his jeans pocket, taking out the strange crystal shard that Madam Mina had given him. He instinctively lashed at the monster's neck with it, noticing in a detached sort of way that the crystal now glowed with an inner white light.

Before the shard even touched it, the werefox let out a bloodcurdling shriek. It squinted its eyes shut, spun around in a disoriented way, and collapsed into a loathsome hairy heap. The crystal promptly dissolved in Dario's hand.

"Well done!" said Leo.

"I'm not sure I *have* done anything." Dario looked at the trickle of water on the palm of his hand where the crystal had been only seconds ago. He shrugged and wiped his hand against his jeans.

"Where did you get that thing?"

"My landlady gave it to me."

"I wish I had a landlady like that."

"Um…you really don't."

Leo leaned carefully over the fallen werefox and squinted at it critically. He studied the monster's features for a few moments and then hung his head dejectedly. "Yeah, that's the one," he said to himself.

"It's what?"

"But I need to make sure," said Leo, ignoring Dario.

He turned to Dario and said, "I know that this is a bit of an awkward question, but may I borrow your belt?"

They tied the unconscious werefox to a beech, binding its front limbs behind the trunk of the tree with Dario's belt. Leo wandered off and came back a few minutes later bearing a freshly cut branch of an ash tree. He crouched down, took a small penknife out of the folds of his cloak, and proceeded to whittle the bark. Wood shavings sprinkled the grass all around him like confetti. Dario hovered near Leo and observed his craftsmanship with cautious curiosity.

"What is that?"

"A Stick of Sylvicolus," said Leo.

"It looks the same as the stick you used to fight the fox."

"That is because it *is* the same kind of stick," said Leo impatiently. "And, in case you haven't noticed, the other stick has been smashed to pieces. Also," he added under his breath, "I need something more powerful."

"So this kind of fiery stick is something you can just sort of make on your own?"

"Of course! If you know how." Leo suddenly looked up with a bemused expression, as if he had only just realized Dario was there. "You know, Dario, I really do appreciate the help you've given me, but I hope you don't feel as if you need to stay here."

"Oh…um…it's really not a problem at all. I can stay."

Leo exhaled with exasperation. "If I have said or done anything that might have given you the impression that I am looking for some sort of assistant, I assure you that this is not the case."

Leo looked up at Dario expectantly, but the latter just stood there like a lost puppy.

"Because I am not," added Leo. "Looking for an assistant."

"Oh," said Dario, blinking with confusion. "I never thought you were."

"Nor do I intend to offer you any sort of formal introduction as to who I am or what I do."

"That's fine," said Dario. "I don't mind."

"And trust me, without a formal introduction, everything that happens next is going to look very perplexing."

"That's all right. I'll manage."

"I also appreciate that since all this is new to you, it may appear interesting and exciting. But believe me when I say that in reality it is not the least bit interesting. Or exciting. So if you feel like leaving right now, please don't hesitate to do so."

Dario was not quite sure, but it sounded as if Leo was making some sort of hint.

"Um…I think I'll stick around for a while."

"Fine, whatever," said Leo and turned his attention back to his arts and crafts project.

Soon the branch was smooth and pale and the air suffused with the scent of fresh wood shavings. The atmosphere was spoiled only by the ominous shape of the fox monster, which still sagged against the tree, its tail sticking out at an odd angle from underneath it.

Once the branch was perfectly smooth, Leo carved a series of strange symbols onto its surface, starting from the bottom of the handle and going all the way to the point of the wand.

"Is this something, uh…magic-related?" asked Dario.

"Don't be ridiculous," said Leo. "Of course it is."

"Why is it called the Stick of Sylvicolus?"

"I don't know. That's what the locals call it because…" Leo paused midsentence and sighed wearily. "…because Sylvicolus used to be something or other in the Withdrawn Realm."

Over by the tree, the werefox moaned and stirred. Leo blew the wood shavings off the wand, gave it a quick expert once-over, and rose to his feet. He strode up to the bound monster, pointing the Stick of Sylvicolus at it. Dario followed a few paces behind, hesitating to come too close in case something of a fiery nature was about to happen. Which indeed it was.

First, the bottommost symbol on the wand started glowing ember red, followed by the one directly above it, and then the next and so forth, until all of the runes up to the top were aglow like miniature furnaces. Finally, an ice-blue blade-shaped flame burst out of the tip of the wand, giving the whole thing the appearance of a flaming sword.

Although Dario was no expert on Sticks of Sylvicolus, he could tell that this was a much higher grade of weapon than the one Leo had used before. This one was like a flamethrower compared to a firecracker.

The werefox came to with a start and immediately began writhing and plead-ing in a surprisingly high-pitched voice made almost incoherent by a prominent lisp. "Make it thtop!" moaned the werefox. "The light ith hurting my eyeth."

"It speaks! How convenient."

Leo crouched over the creature, Stick of Sylvicolus held out before him, making the werefox wail pitifully.

"No problem," said Leo. "I'll make it stop. As soon as you tell me every-thing I need to know. What are you? How did you get here? Where are the oth-ers? Please feel free to answer the questions in whichever order you prefer."

The werefox let out a growl, although it might have been a coarse laugh. "Tho you thtill haven't figured it out? Thtupid thtar demon!"

Leo took a deep, simmering breath. At the same time, the symbols on the wand became brighter. They now burned with a hot yellow glow, while the blue flame at the tip grew bigger. It was like turning up a boiler.

The werefox hissed and tried to bolt, but Dario's belt held it in place.

"Let's not make this any more tedious than it has to be," said Leo. "Now answer my questions."

The monster hissed. "I am a thervant of thomeone far more powerful than you could ever imagine. Thomeone who ith a thworn enemy of the thity. Thome-one who will thoon cruth both you and the thity to dutht."

"I'm sorry," said Leo with exaggerated politeness. "I'm afraid that doesn't quite ring a bell. You will have to be more specific."

The fox growled but did not seem any less reluctant to keep talking in rid-dles. "It ith thomeone ath ancient ath darkneth. Thomeone who dwellth with the shadowth. Thomeone who ith…"

"The Black Queen of Bear Fortress? Yes, I knew that. I asked you what you are and where I can find the others."

The werefox cackled. "I'm thertain you already know that—we are the Four."

"Is that so," said Leo acerbically, but his face was grim.

"Yeth," said the werefox. "You might have thtruck down one of uth, but you have no chanthe againtht the otherth. The thpider will cruth you like a fly if you go near it. And the other…"

The monster cackled again. "The other ith a thubtle one," it said. "You can thearch all you like, but you'll never find her. And if you do, it will be too late."

"Oh, really." Leo tried to sound unimpressed, but by now even Dario could tell that he was deeply troubled.

The fox answered in an ominous stage whisper. "Yeth. The other one will let the Black Queen in, and the Black Queen will unleath all of her fortheth upon the thity." The fox burst into a breathless cackle.

A faraway look momentarily crossed Leo's face, his grip on the wand faltering for a fraction of a second. This was all the opportunity the werefox needed. The monster ripped off its bonds and lunged at Leo with all its might. Leo snapped back to reality just in time to send a powerful bolt of ice-blue fire out of the glowing wand. The flames enveloped the werefox in midair, burning it to a crisp before it even hit the ground. The charred carcass collapsed in a smoldering heap at Leo's feet.

With a weary sigh, Leo wandered off to the side and sat down heavily on the ground, propping his forearms against his knees and his forehead against his forearms. He looked like a man who had just finished running a triathlon only to find out that his house was getting foreclosed.

Dario approached hesitantly.

"So…" he began. "I don't know exactly what's going on, but it looks as if you've just destroyed another one of the Black Queen's…animals that have escaped from her…tunnels. Or something. And that's good, isn't it?"

But Leo only shook his head wordlessly.

15

LEO'S BEACON

Leo did not like appeals or any other formalities. This was why when he stepped into the walled garden of the Hidden Tower, detached the star off his belt, and tossed it up in the air, where it began to glow like a gold meteor, he did it with a mixture of reluctance and self-consciousness. But he desperately needed a star daimon of authority, such as Star Councillor Alnair, to tell him that now that he had valiantly defeated the Fox of Destruction, his mission was complete. That there was no need to go to the Underworld after all. Therefore, as he gazed up at the star, it was Alnair's name that Leo uttered as a calling signal.

It didn't take long for his celestial beacon to be noticed by the Celestial Realm. Within a few minutes, there appeared an answering flash, and then a pillar of light shot down from the sky into the garden. As the bright light slowly condensed into the form of a man, Leo felt happier than he had been since arriving in the city. Finally he would be able to talk to someone sympathetic. He even allowed himself a smile. But the smile faded abruptly once the form had fully revealed itself.

The brown-clad star daimon standing before him was not Star Councillor Alnair. He was not anyone Leo wished to see. Not now and preferably not ever. The new arrival had a broad face, small bovine eyes and the overall look of someone who had just milked a goat.

"Aldebaran," said Leo, his every syllable oozing with dissatisfaction.

"Leo." Aldebaran's voice was as thick as his neck.

"What are *you* doing here? I called Alnair directly."

"The Star Councillors are busy organizing a defensive against the latest barnacle invasion. So they sent me instead."

Leo did his best not to let his despair show. "Is that so? Well, then they might have told you why I still haven't been given the all clear."

"Your work is not yet complete. You are expected to bring this mission to a satisfactory conclusion." Aldebaran's voice had the droning monotone of someone reciting lines memorized by heart. The only thing stopping Leo from punching him in the face was his surprise at the fact that Aldebaran had managed to commit something to memory in the first place.

"Only when your mission has been completed will you be given the all clear."

"Says who?"

"It's all clearly stated in the terms of your indictment. Alnair went through it again this morning because he anticipated you might call. There is no doubt that you will have to see this crisis through, no matter what it takes."

Aldebaran's dull droning was interrupted by a sudden flash of white light. Then a luminous being with long white hair and an ageless face appeared before them.

"Alnair!" Leo felt faint with relief.

"Sorry about this, Aldebaran," said Alnair, "but we've just had some unexpected news, and I thought it best to speak to Leo myself. You needn't stick around if you'd rather be elsewhere."

Aldebaran said that he would indeed rather be elsewhere and promptly swooshed back into the sky.

"What is this about?" asked Leo, his relief quickly turning into anxiety.

"It seems," said Alnair, "that the two creatures you have dispatched have recently reappeared near the asteroid belt."

"What!"

"Auriga found them during one of his routine patrols of the solar system. The two looked shocked and disoriented, as if they had just been reintegrated from a corporeal form into a celestial one. Apparently they have been away for such a long time that they forgot who they are."

"And who are they?"

"We think they might be star daimons—Corvus the Crow and Vulpecula the Fox."

Leo gasped.

"And," continued Alnair, "there is reason to believe that the other two might be star daimons too."

"But...but..." Leo suddenly felt as if he had drunk a vat of Lower Town coffee. "How could this have happened?"

"Frankly, we have no idea. This is a matter that will require further investigation. What is important is that, while we do this, you keep matters under control on your end."

"How?"

"I would suggest focusing on the Black Queen herself. Make sure that, whatever else might happen, she doesn't break out of the Underworld during the coming All Hallows' Eve. Then you can worry about dealing with the remaining two star daimons, if they haven't been dealt with already by then. Their role seems to be closely bound with the Black Queen's plans for All Hallows, and it's highly probable that preventing her planned breakout will also serve as a solution to the problem of stopping the missing star daimons."

This sounded annoyingly similar to what the goldsmith had said, and Leo felt his temper rise accordingly.

"Why doesn't the Star Queen do something about this?" he burst out. "Why doesn't she stop the other two star daimons? Why doesn't the council deal with them directly?"

"We can't. All four of the star daimons in question have been earthed. Like yourself."

Leo winced.

"The Fox and the Crow," continued Alnair, "have been inadvertently restored to their star daimon forms, but the other two still remain on Earth. What this means is that they are outside our jurisdiction. Whatever is of the Earth belongs to Earth. And I needn't remind you that one of our strictest rules commands us not to interfere directly with earthly affairs. This means that until the remaining two star daimons have been released from their earthly bondage, there is nothing we can do about them. In other words, it's all up to you."

"But that is so...unfair!"

"That is the truth." Alnair's form began disintegrating into blinding light.

"Wait!"

The councillor came back into focus.

"My mission has proved to be far more demanding than it initially appeared. I am unable to complete it with my artificially limited powers. I either need backup or to have my powers restored!"

"I agree," said Alnair. "And if it were up to me, I would do either or both of those things. But it's not up to me." He let the implication quiver gently in the air between them.

"Why is the Star Queen doing this to me?" asked Leo. "Why does she treat me—*me*, of all star daimons—with such abject, arbitrary cruelty? She would never do this to anyone else."

"Because you are the one who has taught her secrets to the unworthy."

Leo felt as if he had been punched in the gut.

"So long, Leo," said Alnair as shiny white particles swirled around him. "I do wish you the best of luck with your mission and a swift return to the Celestial Realm."

Leo watched miserably as the last of Alnair dissolved and shot up into the sky. He barely noticed when his own gold star fell down from the sky and landed on the ground with a hollow clink.

16

THE JUNCTION OF WORLDS

Whether intentionally or not, the layout of the East Central Primary and Secondary School building conveyed some deep-seated truths about the eternal order of the universe and man's unending quest for knowledge, including his place in the grand scheme of things.

The primary school, with its location on the lower two stories of the building, was a symbol of childhood ignorance. The playground, as the extension of the lower ground floor, signified the earthy innocence of the ignorant—a primal state, still untouched by the uplifting force of reason that would eventually raise them up from the baseness of their early years to the higher level of secondary education.

And what better way to communicate this elevation than by having the higher level correspond to the upper floors of the building, which was exactly where the secondary school was. However, for reasons unknown, the second floor also contained an element of the lower plane—the primary school library. This made the library a sort of transitional space between the two worlds.

Transcending all this, on the top floor, was the school auditorium. It was a big semicircular room with an impressive wooden stage, which was where secondary school graduation ceremonies were held. Thus, as the highest point of the entire building, both physically and metaphysically, the stage represented the attainment of ultimate knowledge.

As soon as Stella set foot on the second-floor corridor, she was struck by how bright and airy it was up there. It was as if the very sunlight pouring in through the windows shone more generously on this level, and the air currents moved more freely. There was also the general absence of Professor Radovan from these parts, which was another major factor that made the place more appealing. It was ostensibly Professor Radovan's swollen legs that kept her from going up to the library; Stella, however, suspected it was because she had never read a book.

The library itself, hidden behind a cloudy glass screen at the end of the corridor, was a semicircular room illuminated by bright sunlight that came in through three narrow windows, giving the room a mystical cathedral-like quality.

Her eyes immediately landed on a huge corkboard suspended on the wall behind a deserted counter. It sported an unseemly mass of children's drawings that showcased the entire spectrum of childish artistic incompetence. If one were to identify the most obvious way to conceal a secret passage, this would be it.

There was only one way to find out.

The librarian was nowhere in sight, which was hardly surprising. She was a perpetually bored-looking woman who had the air of someone who would barely raise an eyebrow if a horde of giant paper-eating book lice invaded the premises and proceeded to devour the entire contents of the library.

In other words, there could be no harm in taking just one quick look.

Stella slipped behind the counter, moved the unexpectedly heavy corkboard a few inches away from where it rested against the wall, and leaned into the gap.

The first thing she noticed was that there was no secret door hidden behind the panel. She let out a disappointed sigh. Then she realized there was something there after all; it was just that it had taken her a moment to see it. When she did, she gasped, nearly losing hold of the panel.

A large area of the wall behind the corkboard was damaged. A door-sized patch of paint had crumbled off, leaving exposed the rough stone that lay underneath. The stone looked ancient—as if it were much older than the rest of the building—and it had the same texture as the rocks that formed the strange alcove of the Dead Zone. Stella thought she could smell the same damp, earthy scent she remembered from those few moments she had stood within that dreadful alcove inside the playground wall.

Two things happened then, almost at the same time. First, the board slipped off its unseen pegs and landed on the floor with an alarming crash. Stella managed to slip out from behind the panel only a moment before it would have crashed onto her. Second, the skinny gray form of the librarian materialized before Stella, having apparently been wheeled in from behind the maze of bookcases like a piece of stage machinery in some sophisticated theatrical production.

"Can I help you?" The librarian's voice was a lazy nasal drawl.

"I am…I was just…it fell."

The librarian stood before Stella like an upright ironing board, hands behind her stiff back, watching Stella squirm with an expression of near-comatose apathy. She wore a dark-gray jersey top and a mid-gray tweed skirt. This was the default outfit she was never seen out of, regardless of the season. Complementing it was her other trademark feature—tidy, straight jaw-length hair that was perpetually suspended in a state of turning gray, without ever actually getting there all the way.

As she stood before Stella, the librarian inclined her head slightly to one side, not out of curiosity, as one might suppose, but rather because she seemed to be half-asleep on her feet.

"Are you here for a legitimate reason or have you come to the library specifically to vandalize its property?"

"Yes. No! I'm looking for a book."

The librarian raised one thin gray eyebrow. "And what book would that be?"

"About the Black Queen," blurted Stella before she had time to think about what she was going to say. The librarian's face remained fixed in its expression of rock-bottom boredom.

"I meant…" Stella paused to gather her thoughts, but her mind was blank. It was as if her brain had gone out for a cigarette break, leaving a "be right back" sign on its desk. She could practically hear crickets humming inside her skull.

"I meant *The Snow Queen*," she said eventually.

The librarian pursed her dry lips in the manner of someone sucking a sour citrus fruit, then turned on one heel and sauntered over to a tall bookcase on the left, languidly retrieving a slim volume from the top shelf. She returned with the same unhurried pace and began to perform the agonizingly slow routine of issuing a book. It was like watching a peninsula gradually detach itself from a continental landmass over eons of time. She finally handed the book to Stella after what seemed like eight geological eras.

"Is that all?"

Stella felt a wave of despair. She only had a few minutes left before the bell rang, and she still hadn't found any secret passages. "Can I just look around a bit?"

The librarian gave her a lazy "what do I care?" shrug. "Just try not to wreck anything else," she said and retreated back into her unseen lair.

As soon as the librarian was out of sight, Stella tossed *The Snow Queen* onto the nearest desk and rushed back behind the counter. The corkboard was now leaning against the wall, and she pushed it away as far as she could in order to take another look.

The crumbling wall was still there—she hadn't imagined it. And it did smell of stale earth.

As Stella pondered over the significance of this discovery, the board slipped out of her grasp and hit her on the back, pushing her toward the wall. Curiously, she didn't bump against it. Instead, she went *through* it.

She found herself in the middle of a crowded square. There were people in shabby, rustic clothes all around her. They were all chattering excitedly in small groups. Clearly, something was going on.

Despite the oddness of it all, there was something familiar about the place. A sturdy white tower rose over many patchy rooftops on one side, while a stone church with a multicolored shingle roof stood on the other. Stella recognized them as Lotrščak Tower and St. Mark's Church, realizing she was in Upper Town.

This, however, was not the Upper Town she knew and occasionally visited on weekend afternoons. This was an unpaved, extremely low-tech version of it.

The strangest thing of all was the presence of an alien-looking tower positioned about halfway between Lotrščak and St. Mark's. Unlike the white Lotrščak Tower, this tower was made of some crude charcoal-black stone, and its only ornaments were iron spikes. It was much taller than any of the surrounding buildings, and its sides tapered from a wide square base to a surreally narrow top which ended in a row of menacing iron battlements that looked like the curled fingers of a giant skeletal fist. Meanwhile, at the street level, two beefy, oddly hunched guards wearing full iron armor stood on each side of a forbidding iron gate, bearing grime-encrusted spears. It was this tower that seemed to be the main focus of the townspeople's attention.

Suddenly from somewhere in the distance, an agitated peasant's voice shouted, "She's coming! The witch of Bear Town is coming!"

The murmur of the crowd became even more restless.

"Make way for the queen!" yelled an uncouth voice.

The ragtag assembly parted, and soon Stella saw why. A cavalcade of grim armored soldiers on horseback was making an imposing entrance. At the head of the party, riding a black warhorse the size of a tank, was the Black Queen. Her black riding dress was part leather, part chain mail. Her black hair was down, and her face was an expressionless mask. She held her head high and barely looked at the masses. But the raven on her shoulder watched intently.

"Heaven help us!" wailed an old peasant woman who looked like a Dolac Market cottage cheese seller. This was followed by a general outpouring of despair made by many voices. Heads were shaken. Prayers were uttered. Rosaries were clutched.

Stella slipped away from the crowd unnoticed. She didn't know if this was because the people were too preoccupied with the sight of the Black Queen, who was now imperiously entering the black tower, or whether it was because they couldn't see her. Either way, she didn't care. All she cared about was getting out of this medieval nightmare and finding her way back to the school. Even Professor Radovan's class was better than this.

She ran aimlessly in the only direction that made sense—away from the Black Queen—and soon found herself in another vaguely familiar place. It looked like a small open church with vaulted ceilings and a floor made of cobbled stones. Many candles illuminated the cavernous interior, most of them clustered around a shrine that held an ancient painting of a lady in a red dress with a golden crown on her head. If it hadn't been for the still-audible distant clamor of the peasants, Stella would have thought this was the same Stone Gate as the present-day one.

A sudden patter of footsteps nearly made her start, but the small, compact man that scurried into the Stone Gate from the other side hardly looked like cause for concern.

"Ah, there you are!" The man blinked at her through a pair of thick round lenses held together by a complicated-looking frame.

"Don't be alarmed," he added. "They're overreacting. I don't think she's going to have anyone thrown to the wolves today."

"I'm sorry, do I know you?" asked Stella.

"My name is Otto Goldsmith, and I am a goldsmith. But I am also a clock-maker. And a lens-cutter too."

The little man peered up at her critically. "Are you sure you shouldn't be wearing spectacles?"

Stella said she was sure.

"Are you quite sure? Not even light, entry-level ones?"

"Yes, I'm quite sure."

"Well, if you ever do find yourself in need of spectacles, may I recommend my humble establishment, which is just round the corner from here?"

Stella thanked the goldsmith for the recommendation and then said, "Do you know what's going on? I mean, why are the Black Queen and the Stone Gate both inside the school library?"

"Ah, that's how it may seem," said the goldsmith, "but we are in fact not in the school library."

Stella asked him to explain. The goldsmith clapped his little hands with relish. "Well," he said, "I don't know if you're aware of this, but that school of yours is not a normal place."

"You mean because of the existence of Professor Radovan?"

"That, I'm sure, is one of the reasons, but what I was actually referring to is the fact that the school has a strange connection to the Black Queen."

"I knew it!" said Stella. "That's why Black Queen One-Two-Three is such an important game."

"Well, yes, there is that, but there's more." The goldsmith took off his enormous glasses, rubbed one of the lenses with his sleeve, and put them back on. "You see, the school grounds were once the site of one of the Black Queen's most terrifying dungeons."

Stella gaped. "How is that possible? I though the Black Queen lived up on the mountain in Bear Town Fortress!"

"True," said the goldsmith, "but at some point, her evil dominion over the city had grown to such an extent that the dungeons of Bear Town were no longer sufficient. And hauling prisoners up the mountain was always a big logistical challenge anyway. So she had something more local built, something to, hmm... *serve* the southeast part of the region."

The goldsmith paused for a few moments to allow Stella to take all this in and then continued.

"The dungeon stood there, bringing terror to the region, until the end of the Black Queen's evil reign when all her dungeons were destroyed. But although the building itself was torn down, some of the Black Queen's evil magic survived in the very stones of its foundations. The site has been a magnet for evil ever since."

Stella remembered the ancient wall in the library and the one in the Dead Zone and shuddered.

"So is all this just an illusion caused by the Black Queen's evil magic?" she asked.

"No, no, no," said the goldsmith before Stella had even finished the sentence.

"This place"—he made a sweeping gesture encompassing all of the Stone Gate—"is very real. And it's a very special place."

"As special as the school?"

"More special," said the goldsmith after careful consideration.

"The Stone Gate is a place," he continued, "that exists at the junction of several planes—the past, the present, the might-have-been past, the couldn't-have-possibly-been past and many other things besides. It is like a knot that holds many separate strands of existence together. And as such, it can be accessed from any of the strands, as you have managed to do just now.

"And it's just as well, since we were counting on it. We were hoping you would find your way here somehow, because we know you need all the help you can get, what with all that's been happening in the aftermath of the playground incident."

"So you know about it? The Dead Zone and the Black Queen's raven and the spider and the...other creatures?"

Otto nodded sadly.

"How could such a thing have happened?" asked Stella. "How did I end up in the Black Queen's courtyard with her staring at me? Was this some sort of afterimage from the past?"

"I'm afraid it's much worse than that," said the goldsmith apologetically. "What you saw that day on the playground was no mere illusion. It was the Black Queen herself."

Stella stared at Otto incredulously.

"The Black Queen," continued the goldsmith, "is still alive. She has been alive all these centuries without anyone being the least bit aware of it."

"What do you mean?"

"She dwells under Bear Mountain, where she has over time built her own secret underground empire. A powerful spell has sealed her in, imprisoning her for all time, turning her into a living shadow—neither dead nor alive. She no longer has any power over the outside world. But she is clever and has many helpers."

"So the creatures that came out of the wall are her helpers?"

Otto nodded gravely.

"How bad is it?" asked Stella. "What's the worst those things can do out there?"

"Worse than you could ever imagine," said the goldsmith. "If those creatures aren't stopped, there is no doubt that they will help the Black Queen herself make a personal appearance. That spider, for example, is probably weaving some sort of artificial body that the Black Queen's shadowy self can inhabit the moment she comes out. It's probably working on it as we speak."

Stella let out a little yelp. "I didn't mean to do it!"

"It's not your fault!" said the goldsmith quickly. "It was bound to happen sooner or later. The border between your world and the Black Queen's evil domain has become quite thin, you see. And every once in a while, there is a crack—a small, temporary crack, big enough for just a creature or two to slip through. It's just that this time, the creatures that came out are more dangerous than the ordinary fare, and it's quite possible that the Black Queen will try to harness their powers to create a permanent crack, big enough for herself to come through as well. And there is no doubt that she is going to attempt to do this on the Night of the Witches."

Cold chills ran down Stella's spine. She remembered the scary dream she had had about the school and knew that it was somehow connected to this, although she had no idea how.

"But surely it can't be that bad. There must be something we can do to stop her."

"That's the spirit!" The goldsmith beamed at her, his hands clasped enthusiastically. "Yes, despite the odds, there's no reason to be defeatist." Then, presumably remembering that the situation was in fact rather dire, he curbed his enthusiasm somewhat.

"As I was saying," he continued, "things are, of course, not all that bad. Unfortunately, they are not all that good either."

"How so?"

"Well, first of all, the creatures that have escaped are extremely dangerous. And, sadly, there is hardly anyone left in the city who has the required skills to fight such powerful beings."

"What about those people outside the black tower?" said Stella. "They looked as if they would give anything to defeat the Black Queen."

"Yes, well…those of us who can occasionally be found in this quaint Stone Gate juncture are unable to act in your present-day White City. We exist in our own little bubble, just as in your world, the Black Queen exists in her own."

"It all sounds very complicated."

"It is, my dear," said Otto with the relieved tone of a sufferer who has finally found a sympathetic ear. "It really is."

"Are you saying there is no one left in the city who can stop the Black Queen?" asked Stella. "That the city is…doomed?"

"There, there now, my dear. Things are not as bad as that. There is still hope, you see, because we've asked for help. Someone who is from…out of town. This individual is very competent, but not even he is able to put out all the fires by himself."

The goldsmith sighed and wiped his glasses once again.

"Stella," he said with what sounded like a heavy heart, "I know that this is outrageously too much to ask of someone so young and inexperienced, but what would you say if we asked you to help us get rid of one of these creatures?"

"Yes," said Stella without hesitation.

Otto blinked, looking surprised and delighted.

"I've been meaning to do it anyway," explained Stella. "To kill the spider."

"Yes, that's the one!" said Otto cheerfully. He suddenly looked concerned. "But, my dear, are you sure? That thing is dangerous. Too dangerous even for our external associate to handle, who is otherwise impervious to danger."

Stella gulped. Then she made herself say that she would do it anyway.

Otto looked relieved and worried at the same time.

"So where is this spider and how do I kill it?" asked Stella. "Am I right in thinking that it's in the Forbidden Cellar?"

"You are," said Otto. "The spider is indeed hiding in the basement. That is the one thing we know for sure. As the hidden channels of the school building overlap with the Stone Gate juncture, we can sense the creature's presence. If only I could say the same for the other one."

"But the cellar is locked all the time—we've tried. So how do I get in?"

"You cannot get into the cellar by any ordinary means. The powers of the Spider of Illusion will keep any intruders at bay for as long as it's there. You have no choice but to wait for the creature to emerge on its own. You will have to wait for the right moment, and that moment should be sometime on the Night of the Witches."

"How will I know that the exact moment has come?"

"Stay alert and be on the lookout for clues. The Black Queen is a bit of a show-off, and she will no doubt look for an opportunity to make a dramatic entrance. What this means is that if there is anything of a spectacular nature taking place at the school on that day, you can take this as an almost certain sign that the Black Queen will use it to trigger her breakout."

"But nothing spectacular ever happens in our school!"

"You never know," said the goldsmith. "Even the smallest event that is out of the ordinary might be enough to pique the Black Queen's interest. Keep your eyes open."

The goldsmith took a huge mechanical watch out of his pocket.

"Good heavens, is that the time?" He looked at Stella. "You'd better be off now or you'll miss your class!"

"How do I get back?"

"Hmm…" Otto looked around the candlelit interior of the Stone Gate. His gaze landed on an ancient iron door to the left of the shrine. "Through here, I think."

He pulled a bolt and pushed the door. It opened with a heavy groan of iron against stone. There was only darkness on the other side. The goldsmith wished Stella farewell, thanking her profusely for her bravery, and ushered her in.

As she was about to step through, Otto slapped his forehead and exclaimed, "The bottle!" He fumbled in his pocket. "I nearly forgot!"

Otto took a small silver vial out of his apparently bottomless pocket. The vessel was exquisitely decorated with finely wrought leaf shapes accentuated with blue gems. "You will need this to kill the spider. Ordinary weapons won't do."

"It's beautiful." Stella was filled with awe as she took the proffered object. "What is it?"

"Oh, that's just a pretty bottle. It's what's inside that matters."

"Poison?"

"Much stronger than mere poison. A very potent magic concoction brewed up specifically to kill that fiend."

"How does it work?"

"All you need to do is uncap the bottle at the right time, and the rest will take care of itself." Suddenly Otto's face looked grave. "But be sure to open the bottle at the right time and not a moment sooner. You see, once the bottle has been opened, the potion must be used immediately or else it will be useless."

His face brightened again. "Fortunately, the bottle has a very helpful feature that will let you know the exact time you need to open it for the poison to work."

He pointed one stubby finger at the blue gems that glistened in the candle-light.

"These will start to glow blue," he said, "when the spider is within the right range. That will be your sign to release the cap. Of course, by then the spider will have grown so much that you won't need a sign. But it's still clever, don't you think?"

Stella gulped and nodded.

"Now off you go, my dear, and take care." The goldsmith held the door open for her, taking a little old-fashioned bow.

Stella thanked Otto for his advice, and this time she really did go through the door. Moments later, she emerged out of the library wall, bumping into the corkboard that hadn't been moved since its crash. She wriggled out from behind it to find herself being stared down at by the almost-surprised-looking librarian. Stella quickly put the strange silver bottle into her jumper pocket.

"You're still here?" said the librarian with something that would have sounded like incredulity on a person with the emotional range for it.

The bell rang. Stella remembered that she was supposed to act like someone who had come to the library for the sole purpose of borrowing *The Snow Queen*, a book she already owned three different editions of, one of which was in a for-

eign language. The library copy of the book still lay on the counter where she
had left it.

"Thank you," she said and grabbed the book. Then she ran out of the library
and down the stairs in the direction of classroom 5B.

It was just as well that the first class of the day was Professor Novak's uneventful biology lesson because Stella could concentrate on nothing other than
staring at the mysterious silver bottle that sat on her desk concealed between a
bulky pencil case and an open notebook placed upside down so that it looked
like a miniature tent.

She was startled back to reality by the sound of Professor Novak's lazy voice.
The teacher had clearly finished doing her crossword puzzle and had been gazing
at the class sleepily, looking for any distraction that might make the remaining
five minutes of the lesson more bearable.

"Stella," she drawled, "as you can see, we're all bored here, but can't you at
least have the decency to pretend you're doing some work?"

"Yes, Professor Novak." Stella covertly slipped the bottle into her pocket.

She forced herself to wait until the end of the school day before spilling the
beans. There was no point describing an experience as incredible as hers during
the break, when there were other kids around who might overhear. No, this was
an occasion for the Bunker, their secret hideout at the back of Dog Sitters' Park.
This was where she took Rea, Ida and Tin after the end of the last lesson.

The Bunker was not really a bunker. It was more like a ramshackle shed that
someone had built in a public park for no apparent reason and then promptly either abandoned or forgot about. This was where they hid their trading cards and
other curious playground artifacts, such as Pez dispensers and transparent glass
marbles with interesting multicolored shapes in the center. Not that there was
any need for hiding, as no one other than themselves ever went into the Bunker
and, besides, even if someone ever did wander in, it was unlikely that the intruder would have been interested in random kids' junk.

"Do any of you believe me?" asked Stella after she had finished telling her
story. They all sat cross-legged on the floor in a loose circle, the jewel-encrusted
silver bottle reverently placed on a box of cheese crackers in the center.

"I believe you," said Ida immediately, her serene face free of any signs of
doubt or any other complex emotions.

"You must be joking," said Rea.

Stella looked at Tin. "What about you?"

"I don't know. I..." Tin began, gazing uncertainly at the tattered toe end of his left trainer. Though he was usually the one willing to give Stella the benefit of the doubt under any circumstances, he seemed to be struggling with this particular case. "I guess it could be true."

Stella looked satisfied enough with that answer.

"What are you going to do?" asked Ida.

"I don't know," said Stella. "I guess I'll just wait for a sign. Some clue as to what's going to be happening on the Night of the Witches. Then I'll make sure I'm there and ready for it."

"Stella," said Rea, "nothing is going to happen! This whole thing about the Black Queen coming out of some school dungeon in the middle of the night was just a dream. Besides, no one is ever there at night."

"Something's going to happen," said Stella. "I don't know what, but I'll be there when it does."

17

BEYOND THE THRESHOLD

The Moon was a perfect white half circle set against the indigo-black sky. First quarter. In exactly eight nights' time, on October 31, the Moon would be full.

The forest was predictably dark—it had not earned the name "Forest of Shadows" for nothing. Or at least, that was its name on the Withdrawn Realm side. It had no particular name on the ordinary world side because ordinary people were not aware of its significance. If they had been aware, they might have assumed that the forest owed its name to the way its tall trees cast oily black shadows on moonlit nights or the way the woods looked like a black abyss on the nights when the Moon was, for whatever reason, absent. But there were other kinds of shadows that lived in the forest—much darker ones—but to see them, one had to cross over to their side.

Perhaps the townspeople did sense the presence of the shadows after all, at least in some unconscious way, which would explain why the Forest of Shadows was not like other woodland areas that peppered the north side of the city.

Few pedestrian footpaths, coffee stands or waste bins could be found within its perimeter. Few joggers or dog walkers could be encountered there, even during the daytime. There was just something about that particular neck of the woods that compelled sensible people to stay away.

Perhaps it was its location—on the lower slopes of Bear Mountain north of Mirogoj, a big nineteenth-century cemetery which, for all its grand cupolas, ivy-covered walls and majestic colonnades, was still a cemetery. Or perhaps it was its history, as those dark woods had long been fabled to be the site of wandering beasts, witches' covens and shady characters that lurked in the dark.

Leo, of course, didn't have any choice in the matter. He didn't have the luxury of being able to avoid the forest or its errant shadows. On the contrary, he was there specifically for the shadows. This being the case, all he wanted was to at least get the whole thing over with as quickly as possible.

As he wove through the maze of tall trees, a black shadow among many, he moved softly but purposefully, the soles of his shoes barely making a crunch against the mossy ground. The occasional swish of a stray branch against his cape was the only sound that accompanied his progress. That and the sinister hooting, chirping, fluttering and shuffling of the many unseen nocturnal creatures around him, but he simply ignored them all.

So far, he was making good progress. To his right, an ancient dead oak tree gleamed bone white in the moonlight. Leo remembered from the last time he was there, many years before, that the oak was a sign that the Threshold was near. But if reaching this landmark made him hope that he would get to his destination unobserved and uninterrupted, he was quickly disappointed.

Dry leaves rustled a few yards ahead of him. It was a deliberate rustling. This was no mere nocturnal shuffling of small tree-dwelling animals.

Leo stopped in his tracks, then watched and listened.

An unseen twig snapped, and a girl emerged from behind a nearby tree. She had very long bleached hair and was dressed in a long purple gown that appeared to be handmade. The style was some kind of neo-Gothic or postpunk or the like—in any case, not something that one could purchase in an ordinary shop—and the dress had many silver crosses and pentagrams sewn onto it.

The girl gaped when she saw Leo and made as if to scream. Leo raised his hands, palms outward, to show her that he was not some prowling maniac, although his dark hooded cape probably wasn't too reassuring. Nevertheless, the gesture achieved the desired effect, and the girl calmed down. Then she squinted at him.

"It's all right. I'm—" began Leo.

"Oh my god, I can't believe it's you," she said in an excited, amicable voice, as if they were two old friends from school who had run into one another at the Square. "You're the Starman!"

"You're mistaken," said Leo. "I am not the Starman. I am his cousin. Now if you'll excuse me—"

"Yes you are! You're some kind of night vigilante with magic powers. We were there at the Crepuscular Immolation gig the other night. We saw what you did."

"Ah." Of course, Crepuscular Immolation fans *would* be in the "most likely to enter the Forest of Shadows after nightfall" category.

"Look, I even took a picture." She took her phone out of her bag and showed him a murky photo of a black blur and a fuzzy trailing thing. Leo winced at the light. In the darkness of the forest, the glare of the screen was blinding.

"Well, it's a bit out of focus," she said, "but I saw it. And my friends saw it too. Although we're not really sure what we saw."

Leo decided that it was best to leave it at that. "I'm sure that whatever it is you saw was perfectly—"

"How do you do that stuff you do?"

Leo sighed. Young people were such a nuisance. He made a mental correction—*people* were a nuisance.

"I'm not sure I know what you mean," said Leo, trying to sound as blasé as possible. "I attended a rock concert as a longtime admirer of the art form. It is not against the law for ordinary people to attend such events, should they wish to do so. The concert featured a truly stunning display of pyrotechnics and other stage effects, which made me very impressed indeed, just as it did everyone else. One must give credit to the young Norwegian band for making such an effort on what must have been a shoestring budget."

While delivering his speech, Leo focused on transmitting a strong stellar mind-ray directly at the girl's brain to make her forget about the whole Crepuscular Immolation episode. This was something that would have been effortless if it hadn't been for the shackles of Leo's present earthbound state. As it were, he had to make a considerable effort, but in the end, it was worth it—by the end of Leo's talk, the girl looked almost bored.

"Now, what are you doing in this creepy place all by yourself in the middle of the night?" Leo asked.

"Oh, it's a kind of dare." She immediately brightened up. "I told my boyfriend I wanted to go to the woods tonight. The Moon is in Scorpio, you see," she said, as if that explained everything. "But he said no way. And I said, 'Well, you don't have to come along then.' You should have seen his face! So of course, he had to say he wanted to go after all because otherwise it would mean that he's afraid, which he totally is. So we came to the forest together. But as soon as we got to where there were lots of trees, I gave him the slip." She laughed as if this were the most amusing story in the world.

"That's a fascinating narrative," lied Leo, "and I do hope that the young man catches up with you eventually. But now you'll have to excuse me because, as much as I've enjoyed this little chat, I'm afraid I must—" Before he had a chance to finish the admittedly overlong sentence, the girl got very close to him and laid her hands on his chest, proceeding to feel Leo's pectoral muscles, which, despite the layers of highest-quality pure celestial cloth, were still unrestrained enough to show off their impressive firmness and definition.

"Do you ever get lonely among the stars?" she whispered.

"Not really."

There was a rustle in some nearby shrubbery, and then a jittery beam of light pierced the space between the branches, sketching a jumbled, nonsensical pattern on the ground. This was followed by the appearance of a befuddled-looking young man with long mousy hair, who stumbled out of the bushes holding out his phone before him like a lantern.

"Mia? Mia?" he called, squinting at the outlines of Leo and the girl in the dark.

"Hi, Vedran," said the girl in a bored tone, but not before she had taken a step away from Leo.

"Who is that?" asked Vedran suspiciously.

"This is the Starman." The girl's voice was once again brimming with admiration.

"Oh." The youth gave Leo only the briefest glance before turning his attention back to Mia. "You left me back there all by myself."

"I thought you would follow," said Mia.

"How could I when you disappeared so quickly!"

Leo discretely rolled his eyes as a petty squabble unfolded before him. Then he saw his opportunity and took it.

"Wait!" said Mia when she realized Leo was getting away. "I was going to ask you about…about…"

"I'm terribly sorry, but I really do have to get going now," said Leo.

Mia, however, was persistent and seemed to want to go after him. Leo sent her another gentle mental nudge to dissuade her from doing so.

"Hey, isn't Dreyer's *Vampyr* showing at Tuškanac tonight?" she said, as if she had just remembered the fact.

"Yeah, I suppose it might be," said the lad.

"So why are we here instead of there?"

"Don't ask me—it was you who wanted to come here."

The two strolled off in the direction of the city. Mia turned back and gave Leo a knowing wink before the couple disappeared among the trees.

It had taken longer than Leo would have thought possible for the after-image of the girl's phone to fade. For a few terrible moments, he thought that the annoying rectangular blotch would remain in his field of vision indefinitely, forever stuck to his retinas like some kind of cattle brand seared into a cow's hide. Fortunately, the rest of the path was quite straightforward and he probably would have been able to traverse it blindfolded if he ever had to. Soon he found himself in a circle of gnarled, ancient trees. This was it. It had to be.

He had been given a proper induction to the Threshold during his infamous first White City escapade some five hundred years before, and despite the fact that this whole period had been one of the worst in his entire long existence, he still had fond memories of Ambroz the Blacksmith, who had shown him the way to the Threshold. Ambroz had been a tall, broad-shouldered man with orange hair who never went anywhere without his dog, a big slobbery mutt called Pretzel. The blacksmith had had a way of talking about such abstract matters as crossing over to the Withdrawn Realm without using any pretentious language.

As Leo entered a ring of ancient trees, the memory of Ambroz's voice came back to him.

See all those trees standing in a circle? This is the foyer, if you will.

There was a stillness in the air that permeated the place like a soothing, fir-scented balm. A gentle mist, soft and unmoving, clung to the ground. The trunks of the trees were knobby and twisted, their branches intertwined with surrounding ones so that they formed a loose ring around the area. Thick blankets of ivy covered the tree trunks, reaching up in some cases all the way to the top of the trees. On the far end, two identical ash trees stood side by side, forming an arch between them with their intertwined branches. A heavy curtain of ivy hung off the arch, reaching all the way down to the forest floor.

Protruding from the mist in the center of the circle was a round, vaguely egg-shaped stone about as high as a traffic cone. Its surface was full of small cracks and holes that made it look like a large dried-up sea sponge.

See that thing? They call it the Stone of Passing. Or Stone of Passage. Or something. Doesn't matter. Anyhow, it's the latch.

Leo walked up to the stone, knelt before it, and scooped up a handful of cool black earth from the ground. He held the dirt between the palms of his hands, raising them up to his face as if in prayer. He stayed like that for a long time. His lips occasionally moved as if forming words, but no sounds came out of his mouth. The earth in his hands gradually became heavy and charged. He could feel its particles vibrating against his skin.

Then there came a moment when he felt uncomfortably weightless and light-headed. His stomach did a somersault.

This is the moment of transition, when the planes start to shift. Pretzel, no! This stone is not for peeing on.

A tendril of water oozed out from between his closed palms and trickled down his wrist, disappearing inside his sleeve. Leo lowered his hands and carefully shaped them into a cup, which was now half-filled with cold, crystal clear water. Tiny silver specks of reflected moonlight glistened on the surface.

You might feel a bit strange for a minute. But you should be all right as long as you haven't had any wine beforehand. At least that's what everyone likes to preach. As for what they practice, well...I for one couldn't bear to go anywhere near this place without first having at least a drop or two, if you know what I mean.

He leaned over the stone and poured the water over it. The drops ran across the porous surface, finding their way into various holes and crevices that drew the water in with a thirsty sucking sound. The slurping went on until every last drop had been absorbed. As the noise subsided, the stone became smooth and glossy. Presently it began to glow with a deep blue light, like a jewel. Then there was a creaky groaning of ancient, heavy things shifting under the earth, and with the noise, the shiny stone began to slowly sink into the ground. At the same time, the ivy curtain suspended from the twin ash trees parted open in the middle, forming an arched doorway into pure darkness.

This is the Threshold, and you'd better believe it.

Leo stepped inside.

First there was a short tunnel entirely devoid of light or sound. In the dark, there was no way of knowing how wide or high it was or whether such categories even existed in absolute, all-consuming darkness.

You might feel an urge to ponder matters of an existential nature. Don't.

When he finally emerged, it was into a forest that at first sight didn't look much different from the one he had left behind, apart from the presence of a faint ultramarine glow that seemed to permeate all but its darkest corners. But Leo knew better—he was now in the Withdrawn Realm.

The Moon was still there, as were the trees, although these were taller and more menacing than their counterparts on the city side. A wide path lay ahead, with thick woods on either side. The blue tinge gave the trees the appearance of mysterious flora in a dark canyon at the bottom of the sea. The bare black branches were in constant motion, swaying hypnotically from side to side as if driven by invisible currents. Their gangly skeletal forms knitted frightening apparitions that cast terrible shadows on the ground. It was easy to see things—unnatural, terrifying things—in those shadows.

A wispy gray cloud, like a great feather in the sky, sailed over the Moon, veiling its lower half. Suddenly the trees around Leo changed. Human shapes grew out of their trunks, the torsos painfully twisted, the heads thrown back and bony arms extended upward in a gesture of petrified agony. Weeds sprouted out of the gaping mouths. Then the cloud shifted, and the grotesque trees changed into something even more ghastly—a forest of stakes with rotting corpses impaled on them like human scarecrows. With another shift of the cloud, the shapes changed into hanging trees. Corpses swayed on their branches like unwholesome Christmas ornaments. There was one massive old oak that held at least fifty hanged men. Then the cloud moved on, uncovering the Moon, and the terrible forms were gone.

A fierce animal howl pierced the night. It could have been a wolf or perhaps something even worse. Soon other howls echoed all around him. There was no sign of the animals themselves, although in the trees to his right, a black shadow stirred. Leo quickened his pace.

Then something scuttled in the dark by his feet.

Leo peered down and saw that it was a fish the size of a large trout—the kind that would, if caught by an amateur fly-fishing enthusiast, warrant a posed photo with the catch displayed proudly in the fisherman's hands—except this fish had the addition of four hairy legs, much like a dog's. Two blank round eyes bulged out of the top of the creature's head like buttons, making it look as if the fish were staring up at Leo intently. But whatever the fish saw, it wasn't interesting enough, as it quickly turned around and scampered off into the woods, its long tail trailing behind it like a lizard's.

No sooner had the quadruped fish left the scene than Leo heard the fluttering of thin, papery wings coming from somewhere behind him. Something dry and unpleasant, like a large moth, brushed against the back of his head. Leo waved it away unseeingly and marched on. The thing fluttered away for a moment but then came back, except this time it hovered only inches above his face. Leo stopped.

The thing was indeed a large moth—a very large moth, about the size of a pheasant—that had what looked like a hideous shrunken human head. The scalp was withered and hairless and the face pale and gaunt, its semitransparent skin pulled tautly over jutting bones. The nose was just two vertical slits; above it, two bulging eyes stared at Leo unblinkingly. A pair of long antennae, jointed like a spider's legs, stuck out at the top of the moth's head. Instead of an insect's mouth, the creature had lots of sharp teeth.

The moth hissed like a feral cat and dived at Leo, snapping its jaws repeatedly with a bony clicking sound. Leo fought the creature off with his forearm, thrusting it sideways with a sickening crunch. A shower of fine gray dust sprinkled his face. But the moth came at him again. One of its hind legs was now drooping pathetically, but its wings worked even harder to make up for the loss, whirring frantically like a fan switched on at the highest setting. Leo whacked the annoying creature with the back of his hand, feeling one of the antennae snap under his knuckles. Before he could move his hand back, the moth bit him. The needle-sharp teeth buried themselves into the soft flesh at the side of his hand, drawing blood. Leo stifled a cry.

The moth was about to advance again but froze in terror as a sudden flapping of large wings disturbed the air. A giant owl with a human face and saucer-sized eyes descended upon the moth, clutching it with its talons and carrying it off into the black sky. A broken moth's wing tumbled onto the ground before Leo's feet. Leo surveyed his wound. It was nothing incapacitating, but he resented the pain nevertheless. It was unpleasant and entirely unnecessary. The wound was healing fast, but just before it fully closed up, three drops of blood oozed out and dripped onto the ground. All around him, unseen wolves howled.

A twig snapped somewhere to his right. Leo turned to see the same shadow he had previously spotted slinking among the moonlit trees. The silhouette had a lithe, fluid shape. Apart from that, he still couldn't tell what kind of animal it was. A fox perhaps, or a hare. Or a wolf.

As if on cue, a wolf howled, followed by another and then another until a whole rumble of wolf howls echoed around him.

A gray wolf emerged from the shadows less than a dozen yards ahead of him. It was a big wolf and clearly a hungry one. Skinny ribs stuck out against its sides and a ferocious scowl contorted its face. Its eyes were like two glinting silver coins.

Presently other members of the pack joined their leader. There were now six pairs of silver eyes watching Leo.

The pack leader started slinking toward him, a low growl emanating from its throat.

Leo reached into his pocket and withdrew his Stick of Sylvicolus. But before he had a chance to charge it, a single plaintive note resonated through the air, followed by a cascade of shimmery strumming. Then a man's voice began crooning a simple but haunting tune. The source of the music was an indeterminate distance away, but it sounded as if it were getting closer.

The melody seemed to have a pacifying effect on the wolves, and the attack formation promptly dissolved into a loose gathering as purposeful as a group of tourists in a souvenir shop at an airport terminal. Then all six of the wolves ran off in the direction of the forest.

Meanwhile, the music had become louder, and the words could now be clearly discerned:

> *Oh what joy it is to sing*
> *Of deeds both vile and fair*
> *Beneath the walls of this white town*
> *That stands beyond compare.*

A buoyantly dressed young man with a lute sauntered out of the woods, his gait light and carefree. He wore yellow hose and a loose tunic made of many different-sized patches of variegated cloth. On his head there was an extravagant hat.

Leo immediately put up his guard. He had no doubt that the debonair vaga-
bond known only as the Minstrel was the person Otto the Goldsmith had meant
by "the one who will lead you to the secret door under the mountain." And he
had no doubt that the Minstrel was qualified for the job. As one of the oldest—
albeit ageless and unchanging—denizens of the Withdrawn Realm, the Minstrel
knew the place better than anyone else. Leo had encountered him before, during
one of his previous reluctant sojourns in the White City, and he knew his insight
was invaluable. But he also knew that the Minstrel was dangerous. Not overtly
but in a subtle, unsettling way. There was something about his airy manner that
filled Leo with unease. In a way, there was a bit of Algol in him—like the demon
star, the Minstrel didn't seem to care about anything. To be fair, Leo didn't care
too much about anything either, but the other two cared even *less*.

When the Black Queen had first come to power, thus bringing about the
gradual but inexorable destruction of the Withdrawn Realm, most of its population had understandably resented Leo for his prominent role in the whole affair.
But the Minstrel had always treated him with the same unchanging cheer. Leo
found this more unnerving than anything.

"Bluestar!" cried the Minstrel joyfully upon seeing Leo. The lively youth
waved delightedly and immediately burst into song:

Here comes a man who's from afar
But where, he will not say.
For he's no man, he is a star
And he'd prefer not to stay.

Despite his unease and mild annoyance, Leo had to admit to himself that
the Minstrel was good at what he did. He had one job—to come up with lyrics
that contained both rhyme and situational relevance, and he did it well, certainly
better than Leo would have been able to.

"I'm glad to see you haven't lost your prosodic predispositions, Minstrel,"
said Leo.

"And I'm glad to see you haven't lost your fashion fortitude," said the Minstrel.

"Why, thank you," said Leo despite himself. He could never remain indifferent to flattery, not even the ironic kind.

Then the Minstrel sang another ditty, making subtle jibes at Leo's vanity.
Leo listened patiently, sporting a tolerant smile.

Before the musician had a chance to begin another number, Leo said, "Any news from whatever's left of the Realm? Is everything still irreparably lost because of…me?"

"Fear not, Bluestar, things are not that bad. They rarely are. Come, let us walk for a while and I'll tell you all about it—well, the good parts anyway."

"Certainly," said Leo.

Now, here was another thing about the Minstrel—he could be an exceptional guide as well as an unlimited source of information, but one couldn't be too direct with him. Stating one's intentions too explicitly was inadvisable. Such an approach would only yield improvised riddles in rhymed couplets. So Leo mentally strapped himself in for the long haul.

They immediately fell into an easy, companionable gait, enhanced by musical accompaniment in the form of the Minstrel's upbeat traveling songs. His mirth, although jarring, made their surroundings appear less dreadful. Even now, a huge spider lurking behind a rock ahead of them, which on closer inspection turned out to be an octopus walking on its tentacles, was scuttling away as they passed.

"And what brings you to these dreary, dispiriting parts this time around?" asked the Minstrel.

"Oh, they're hardly dispiriting," said Leo. "And I was just stretching my legs. It always helps whenever there's something on my mind."

"Anything that might be of interest to a wandering troubadour?" The Minstrel's eyes shone with an uncanny light.

"Oh, you know, just the usual. Expedited interstellar travel, interplanetary fieldwork, Star Council politics. A bit dull really. Although, come to think of it, there was this one little thing." Leo's tone was carefully neutral. "It's a bit of a mystery."

"A mystery!" said the Minstrel breathlessly and then performed a short accompanying piece:

Beyond the sea, beyond the dale
A temple lies so fair.
Its vaults are locked, but what they hide,
We neither know nor care.

Leo smiled politely, clenching his fists behind his back so as to prevent them from grabbing the Minstrel by the neck and shaking him like a rag doll. Once his annoyance had subsided, he said, "I'm afraid this particular mystery is a bit closer to home."

"Is it really?" The Minstrel's eyes were wide with childlike curiosity.

Leo racked his brains for the right phrasing of what he was going to say next. Then he noticed that they had emerged into a barren valley of gray dirt and brittle rock near the foot of Bear Mountain. A bizarre road with many bends that wound round and round but led nowhere formed a nonsensical looped pattern in the middle of the plain. Multitudes of dejected people wandered aimlessly down this path—old men with walking sticks, younger men in uniforms, peasant women with red-and-white aprons, beggars in tattered rags and other sorts of wretches. Leo immediately recognized it as the Valley of the Lost.

This was a curious place indeed. It was a region of the Withdrawn Realm where people from the ordinary world, those who had given up on life, sometimes ended up. One day they would be struggling through a miserable pseudo-existence in the ordinary world, barely making ends meet and seldom being able to see the outside world from behind their cloud of misery, and the next day they would simply find themselves in the Valley, not knowing or even caring how. There they would simply continue with their miserable pseudo-existence, wandering around in a lifeless daze, barely even noticing the difference.

Most of these wretches were lost souls stuck in the modes and ideas of some bygone era, unable or unwilling to adapt to a changing world. And so they drifted, treading the road despondently, going around an endlessly curving path that always seemed to take them back to where they had started.

"Look at that," said the Minstrel. "Isn't it a poignant sight?" And he burst into a heartfelt elegiac ballad.

Not far from them, a slow procession of downtrodden old people walked behind a horse-drawn cart loaded with a coffin. The hunched forms of the people cast long black shadows against the Moon-bathed valley. Suddenly one of the shadows peeled itself off the ground, soared into the air, and swept over the procession menacingly. With its kitelike shape and long tail like a flagellum, it looked like a giant spectral devilfish.

"Mary's blanket!" cried Leo. He had no idea why those things were called Mary's blankets and he didn't care. All he cared about was not being anywhere near one.

Mary's blankets were vicious predators that preyed on the lost and helpless, which was, incidentally, how Leo now felt. In appearance, the creatures were constantly changing sheets of sheer darkness that looked like nothing so much as the complete absence of matter. They moved with unsettling twitchy movements, their speed frightening. If they set their sights on someone, the victim's fate was pretty much sealed. Leo didn't know just how far his present earthbound vulnerability extended and he didn't care to find out. He cast a nervous glance at the Minstrel, but he was watching the spectacle with an expression of pure bliss.

The preying Mary's blanket flicked its flagellum at an old widow at the back of the procession, coiling the whiplike appendage tightly around her waist.

The old woman didn't even try to resist. Instead, she passively allowed herself to be dragged toward the creature, apparently indifferent at the prospect of plunging into a void of black matter. As she did so, the Mary's blanket expanded to a rotund blob, absorbing the hapless widow like a black amoeba, and then shrank to its previous size with an audible whooshing sound, as if something had been sucked out of it.

Leo felt his knees turn to water, but for the time being at least, the sensation was only a figurative one.

"Watch this," whispered the Minstrel. Turning to the Mary's blanket, he yelled, "Hey, sperm-tail! Come here!"

The Mary's blanket twitched its flagellum.

"Is this wise?" whispered Leo out of the side of his mouth.

"Fear not, Bluestar, I do this sort of thing all the time."

A ripple ran through the Mary's blanket, indicating the turning of the creature's attention to the Minstrel. The loathsome black shape spun around and glided over to the two of them like some hellish helium balloon, propelled by the lashings of its tail. Though he knew it would be of no use, Leo instinctively reached for his Stick of Sylvicolus. The creature got to within a few yards of them, then paused and hovered there ominously. It seemed to be trying to decide which one of them to annihilate first.

Leo had never seen a Mary's blanket up close and was surprised to see that the shapeless thing had a rudimentary face—eyes like two silver pinpricks and, underneath them, a small maroon triangle, which could have been either a nose or a mouth or both. The creature stared at the Minstrel's colorful form with something akin to suspicion, or perhaps it was just shortsightedness.

Beaming at the attention, the Minstrel played a spectacular theatrical flourish and then delivered a feverishly upbeat little tune, strumming the strings so energetically that his hand looked like a motion blur. As he sang, he hopped up and down to the imaginary beat of a merry jig like a peasant at a village fete. He ended the performance with a dramatic high note.

Even before the song was over, the Mary's blanket swished backward as if singed and dived headfirst into the earth. The end of its long whip-appendage lingered behind for a second, wriggling like an earthworm, and then disappeared with the rest of the creature.

"That was fascinating," said Leo. "I had no idea Mary's blankets reacted to music in such a visceral way."

"Only certain kinds of music," said the Minstrel in an expert's tone of voice. "They can't stand anything with positive vibes."

"Fascinating," said Leo. He didn't want to ask the Minstrel why he hadn't intervened before the monster had devoured the old woman. He thought he already knew the answer.

"But I hope this little incident hasn't marred your meditative walk," said the youth. "You were about to ask me something before we were so rudely distracted."

The Minstrel looked at Leo with something akin to evil amusement. But this could have been just Leo's imagination, which was still reeling from the trauma of encountering the Mary's blanket. Either way, he could feel his patience, not to mention his capacity for verbal subtlety, fading.

"Any news about Barbara?" he blurted.

"Ah!" The mischievous sparkle in the Minstrel's eyes left no room for doubt that this was the question he had been expecting.

"Any rumors from the Underworld?" asked Leo. "Did you hear anything about any odd things...stirring in there?"

"Did I ever."

"What do you mean?" Leo didn't like the sound of that.

"From what I hear"—the Minstrel lowered his voice as if to avoid being overheard—"whatever it is that Barbara's been engaged in all these years, it hasn't been the cultivation of philosophical idleness."

"You don't say. Has she taken up jogging, bookkeeping or…spelunking?"

"In a manner of speaking. Rumor has it that she has built a replica Bear Town Fortress down there, except bigger and more terrible than the old one."

"How industrious of her." Leo didn't want his tone to convey the fact that his blood had turned to ice. Then, as if to reassure himself, he added, "Are you saying that she has her own private workforce down there?"

"That is exactly what I'm saying." The Minstrel flicked his fingertips across the strings of his lute to accentuate his point. "And there's more." He paused for dramatic effect. "The underground Bear Town Fortress lies beneath the old one. And there is a well in the center, just as there is one in the old fortress. They say that the Underworld well is aligned with the other well aboveground. As if it's some sort of passage."

Leo made a small choked sound at the back of his throat.

"And it sounds," continued the Minstrel mercilessly, "as if the only thing she lacks is the opportunity to use it. But it seems this might happen sooner than she expected."

The Minstrel picked a few notes on his lute. They sounded chilling. Then he added casually, "Of course, you must have heard about the missing Four. And how one of them is likely to help her open the passage when the time comes."

Leo cleared his throat. "Yes, the matter has been brought to my attention."

"But, frankly, Bluestar, you shouldn't take my word for it. Now that you're here, you can see for yourself that every word I say is true." This time when the Minstrel looked at Leo, the spark in his eyes was unmistakably evil. "You know, there is a door—a door at the foot of the mountain that leads straight into the Underworld."

"Is there?" said Leo coolly. "I might check it out sometime if I feel inspired. Thanks for the suggestion, Minstrel."

"Always a pleasure." The Minstrel took a histrionic bow.

"You don't happen to know how to get there? Perhaps there is some convenient shortcut you could suggest?"

"I know something much better than a shortcut." The Minstrel put his thumb and index finger in his mouth and whistled. The clear, piercing sound that came out was the aural equivalent of a laser beam. If there had been any delicate crystal stemware in sight, not that there was any demand for such things in the Valley of the Lost, it would have surely cracked.

From the woods behind them, there came a rustling, crunching sound. This was followed by the sniffing and huffing of a large animal.

What appeared before them was like a cross between a giant snow-white squirrel and a unicorn. It was shaped exactly like a squirrel, an elephant-sized one, except it had a long rainbow-striped tail like a unicorn's. Of course, since no one has ever laid eyes on a real unicorn, meaning there has been no factual evidence showing that unicorns do in fact have rainbow tails, there was no way of knowing whether this particular tail really *was* like a unicorn's. Which meant that the creature standing before them might have been nothing more than a very big squirrel.

The Minstrel went up to the squirrel. The creature promptly nuzzled his hat.

"This is Squirrely," said the Minstrel, patting the side of the creature's neck. "Squirrely is a marmotaur. I trust you are familiar with marmotaurs?"

"I've heard of them," Leo lied.

"So you know that you should never feed them chestnuts?"

"Of course," said Leo. "I wouldn't dream of it."

The Minstrel whispered something in Squirrely's fuzzy ear, and the creature waved its tail eagerly in response, sending sparks of rainbow colors in all directions. Then the youth turned toward Leo.

"Squirrely will take you up to the secret gate," he said. "But after that, you're on your own, Bluestar. You shouldn't have any trouble getting in. Just look for the key hidden under the doormat. And don't forget to put it back before you go in. If you change your mind though, and I wouldn't blame you if you did, Squirrely will bring you back here, no questions asked."

Leo thanked the Minstrel, mounted the marmotaur, and then the two of them, star daimon and giant squirrel, were off.

18

THE DRAGON KEY

Dario had been in high spirits since the werefox showdown, which he had taken as an unofficial initiation into the mysteries of the city. The only problem was that he didn't know what was supposed to happen next. In an ideal world, Leo would have immediately appointed him a sort of magic apprentice and provided him with special training that would have looked as seamless as a 1980s movie montage. By now, the two of them would have been prowling the streets of the city in matching star-themed outfits, fighting all manner of supernatural evil.

None of those things had happened though. Dario hadn't heard from Leo since the aftermath of the werefox battle. The scene of the showdown had not been discovered, and the news reports on the mysterious escaped beast had simply petered out. The few remaining references to the event claimed that the whole incident had been nothing more than a case of some wild animal, possibly a hyena or a tapir, escaping from the Maksimir Zoo.

And Leo himself had apparently disappeared. There had been neither any new Starman sightings in the city nor new text messages on Dario's phone (he still wasn't convinced by Leo's claim that the mysterious text hadn't been sent by him). Dario had waited patiently for a few days. After all, he wasn't pushy. He didn't like to pester people. But on the fifth day after the werefox battle, when it became obvious that no further communications from Leo would be forthcoming, he decided to take matters into his own hands. He decided to pay Leo another visit.

However, as soon as he set foot inside the courtyard of the Hidden Tower, he knew that Leo wasn't there. It wasn't just the fact that there was no sound of Leo talking to himself. The place simply felt lifeless and abandoned in a way that no place could possibly feel if the Starman were in or at least near the area.

"Leo?" he called, but the only answer he got was the stirring of dust motes in the still air around him.

A patch of brightness grabbed his attention from the periphery of his field of vision. It was a letter-sized piece of yellowish paper that had been attached with a pin to a door on the ground floor.

Dario approached the object cautiously. In the top right corner of the letter there was an elegantly scrawled *October 21st*—the day of the werefox incident—and underneath it, a note written in an equally extravagant looping hand read,

> *Dear Dario,*
>
> *Just a quick note, in case you drop by again, to let you know I've had to go away on what you might call "business." I know that after everything you've seen, trying to convince you that none of it is real would be pointless, especially now that I've told you more than I should have done about the Realm (I've always had a bit of a problem with keeping secret things secret). And, while you obviously are a competent lad with an admirable grasp of what is going on under the surface of the city and an even more admirable enthusiasm for action, at the moment there is simply no way to include you in the goings-on currently brewing in the city without considerable risk to your person.*
>
> *The matter is simply too dangerous for anyone with less than five centuries' worth of experience fighting this particular archvillain. Therefore, I must ask you not to attempt to intervene in any way, whatever circumstances may arise in my absence. For better or for worse, I must bring this little drama to completion on my own.*
>
> *In the meantime, you may wish to consider going away for a while, as the city will not be the most peaceful place in the galaxy for the next ten days or so (not that it ever is—that title is reserved for Enceladus. Although, to be fair, it's not that hard to be peaceful when you're nothing more than a big ball of ice.). If you have an aunt who lives someplace outside the city, such as Australia, now might be a good time to pay her a vis-*

it. Whatever you do, stay away from Bear Mountain on the Night of the
Witches.

Wishing you success in all your self-preservation endeavors,
Leo

Dario stared at Leo's signature for a long time. The whole word, written in
Leo's unique hand, had the appearance of a crouching lion. The top of the *L* had
a curve that looked like a tail, the *e* was a bit squashed so that it looked elongat-
ed and trunk-like, while the *o* had two curls on top that looked like a stylized lion's mane.

Careful not to make a noise (not that there was any rational reason for the
stealth), Dario plucked the note off the door and slowly folded the paper before putting it into his pocket. Then, driven by an odd impulse, he went up the
wooden steps to the first floor and entered the main hall. The book he had been
after on the day of the werefox incident sat on the table. This time he was sure it
was the right one. It looked smaller than he remembered—no bigger than an address book—but its matte black cover was unmistakable. He didn't open it—he
dared not do it without a reason. Instead, he carefully picked it up and slipped
it into the inside pocket of his jacket. He had decided that whatever was going
to happen in the city in the following few days, he was not going to hide from
it. He was going to help whichever way he could, even if that meant pinching a
weaponized magic book that he didn't know the exact use of.

"Hello," said a soft crooning voice behind him.

Nearly jumping out of his skin, Dario whirled around expecting to see a
fearsome servant of the dark side lurking behind him with an axe. But the pale,
amused-looking man in the strange black outfit who stood there didn't look like
a servant of anything.

"Who...who are you?" asked Dario, blinking myopically. There was something about the stranger that gave Dario a headache—it was as if his image was
flickering on and off.

"I'm a friend of Leo's. He asked me to drop by to check that he hasn't left
the oven on."

"Um...so you know he's gone away? Has he told you where he's gone off
to?"

"No, he never tells me anything," said the flickering man airily. "But he did give me this." He strolled up to Dario casually, taking a small glinting object out of his pocket.

"Um…what is that?"

"No idea. He said you should keep it with you while he's away. It's some sort of talisman, I think."

Dario took the proffered object. It was an antique key shaped like a dragon's head with red eyes made of gems. It felt heavy in his hand.

"Um…thank you," he said.

But when he looked up, the flickering man was gone.

Whenever there were big things on his mind, especially if those things were of a philosophical nature, Dario had the tendency to take his problems out for a stroll up and down the streets of Upper Town. There was something about the brooding medieval ambience that helped his thoughts fall into place. And so, as he left the Hidden Tower, he immediately set out on his meditative walk, heading first to the statue of the city's patron saint, St. George, who sat astride a dejected-looking horse, then through the Stone Gate and from there to the streets of Upper Town. His mind was bursting with stuff—stuff he didn't know the true significance of.

On this occasion, however, the walk failed to produce any beneficial results. If anything, it only made him feel even more confused. He was still wandering around the narrow streets as night fell and the crescent Moon rose over the ancient roofs of Upper Town, covering them with its silver light. There was something else there too, besides the Moon. The back of his neck tingled, the way it always did when he felt he was being watched. He could almost feel a pair of unseen eyes upon him.

A chill went down his spine as he went past the Stone Gate once again. In the chilly light of the Moon, its arched entrance was like the gaping mouth of a giant subterranean beast. For a moment, Dario felt a surge of supernatural dread. The Stone Gate and the surrounding buildings looked the way they must have done centuries ago, uncanny and unchanged. If he had been standing in the same spot in the Middle Ages, the view before him would have been the same. What if he now went through the gate and slipped into some medieval wormhole? No one would ever know.

This thought was so disturbing that Dario turned instinctively in the opposite direction only to bump into something small that promptly let out an agitated yelp. Unthinkingly, Dario reached for Leo's banishing book in his pocket.

Two tiny men, barely three and a half feet tall, dressed in identical monastic robes, stood before him. The older of the two gasped when he saw the black book. Dario put it away with an apologetic grin.

"Did you see that, Brother Gregor?" asked the elder monk.

"Yes, I did, Prior Dominik," said the other.

They gave Dario matching judgmental looks.

"Wh-who are you?" stammered Dario.

"I am Prior Dominik," said the elder monk peevishly, "and this is Brother Gregor. We are of the Order of the Little Brethren. As for who *you* are, it is plain to see. You are someone who has foolishly chosen to associate with that demon."

The other monk made a contemptuous sound.

"What demon?" Dario stuttered. "You don't…you don't mean Leo?"

"I knew it," said Prior Dominik. "It figures."

"I should have known," said Brother Gregor practically at the same time. The two of them exchanged a look of disapproval.

"Wait, you two know Leo?" asked Dario.

"Of course we know Leo," said Prior Dominik. "He is *notorious*."

"So you, um…work with him?"

"Absolutely not," said Prior Dominik. "We do not approve of his methods."

"That man is reckless," said Brother Gregor. "And he's not even a man."

"You mean he's a…"

"Demon," cut in Prior Dominik.

"Well, he did say he was a star daimon," said Dario with more confidence than he felt. He still had no idea what exactly a star daimon was.

"A mere technicality," said Prior Dominik.

"A matter of nomenclature," said Brother Gregor.

"He is an ancient entity without any morals or sense of allegiance."

"But…but surely he can't be that ancient," said Dario.

"Very ancient," said Brother Gregor "He is thousands of years old."

"Hundreds of thousands."

"Millions," added Brother Gregor helpfully.

"He is as old as the Earth."

"Possibly older."

"But it cannot be," said Dario. "He doesn't look a day over thirty."

Brother Gregor slapped himself noisily on the forehead.

"Mark my words, laddie," said the Prior, "that man—that *being*—is ancient and it's dangerous. It nearly brought the city to ruin many years ago."

Something clicked in Dario's mind. He remembered Leo's story about a powerful being who accidentally instructed the Black Queen, and he also remembered his recent admission of not being able to keep a secret.

"Wait," he said. "That was him? It was Leo who told the Black Queen all those things that gave her power?"

The two little monks covered their ears and started shaking their heads at the same time.

"We don't speak of that person," said Prior Dominik.

"We don't utter that name aloud."

"Right," said Dario, feeling more baffled by the bizarre head-shaking than by what he had learned about Leo. "Well, I'm sure he meant no harm." As soon as he had said it, he believed it. Whatever Leo was, Dario knew he was not evil. "He must have made a miscalculation."

"Yes," said Brother Gregor, "that's what he'd *want* you to believe."

"A word of warning, young man," said Prior Dominik, holding up one tiny index finger, whose tip only reached up as far as Dario's belt buckle. Despite his waist-level height and child-sized robe, the little friar somehow managed to look imposing. "You stay away from that reckless man. He is not who you think he is. And the city is not what you think it is. I assure you that whatever he might have told you about the magic realm, it is only a part of the picture."

Dario gulped. "I'll keep that in mind."

Prior Dominik gave Dario a stern, appraising look that made him shuffle his feet.

"Come, Brother Gregor," said the prior. "There is nothing more we can do to help this young man. If he chooses to be led astray, then that is what will come to pass, regardless of what we say or do."

"He has been granted the gift of free will like the rest of us," said the other. "He can make his own choices."

"Indeed."

Then came the sound of a distant church bell. The two little friars perked up their ears.

"Dinner!" said the pair in unison.

"Well, we'd better be off," said Prior Dominik. "It's been nice talking to you."

"So long," said Brother Gregor.

The two monks departed with a spring in their step.

19

INSIDE THE MOUNTAIN

I t was exactly how Leo always imagined riding a giant squirrel would be. The marmotaur moved with surprising agility—switching between two legs and four with a spontaneity that Leo was not entirely comfortable with, but this was only because it put him under constant threat of whiplash injury. The method did, however, enable the squirrel to cover a lot of ground. The creature cleared the Valley of the Lost with a few long leaps, ignoring the confusing spiral path and simply cutting diagonally across. Then the squirrel entered a thick cluster of tall trees on uneven ground and crossed it effortlessly, hopping over the trees with the ease of a hare jumping over a vegetable patch. Leo barely managed to hang on.

They reached a small clearing at the base of the mountain, where the squirrel made an abrupt stop. With a surprised yelp, Leo slid off its back and tumbled in an undignified heap to the ground. To add insult to injury, the ground was soggy and strewn with half-open chestnut pods that stuck to his clothes. The squirrel sat down on its haunches like a dog and stared at something behind Leo, its nose twitching.

"Why, you little—" began Leo and then realized there was no point talking to a giant squirrel, not even to shower insults on it. He sprang to his feet, brushed the dirt off his cape, and turned in the direction of the marmotaur's gaze.

On that side there was what looked like an entrance to a cave, quite possibly a cave leading into the mountain, and it would have looked like a fairly ordinary cave if it hadn't been for the fact that its entrance was a proper door.

"Oh," said Leo. "Well, that wasn't *too* hard to find."

No sooner had he uttered the last word than the stillness of the grove was disturbed by a piercing howl, followed by a whole choir of them.

"Not again," moaned Leo.

Moments later, the undergrowth around him was dotted with glinting spots of silver. When the first wolf emerged from the cover of darkness, it was growling and its fangs were bared.

This time, Leo didn't hesitate to reach for his Stick of Sylvicolus. He did, however, still feel reluctant to use it so soon for something as common as a pack of wolves—these weren't even mutant wolves bred by the Black Queen, but ordinary wolves of the *Canis lupus* variety.

Then he remembered what the Minstrel had told him about not feeding chestnuts to marmotaurs. There was only one reason why certain foods should be kept away from a Withdrawn Realm animal—because, if eaten, such foods made the animal in question act in strange, unpredictable ways. Leo decided that, under the circumstances, this was a path worth exploring.

Never taking his eyes off the wolf, he cautiously crouched down and scooped a handful of chestnuts off the ground.

"Squirrely," he said, rising slowly and extending his chestnut-laden hand to the beast. "Here, Squirrely."

The giant squirrel gave the chestnuts a single exploratory sniff and then scoffed them all in one go.

Leo immediately regretted what he had done. The marmotaur towering above him first shuddered and twisted, then transformed into a steroid-fueled version of itself. The wolves froze in place. The giant squirrel let loose a terrible guttural growl and charged at them with the force of a speeding steam engine. The wolves scattered like field mice.

Leo nodded once, satisfied. He strode over to the door, which was a poorly maintained medieval-looking thing. There was no doormat though, and Leo huffed, annoyed, because there always had to be something, some annoying little thing that made everything else needlessly difficult.

Then he saw a moss-covered rock about the size of a cushion lying on the ground, and, nudging it with his foot, he realized that the moss was in fact a fluffy green doormat. Concealed under it was a rusty antique key. Leo picked it up and put it into the equally rusty and antiquated lock. It took a bit of wriggling, shaking and cursing, but in the end, the lock did yield. The door opened.

Leo put the key back in its place and went into the Underworld.

It didn't take long for his eyes to adjust to the gloom, mainly because it wasn't that gloomy. The same ultramarine glow that permeated the land outside was also present inside the mountain. A faint bluish glow hung in the air, while brighter highlights of the same color outlined the cracks in the cave walls. Ahead of him, there was a long tunnel leading into the dark. Above him, the cave formed a high cathedral ceiling. There was, however, no sign of the Black Queen's alleged underground fortress. So Leo set out down the tunnel, following the trail of blue light that he hoped would eventually lead him into the heart of the mountain.

As he treaded the path, he felt himself moving steadily downhill. The air gradually got cooler and the blue light icier. Every once in a while, he would come across another path branching off in a different direction, but he always followed the one where the light was brighter. On one occasion, the walls of the tunnel disappeared, giving way to a deep, dark chasm with only a single narrow path stretching across it like a bridge. Leo thought he could just barely see a ripple of water down there in the deep, as if at the bottom there lay some kind of underground lake.

Then he was back in the tunnels, which kept getting narrower and more labyrinthine by the minute. Every few paces, there was a sharp turn, and he found himself going left and right in a random pattern, wondering whether he would ever find his way out of the maze he was in.

After one such turn, he found himself in a tunnel that was darker than any he had seen so far. However, unlike other parts of the cave, this one wasn't sepulchrally silent. A whispery rustling was coming from somewhere ahead of him. He took a step forward and blindly stumbled into an unseen obstacle.

"Ow, careful," said a nervous voice.

Leo grabbed his Stick of Sylvicolus and held it up as part weapon, part torch. Its flame illuminated a group of pale, willowy long-haired beings huddled together in a nook formed by two jutting rocks. The creatures blinked up at Leo fearfully, looking as if his torch were the brightest thing they had ever seen, which Leo thought was highly probable. They all wore long tattered tunics that might have once been blue. Stones, sticks, small animal bones and various other objects such as pots, shoes and empty cigarette lighters were scattered all over the floor.

"Who are you?" asked Leo sharply.

"We are the tram fairies," answered a timid voice that belonged to a yellow-haired creature in the middle of the group.

"Well..." That wasn't the answer Leo had expected. "Well, what are you all doing here?"

"We are huddling," said the yellow-haired fairy. The others nodded in agreement.

"Fine, but why are you huddling *here*?" Leo dimmed the glow of his wand, since the creatures were clearly harmless. "You won't find any trams in this place."

"Do you really think so?" said another fairy, a feeble hunched thing, before fearfully lowering its head once again.

"You see, we're not sure," said the other fairy.

"What do you mean you're not sure?" Leo suspected that whatever was coming, it wasn't worth his time. But he decided to humor the pathetic creatures anyway, since it was obvious that none of them had spoken to anyone outside their circle for a very long time.

"We're not sure if there are any trams here because we have never seen a tram."

Leo wrinkled his brow. "Isn't that a bit odd, given that you're tram fairies?"

"I agree it is a bit awkward," said the yellow-haired fairy with something akin to enthusiasm. "You see, we are ancient beings, created at the dawn of time with the rest of the beings of the Withdrawn Realm. The only problem is that at the dawn of time, there were no trams around!"

"Ah." Leo was starting to see the problem.

"At first," continued the fairy, "we assumed that if we waited long enough, trams would eventually present themselves. And so we waited for years and years and years and centuries and centuries..."

"And centuries," added another fairy.

"But there were no trams to be seen, nor did we know what they were supposed to look like. None of us knew—not the great tram fairy sages Tramson and Tramwin, not the lauded poet Trammerlaine, not even the ruler of the tram fairies himself, the late King Bertram."

The others sighed mournfully.

"And then," continued the tram fairy, "the Black Queen took over the Withdrawn Realm, and then Nestis cast the spell that trapped her under the mountain. Alas, the spell trapped us in too! We were just strolling by looking for trams in the woods when the whole thing happened, and we got caught in the middle."

"I see," said Leo.

"Please, kind sir," said the hunched fairy, "would you tell us if any of these things are trams?" The pitiful creature hunched down and started picking things up off the floor one by one, showing each one to Leo. Among them was an old picture frame, a discarded AA battery, an old toothbrush, a rubber duck and an empty beer can.

"No…no…no," said Leo.

"How about this?" asked the yellow-haired fairy, pointing at a broken vinyl record.

"No."

Then the others joined in and started showing him random items hoarded in the tunnel. Leo kept saying no. The more objects he dismissed as nontrams, the more dejected the tram fairies became. After a while, Leo began to see the futility of his current strategy. First of all, if this went on much longer, he would be delayed in this tunnel indefinitely while the tram fairies went through their entire accumulated garbage inventory. Second, if Leo crushed all their hopes, the tram fairies might choose not to cooperate. And he needed all the help he could get.

So he decided to adopt a different approach. The next time a tram fairy picked up a random object and presented it to him, Leo said yes.

The tram fairies let out a collective gasp. The yellow-haired fairy held up the object in question reverently. It was an unopened can of dog food with a picture of a Yorkshire terrier on it.

"*This* is a tram?" said the fairy in a breathless half whisper.

"Yes." Leo nodded. "That is a tram."

The tram fairies burst into animated chatter. There were even a few whoops of joy. The yellow-haired tram fairy held up the canned dog food triumphantly and made a short cringeworthy speech. There was more cheering. Leo waited patiently for the jubilation to subside.

"You have restored purpose to our existence," said the yellow-haired fairy. "Is there anything we can do to repay you?"

"Well, now that you mention it, there is. Any chance you could show me the way to the Black Queen's hideout?"

The collective ecstasy fell off the fairies' faces like a pensioner tumbling off the highest step of an old number seventeen tram.

"This is as far as we dare take you," said the yellow-haired fairy, whose name turned out to be Tramkins. They had emerged out of a network of tunnels into an open, mist-covered underground plain, which, according to Leo's calculations—many of them based on the downward trajectory they had taken—was somewhere near the center of the Earth.

On the far side of the plain, an enormous rocky elevation rose out of the ground, its shape reminiscent of Bear Mountain. A hellish double of Bear Town Fortress, bigger and much more terrible than its aboveground version had ever been, towered on top of it.

"None of us has ever ventured beyond this point," said the hunched tram fairy, whose name was Tramwise, "because this is where the Black Queen's evil domain truly begins."

Leo said that he would be fine on his own, thanking them all for their kind help.

"And, you know," he added, "if you ever decide to get out of here, there is a secret door…over there somewhere." He gestured vaguely in the general direction of where he remembered the door under the mountain to be.

"Oh," said Tramwise, looking surprised. "We should be all right in here, I think."

"Now that we've finally found a tram," said Tramkins, clutching the can of dog food protectively against his skinny chest, "we've got everything we could ever wish for."

"Right," said Leo. "Well, so long, Tramkins and Tramwise."

"So long, kind sir," said Tramkins, "and thank you for everything you've done for us."

Leo assured Tramkins that it was not a problem at all and then turned to the other tram fairies. "So long, Trammy, Tramberwell, Tramembert and Tram-Tram."

"So long, Leo." The tram fairies mumbled their farewells and then scuttled off.

20

BEAR TOWN FORTRESS

I f someone had asked him only a few minutes before whether he would ever miss the tram fairies, Leo would have scoffed at the idea. But as he approached the dark edifice rising above him from beyond a veil of blue mist, he found himself longing for the company of the silly creatures. He found himself longing for the company of *any* creatures. Even the Little Brethren would have been welcome.

No, thought Leo with a shudder. *Not the Little Brethren.*

The blue light that seeped out of every pore of the Underworld was gathered in an even higher concentration in the areas around and above the fortress, clinging to it like a cloud of iridescent smog. In contrast to the blue radiance, hundreds of torches surrounded the fortress on all sides, flickering with a demonic orange-red sheen. Despite the multiple light sources, the hulking form of the fortress was an almost opaque black, as if reluctant to reflect any light.

Leo stopped when he reached the foot of the rocky underground mountain. The elevation was surrounded by a moat filled with murky water, whose oddly glazed surface was covered in many speckles of reflected blue light. As for the fortress itself, gone was the simplicity of its aboveground counterpart. Instead of clean lines and boxy buildings, this fortress was all nightmarish high towers, dark crevices and sprawling walls that seemed to contain an entire city within. Instead of battlements, strange uneven spikes lined the top edges of the walls, and many limp, tattered things hung off their lower reaches. From where Leo stood, the hanging things looked like rags. A single narrow path led up the hill and into the fortress. But in order to reach it, Leo first had to cross the moat, and this was a nuisance. He got to the edge. The water didn't look dramatically deep, but he was bound to get at least partly wet nevertheless.

He sighed. Then he stopped. The moat had moved. Not in a rippling sort of way that one might expect from a body of water but in the ponderous way of a large solid object.

Then an enormous snake's head arose from the ground, where it had been lying concealed behind a huge rock, and hovered above Leo menacingly. The snake's hiss was like the sound of a deflating zeppelin and its two fangs were as big as broadswords. A greenish drop of poison clung precariously to the tip of one monstrous fang, glistening in the blue light like some famous jewel that has its own proper name and criminal history. The rest of the snake's body stirred, causing a wave of shimmering silver sparks to run all around the foot of the hill. It truly was an enormous snake—a proper fortress-encircling snake if there ever was one. With a snake like this, one didn't need a moat. Leo was slightly annoyed with himself for not noticing this little detail sooner.

He quickly retrieved the Stick of Sylvicolus out of his pocket, his mind so focused on the task at hand that the tip began to glow a mesmeric purple before he even had a chance to point it at the reptile's leathery yellow eyes, which were immediately drawn to the glow—definitely a poor decision on the serpent's part. The snake froze in a kind of open-mouthed, wide-eyed half lunge and remained that way. Even the drop of poison froze. Leo chuckled. The Stick of Sylvicolus, normally a simple weapon of the rudest sort, had, in the hands of an expert, other potential uses—uses far more sophisticated than blowing things up. Leo kicked the reptile's scaly side to test the effectiveness of his hypnotic spell (it was effective), then climbed over the stupefied serpent and proceeded up to the path.

Even before he had made it halfway up, Leo was overcome with a repulsive animal stench that came in waves from inside the fortress, mixed with the odor of drying blood, putrefaction and something hot and metallic. Chilling screams, some of them human and some of them not, resounded from the same direction.

As he got closer to the fortress, he could see that the tattered things hanging off the walls were not rags but rag-like cadavers of emaciated humans that had been nailed there. Some of the corpses had been hanging there for such a long time that there was nothing left of them other than bones and bits of cloth. And above this gruesome display, all along the top edges of the walls, what had looked like spikes from below turned out to be rows of bones, mostly ribs, sharpened into points and arranged side by side so that they looked like razor wire.

The path led to an arched gate that opened into a spacious outer court packed with soldiers, servants and beggars. There were so many people walking, standing, crawling or loitering about that no one paid Leo any heed as he stood there at the entrance. He briefly wondered what all those people were doing there. Then he pulled up his hood and stepped into Bear Town Fortress.

The stench that he had got a small sample of on his way up hit him with full force and he nearly gagged. The ground was strewn with gruesome pieces of half-chewed rotting meat and severed body parts, both animal and human. All kinds of tiny, unpleasant creatures—worms, insects, spiders and other things that Leo didn't even want to think about—teemed all over the grisly remains. There was hardly an empty, noninfested spot to place one's foot on. Every step caused a sickening crunch of crushed bone or cracking exoskeleton.

Forcing his revulsion aside, he ventured farther into the courtyard. The place was like a combination of a military camp, a bonfire party and a horror show. A semicircle of crackling pyres lined the entire perimeter of this open space, bathing the whole area in a warm glow that was almost as bright as sunlight. Within this area, there was another semicircle of tall wooden posts supporting a network of chains that hovered above the ground like electrical cables. Hanging suspended from these chains were many cages, each occupied by at least one wretched emaciated captive.

The cages, however, were not the only spectacle of horror on display in the courtyard, for the place boasted many other attractions as well. Among them were a number of severed heads impaled on stakes; shrieking people being roasted alive over improvised iron grills while other groups of prisoners, watched over by guards armed with red-hot iron blades, crouched miserably in small wooden pens at the side; people being mangled like rag dolls by terrible beasts or being eaten alive by giant snakes (giant if compared to ordinary snakes, tiny if compared to the one that lay outside the fortress); snakes walking around on two legs as if this were common practice for the species; inordinately large black spiders spinning webs in the corners, some of which sported bulging human-shaped cocoons; and men and beasts fighting over pieces of torn flesh lying on the ground.

And all around there were ravens—ravens circling ominously over the fortress, ravens perching on walls and cages, ravens preening, ravens squawking at other ravens, ravens poking at the messy scraps on the ground with their curved black beaks, ravens plucking pale flesh off dangling lifeless limbs. These were not huge red-eyed monstrosities like the Raven of Despair, but Leo had already had enough of ravens in general, red-eyed or otherwise.

Among these unwholesome sights, there were also what appeared to be totem poles. These were about ten feet high and ornamented with crudely carved animal shapes. On top of each pole sat a misshapen animal skull. Strangely hunched soldiers clad in bulky armor made of iron, leather and bone congregated around the poles in packs. For these were actual packs. Despite the full armor that obscured their features, the soldiers' manners revealed them to be the Black Queen's infamous animal hybrids, mainly wolves, although the Black Queen seemed to have developed several other varieties while in captivity.

Some were lean and edgy, some tall and taciturn, others bulky and brooding, but they all moved in an awkward, stilted way, communicating only in grunts. As Leo slunk past a group of skinny, hungry-looking soldiers sitting around a totem pole with a wolf skull on top, gnawing on bones and scraps of meat picked up from the horrible mess on the ground, he saw wolf snouts and glinting wolf eyes showing through the grille-shaped visors of the helmets.

Staggering or crawling among the various torture exhibits and the lounging soldiery were hundreds of wretched, starved peasants, begging or trying to scavenge food among the grim heaps scattered on the ground. Suffering had contorted their features beyond what should have been possible, turning their faces into expressionist masks of agony.

Something clutched the hem of Leo's robes. It was an old beggar in bloodstained rags. One of his arms was unnaturally bent and his legs were two gore-covered stumps.

"Won't you help a poor beggar, kind sir?" he said with his nearly toothless mouth. "Please help."

"How did you get here?" Leo asked.

The beggar looked taken aback. "Same as everyone else," he said. "One of 'em Mary's blankets got me. But instead of sweet oblivion, it brought me this. And there ain't even any proper booze here." The beggar croaked out a bitter laugh and crawled off.

Before Leo had time to process what he had just heard, something bumped against the side of his head. He whirled around alertly, but it was only a limp, bone-thin arm that dangled gingerly from one of the horrid cages. The arm was attached to a young woman that had been so worn out by captivity and starvation that she now looked like a hag. Her blank, lifeless eyes stared at Leo. Suddenly they blinked. Leo winced.

"Antonio," said the woman in a coarse, broken voice, her arm stirring feebly. "Antonio!" she called with a bit more force, but Leo had already moved on.

A violent commotion had broken out ahead of him. A pack of snarling wolf soldiers were chasing a group of three men who had somehow managed to escape from one of the pens. The men were running for the gates as fast as their bare feet would carry them. The sudden surge of activity caused a general outburst of growling, barking and yelling. The circling ravens cawed excitedly. Then one of the men slipped on something particularly slimy lying on the ground and fell down. His pursuers were upon him within a second, tearing him to pieces with their sharp knives. The second man didn't even have to slip first. He simply collapsed from exhaustion and allowed himself to be ripped apart without a shred of resistance. But the third one kept rushing toward the gates without looking back, outrunning even the fastest of the wolves.

He had nearly made it to the gate when a big brawny soldier with a helmet the size of a gas stove stepped out of the guard post by the gate, carrying something that looked like a crossbow, except it had a flame instead of an arrow at its tip. The guard pulled the trigger, and the flame turned into a roaring blaze, instantly burning the would-be escapee to a charred crisp. Fierce howls erupted among the wolves. The big soldier retreated calmly back to his tower, leaving the smoldering remains lying on the ground.

Leo decided he had seen enough of the outer court. As fascinating as it had been to observe the Black Queen's subjects in action, to get to the core of her evil master plan, he would have to advance farther into Bear Town. And, using the clamor of the near escape to slip past several packs of wolf soldiers unnoticed, he did just that.

A single narrow gate, little more than a tall vertical crack in the wall on the far end of the outer court, was the only passage into the interior of the fortress that Leo could see. Two guards who had been lurking on either side momentari-

ly turned their heads toward the source of the commotion. This was all the time
Leo needed to slip through to the other side.

Once there, he found himself in a deserted enclosure that was part clois-
ter and part armory. Half-buried in a mound of black earth at the center, a big
sphere that looked like a miniature crack-riddled sun glowed with an angry red
light. Swords, knives, arrows and other weapons had been driven in, point-first,
all over its surface like pins sticking out of a cushion. The blades were red where
they met the fiery globe, but they were not melting. Rather, they seemed to be
charging.

The stillness was broken by the sound of iron shoes scraping against the
ground as a soldier wandered in from the outer court. It was one of the hybrid
wolves, but not a very fearsome one. If anything, this one was leaning toward
the runt end of the spectrum. The scrawny thing had nervous, twitchy eyes and
clearly struggled with bipedal motion. He looked as if he might topple over any
second. In his skinny front paws, he carried a small sword that was presumably
empty or low on power or whatever the appropriate technical term was. In any
case, it was not red.

"Hey!" yelped the unfearsome wolf when he saw Leo standing before the fiery charger. "What are you doing here?"

Leo quickly decided that the best course of action was to blend in with the
environment and try not to arouse the wolf's suspicions.

"Nothing, I swear!" he whimpered pathetically, raising his empty hands. "I
am just a poor harmless beggar. Please have pity on me…sir." As he spoke, he
was eyeing another, even narrower, gate looming at the opposite side of the enclosure. He hoped this was the passage into the innermost circle of the fortress.

"Well, go back to your dung pile, beggar," said the wolf, pointing one un-
derdeveloped paw at the other gate, the one leading back into the outer court.
"You have no business being here."

"Yes, sir. Thank you, sir." Leo bowed his head in deference and waited for
the wolf to drop his guard. Then he quickly slipped through the gate on the opposite side.

"Hey, wait!" shouted the wolf after him. "You're not supposed to go in
there!"

Leo ran without bothering to turn and check how bad things were. He was
now in a muddy makeshift village where malnourished two-legged wolves, bears

and even a few humans worked in smithies, poked about in vile-smelling stables or huddled in primitive stone huts. Whatever these creatures were, they were not soldiers, and they gave Leo indifferent looks as he rushed past them. But he could still hear the voice of the rookie wolf yelping agitatedly in the distance behind him, and soon the agitation had spread to the haggard faces around him.

"Fugitive!" shouted a voice behind him. "Stop him!"

Casting a quick look over his shoulder, he saw a whole stampede of wolves chasing after him. Without thinking, he quickly turned into a random alley, where he promptly bumped into something solid. It was another wolf, except this one was bulkier. This wolf looked as if he had been fed on higher-quality protein than the others. In his iron-gloved hands, he held a glowing red club at the ready.

The wolf wasted no time in taking a swing at Leo. The latter drew his Stick of Sylvicolus and made a brilliant blade of fire shoot out of it just in time to fend off the burning club. Nevertheless, he was stunned by the force of the blow. Clearly, not all wolves were useless.

Although this wolf had the element of surprise on his side, Leo quickly found his bearings and took down his opponent with three swift strokes. But then the rest of the pursuing pack was upon him.

They filed into the alley like rats through a drain, attacking him with all manner of swords and knives, none of which would have been too much of a problem had the weapons not been enhanced with the inner fire. As it were, fighting the souped-up wolves was a nuisance. Leo had to whirl his Stick of Sylvicolus around with dervish-like speed to fend them all off. This was not only tiring but also ruffled his hair in a most unsatisfactory way. And so, with an annoyed groan of exertion, he shot a massive fireball out of the stick, knocking over the remaining wolves like scattered dominoes with one sweep. He promptly turned and ran farther down the alley without looking back.

A hand shot out from one of the side huts and pulled him into a gloomy room.

Leo was quick to react, raising his weapon to fight off the latest attacker, but he lowered it when he saw that the hooded figure standing before him was not one of the Black Queen's hybrid minions. There was nothing misshapen about the figure other than the hood itself, which was part of a dirty brown robe that had obviously been thrown on to conceal what lay beneath. When the hood was pulled back, Leo saw a familiar rugged face with green eyes and a straw-colored fringe.

A wave of surprise, disbelief and, above all, relief washed over him.

"Betelgeuse!" he said.

21
THE THREE OF THE SEVEN

The headquarters of the Star Council were located on a medium-sized converted sun whose surface temperature had been turned down to a pleasant twenty-two degrees Celsius. (While nearly all star daimons could withstand the entire range of cosmic temperature conditions, not all of them were keen on extreme heat.) The HQ building itself looked like a cathedral-sized crystal iceberg with many unevenly sized spire-like peaks protruding out of it at irregular intervals, making the whole thing look from a distance like an erratic bar chart. Multitudes of small circular platforms projected from various parts of the structure in a seemingly random way. These were landing pads that enabled star daimons to directly access specific parts of the building. Although there was a front door, and a rather monumental one at that, star daimons did not like the hassle of having to walk through a door and then go up the stairs when they could simply fly up to a particular chamber from the outside.

The three star daimons that landed on the highest platform, the one that led into the private office of Star Councillor Alnair, looked tired, in a rush, and overall worse for wear. Two of them, Carina and Ara, were female warriors with lots of scratches and dents in their armor, and the third one, Ret (short for Reticulum), was a nerdy youth in baggy clothes who looked as if he might have been their kid brother, although he wasn't. They were all members of the unofficial star daimon police, aka Star Force Seven.

The trio headed straight into the office, an impressive crystal dome not unlike a fancy space igloo, that was nested inside a forest of glassy spires on the top level of the building.

They found Alnair sitting cross-legged on the floor playing with what looked like a handful of glowing blue marbles.

"Ah, there you are!" he said and invited them to take a seat. Seeing that Alnair had no intention of moving to the exquisitely designed conference room part of the office, the three sat down on the floor in front of him.

"Apologies for calling you at such short notice," said Alnair. "I know you're all very busy fighting the barnacles. How's that going, by the way?"

"It's a madhouse out there," said Carina. "We've wiped out thousands of them, but new ones just keep coming."

"We found a whole cluster of them under the tail of Little Bear this morning," said Ara.

"It's looking almost as bad as the Great Barnacle Blockade of the year 1,117,895," said Ret.

"The good news," said Carina, "is that Auriga and the Herdsmen have made some headway near the Crane. And Altair and the Horsemen have cracked a whole barnacle cluster at the Whirlpool."

"That is good news indeed," said Alnair. "This is why I hoped the three of you might be able to spare a moment of your time."

The others looked suspicious.

"I'm afraid I've got a bit of a side gig for you."

"What sort of side gig?" asked Carina, sounding wary.

"I'm afraid it's the White City again."

The others didn't answer.

"You know," said Alnair, "the one on Earth, just round the corner from Alpha Centauri. The one that Leo fell foul of some time ago."

"Yes, we know," said Ara flatly.

"Now, I know what you're all thinking," said Alnair in a conciliating tone. "You're thinking that you're being unfairly taken away from the center of the action in order to be sent to some irrelevant backwater."

"Aren't we?"

"Well...yes. And no. I realize Earth isn't exactly one of the most exciting places in the universe—"

"You can say that again," said Ret.

"—but this is a delicate mission with potentially far-reaching consequences."

"Potentially?"

"Well, we are still not quite sure, but we believe that the White City might be harboring certain star daimons of darkness that went missing many years ago. There were four of them—do you remember?"

The others looked blank.

"You don't. Never mind." Alnair sighed. "At first, I couldn't remember it myself either. Those four were never the most sociable of star daimons, and hardly anyone saw them on a regular basis even while they were still among us. This is why when they disappeared, no one even noticed. It was only through talking to two of them, Corvus and Vulpecula, who were recently rediscovered after some… altercations with Leo in the city, that we have been able to form a more complete picture of what might have happened. And the picture is not a pretty one. There is now no doubt that the disappearance of the four was not voluntary."

Alnair paused, as if to give his small audience a chance to ask questions, if there were any. There weren't.

"Through interviews with the two who have returned, we have inferred that the manner in which they initially went missing involved being summoned— some might call it 'ensnared'—by the so-called Black Queen of the White City."

He paused to see if what he had said had managed to arouse interest in any of his listeners. It hadn't.

"We have also inferred that the other two missing star daimons must be Tarantula and Cora Serpentis. This is bad news indeed, not least because this Cora is suspected of being in possession of a certain key, which makes her presence in the city all the more dangerous. We have dispatched the Hunters to find the key, and Leo is, as ever, bound to restore balance in the White City. We need you to go down there and make sure that while all this is being played out, no star daimon rules end up getting breached. The disappearance of the four is one of the worst offenses against star daimons in recent memory. For a star daimon to be entrapped by an earthling and turned into their agent is very rare. For four of them to be entrapped at the same time is unheard of. We must make sure that no offense of that order of magnitude happens on this occasion or, indeed, ever again."

"Why?" asked Ara dejectedly. "Why does it have to be us?"

"Yeah," said Ret. "Why don't you send Altair? He'll get there faster than any of us."

"I'm afraid we need Altair on the barnacle front."

"And Hamal?"

"He is…not entirely suitable for this kind of job. This is an inhabited planet we're talking about. Actual Earth-plane entry might be required. We cannot send someone who would draw too much attention to himself." Alnair was politely referring to the fact that Hamal had a pair of enormous ram's horns on his head.

"It's so unfair," said Ret.

"Well, it's a tough job," said Alnair, "but someone's got to do it."

22

THE HUNTERS

The last thing Leo would have expected to find in the Underworld was another star daimon, let alone six of them. And yet this was precisely what he had found. Betelgeuse had not come to Earth by himself. Also with him were Rigel, a sturdy Hunter who looked as if he had been made from a single piece of rock; Bellatrix, a warrior-Huntress who lived by the credo "shoot first; ask no questions later"; Alnilam, whose senses were as sharp as a greyhound's, and the male-female twins Min and Taka.

The six of them were members of an awe-inspiring group called the Hunters, although some called them Star Force Six (oddly enough, Earth people, for some reason unknown to the Hunters, collectively referred to all six of the star daimons as "Orion"). Their job was to track down and find or kill whatever needed to be found or killed at a given time. Needless to say, they were an excellent resource in the star daimons' ongoing battle against the barnacles, but they had other uses too.

As they sat in a circle around a small floating yellow orb that Alnilam always carried with him on distant missions as part heater and part novelty lava lamp, Betelgeuse explained to Leo that the Hunters had been sent to the city by the Star Council in order to track down a certain missing artifact.

Apparently one of their fellow star daimons, Draco, who had a childish fascination with all things secret and forbidden, had once owned a sort of dragon-shaped key that could unlock doors to secret, forbidden places. One day, he met the mysterious Cora Serpentis, the shape-shifting reptilian star daimon who dwelled in the dark places of the universe. One thing led to another, and at the end of it all, Draco found himself jilted and keyless. The snake daimon had stolen his precious dragon key!

All this happened quite a while ago, but Draco had felt too embarrassed at the time to admit to anyone what had happened. It was only after he had overheard rumors about the recent reappearance of Corvus and Vulpecula and the possibility that one of the remaining missing daimons might be Cora that Draco decided to finally come forward and fess up.

Being a tireless bunch of handwringers, the Star Council immediately decided that the dragon key had to be retrieved without further delay. They did have a brief debate as to whether this matter was under their jurisdiction, since the missing star daimons had become earthed, but in the end decided that whereas the missing star daimons themselves were earthed, the dragon key was not—it was still a genuine artifact of the Celestial Realm. And so they promptly dispatched the Hunters to the White City to find the stolen key.

In other words, the Hunters were there on a very important mission. This was why, when Leo asked them to help him with the Black Queen business, Betelgeuse flatly said no.

"But…" Leo knew his chances were microscopic. The Hunters were a straight-shooting bunch, and they were unlikely to bend the rules for him. "Please?"

"I'm sorry, Leo," said Betelgeuse, "but we were sent here by the council specifically to find the key as quickly as possible. We were not asked to engage in skirmishes with fallen stellar entities. We are only here because we've just arrived and this seemed like a logical place to start our search. If we don't find anything in these subterranean regions, we will move on to the surface level of the city."

"But…" Leo was at a loss for words.

"Fear not, friend," said Alnilam kindly. "You will be fine on your own. If it's any consolation, these wolf guards are all useless. They are no match for you."

"They are stupid and disorganized," said Taka. "We were able to find this hiding place without much effort. They never even bothered to go after us."

"Get some sort of disguise, like one of these things"—Betelgeuse pointed at his brown rags—"and you'll easily slip past anyone unnoticed. They never look too closely."

The Hunters rose to go.

"So you're off then?" asked Leo, feeling a silly sense of abandonment.

"The sooner we get this done, the better," said Betelgeuse.

"By the way, how did you manage to get here directly?" asked Leo. "Did you have to go through the secret door too?"

"Leo," said Betelgeuse with a cautiously compassionate tone, "we are not earthed like you."

Of course, thought Leo miserably. Every other star daimon coming down to the city would be able to use the full extent of their powers, including effortlessly beaming themselves directly into the Withdrawn Realm.

The Hunters slipped out of their hiding place one by one. Under their dirty cloaks, further obscured by the blue gloom of the fortress, they looked like ordinary wolf guards on their way to their posts. On his way out, Betelgeuse gave Leo a spare cloak he had salvaged from some Bear Town dust heap. Leo accepted it gratefully, glad to see that it even had the added bonus of being his size.

"Don't worry, Leo," said Betelgeuse, "I'm sure we'll meet again soon."

23

THE NATIVE ELEMENT

After the little friars had left, Dario did another quick round of Upper Town landmarks and then decided it was time to go home. Even with the voices of the monks still ringing in his ears, he was unable to shake off the feeling of being watched. If anything, the sensation had become even more intense. His palms were starting to sweat and his pulse was becoming fluttery. He couldn't stand the suspense anymore. But he didn't want to take the shortcut through the Stone Gate. Having to go through its eerie candlelit interior would have been too much for one night. So he turned the other way, deciding to take the longer, safer path that would take him past Lotrščak Tower and then down to the Square.

As he glanced down, he caught sight of a pair of silver eyes staring at him from behind a rubbish bin farther down the street. His heart clenched inside his chest. But then a ray of moonlight passed over the two silver disks, revealing a small triangular face, and a black cat jumped off the bin, landing softly onto the pavement. It gave Dario a haughty look and then silently padded off into the shadows. Dario exhaled a shaky breath and moved on.

All around him, trees were whispering—ancient trees that stood half-hidden behind the walls of the many secret courtyards of Upper Town—wild trees that would not suffer themselves to be contained by the walls. Their branches reached over the rooftops and crept up the sides of the surrounding buildings, splaying out in every direction.

Ahead of him, a gnarled tree leaned over a semicircular wall that enclosed a mysterious garden, its branches reaching down and spilling out over the street in a leafy cascade. The shadows cast by the sprawling tree were ink black, and Dario took a wide berth as he hurried past them.

"Dario?" said a soft, melodious female voice from somewhere behind him—from the direction of the shadowy tree. "Oh my god, *Dario*?"

Dario stopped. It was not often that his name was uttered in the street by soft-spoken women, or, for that matter, *any* women.

He turned to see a beautiful pale girl dressed in a black velvet gown that brushed against shapely curves and reached all the way to the ground, where it merged with the shadows. She stood bathed in the light of the Moon, its rays glowing around her like a silver aura. Her skin glowed in the spectral light as if the Moon were her native element. Her face was a perfect ivory-colored oval, framed with long silky hair so black that its highlights looked electric blue. Her eyes were a very light, clear blue, the kind of blue that Dario, had he been more poetically inclined, might have compared to sapphires. Around her eyelids there was a fine web of tiny purple veins that made her look as if she were wearing eye shadow. The effect, further accentuated by overlaying shadows cast by her eyelashes, was strangely bewitching.

"Um," he said.

"Don't you remember me?" said the girl. "Cora—we met at the Crepuscular Immolation gig."

A light bulb flashed in Dario's mind. "Of course! Cora. You were at the Ditch with the…"

Dario's brain stammered. He realized that the flash was not a memory at all but more like a short circuit, and that he genuinely couldn't remember ever having seen the girl before, but right now that didn't matter.

"That's right!" said Cora.

They exchanged a few pleasantries and how-have-you-beens like old friends.

"So what brings you here at this hour?" asked Cora.

"Oh, I was just…um, sort of wandering around. I like walking around Upper Town at night. It's very…atmospheric."

"I think so too!" Cora's eyes flashed with an icy spark. "I also like walking by myself at night. That's exactly what I was doing just now."

"You were? What a strange coincidence!"

"Want to show me around a bit?" She walked up to him and took him by the elbow old-fashioned-style. Her eyes were like pools of quicksilver, and she smelled of mountain streams and wildflowers. Dario felt light-headed.

"Um…sure."

They strolled down the dark streets for a while, going around in a circle, until they found themselves at Katherine's Square. At the far end of the square, the white baroque church of St. Katherine, whose shape never failed to remind Dario of a giant bell, looked cold and cryptic in the moonlight, like a huge deformed skull. Cora led them past the square and toward the edge of Grič Hill, where the chalky-white Lotršćak Tower sat overlooking Lower Town below.

They sat down on one of the wooden benches along the tree-lined promenade that spanned the edge of the hill. Cora wanted to know everything about Dario, and he told her as much as his brain could muster. He talked about his childhood in Samobor, the small town he was from, mentioned his failed philosophy studies, and even briefly touched upon his reluctant tenancy at Madam Mina's. Cora watched him raptly the whole time, her mesmeric eyes never leaving his. It occurred to him that he was doing all the talking and that he still didn't know a thing about her, but he didn't mind. He stopped when he realized he had nothing left to say. His life was a depressingly simple, boring one. His entire life story could fit onto the back of a used tram ticket.

But Cora didn't seem to mind.

"Fascinating," she said in a strange voiceless way that sounded almost like a hiss.

"You think?" Dario was genuinely surprised that anyone could find him interesting.

Cora smiled. She looked up at the Moon and languidly reached up with both hands. Her long fingers unfurled one by one like the petals of some exotic flower. She drew her hands together so that they formed a cup. The moonlight poured into it.

Finally she lowered her still-cupped hands. There was now a small pool of crystal clear water inside. Shards of moonlight glittered like jewels against its surface.

"What is that?" asked Dario, feeling numb.

"Moon water," said Cora in a reverent whisper. "Give me your hands."

Dario was not at all sure what this could mean in the present context, which was a context that included, among other things, a person holding a quantity of water that had seemingly materialized out of thin air, so he held out his hands awkwardly, like a five-year-old showing his schoolteacher that he had washed his hands before lunch.

Cora immediately poured out the mysterious Moon water over his hands. The water ran in icy cold trickles down the lines of his palms and then, bizarrely, under his sleeves and up his arms. He could even feel a trickle of water spreading over his chest. For a moment, his wet hands glistened in the moonlight, glowing a sort of translucent white. Then he realized his whole jacket was transparent where the water had soaked it, suddenly looking as if it were made of glass. The contents of his inner pocket, including the strange dragon key, showed like bones on an X-ray image. But the wetness was gone in an instant and then his jacket looked normal again.

"Um...what just happened?" asked Dario in a dreamy, bewildered voice. "What does this mean?"

"It means I want to see you again."

"Oh." Dario's heart started beating really fast inside his chest. "That can, um, be arranged. When?"

Cora smiled, and her eyes were like silver-specked crystals. Dario was too distracted by their brilliance to see the forked tongue, whose double tip flicked out of her mouth for a fraction of a second.

"On the Night of the Witches," she said.

24

LEO CALLS THE ARCHERS

The cloak that Betelgeuse had given him worked well. Leo had been making his way steadily through Bear Town Fortress without anyone noticing that he didn't belong there. He hadn't seen the Hunters at all since that time at the hideout. They were either being remarkably inconspicuous or had perhaps already finished their search of Bear Town.

The fortress itself was a maze of concentric circles. Each ring was separated from the next by an unscalable wall. The hellish outer court, with its captives, peasants and beggars, was only the outside circle. The next inner ring, where he had stumbled upon Betelgeuse and the Hunters, was a downtrodden village populated by the more useful members of the peasantry, who were made to use their meager skills from their past aboveground lives to provide the residents of Bear Town with clothing, primitive furniture, pottery and other nonlethal everyday items. The next circle was a smithy, the one after that a hideous outdoor feeding pen for the wolves and bears, while the next few rings were reserved for the practice of various unsavory blood sports.

It was impossible to tell where exactly he was at any given moment within Bear Town. All he could do was keep going. The one thing that was obvious was that each circle had fewer humans and more animal hybrids than the one before. By the time he reached the eighth inner ring, the human serfs that could occasionally be seen in the outer circles were all but gone. The upside of this was that the gates of the inner circles were mostly unguarded. The wolves and bears clearly didn't expect anyone other than their own kind to move among the innermost levels. Nevertheless, Leo made sure to keep his hood up at all times.

When he reached the next wall, he knew he was close to the central circle of Bear Town because he could see the main tower looming over the top. But nothing could have prepared him for the sight he saw when he reached the gate to the inner circle.

The Black Queen's castle was a colossal edifice whose many towers and side wings sprawled all over the central ring like a small city. Ominous red light poured out of its many narrow slit windows. An entire ring of glowing red power stations surrounded the perimeter.

In the midst of the castle there was a circular courtyard, and in the center of it gaped the black pit of the Queen's Well. Hanging around the outer edge of the circle was the usual assortment of wolves. But they were not alone. Stationed at various posts around the castle were hundreds of nasty-looking bears, all of them armed with heavy weaponry that made the wolves' clubs and bows look like props from a junior archery competition. The bears had massive swords and crossbows that glowed red. A group of bears guarded the well, all of them looking ready to maul, shoot, blow up, or generally kill anyone who came within spitting distance of it.

Leo realized with amusement that bordered on frustration that he had underestimated the Black Queen once again. All this time he had thought he would simply swan into her inner sanctum, fight off a handful of haggard wolves, and perhaps blow up the well for good measure. But he had never expected this. The Hunters may have had a point when they said that the scrawny wolves were no match for Leo. But these bears with their heavy-duty weapons were a completely different ball game. In his crippled earthed state, armed only with his feeble Stick of Sylvicolus, Leo could barely light a barbecue, let alone take out a whole legion of the Black Queen's toughest ursine bodyguards.

Leo's mind worked feverishly. It was as clear as day that he couldn't take on all the bears by himself. If it had been a few or maybe even a few dozen, perhaps he might have had a chance. But hundreds—no. If he tried to take on hundreds of bears armed with catapult-sized crossbows by himself, he would be a sitting duck. He needed backup. The Star Council was out of the question though. They would pester him with questions and in the end might still decide that this was another matter he had to deal with on his own. No, official channels would be of no use in this case. He would have to use unofficial, somewhat illegal ones.

Slipping back into the quieter eighth circle and retreating into a secluded spot behind a utility building, Leo plucked the eight-pointed star off his belt and flung it into the air, careful not to let it rise all the way up to the roof of the mountain where it might be visible to the guards.

He uttered a calling name, and the star began to glow. Even though he was underground, his star beacon was still perfectly usable. Star daimons had acute senses, and they could usually pick up signals even if someone tried to reach them from the farthest corner of the universe. They didn't, of course, have to respond. If a star daimon sensed that a particular signal might be coming from a potentially dangerous location, they could simply ignore it. But the Archers, a band of swift-footed space adventurers with a penchant for risk, were a group Leo could always rely on when he was in a tight corner. They did often expect a return favor, typically one that involved Leo being used as bait to lure some bulbous, flesh-eating space monster, but since he had exhausted all other options, he was adamant not to let such worries bother him for the time being.

Presently a faint purple beam came down through the roof of the mountain and landed before Leo. The figure inside it was barely visible.

"Rukbat?" asked Leo. "Is that you?"

"It's Nunki," said a clear, resonant voice. The purple beam wobbled a bit and then became sharper. Leo could now see the familiar shape of a slight, bird-like star daimon dressed in a purple-and-orange outfit. Nunki, whose eyes were like two quickly shifting sparks, had the best aim of all the Archers.

"Rukbat and the others are neck-deep in barnacles. So am I, actually, but I thought I could use a break, at least a halfway one." Nunki had the unique ability to be in several different places at the same time.

"Is it that bad?"

"There's more of them than usual—you should see the size of those barnacle barricades! But it's nothing we can't handle." He darted a swift silver glance around him. "Leo, what in Jupiter's Red Spot is this place? It feels like being inside a crater on Desolation Planet's darkest moon."

"That is actually not very far from the truth."

"What's going on?"

"Black Queen business."

"Again?"

"Yes, again. Listen, Nunki, I don't have much time to explain, but I really need the Archers' help. Can you guys spare a few minutes of your time whenever there's a lull on the barnacle front?"

"What do you need?"

"See all those big bears with crossbows?" Leo pointed with a slightly unsteady finger. "When I try to stop the Black Queen's evil master plan, they will all start shooting at me at the same time. And all I've got is this stick."

"It looks as if you're a bit outnumbered."

"I knew you'd understand."

"I wouldn't mind giving you a hand here, Leo. And it would be a welcome change from the barnacles."

Leo allowed himself a hopeful smile. "So is that a yes?"

"I'll ask Rukbat, but I can't make any promises. The way it's going, there won't be a lull anytime soon."

"Please, Nunki, you're my only hope."

"I'll see what I can do. But it might be a while before we're able to come to the rescue."

"Thank you, Nunki."

"Hang on in there, Leo," said Nunki as he started fading. "And just remember, whatever happens, it can't be as bad as decompressing a quasar."

The purple beam vanished. Leo retrieved his star and took a step back, stopping when he bumped into something big and solid. A strong, heavy paw landed on his shoulder, clutching with a painful grip. Leo slowly turned to see a huge bear in a leather tunic standing behind him. A massive rib helmet was mounted on the bear's head, and through its gaps, Leo could see a snarling mouth full of teeth.

25

THE THING ITSELF

The one positive result of Stella's newfound sense of purpose was that Professor Radovan's classes no longer felt so daunting. There was no longer any nauseating sense of anticipation before the start of each class. In fact, as Stella sat at her desk, she was so absorbed in her thoughts about the Black Queen and everything the little goldsmith had told her that she didn't even notice when Professor Radovan called her name.

She only realized there was something going on when she felt something light strike her arm. It was a tiny crumpled piece of paper, and it had come from the direction of Tin's desk. She turned and saw Tin staring at her with a panicked expression, motioning toward the teacher's desk with his eyes. Stella looked up to see Professor Radovan glaring at her with eyes like the butt ends of two poisoned daggers.

"I have called your name twice, Feglar," said the teacher with a low, dangerous voice, "and I am not going to call it again."

Stella picked up her notebook and sprang out of her seat. She had barely made it all the way to the teacher's desk when Professor Radovan's meaty arm shot out like a cobra and snatched the notebook out of her hands. The teacher flipped through the notebook impatiently, giving each page a noisy slap and accentuating each interval with a rasping porcine grunt. When she finally reached Stella's most recent homework assignment, it was as if for a few weighted seconds all sounds faded out.

"What is the meaning of this, Plegar?" said Professor Radovan eventually, her voice flat and icy.

Stella blinked. The notebook lying open on the teacher's desk looked light-years away, like something on the other end of a wormhole.

"Are you dumb, Felgar?" Professor Radovan was now practically snarling. "Answer me!" The last word was accompanied by a loud bang as the teacher's huge fist hit the desktop. The fist was the size and shape of a pork joint. Stella's notebook jittered nervously with the force of the impact. Somewhere in the back row, a pen rolled off someone's desk and tumbled onto the floor with a clattering crescendo. This seemed to happen a lot.

Straining to see through what felt like vast stretches of space that separated her from the notebook, Stella finally noticed that the page where her latest home-work should have been was entirely covered in jagged spidery drawings of things that did indeed resemble spiders, but in a vague, associative way, the way a stick figure vaguely resembles a man. These were quick, messy sketches full of ugly, urgent strokes made with a black pen.

How interesting, thought Stella. She had no recollection of making those drawings. She was sure she didn't do anything of the sort the previous night, although she couldn't quite remember what she did do.

Stella made a drawn-out nonverbal sound that was halfway between an *a* and a vocalic *r*.

"You will get a one for this," growled Professor Radovan. One was the low-est available grade, the fail grade (the highest being five), and a sort of kiss of death for a pupil's grade point average. To counterbalance its toxic effect, the pu-pil with a one would have to get at least two more fives by the end of the term. And the probability of Stella getting two fives from Professor Radovan was as high as the likelihood of Professor Radovan hosting an Emotional Intelligence in Educational Environments workshop.

Professor Radovan snatched a special red pen that she used specifically for entering bad grades and scrawled a ferocious red *1* on a page in Stella's part of the register. The figure looked like a stake dripping with blood.

"Get out of my sight," growled the teacher.

Stella retrieved her notebook from where it lay on the teacher's desk with the hesitation of Flash Gordon sticking his hand into the Wood Beast's stump at the urging of Prince Barin and then went back to her seat. Tin gave her a sym-pathetic look.

Professor Radovan watched Stella's retreat with her beady evil eyes and then, satisfied that Stella had been adequately subdued, grunted contentedly and began trawling through the register book once again like a sow nosing for truffles.

❦

As Stella tied her shoelaces later that same day, she was certain that the worst thing that could have happened that day had already happened. But then Tin returned from the boys' toilets with a dazed look on his face.

"Stella, I think you should see this," he said. "You too," he said to Ida and Rea.

He led them to the boys' toilets side of the corridor where a new poster had just been placed on the wall.

It was a huge thing, the size of a beach towel, which would have been an unusual sight in itself in the normally posterless primary school corridor even if it hadn't been for the stark black background and the glaring title that said *The Night of the Witches* in bold red font. There was more text underneath, in smaller white letters.

Stella strolled up to the poster, taking in all the details:

THE NIGHT OF THE WITCHES

WHAT?—The first EVER official Night of the Witches party

WHERE?—The school auditorium, top floor

WHEN?—October 31, 7 p.m. onward

WHO?—East Central Primary School students

WHY?—Just because

Underneath all this, there was a white-against-black silhouette drawing that showed the school building as a haunted house with broken windows, crumbling walls, a crooked roof and tiny bat shapes fluttering around it. Stella stared at the whole thing with wide-eyed wonder.

"This is it," she finally said. "The thing itself."

"Yup," said Tin.

PART THREE

THE
NIGHT
OF THE
WITCHES

26

AN APPALLING WASTE OF TIME AND EFFORT

When the idea for a proper Night of the Witches celebration for primary school pupils was first brought up at a staff meeting in early September, some East Central Primary School teachers had strongly opposed the motion. For example, Professor Beli, the physics teacher, countered the initiative on moral grounds, proclaiming the whole idea of that particular holiday to be nothing more than a consumerist confection, whereas Professor Palčić, the school secretary, felt that the idea neither served a meaningful purpose nor contained educational value. Needless to say, Professor Radovan was quick to take the opposition's side, becoming within a very short span of time the initiative's most vocal critic. The pro-event faction, on the other hand, counted among its ranks practically all of the younger teachers, who mystified the old guard with such baffling concepts as "a creative outlet" and "social media followers."

Professor Mira Novak was not one of the teachers who strongly opposed the Night of the Witches event, but this was only because she was too indifferent to strongly oppose anything. Her indifference extended to people, things, ideas, school events and life in general. She did, however, deign to invest enough time and energy into deciding that the whole Night of the Witches thing was pointless, as well as being an appalling waste of time and effort.

As it were, the rest of the teachers had not been as willing to practice the philosophy of nonattachment as Professor Novak, and so what had started as a peaceful meeting had soon erupted into a fierce verbal battle such as had never been seen in that particular teachers' lounge before. Harsh words were exchanged, including "nonsense," "snotface" and "damn." Every attempt at reaching an agreement failed. In the end, the principal made an executive decision in favor of the event, citing such things as "public image," "parental pressure" and "keeping up with the times" as his main arguments. The older teachers had been, according to eyewitness accounts, "infuriated and appalled," and none more so than Professor Radovan. Had her various cholesterol-related conditions been less debilitating, she would have taken up arms and organized a mutiny right there and then. In the end, however, not even her indignation could sway the pendulum to the anti-event side. The principal's word was final—the event was a go.

As she strutted out of the teachers' lounge at around seven p.m., just as the Night of the Witches event was about to begin, Professor Novak rolled her eyes at the sight of the various seasonal drawings, figurines, banners and other disposable rubbish that the pupils had bothered to put up during the short interval between her last lesson and the last slow latte she had had with the school speech therapist in the lounge before the latter had gone home for the night.

"What is that?" she asked a hapless fourth grader who was in the process of pinning a cardboard cutout of a witch onto one of the large corkboards in the corridor.

"J-Just some things we made in class, Madam Teacher," stammered the fourth grader, his eyes looking huge behind thick glasses.

"How long did it take you to make that?"

"Oh, about two days." The kid sniffed wetly.

Professor Novak rolled her eyes and went on her way.

The whole ground floor was a display of wasted labor. Drawings of witches, cauldrons, haunted castles, cartoon skeletons and the like covered the wall panels. And sitting on the cupboard shelves usually reserved for sports trophies and school photographs, there was now a row of figurines made of corncobs, chestnuts, apples and other seasonal produce.

The sight of those strange effigies sent a slight ripple of discomfort down the thick curtain of Professor Novak's listlessness. There was something pagan and altogether inappropriate about those things. They did not belong in a school. But she quickly dismissed these thoughts, deeming them unworthy of any further applications of her cognitive functions.

Tinny music mixed with the chatter of schoolchildren resonated through the building as Professor Novak headed up the main staircase. With exaggerated effort, she climbed all the way up to the top floor, then turned left and entered the auditorium.

It was an unsightly mess. All the seats had been cleared away to provide space for the many mingling, dancing and chatting pupils dressed in a variety of bizarre handmade costumes, including someone wearing what looked like a shower curtain with an actual showerhead sticking up above his head.

"And what are you supposed to be?" asked Professor Novak sternly.

"A shower," said the child with a bemused expression.

"Whatever, forget I asked," said Professor Novak and then sighed the deep, shaky sigh of the long-suffering. How was she supposed to survive the next few hours?

The stage had been decorated with banners and papier-mâché figures. A long table stacked with food and soft drinks had been placed by the wall. This was, Professor Novak was pleased to note, the area where a large majority of the teachers had congregated. The fat Professor Anić seemed to be particularly at home near that part of the table where all the apple pies, chestnut cakes, Jelačić slices, walnut roulades, Sacher tortes and other baked goods provided by the parents were stacked on large trays borrowed from the cafeteria.

Professor Novak made a beeline for the table, her eyes set firmly on a particularly scrumptious-looking slice of sour cherry strudel. She might manage to make it through the night after all.

Stella hadn't bothered dressing up for the Night of the Witches. She knew she wouldn't be attending the main event. The only prop she took with her was the silver bottle.

As she left the house at five minutes to seven, a number seventeen was waiting at the tram stop outside, its single round headlight casting a fan of white light through the night. She crossed the tracks in front of it, the headlight watching her silently. Tiny motes floated around in the glow of the light. As she headed down the main road under the tall chestnut trees, the tram left the stop and soon caught up with Stella. It rolled slowly down the tracks for a few seconds, its front carriage level with Stella's side, as if strolling along with her. Then it gained speed and was soon gone, disappearing silently into the night.

❧

As he got ready to go out for the Night of the Witches, Tin did his best not to look at the full-length hall mirror for fear of seeing the ridiculous reflection therein. He found it hard to look away though, the way people passing by the site of a car crash are said to find it hard to look away. He hadn't been sure whether he was supposed to dress up at all or not, but to be on the safe side, he had decided to make at least some effort at it. So he was going dressed as a car mechanic—for no other reason than that there were still things from his dad's car mechanic days lying around the house that his dad didn't mind Tin using. His outfit consisted of a checkered shirt, dark-blue overalls and black boots. A single size nine spanner stuck out of one of the baggy pockets of his overalls as a kind of prop. A tattered fake moustache was stuck to his upper lip. It wasn't a dignified sight.

His dad was currently parked at his favorite place, in front of the TV, six cans of beer at his side, all set for a big football match taking place in the stadium a few blocks away. A heady aural stream of studio forecasts, prematch stadium chanting and beer commercials poured out from the living room.

Tin looked at the gray plastic watch on his left hand. Five to seven. He had to get going. He was supposed to meet Stella at seven p.m. outside the school's playground-side entrance. The plan was to keep watch over the cellar door and ambush the Black Queen's spider when it attempted to come out. Hopefully, Rudi the janitor would be too distracted by the noise coming from the auditorium to notice the two of them. Meanwhile, Rea and Ida would be in the auditorium to keep an eye on things.

Having ascertained that he looked as stupid as he felt, Tin shouted a quick goodbye in the direction of the TV room and stepped outside, the sounds of ecstatic stadium chanting accompanying his exit until he closed the door.

It took him a moment to realize that, even with the door closed behind him, he could still hear the chanting—or at least a certain kind of it. It was a continuous simian hooting devoid of any meaning or intelligence. When he stepped out into the street, he could see the source of the noise.

Farther down the street, four football hooligans monkeyed about by a metal bin they had set on fire. Two of them he recognized as Alen and Borna, but the other two idiots were unknown to him. They looked like older idiots, perhaps in their twenties. They must have randomly stumbled into the street on their way to the stadium. Such things did occasionally happen. Maksimir Stadium was nearby—halfway between their street and the zoo, although Tin had always thought that it would have been much more fitting for the stadium to be located *inside* the zoo.

One of the older idiots was beefy and had a face like a stunned ox. The other one was skinny and had a face like a constipated goat. Both wore jeans and denim jackets, and there were blue scarves tied around their necks. They were kicking the smoldering bin while trying to produce what sounded like parts of a football anthem in between bursts of nonverbal hooting. Even Alen and Borna looked uncomfortable in the presence of idiots of such caliber, although they were doing their best not to let it show.

Out of all those details, the one that was of the highest priority to Tin was the fact that the hooligans had established their temporary cheering and bin-kicking territory at the exact spot he had to pass in order to get to school. Tin had no choice other than to try to slip quietly by, hoping he would not be noticed.

No sooner had he started thinking he would get away unobserved than the kicking and hooting suddenly stopped. He turned his head to see Stunned Ox and Constipated Goat staring at him in mock surprise.

"Look at that!" yelled Stunned Ox. Constipated Goat snickered.

"What are you?" asked Stunned Ox. "A gigolo?"

Beside him, Constipated Goat exploded in a high-pitched burst of hysterical laughter.

Borna and Alen laughed nervously. While trying to come up with an answer, Tin had time to notice that Borna was for once standing in a way that was not astride his bike. There was no bike in sight.

Tin considered his options. When faced with this type of idiot, there was no right answer. The best choice was to start running right away. It would take him less than two minutes to run to the school.

But before Tin could make a decision, Stunned Ox sauntered cockily away from the bin and planted himself in front of Tin, blocking his way. He was now so close that Tin could see a lump of dried snot hanging out of his left nostril.

"I asked you a question," said Stunned Ox, and this time there was a look of obstinate moronic menace on his bovine face.

"I'm a car mechanic," said Tin.

Constipated Goat laughed again. "Come on, let the kid go," he said in a high-strung voice.

Stunned Ox was still staring at Tin. "Are you trying to be funny?" he said after a menacing pause. His idiotic eyes narrowed into evil slits. A vein popped out on his thick neck. His cretinous mouth fell half-open, exposing a set of teeth as ugly as they were incomplete—at least three of them were missing, and that was just the lower jaw.

You loser, thought Tin. It was only after the face of Stunned Ox became a livid mask of murderous hate that he realized he had said it aloud.

"I'm going to fucking kill you," mumbled Stunned Ox in a low, homicidal voice.

This time, Tin's unconscious mind made an executive decision, and he found himself bolting in the opposite direction. Running to the school was no longer an option. It was time to come up with plan B. Running back home was out of the question—his house was too far. By the time he reached it, Stunned Ox would have caught up with him, despite the former's obvious intoxication and his heavyset, unathletic bulk. Or even worse, if he made it to the house, the hooligans could smash the windows or set the house on fire as they had done to one of those bins, and he didn't want his mom to get upset when she got home from work. His only chance was to try to lose the hooligans in one of the many side alleys, all of which he was familiar with by virtue of having lived in the same neighborhood his whole life. This gave him a tactical advantage over Stunned Ox, who was not a local.

From behind him, there came a barrage of explicit curses followed by the sound of a bin being knocked over, but Tin had no idea what this indicated in terms of the hooligans' proximity to himself. He didn't dare look behind him though.

To his left, a narrow side alley led to an abandoned building site that had existed ever since he could remember in a state of perpetual unfinishedness. The alley, which was a dead end, had no name that he knew of, but in his mind he always referred to it as Incomplete Street. It was here that Tin decided to seek refuge.

He could no longer hear what was going on behind him. All he could hear was his heart thudding in his ears.

Tin's eyes darted over the planes and corners of the site desperately. The place hadn't changed since the last time he had been there. It was still nothing more than a patch of uneven ground, in the midst of which stood the skeleton of a two-story building. In the front yard, a rusty cement mixer lay toppled over on a pile of grimy bricks. Farther back, in a dark, easily overlooked corner, a blue chemical toilet leaned against a half-finished wall at an odd angle. Of course! This would be the perfect place to hide.

Quickly, Tin scrambled into the blue box and shut the door silently, leaving open a thin crack so that he could see outside. There was no one out there. He sighed with relief. Then he nearly gagged as the chemical stench of his hiding place reached his lungs.

27

THE BLACK TRAM

"What did you think?"

Dario and Cora ambled through the woods surrounding the arty cinema near the city center where they had attended a Night of the Witches special. The program had been running all day, but they had only turned up for the last movie, which had been the most recent cut of *The Exorcist*.

If there had been any capacity for coherent thought left in Dario, he might have said something to the effect that, in his view, the new cut was the same as the old one apart from the scene where the girl walks down the stairs on all fours headfirst, which was indeed creepy in a way that projectile-vomiting peas never had been, but that otherwise he didn't see much point in the new cut's existence. Instead, he only let out a dreamy hum.

Since the night he had first met Cora in Upper Town, Dario's priorities had experienced a shift. It wasn't an earth-shattering, seismic shift—rather, it was more like the slow oozing of honey down a silver spoon. He had barely noticed the change himself, but this was only because, as of late, he barely noticed anything—anything, that is, apart from Cora's moonlit sapphire eyes. Their image had carved itself into his mind with such intensity that during the endlessly long days leading up to All Hallows' Eve, it had felt as if it was all he could see.

He still remembered that there was something going on with the Black Queen, but he was no longer quite sure what. And he remembered that Leo had gone off somewhere, but he had no idea where to or why. He still carried in his pocket Leo's banishing book and the strange key Leo's mysterious friend had given him, but this was mainly out of some vaguely understood sense of duty. In any case, he no longer felt any sense of urgency. How could he, when Cora's voice was so soothing?

"Can you feel the energy of this place?" she said.

They had been walking slowly in order to let the other cinema-goers stream past them. Once most of them had gone, Cora had stopped by a particularly dark copse of mossy old trees.

Dario was mesmerized by the way the deep shadows seemed to blend seamlessly with the lines of Cora's opaque black dress and the way her face as well as the exposed pale skin above her neckline seemed to glow all the time. It took him a while to realize she had asked him a question.

"Um..." His brain practically creaked with exertion as it tried to catch up. "Well, it is a bit spooky."

"They used to burn witches at this exact spot." Cora sighed and smiled dreamily, as if reliving a fond memory.

"Really?" Dario blinked sleepily. "Well, that explains the spookiness."

"I know a place that's even spookier."

Dario gazed into her iridescent eyes. Her eyebrows were arched mischievously. "You do?" His tongue felt thick. "What place might that be?"

"Do you want to see it?" Cora's eyes were huge.

"Uh...sure."

Cora looked pleased. "I can take you there," she said mysteriously.

Dario said, in as many words as he could muster, that he was all for it.

"We'll need to take the tram though," she added in a mock-ominous way.

"That's all right—I have a ticket," said Dario automatically and, despite his mental haze, immediately felt like an idiot.

But Cora only smiled.

She led him to the Ilica Street exit and across the road to the Frankopan Street tram stop. They got on a cosily warm number fourteen. The tram took a right turn into Ilica, stopped at the Square, let out a group of loudly gossiping middle-aged women who seemed to have only the most disparaging things to say about someone called Jasna, and then headed north. As the tram went past the familiar sight of the Fishpond Street stop, Dario's mind momentarily stirred into action, producing a paranoid mental image in which the spooky thing that Cora wanted to show him turned out to be Madam Mina.

In his vision, Cora took him to the very flat he shared with Madam Mina, where, within seconds of going through the front door, they were greeted by the sight of his landlady's squinting, grinning head popping out of the piles of clutter like a hellish jack-in-the-box and screaming "Surprise!" in a manic voice. What could be spookier than that? It was an absurd thought, but he nevertheless felt almost light-headed with relief as the tram sped past his stop.

Then Cora said something mellow and meaningless in her melodious voice, leaning against him where they stood at the back of the tram, and Dario could no longer remember the thought that had troubled him only moments before.

The territory that lay beyond Fishpond was mostly unknown to him. Dario had rarely had the need to go farther north on the number fourteen route. He knew there was a historic cemetery up there somewhere and, even farther north, Bear Mountain, but he had never visited either.

When they disembarked a few stops later, Dario found himself in an unremarkable street with two tram tracks running down the middle and a three-lane highway on either side. A row of tall trees—fir, beech and chestnut—lined the street, forming an arboreal path that led all the way up to the mountain, whose black silhouette was visible in the distance against the background of moonlit clouds. The traffic was scarce. It was quiet and moody, but hardly spooky.

"Where are we?" asked Dario as he followed Cora to the other side of the road.

"The Star of Gubec."

"Um…does the Star of Gubec have anything to do with Gubec?" mumbled Dario. Despite being considered by some to be an honorary *purger*—that is to say, a native of Zagreb, i.e., someone who should know these things—Dario didn't. His mind quickly went over the information he was familiar with.

Matija Gubec was the leader of a peasants' revolt that took place in the rural areas around the city sometime in the sixteenth century. Himself a former serf, Gubec wanted to liberate the peasants from the terror of parasitical landowners. He was rewarded for his efforts by being captured and taken to Zagreb, where he was publicly tortured and quartered in the overly exhibitionist manner so dear to feudal overlords.

"Why, yes," said Cora. "This is where he died." They were walking on the right-hand side of the main road, which was now starting to curve to the right.

"I thought he was executed at St. Mark's Square."

Instead of replying, she gave him another one of her mysterious smiles. She stopped at the foot of a small hill where a leafy road branched off the main street on the right. She had an open, attentive expression, as if listening out for something. Then she moved on, leading Dario farther up the road.

It was pleasant, apart from the eerie stillness. The soft crunching of fallen leaves under the soles of their boots was the only sound that disturbed the quiet. The night kept getting chillier, and soon a faint trickle of white mist appeared on the road, quickly turning into a thick opaque carpet that completely covered the ground. And it kept getting thicker. The fog seemed to be pouring out from the darkness behind the trees that stood on either side of the road.

"Uh…why are we here?" asked Dario, suddenly uneasy.

But Cora ignored him. She was looking at something farther ahead. Dario followed her gaze and was startled to see a cluster of many points of warm golden light glowing through the carpet of mist where the pavement gave way to the trees. As they approached the lights, Dario could see that these were candles.

"This is what I wanted to show you." Cora's voice was a whisper.

"What is this?" Dario whispered back.

"A terrible tram crash happened here on this day, All Hallows' Eve, many years ago." Cora's voice had dropped an octave, and Dario's spine was awash with chills.

"It was a Sunday morning, and a tram was going down this road, on its way back from Mirogoj Cemetery.

"At first, things were calm and uneventful. But then something happened. The tram started going very fast, and it couldn't stop. It just kept on going faster and faster. The driver tried to slow down, but no matter how hard he tried, the tram just kept on going. It went faster and faster the farther it went down the hill. When it reached the bottom of the road, it jumped out of the tracks and smashed into these trees. It crashed so hard that it pulled the trees out of their roots. Many people died."

Cora made a portentous pause. "The tram was a number thirteen."

There was a long, uncanny silence as Dario soaked up all the information.

"But…but wait a minute," he said eventually. "There are no tram tracks on this road."

"There used to be," she said.

Dario gulped.

"They say," she continued, "that it was the most beautiful tram route in the entire city. But after the crash, people started avoiding it. They feared that something bad might happen again. And so the Mirogoj route was shut down. Soon the tracks became a ghost road, until they were finally dismantled for good."

Dario stared at the flickering candles, suddenly feeling unbearably sad. He blinked a few times, hard, and looked up at Cora. She stood as tall and still as a black obelisk rising out of a white pool. Thin rivulets of fog flowed around her ankles like a phantom river. She continued with her narrative, the words flowing past her lips like the mist streaming on the ground.

"They say that sometimes at night, when it's very quiet"—Cora was now standing very close to him, and her eyes were like iridescent moonstones—"if you listen carefully, you can still hear the echo of the crash."

She fell silent. All around them there was only deathly silence. Even the traffic on the main road was now out of earshot. A shudder ran down Dario's spine. He wanted to say something but found himself unable to speak. Cora's bright eyes were captivating and terrible at the same time. Mesmerized, he took a step to close the short gap between them, and then another, and another, and he should have closed the distance by now, but no matter how many steps he took, the gap remained the same. It was as if underneath the pool of mist, there was no ground at all.

Cora suddenly looked up into empty space, as if listening.

"Can you hear it?" she whispered.

Dario gave up on his attempt at getting closer. "W-What?" he managed to say. Then a loud snap nearly made him jump. But it was only his own foot crunching a stray chestnut.

Cora still listened intently. "It's coming," she said.

The chill that had run down Dario's spine was now spreading though his extremities. He tried to tell himself that he was merely under the spell of Cora's fanciful yarn, making a mental note to tell her that she should try doing one of those ghost tour things that tourists everywhere seemed to love. He was going to tell her that first thing, as soon as they extracted themselves from the clutches of the macabre atmosphere of the place.

All of a sudden, he thought he could hear a faint grinding noise, like the sound of metal wheels making a turn in the tracks. It was probably one of the trams going past the Star of Gubec stop on the main road. Except there were no turns there—or at least there weren't anymore.

He glanced down toward the main road nevertheless and nearly cried out. There couldn't have possibly been a tram there, since there were no tracks on Mirogoj Road. And yet, there it was.

A spectral black tram had just turned into Mirogoj Road at the foot of the hill from Ksaver Road. It glided toward them over the carpet of white mist ever so slowly on unseen tracks that no longer existed.

It was one of the boxy early-twentieth-century trams, even older and boxier than the old number seventeen stock. Like the seventeen, it had a single round headlight, but unlike the seventeen, its angular main body was mounted on a massive ungainly pedestal of complicated machinery. The box containing the wheel mechanism was flanked on each side by two metal fenders, while a third fender jutted out like a snowplow's blade at the front. A thin, spidery pantograph projected from the roof like a giant insect's antenna, wobbling slightly as the tram moved, but there was no electrical cable to be seen above it.

The inside of the tram looked empty. The trees in the background were visible within its skeletal window frames. Apart from that, the apparition, for that was what it had to be, was completely black. But it was not an ordinary blackness of black paint. Its blackness was something more elemental. It was a complete absence of light. Neither streetlight nor moonlight was reflected off its surface. There were only two points of light on the spectral tram, both of them looking entirely unnatural. One was the single round headlight, which cast a faint beam of ghostly silver-white light onto the mist-covered street. The lamp's glow, however, was not electric. Instead, it seemed to be made of the same ephemeral substance as moonlight. The other point of light was a shimmering silver plate in the top left corner of the windshield. On it, a black "13" stood out clearly.

Dario made a tiny choked sound at the back of his throat. He glanced at Cora, who stood next to him as still as a statue. She was staring at the tram with a strange magnetic gaze. The black tram was now only a few yards from them. It made no sound as it sailed across the sea of white mist. Its towering black bulk looked heavy and weightless at the same time.

When it reached them, the tram stopped and waited silently in the moonlight while tendrils of pale mist rolled around it like waves. Its three doors were open, but then again, they always were. It was one of those old models designed before health and safety existed as a concept, and its doors did not have shutters. The open doors gaped at them invitingly.

Inside the carriage, a row of light bulbs on the ceiling suddenly flickered on with a phantom silver light. It filled the interior with an icy, insubstantial aura that reminded Dario of the glow of a black-and-white television set playing one of the old episodes of *The Twilight Zone*. Despite this variety of details, or perhaps because of it, Dario was now convinced that he was having a dream. He would undoubtedly wake up anytime now to the sounds of Madam Mina's typewriter.

He nearly jumped when Cora clutched his wrist. "Let's get on," she said and tugged. Before he even had a chance to protest, he found himself walking up the steep, narrow steps of the tram's driver-side door.

Cora led him to the wooden seats, and they sat down side by side in the front row. For a dream phantasm, the tram had a startlingly vivid level of solidity. Dario had actually managed to bump his leg against the edge of his seat before plonking onto it inelegantly.

There was a faint chime, and then the tram was moving again, gliding smoothly up Mirogoj Road. There was no side-to-side rocking nor any other tugging or swaying motions that normally accompanied an ordinary tram ride. The tram made its way up the hill effortlessly, without any interference of physical forces, as though it were made of air.

A flash of lucidity reminded Dario that now was probably a good time to ask Cora why she had dragged them into this improbable vehicle and what exactly was going on, but then he remembered that this was a dream and that dreams had their own logic. If a ghostly tram appeared to a person in a dream, then of course the person would get on board. That was the whole point. The best thing to do now, he decided, was to be on the lookout for symbols. Freudian, Jungian, Lacanian and other kinds of symbols. There were bound to be at least some of them.

But perhaps his expectations were too high, because the landscape he saw outside was the continuation of the same old Mirogoj Road. There were no symbols representing various aspects of consciousness, only more trees. Trees lined the road on either side—tall pointy pines, gnarled old chestnuts, slim sinuous saplings, sturdy leafy beeches. The barks of the trees reflected the silver moonlight, the wavy branches casting long dark shadows on the pavement. Every once in a while, he would catch a fleeting glimpse of a building or two hidden behind the trees, but those were always semi-obscured by the shadowy branches.

Dario blinked and looked down at his lap. He was surprised to see that Cora was still holding his hand. That was strange. Her hand must have been as light as air. Maybe the tram had that kind of effect on all of its contents.

The trees became thicker the farther up the tram went. Where there had previously been a varied but neat line of trees, there were now thick black patches of them that might have been parts of a real forest. The road became more sinuous, the turns wider. But the tram traversed the new terrain as effortlessly as before.

After a while, they reached the high, ivy-covered wall of Mirogoj Cemetery. The tram went past its many cupolas and arcades, and then moved on, going farther and farther up the mysterious road toward the slopes of the mountain.

This was no longer a ghost of the Mirogoj Road tram tracks. There had never been any tracks beyond this point.

Suddenly Dario felt a lurching sensation in his stomach, the kind that sometimes happens when you're in a lift that goes up too fast. He looked out of the window and saw only the tops of trees. The tram had soared into the air and was now gliding above the forest that began at the foot of the mountain.

The tram went higher and higher, getting ever closer to the mountain. It seemed to be heading toward one of its upper peaks—a familiar sight for tourists and day-trippers, since the ruins of Bear Town Fortress sprawled all over it.

This indeed turned out to be their destination.

The airborne number thirteen started descending once they were in sight of the tree-lined path that led up to the outer wall of the fortress. It landed softly at the foot of the path, directly in front of the crumbling ruins of the main entrance into Bear Town.

"This is the last stop," said Cora, sounding like an ETC conductor announcing the terminus of a standard route.

They stepped outside, and the tram immediately soared up once again. It sailed away through the air with a dreamlike slowness, its black silhouette gliding in front of the big yellow full Moon, and then disappeared into the night sky.

"I had no idea trams went all the way up to here," said Dario numbly.

Cora gave him an elusive smile. Then she led him into the abandoned ruins of Bear Town Fortress.

28

THE STAR WARRIORS

A red blaze shot through the vaulted ceiling above the Underworld Bear Town Fortress. Five star daimons materialized in an inner-circle clearing. Each was tall, brawny and outfitted in a combination of red tunic and overelaborate iron armor. They were the Star Warriors. The tallest and brawniest of them all, Antares, had a polished helmet with an enormous red plume on it.

"Ha ha ha!" laughed Antares triumphantly. "What did I tell you? The place really does exist, just as described."

"Are you sure this is the right place?" asked Lesath, the Star Warrior standing directly to his right.

"Of course it is! How many secret underground fortresses can there be on this petrified centaur testicle of a planet?"

"But how do you know he is underground?"

"Because Algol said so. He specifically said we would find him *under* the city, not *in* the city. And it's just as well. In this dump, he'll be like a barnacle in a barrel."

"Do you still mean to kill him, boss?" asked the star daimon on the left, whose name was Shargaz.

"No," said Antares ominously. "Death would mean nothing to that sun-blasting bastard, not even in his current state. No, I propose to do something much worse."

"What, Antares?" asked Shargaz, his eyes glowing with evil eagerness. "What will you do?"

"I will shave off his hair."

The others stared at him in stunned silence.

"You wouldn't do that, would you, boss?" said Lesath eventually, his tone hushed.

"I would. And I will."

"But what will you use for shaving?" asked another one of the star daimons, Sharur, in a thick, idiotic voice.

"I don't know. I haven't thought of that. I guess I'll…I'll just have to use my sword."

"But you can't get a clean stroke with a sword," said a brooding Star Warrior called Akrab.

"The point isn't to give him a new hairstyle," said Antares with indignant patience. "The point is to *cut off his hair.*"

"Oh."

"Where is he, by the way?" asked Lesath.

Antares swiveled his plumed head, taking in the sight of many ragtag wolf soldiers, some of whom had noticed the arrival of the warriors with fearful curiosity, as if unsure whether to shoot at the unexpected arrivals or offer them a drink.

"No idea."

29

THE CHARGE OF THE GREAT WEREPIG

The school loomed over her like the hull of an enormous tanker in a cutting yard. The full Moon hung in the night sky halfway between the peaks of the school's two towers, casting a net of unearthly silver light over the roof's shingles. The glowing yellow rectangles that were the top-floor windows were the only other points of light. Tinny music drifted through the chilly autumn breeze from the direction of the top-floor auditorium. The noise was accompanied by a steady bounce-bounce-whoosh-bounce sound of a middle-aged man shooting baskets under the single electric light of the basketball court.

The man, who wore a blue tracksuit with a big figure eight on his back and whose head had a greasy bald spot that looked like a tonsure, was shooting baskets in the most monotonous, desultory way imaginable. The game clearly bored him out of his wits, and yet he kept on shooting basket after basket nevertheless, always in the same way—first a brief preparatory period of ball-bouncing, followed by a two-second silence as he launched the ball, sending it gliding through the air in a perfect parabola. And then, either an elegant whoosh as the ball slipped through the hoop or a thump if the ball hit the wooden frame instead. Whatever the outcome, the man would pick up the ball indifferently each time, and then the whole process would begin anew. It was as if he secretly hoped this activity would bring him some sort of illumination if only he persisted with the boring, repetitive drudgery of it long enough.

Tin, however, was nowhere in sight. It was very uncharacteristic of him to be late, and Stella briefly considered the possibility that the middle-aged basket-

ball player might in fact be Tin in disguise before quickly dismissing the idea as
absurd. She didn't know what kind of costume Tin had chosen to wear, but whatever it was, it couldn't have been that convincing.

There was a more probable explanation—Tin might have already gone inside. That had to be it. He was probably already keeping watch outside the Forbidden Cellar, waiting for her to turn up. And so Stella swung open the heavy
school door and went inside.

An enthusiastic electric guitar solo mixed with the chatter of many voices
resonated through the school building in time with her steps, but as soon as the
door banged closed behind her, the music stopped and all the lights went out.

She found herself standing alone in the dark ground-floor corridor of a
building that suddenly felt strangely deserted. The sudden silence wasn't that of
a brief pause between two songs. This was something much eerier. The voices of
the pupils were gone too, as was the sound of the bald man shooting baskets.
Stella was struck by the certainty that she was alone in the school building. She
didn't know how this was possible, but she knew it to be true.

The realization made her rigid with dread. For a moment, she stood motionless in the middle of the corridor like some strange upright vacuum cleaner
that had been left behind by the cleaner. The next instant, she recovered with a
start and immediately ran back to the door. She clutched the ice-cold metal handle, but it wouldn't give. There had been no one there, either inside the school
or out, to lock the door during the few seconds since her arrival, but that didn't
change the fact that it was now locked. She shook the bulky handle, but the massive door wouldn't budge. After a while, she gave up, turning around to face the
gaping darkness of the school building once again.

Once her eyes had adjusted to the gloom, she could see that far from being
pitch-dark, the school corridor was radiant with the bright light of the Moon
that poured in through the windows, making the polished stone floor glow like
a river of silver.

In the uncanny moonlit schoolscape around her, not a shadow stirred. But
at the same time, it was as if every single thing, both seen and unseen, moved.
Strange currents whirled around her, brushing against her legs and playing with
her hair, as if the river of moonlight were a real river and she a tiny creature immersed in it. The very air felt electric and alive.

Straight ahead of her, the main stairwell glowed in the moonlight like the stage stairs in some music video. There was nothing else to do but go up. Going back the way she had entered was no longer an option.

Stella slowly climbed the stairs until she reached the familiar first floor of the East Central Primary School. Through the big windows that lined the corridor, moonlight descended in thick white beams that looked like the flying buttresses of some spectral cathedral.

She paused, pricking up her ears as a strange echo trickled down the stairs from the top floor. It was the sound of the Night of the Witches party, a mixture of music and chatter that had been so mysteriously cut off only a few minutes before, except this time it sounded faint and ethereal, like the ghost of its former self. The volume rose and fell, rose and fell, white noise humming in the background, as if some invisible hand were trying to find a signal on a spectral radio. Then the noise stopped just as unexpectedly as it had begun.

A door banged to her left. An echo of rubber soles creaking against the polished floor came from the cave-like corridor leading to the teachers' lounge. A few seconds later, the ominous bulky form of Professor Radovan emerged from the shadows. The moment she spotted Stella, the teacher froze in place, her timber-like legs planted in a wide stride that made her look like the supporting frame of a barn.

"What are you doing here, Flegar?" Professor Radovan's rough, grunting voice resonated through the building like the clang of a massive medieval church bell tolling in a village ravaged by the Black Death.

Stella froze, unable to either speak or flee.

"Answer me, Flegar!" The teacher had never looked as boar-like as she did at that moment. Her jowls shook as she growled furiously, her nostrils flaring out.

This must have been what finally made Stella's instincts come to life. Turning on her heel, she fled down the empty corridor, cutting through the slanting shafts of moonlight that seemed to have a cobwebby physical presence.

She had barely made it halfway when from behind her there came a ferocious thundering that sounded like a stampede. Stella risked one brief over-the-shoulder glance and saw an image from her worst nightmares: Professor Radovan had charged.

Stella's trainer-clad feet pumped like pistons, but the faster she ran, the longer the silver-lit corridor became. She sensed the teacher catching up with her. She could hear her feral panting behind her. But surely Professor Radovan couldn't run that fast.

She cast another quick glance behind her and nearly screamed when she saw that the thing charging after her was no longer the teacher but a giant wild mutant pig—a werepig—as big as a minibus, with spiky hair and bulbous warts oozing pestilent pus. Frothy slime dripped out of a mouth that was as big as the business end of a bulldozer. Some remnants of Professor Radovan's features were still there. For one thing, the monstrous sow had the teacher's rigid swollen limbs, and there was even a close resemblance to Professor Radovan's crew cut in the bristles at the top of the creature's head. The expression on the werepig's face was that of intense idiotic murderousness.

When Stella faced ahead once again, the remaining stretch of corridor looked shorter than before and the darkness at the end more cavernous. It was only then that she realized that the looming darkness was the mouth of the dirty staircase going down to the Forbidden Cellar. Her first instinct was to panic, but she immediately made herself calm down. After all, she had come to the school on this very night, at this hour, specifically because of the thing lurking in the basement. She was going to go down there sooner or later anyway. She was only worried that it might be too soon—if the cellar door was still closed, the hideous werepig that had once been Professor Radovan would ram her into the wall, crushing her like a bug.

There was no time to worry about such details though. She could already feel the beast's foul breath upon her. She sprinted down the remaining few yards of the corridor and leaped down the murky staircase. The werepig followed, huffing and grunting as it tried to squeeze its fat bulk down the stairs. The banister cracked under its weight.

What awaited her at the bottom of the stairs was so unexpected that Stella would have paused and gasped if there hadn't been a deranged werepig at her heels. The door to the basement was indeed open, standing ajar and barely hanging on its hinges. It had been broken through, or more precisely, *exploded* through from the inside. The padlock lay broken and twisted on the floor, as if it had shot out from the force of the blast.

There was no sight of the spider or any other creature. The crack of the open door showed nothing but darkness inside. But this was what she had been drawn to all this time. It was this tempting darkness that had first called her to the cellar.

With this thought, she stepped into the unknown depths of the cellar without further hesitation. The door, suddenly restored to its pre-blast state, closed behind her with a dramatic bang, and the darkness swallowed her.

30

OCTOBER 31, 1954

I t was a chilly October morning, and a somber crowd had assembled at the tram stop outside the walls of Mirogoj Cemetery. The streets were wet with the previous night's rain, and a blanket of sodden yellow leaves covered the pavement.

The size of the crowd was hardly surprising, since it was the eve of All Hallows, the day when people made their annual pilgrimage to the graves of their departed. Whole families as well as a few solitary older people were gathered at the Mirogoj tram stop. They had all undoubtedly come to the cemetery a day in advance to check the state of their family tombs and see if anything needed to be cleaned, fixed or trimmed before the Day of the Dead.

The youth in the worn brown suit was just another face in the crowd. He stood next to a young mother and daughter, both of whom wore identical shades of blue, although the girl's coat was highlighted with a white pelt lining. A casual observer might have thought that the young man was in some way related to them, but that conclusion would have been completely wrong.

He had come there to do an errand for his mother. Her sister was coming to visit from abroad for All Hallows' Day and his mother wanted to make sure their parents'—his grandparents'—graves were in a presentable state. But since working outside in the cold weather would have made the arthritis in her hands even worse, he had volunteered to go in her stead. His mother had been so grateful. He had always been such a good boy.

Presently the tram appeared at the top of the slope where Mirogoj Road ended. It was an old model from the 1920s with a single sturdy blue carriage, three open entrances and one round headlight, which for some reason always reminded him of mine carts. Its route number, thirteen, stood out clearly, white against black, on a square plate at the front.

The tram made a turn around the obelisk outside the main cemetery entrance and then pulled over at the stop. It was crowded inside, but this stop was the end of the route, and most of the passengers would disembark shortly. The first stop was also the last.

The number thirteen let out its load of passengers, who promptly headed for the cemetery gates in a loose, disjointed group. The people waiting at the stop began to slowly board the tram. The young man was among the last to get on. The tram was already half-full and all the seats had been taken. He was glad to see that the mother and daughter had found a seat. They sat by the window near the middle entrance, looking out at the green cupolas over Mirogoj's arcades while the mother talked to the daughter in a voice too low to be overheard. He remained standing just behind the driver's cabin, holding on to a vertical bar by the door.

There was a single chime, and then the tram slowly pulled out of the stop. Moments later, he saw a boy of about fifteen run toward the departing tram from the direction of the cemetery gates and hop effortlessly on board through the back entrance. As the tram swept past the many flower stalls lining the cemetery walls, he saw another would-be passenger race after the tram—a small street urchin in tattered clothes who had been tending one of the flower stalls. The tiny flower-seller swiftly caught up with the moving tram and climbed on board as deftly as a mountain goat.

As if finally satisfied that it had picked up all the passengers it intended to carry on that occasion, the tram surged forward. With a screeching of wheels against tracks, the tram made a wide semicircular turn outside the tall cemetery arcades and headed right into Mirogoj Road. It glided smoothly down the hill, gaining speed by the second.

The young man glanced at the new arrivals, both of whom had quickly blended in with the rest of the passengers. He immediately felt like an intruder, standing there at the front of the tram. He rarely went to town—his ailing mother needed him to be on hand at all times—and when he did, he always felt out of place. If it hadn't been for the cemetery, he would probably never have gone to this unfamiliar part of town with its unfamiliar tram routes. He could never remember where he had to get off.

Awkwardly, the youth leaned into the opening of the driver's cabin and said, "Excuse me, where do I need to change for number seventeen?"

The driver winced as if stung, his hand momentarily freezing in midair over the hand brake. "In Drašković Street." The voice was abrupt and, to the young man's ears at least, somewhat unsteady.

"Thank you." He hadn't realized how agitated the driver had been. If he had known, he never would have interrupted him.

The tram was now going alarmingly fast. Not only was it not slowing down, but it also seemed to be accelerating. From the driver's cabin there came a barrage of impatient thuds as the driver worked the unresponsive brakes.

The young man caught a sudden movement with the corner of his eye. The little flower-seller had jumped out of the speeding tram. He saw the urchin land on the damp, leaf-covered pavement. A few elderly women gasped.

The comfortable murmur of many quiet, intimate conversations died down as the passengers began to realize that something was wrong.

Moments later, the older boy, the one who had hopped on board just before the flower-seller, also jumped out.

At the same time, the tram surged down the slope of Mirogoj Road with roller-coaster speed. Desperate sounds of the driver struggling first with one type of brake and then another came from inside the cabin, but the tram only kept accelerating. The endless rows of chestnut trees that lined the road on both sides had turned into a greenish-brown motion blur.

When the tram was about halfway down the hill, the driver yelled, "Everyone, jump out if you can! I can't stop the tram!"

There was a collective gasp. The young man saw the passengers look around helplessly. Most of them were average people on their way back from the cemetery, not stuntmen trained to leap out of speeding vehicles. The street outside flew by with head-spinning velocity. Jumping out under these circumstances would have spelled certain death. And so everyone stayed put, choosing to hope for the best—perhaps the brakes would start working again or the tram might somehow slow down at the foot of the hill. A few older women clutched their rosaries and mumbled urgent prayers. The girl in the blue coat had buried her head in her mother's neck.

Even though he was now probably the most agile passenger left on board, the young man felt just as powerless as everyone else. He was numb all over. If only he hadn't disturbed the driver with his stupid question, he thought. If only he had never left the house.

The speeding tram was now nearing the foot of the hill, where Mirogoj Road ended and Ksaver Road began at the junction known as the Star of Gubec. The unstoppable number thirteen sped relentlessly on, swaying from side to side with a terrible clattering racket. The windowpanes shook. A few people screamed. Someone was whimpering, but it was hard to tell whether it was a child or an adult. Meanwhile, the tram kept on going faster and faster.

The noise of the rampaging tram had grown to a kind of cacophony of destruction. But for a few seconds, moments before the tram reached the turn at the foot of the hill, there was only silence. It was as if everyone on board held their breath, envisioning a hundred different scenarios of what might happen next, hoping for the best.

But what happened next was the worst.

As soon as the number thirteen reached the turn, the savage force of kinetic energy catapulted it out of the tracks. The airborne tram glided over the road and smashed into a barrier of trees that sent the tram rolling over and over on the ground. People screamed while the metal container that enclosed them groaned and cracked.

But for the young man, it was as if time had stopped. Everything unfolded in slow motion. The whole world slowly spun around him. Someone's umbrella whizzed past his ear. Somewhere above him or under him (it was hard to tell at that point) there was now an enormous hole. Small pieces of debris scattered around him.

His gaze landed on the only fixed object in sight—his wristwatch, which he had inherited from his late father. The hands showed 8:35. He felt a morbid sense of calm because at least now he knew the exact time when he was going to die.

The tram kept rolling until it encountered another cluster of trees, which it promptly knocked over, tearing down the trees like a lawn mower slashing through a few blades of grass. There was a tremendous crash that shattered the tram as if it were nothing more than a toy, propelling it even farther until its remains finally collapsed at the foot of a lamppost.

The impact thrust the young man through a hole in the roof, and he thought, *this is it*. But he landed on the grass among the broken trees and somehow, it was not the end. His eyes were still able to see the torn-off branches and his lungs still pumped the chilly autumn air. There was a throbbing pain in his right shoulder, but apart from that, he felt fine. He flexed his fingers and toes. All fine. Even his numbness was subsiding.

Slowly, he got to his feet, holding on to a fallen tree trunk for support. It was only then that he could fully see the devastation.

The tram was a blackened husk lying on its side like a dead animal. It was surrounded on all sides by piles of debris. The enormous hole in its roof revealed the shattered interior and the unmoving forms of the passengers trapped inside. Several mangled bodies lay on the ground before the wreck. Among them, there was a tattered scrap of what had once been a fur-trimmed blue coat.

Rudi woke up shaking and perspiring in his tiny janitor's apartment. An empty bottle of šljivovica lay on his chest. Faint sounds of music were trickling in through the walls from the school auditorium, but he could barely hear anything. He could barely remember what day it was. All he knew was that it had all been his fault. If only he hadn't bothered the driver! If only he hadn't distracted him with his stupid question, the driver would surely have been able to stop the tram on time. He clutched his head and let out a growl as loud as a crashing tram.

The floor began to rumble.

31

THE EARTHQUAKE

The auditorium lights went out and the feeble music stopped. There was a collective gasp, followed by a few moments of silence that would have been complete if it hadn't been for the rustling of several bags of potato chips. Apparently, some people could eat under any circumstances.

After a few more awkward moments of this, the silence gave way to an outburst of excited chatter.

The flock of teachers assembled around the food table had remained frozen in midbite. Professor Anić, the geography teacher, sat wide-eyed with her cheeks stuffed full of cake to near-bursting point. It was heartbreaking that someone who had been tending to the delightful walnut and raisin roulade with such selfless devotion should be so cruelly interrupted.

Professor Novak was the first of the teachers to react. Putting down her half-eaten chocolate éclair, she rose from her chair and said "Wh—," but before she could finish the sentence, the floor began to tremble. Some of the pupils screamed.

"Don't panic!" bellowed Professor Novak, having found her voice again, but the tremors had already turned into a violent quake. This was accompanied by a loud groaning, tearing noise, as if the building were being ripped apart. At this point, Professor Novak gave up on the idea of taking charge of the situation.

The terrified pupils started running out of the auditorium, accompanied by the teachers. The steady stream of screaming children and befuddled teachers, some of whom were still eating cake, poured down a stairwell that was now as dark-stricken as the auditorium. Not a single light was left on in the entire building, but this was not the time to worry about such things, as windows were bursting, walls collapsing and the stairs cracking beneath their feet.

The crowd poured out through the main entrance and dispersed in various directions, although many assembled outside in the street to watch the unfolding spectacle.

The school was turning itself inside out. The walls were contorting and changing angles. The towers were growing taller, their conical roofs steeper. Strange shapes were springing out along the top edge of the building. In the dark it was hard to see what they were, but they looked almost like jagged, claw-shaped battlements.

The transformation was both terrifying and surreal at the same time. Its significance seemed to shift with each shimmer of moonlight, changing with the passing of each cloud that drifted before the uncannily bright Moon. One moment the building looked like an imposing alien edifice. The next, its strange shapes seemed to be nothing more than a trick of the moonlight.

32

ALL-CONSUMING MASS OF THE UNCONSCIOUS

Cora had the air of someone who knew exactly what she was doing, which was more than Dario could say for himself. Grabbing his hand, she led him confidently farther and farther into the benighted ruins of the fortress, and Dario allowed himself to be led.

The ubiquitous mist had found its way into every corner of the site, creeping over narrow paths, running over grassy slopes and trickling out through the battlements. It was, however, possible that the mist was nothing but another dream symbol. Dario certainly considered this possibility. Had he been asked to venture a guess as to the symbol's meaning, he would have gone for "relentless, all-consuming mass of the unconscious." This was the state his mind was in anyway.

From the moment Cora had led him into the fortress, he had been overcome with a sense of inevitability. There was something going on here, something that he didn't understand, but he was powerless to do anything other than allow himself to be swept in whichever direction the inexplicable forces around him decided to take.

"Um…where are we going?" he mumbled as they passed through the arched stone entrance to the inner courtyard.

"You'll see," said Cora.

She led him up to a creepy derelict well that stood in the center of the courtyard like a buoy in a sea of mist. Cora was staring at it with an expression so intense that it was frightening. Her eyes were very bright and her pupils had shrunk to pinpricks.

"It'll do," she said. Then she threw him down on the ground before the well.

33

THE BLACK QUEEN

The dungeon was predictably dark apart from a few dusty shafts of reddish torchlight that trickled in through the bars. The cell was windowless; crumbling walls surrounded him on all sides. Outside the door, a constant scraping of iron boots against the floor signaled the presence of a guard, but no one had come in to check on him yet.

Leo lay on a pile of rotting rags where he had collapsed shortly after being tossed in by a bear soldier with poor interpersonal skills. As he blinked at the darkness, coaxing himself into consciousness, he realized for the first time since he had landed at the Prečko turning circle that the prospect of his being stuck on Earth forever was no longer just a worst-case-scenario to be used for dramatic effect in his diatribes against the city but a highly probable outcome of his present circumstances.

A flurry of movement that suddenly arose outside the door stirred him into full wakefulness. This was followed by the rasp of a key being thrust into the rusty lock. The door opened with a noisy screech. Two bear guards armed with halberds burst into his cell and stopped by the door, one on either side.

The Black Queen stalked in. She looked just as Leo remembered her, except skinnier and taller. In fact, she looked at least ten feet tall, but that might have been just an effect of Leo's low-angle perspective. Her stern face had become even more angular than before, and her flashing eyes had shrunk into deep, dark pits. Her black hair was pulled up in a bun so severe that it looked ready to peel the scalp off her skull; her black gown hung off her bony frame like a monk's habit;

the black semicircle of her raised collar looked like the negative of some Egyptian deity's solar disk.

"Hello, Barbara," said Leo with feigned amicability. "Long time no see."

"You." The Black Queen's voice was as hard as the walls of Bear Town Fortress.

"How have you been? You look well."

"You piece of filth," hissed the Black Queen. "How dare you speak to me this way? How dare you speak to me at all? How dare you show your face before me after everything you've done?"

"Wait—what was the first question?"

"You've killed two of my servants. They were invaluable to me."

"Would it help if I said they tried to kill me first?"

"You are going to pay for it. All of it."

Leo let out a jaded sigh. "I presume you're going to kill me now?"

"Don't try to trick me again, demon." The Black Queen's stare was as icy as Mirogoj rain. "I know you can't die. No, I will not provide you with the convenience of a temporary death. You will instead be made to spend the rest of your life as I have done all this time—as a prisoner. But unlike me, you are not going to have anything other than this tiny cell in which to rot for all eternity all by yourself."

"That doesn't sound too bad," said Leo. "After all, I *am* an introvert."

The Black Queen gave him a look of such bitterness that it could have curdled milk into cottage cheese even more pungent than the fare sold by overassertive peasant women at Dolac Market.

"But first," she said, "I am going to make you watch as I break out of my prison, which will surely seal your fate when your all-knowing Star Council finds out."

"I wouldn't count on it," said Leo. "The council is hardly that consistent."

But the Black Queen did not respond to his jibe. Instead, she turned briskly, with an impressive swoosh of black cloth, and strode out. The heavy door slammed shut, and once again he was alone in the dungeon.

Leo sighed.

The Black Queen went down a torchlit corridor and then up a spiral staircase to the top of the tower. She slipped into her bedchamber. Antares was sprawled on her bed, his wrists and ankles bound to the bedposts with leather straps.

"What is this?" His wide, panicked stare was darting all over the room. "Where am I?"

The Black Queen smiled mysteriously.

"Where are the others?"

"Fear not," said the Black Queen, her voice soft and treacly, "the others are being well taken care of."

"What have you done to me? Why am I feeling so dizzy?"

"I've merely given you something to calm your nerves."

"You can't do this to me! I demand to be released this very instant!"

"You will be, in a moment. But before you go, I need you to do a little something for me."

She started rubbing his chest.

"Yeah…what?"

"We have had some…intruders coming in. I'm afraid there are too many for my soldiers to handle. Would you deal with them for me?"

34

THE HOOLIGANS ARE COMING

Tin was having a hard time keeping track of time, space or any other dimension in the dark, foul-smelling chemical toilet that he was still huddled in. There was something about the shape and size of his improvised hiding place that muffled and distorted external noises in a way that made them all sound alike. Every murmur made him prick up his ears and curl into himself like a frightened hedgehog, but as to whether the noise was a passing car, a cooing pigeon or a snarling hooligan, he couldn't tell.

For all he knew, there might have been a whole load of hooligans, or whatever the collective noun for a number of hooligans was—herd? Pack? Shoal?—coming for him.

What if Stunned Ox or Constipated Goat had called for backup? Was there such a thing as backup in the hooligan kingdom? Maybe they were grouped in squadrons or whatever an organized unit, as opposed to a disorganized pack, of hooligans was called. And maybe one of his persecutors had called or texted the nearest unit.

There were bound to be lots of them nearby. Whenever there was a football match at Maksimir Stadium, it was not uncommon to see whole shoals of hooligans packed into a number eleven or any other tram unfortunate enough to run anywhere near the place. In such cases, the hooligans would inevitably end up with the whole carriage to themselves, as any sensible members of the nonhooligan population would make sure to vacate the carriage shortly upon the hooligans' arrival. And the hooligans would always make the most of their temporarily occupied territory, turning it into a mobile football cheering unit. Before long, the carriage would be thrumming with the singing of many throats, shaking with the bouncing of many boot-clad feet and shimmering with the waving of many blue flags. If the hooligans were in a really good mood, they might even smash a window or two.

In his frightened state, Tin could easily imagine just one such carriage unloading at the nearby station its loathsome cargo of chanting idiots, who would then inevitably proceed to march toward him. He could see their idiotic gapmouthed faces and their blue hoodies and their cheap earrings and their dirty jackets covered in pseudofascist symbols whose meaning the idiots didn't even understand and Tin didn't care about. He could practically hear their boots stamping on the ground in a maddeningly monotonous yet deadly rhythm.

What would the hooligans do to him if they found his hiding place? They would probably start by taunting him and kicking the sides of the shelter. The kicking would gradually become more aggressive until they knocked the whole thing over and started bashing it indiscriminately from all sides. Maybe they would keep on kicking it and stamping on it until it collapsed in on itself, flattening Tin to a smear of greasy pulp. Or maybe they would drag him out and hang him off a branch of the nearest tree with his own belt. Except he had no belt, since he was wearing overalls.

It took him a while—it was impossible to tell how long—to realize that he was being ridiculous. There he was half suffocating and scaring himself to death when the hooligans were almost certainly long gone. They were probably halfway to the football stadium by now. They had to be if they were going to make it before the start of the game. And besides, Stella was probably waiting for him outside the school, wondering why he was running late. There was no point hiding here in the dark anymore. Tin reached for the narrow plastic door.

Before his hand could touch it, the door was pulled violently open from the outside. A wide-necked mouth-breathing figure with short curly hair and a low forehead stood in front of him. A sharp switchblade glinted in the creature's right hand.

"You're dead," said Stunned Ox.

35

INSIDE THE CELLAR

At first there was nothing but darkness, and for a moment, Stella felt like an astronaut who had ventured out of her spacecraft to fix a broken solar panel or some such thing only to find herself sucked into another dimension, one where there was neither light nor sound. But then she stepped into a puddle of something sticky and realized that she was still in the ordinary material realm after all.

Something light and silky brushed against her hand, drawing an involuntary yelp of surprise out of her throat. Then another strand caught her on the cheek. The invisible diaphanous threads were everywhere, crisscrossing the cellar from all directions like ghostly laundry lines. They slid up her face and crept over her hair, reminding her with every odious touch that she was now in the spider's lair.

Stella reached for her magic silver bottle and held it up like a torch. If she had been expecting its blue gems to flash like miniature lightning bolts, bathing the cellar with brilliant light, she would have been disappointed. Because the gems did precisely nothing. The magic bottle was just another unseen object in the pitch-dark cellar, indistinguishable from the rest of the darkness. She tucked the bottle back into her pocket and took a few cautious steps farther into the cellar. Her eyes slowly began to adjust to the dark, and she realized that there was some light in the lair after all. After a few more steps, the source of the light revealed itself to her—the Moon, whose rays came in through a few slits on the ceiling at the far end of the cellar. This, thought Stella, had to be the grating at the top of the northern tower stairs where she had spent so many hours peering into the darkness, wondering what was concealed below.

Only a tiny fragment of the Moon could be seen through one of the corners of the opening, a single speck that glowed like a brilliant white gem. A thick beam of moonlight descended from it into the cellar, filling it with a spectral luminescence that made Stella feel faintly light-headed. Her eyes dreamily followed the straight line of light until her gaze landed on a strange pale bundle that lay on the floor at the foot of it.

She blinked.

The thing on the floor had the shape of an adult lying on one side in a fetal position, but it had no other human features—no face, no hair, no fingernails. All it had was a smooth milky-white film that enveloped the prone shape like a cocoon.

Stella stood above the figure motionlessly, her mind and body overwhelmed with awe. She bent over the cocoon and reached out with one trembling hand, touching its shoulder cautiously. The pod was surprisingly light—almost as light as air—and even something as gentle as Stella's featherlight touch made it turn over on its back. Stella gasped. A dark gash ran along the front from the top of the head to the tip of the toes, the edges ragged as if the pod had been torn open.

Within a few moments of turning over, the cocoon collapsed into a crumpled mess like a deflated air mattress, letting out a puff of stale ice-cold air.

Stella straightened up. Then she gasped.

The Black Queen was standing before her.

The dreadful yet familiar figure with the high collar loomed half-hidden in the shadows a few feet away from the cocoon.

Now that Stella stood face-to-face with what she began to realize was the very thing that had compelled her to go into the Forbidden Cellar in the first place, she had no idea what to do. She grabbed the silver bottle again, but it was still not glowing blue. The apparition standing before her was not the spider. It was the product of the spider's weaving—the very thing that the goldsmith had warned her against.

She took a step back. The Black Queen took a step forward. It was a fluid, weightless step, as if the figure were gliding over the floor. And, indeed, there was something ethereal about the silent form that made it look as if it were hardly more substantial than the darkness.

Stella took another step back, tripped, fell, and landed on a pile of cardboard boxes. From her new vantage point, the towering shadow before her looked at least ten feet tall.

The Black Queen stepped into the moonlight. There really was something insubstantial about her. Stella could see the wall in the background straight through her.

The only solid thing about the Black Queen was her face, which stared down at Stella with two soulless eyes like black pits. Stella blinked hard to make the vision go away.

When she opened her eyes again, the black eyes were still staring at her, except there were now more than two. The monstrous predatory head looming over her had at least a hundred of them.

36

THE STUNNED OX

The hooligan with a striking resemblance to a stunned ox held Tin by the collar in a brutally tight one-handed grasp. With his free hand, he held the knife against Tin's throat. The miscreant sneered in a manner that was typical of that breed, spitting out a variety of vulgar insults in a vicious low hiss.

As Tin felt the sharp blade press into the soft flesh under his chin, he wondered with a sluggish detachment how it had come about that he was about to die. How could it have come to this? He had been on his way to school, on an errand of questionable legitimacy, to be sure, but nevertheless a nonlethal one.

Had he been asked earlier that day about his opinion on the worst thing he was likely to experience that evening, he would have said something like feeling embarrassed for Stella if she failed to find her imaginary spider. He certainly wouldn't have said being the victim of a cold-blooded murder outside a broken-down chemical toilet in an abandoned building site in a side alley at the far end of the road near the school.

It must have been the unexpected and almost surreal nature of his situation that made his brain so slow. His brain clearly didn't believe that what was happening was real, and therefore it, his brain, didn't see a need for any kind of preventive action. It—his brain—was in fact far more interested in trying to come up with additional adverbials that would further expand the description of the location of his imminent demise—around the corner from the car with no wheels under the full Moon after school before supper. Tin's hand was the first part of him to recover from the general numbness, stirring into action apparently of its own volition.

Deftly and with great subtlety, it climbed into Tin's pocket like a trained mongoose, curling itself around the biggest object therein, which happened to be his dad's spanner. Tin felt the cool handle and wondered briefly why it was wet. Then he realized that his palm was dripping with sweat.

Stunned Ox hadn't noticed Tin's little maneuver. His stupid beady eyes clearly couldn't handle peripheral vision. Besides, Tin was bound to have been classified in the hooligan codex as helpless prey and therefore warranted no caution. It would be easy now, thought Tin, to take out the spanner and whack the brute in the teeth. This was the sort of thing that would have worked for sure in the movies. Stunned Ox would howl in pain, drop his knife, and Tin would make a run for it. Afterward, Stunned Ox would just stand there, shaking his fist in anger, and that would be the end of it. But would it work in real life? Tin wasn't so sure. The blade was dangerously close to Tin's throat, and any sudden movement might make the beefy hand that held the knife give an involuntary jerk and slash him. Besides, Tin wasn't a natural-born street fighter. He would probably have missed his target.

But such considerations became less relevant as Tin's brain finally tuned in and registered the dark, deserted alley he was still in and the mindless face staring down at him, its grimace looking demonic in the moonlight. There were no streetlamps in this dead end of a street to soften the hooligan's appearance or to trick Tin into thinking that he was anywhere other than in a corner of Hell. There were no other people around either, no witnesses, and none of the many big, menacing shadows poking out of the deserted building site managed to look like anything other than a potential place to hide a dead body. Stunned Ox really was going to kill him.

"You little shit," hissed Stunned Ox. "I'm going to chop you into a million pieces. They will be collecting your remains in Tupperware dishes."

Tin felt the blade of the knife move even closer to his throat. He winced as it cut into the skin of his neck. There was a warm tickle around his collarbone as blood began to pour down his neck.

There was nothing for it. He had to do something. He was going to die either way.

Tin furtively tightened his grip on the spanner and prepared to strike.

37

ALGOL IS BEING HELPFUL

Leo lay in a semiconscious daze on the cold heap of grime that was the dungeon floor, staring up at the dank ceiling. He rubbed his eyes with the palms of his hands, making a long throaty sound of utter exasperation.

A handful of glowing silvery particles emerged out of the darkness and, moments later, Algol appeared before him.

"Leo," said the daimon with a nod of greeting.

"I don't believe it," moaned Leo. "What are you doing here?"

"May I ask you the same question?"

"Please don't make this worse than it already is. Obviously I didn't choose to be locked inside Barbara's wine cellar."

"Have you dug out your escape tunnel yet?"

"Not really. Without realizing it, Barbara has done me a favor. She means to drag me off to watch her crossing-over ritual. This will save me the trouble of figuring out how to sneak in there incognito."

"And how are you going to stop the ritual? Do you have a plan?"

"Yes," said Leo. "First, I'm going to single-handedly fight the entire Bear Town army with my wooden stick, and then I'm going to grab Barbara by the hair and pull her back before she's able to cross over."

"Sounds very sophisticated," said Algol. "It might work."

"Well, I'm lucky that I at least still have my Stick of Sylvicolus with me, as useless as it is. This is only because Barbara's soldiery is so backward they don't even know what it is. They probably thought it was some kind of shepherd's flute."

"That is indeed lucky. But you might also want to try this." Algol produced a small shiny object from his pocket and tossed it to Leo, who caught it with one hand. He looked at it closely. It was a glowing golden star, as delicate as a snowflake, floating inside a small glass sphere held on a chain.

"What is this?"

"It's just a little something I got from Ophiuchus. It's one of his next-generation healing gadgets, very cutting-edge. It can restore a star daimon's strength faster than a trip to the Red Dwarf Spa. But it has other potential applications too."

"Have you tampered with it?"

"Of course not!" Algol looked outraged. The next instant, his expression was mildly apologetic. "Well, maybe a little."

"What does it do now?"

Algol's eyes sparkled. "Something that might come in handy. You see, it can restore the powers of an earthed star daimon for a brief moment. Just the briefest of moments. Maybe a second or two. Nevertheless, in your current situation, even a moment as brief as that could prove to be decisive. Of course, you would have to choose the right moment to use it."

"How does it work?"

"It's very easy. To activate it, all you have to do is crush the glass globe in your hand. But remember, you can only use it once and only for a single moment."

"Have you tested it?"

"Of course not. But I'm hoping you will."

"That's very reassuring."

Algol shrugged. "No pressure; you don't have to use it if you don't want to. This is just a little alternative option in case you lose your stick." His flickering image was starting to disintegrate.

"That's it?" said Leo. "You're just going to disappear now? You do realize that you could probably get me out of here without too much effort?"

"Yes, but that would be too helpful," said Algol. "It would tarnish my reputation as a demon star."

Leo groaned with frustration.

"As I'm sure you're aware," Algol continued, "in order to maintain my status as a demon star, I can only be helpful *some* of the time. And only if those times that I am being helpful are counterbalanced by the times I am *not* being helpful."

"That sounds complicated."

"It is."

"In that case, how do I know whether by giving me this Ophiuchus dongle you are being consciously helpful or merely setting the stage for being unhelpful?"

"You don't. That's the beauty if it."

Leo groaned.

"You can always say no," said Algol helpfully.

Leo considered. The little golden star, almost the same shape as the one on his belt, sparkled like a miniature sun in the gloom of the dungeon.

"I guess I'll hang on to it. Just in case. I probably won't need it anyway."

"Probably." Algol grinned. Then he disappeared.

38

THE SPIDER OF ILLUSION

Stella's eyes had become perfectly adjusted to the darkness. She could see, for example, that the huge black spider towering over her was suspended from a structure of cobwebs as intricate as the vaulted ceiling of a Gothic cathedral. The spider's body was as big as a small car and its legs the size of construction site cranes. Its many bulbous arachnid eyes glowed red in the moonlight, regarding her with deadly cunning.

It must have been the eyes, or possibly the legs, that made Stella's bottle finally start glowing as promised. The gems turned into points of blue light with such suddenness that she nearly dropped the thing. As the glow grew brighter, it became obvious that the gems themselves were not its source. Instead, they had turned into tiny transparent windows that enabled what looked like boiling blue lava that had apparently been contained inside the bottle the whole time to shine through.

The blue glow cast a fan of light on the monster above Stella, revealing all the grim details that had previously been obscured by the dark. The giant mandibles, as big as a bear trap, were by far the most prominent one. They looked ready to snap her in half. And whereas spiders didn't normally have fangs, this one did. They were as big as stakes and protruded out of its gaping maw at irregular intervals like a vandalized picket fence. The Spider of Illusion might have been a weaver of phantasms, but its terrifying presence was all too real.

The horror of the sight before her was a reminder that now was the time to open the silver bottle and allow it to do its work, that this was perhaps her only chance. But no sooner had her hand reached for the cap than the Spider of

Illusion sprang down at her from its perch. With effortless agility, the monster knocked the bottle out of her hand, sending it spinning through the air. For a moment, the blue rays danced around the cellar as if coming from a novelty disco ball; then the bottle crashed into the wall. Stella watched with dismay as the silver bottle landed on the floor about ten feet away from her.

She instinctively turned to go after it, but the spider made a sudden leap, ramming the points of its legs into the floor on all sides. Stella found herself trapped inside a hideous cage. She grabbed two of the legs like a captive clutching the bars of her cell and tried to pull them apart. Touching the sickeningly coarse, bristly legs made her shudder with revulsion. The effort was useless, since she couldn't move them so much as an inch, but she did manage to provoke the monster. It lurched its bloated body back, never moving its obstructing legs, and snapped its vile jaws at her. She ducked just in time to avoid decapitation.

Suddenly she felt a surge of anger. *No one tries to bite my head off,* she thought. One of her boot-clad feet shot out, aiming for a crooked, prickly leg. It kicked a knobby joint with a sickening crunch. The Spider of Illusion let out a hiss like a decompressing pressure pot. The broken leg sagged for a moment, opening up a crack big enough for a medium-sized person to crawl out of. The spider's leg quickly sprang back into place, as strong and menacing as before, but not before Stella had bolted out of the gap and snatched the still-glowing silver bottle.

She tore off the cap with one quick, violent gesture. The spider stared at her with a look that was as close to bewilderment as possible for a creature that had a hundred eyes. It was then that Stella realized she didn't actually know what to do with the bottle. Was she supposed to simply splash its contents at the spider's face like some acid attacker?

But the bottle itself provided the answer. A tendril of bright blue light snaked out of the opening like a genie out of a magic lamp. It kept swirling out until it was about five feet high and then stopped. Its sinuous pose was alert, as if the tendril were waiting for something to happen. As the coil of blue lava unspooled itself into a glowing whip, she understood what it was that the swirling thing was waiting for—to be used.

The spider, however, was not happy with this turn of events. It lurched at Stella like a charging eight-legged bull. She leaped to the side, only barely managing to avoid getting trampled. Impulsively, she cracked the fiery blue whip against the floor. It made a satisfying electric snap. The spider swiveled around to face her, its eight legs working frantically. Stella lashed the whip at the spider's abdomen.

The burning whip struck its target with remarkable precision. There was a high-pitched sizzling sound then the spider shrieked. Where the fiery whip had hit it, there was now a smoking gash. Slimy ichor oozed out of the wound.

As the monster reeled from the blow, Stella rained a shower of lashes all over its hideous, bristly, slimy body. It fought back, but she was relentless. In fact, she was starting to enjoy it. She had never liked spiders.

Soon the Spider of Illusion was reduced to a smoking mess. Finally, it let out one long chilling shriek and slowly collapsed in on itself, its legs curling up around its battered, half-roasted body like the dry petals of a dead flower. Stella allowed herself a small sigh of relief. She gazed at the beaten spider with the pride of a craftsman admiring a fine piece of work.

But just as she was about to turn around and walk away, a single broken spider leg sprang up with a disturbing jerky spasm, its sharp tip shooting out at her like a javelin. The movement was so sudden that she barely had time to register a stinging pain in her thigh.

The tough fabric of her jacket had prevented the spider's leg, which now lay lifeless on the floor along with the rest of the creature, from splitting her open like a fish fillet. But her jeans were made of less durable stuff, and the side of her thigh where the spider's claw had ended its stroke now had a throbbing cut. It wasn't a deep cut—the bleeding was negligible—but Stella knew from the sudden drowsiness that washed over her that she had been poisoned.

As the remains of the spider continued to sizzle, her vision started to black out. She only had time to see the glowing whip receding back into the bottle before she lost her balance and collapsed onto the cold stone floor.

39

THE AUDITORIUM

The vacant husk of the Black Queen glided through the darkness of the abandoned school building. In the wake of the earthquake, which had cracked the walls and overturned cupboards, all was quiet. The silent shell could have been just another one of the many shadows that moved in the dark.

The silence was suddenly interrupted by the sound of frantic stomping footsteps.

A gaunt, bedraggled man who looked as if he had just lived through his worst nightmare stumbled up the central staircase. He stopped and looked frantically first to the left, in the direction of the teachers' lounge, and then to the right. When he saw the stealthy figure of the Black Queen approaching him, he looked almost as if he had been expecting this.

"Don't take another step," said Rudi, holding up his hands like a traffic policeman. "You're not going anywhere."

The empty-eyed form of the Black Queen kept on advancing unseeingly. Rudi froze, his mouth half-open. He looked as if he had said everything he had to say and couldn't think of what to do next.

"I…won't let you do to anyone else what you've done to me," he added.

Directly above his head, there was a heavy halogen tube that had become detached during the earthquake and now clung to the ceiling by a single wire.

The wire suddenly snapped and the tube fell off, hitting him on the head with one of its hard edges. Rudi collapsed like a felled tree.

The shell of the Black Queen continued her journey down the corridor, sliding effortlessly over the janitor's motionless body.

When she reached the main stairwell, she slowly began to ascend. The moonlit highlights on the stairs created a ladder of glowing silver rungs.

The Black Queen climbed all the way up to the top floor, then calmly turned left and swept into the auditorium.

The setting of the inaugural East Central Primary School Night of the Witches festivity was a mess. The combined forces of the earthquake and the revelers' hasty departure had left the place in shambles, although it was hard to say which factor had caused more damage. Chairs and tables lay scattered across the floor like fallen dominoes. The old grand piano lay upside down with its legs in the air like a dead insect. Parts of the ceiling had fallen off.

Moving with ease among the rubble, the thing that looked like the Black Queen glided toward the semicircular wooden stage, where a ripped-up black banner with the words *The Night of the Witches* written in sparkling silver letters hung suspended between two poles that had been hauled up from the gymnasium.

Silently, the dark figure ascended the stage. The wooden boards, usually creaky, made no sound beneath her feet.

She stopped in the middle of the stage and raised her hands to the ceiling. There were already cracks in it, but as she stood there, the cracks deepened, running in every direction like a web until the roof above her collapsed. The Black Queen stood still in the shower of rubble, which fell everywhere except directly onto her, and waited for the dust to settle.

Outside in the street, some of the children still hanging around outside made a cheering sound as the roof of the northern tower caved in. But no one could see the Black Queen standing at the top like a figure on a pedestal—no one but the Moon, which now hovered directly above her, illuminating the exposed auditorium like a spotlight.

The icy silver light of the Moon cascaded all around the Black Queen. She reached out one pale hand and grasped a silver ray. She gave it a quick tug, as if testing it, and then, apparently satisfied, climbed onto the delicate web of moonlight as deftly as a spider.

40

THE SERPENT

Dario's brain felt like a fuse on the verge of bursting. Cora was all over him, in more ways than he'd ever thought possible. At some point, she slowed down and then threw her head back, exposing her pale white neck that glistened like an ivory column in the moonlight. She stayed like that for a while, and Dario glowed with a sense of achievement for leading someone to such protracted ecstasy.

He soon realized, however, that whatever it was that was keeping her in this position, it had nothing to do with him. She was in fact staring at something in the sky.

Dario followed her gaze and saw something that his mind couldn't process at first. The sight did not compute. It looked like a ghostly figure in black climbing down from the sky on a ladder of moonlight. It descended slowly but deftly, taking its time to choose the right footing like some fastidious spider.

"Just in time," said Cora in a throaty voice as the descending figure landed softly on the ground a few yards away from them. It was the Black Queen, Dario realized, or at least a fairy-tale idea of her. She had the preconceived black robe, the black hair and the pale face, except the face had no features other than two dark pits for eyes. The figure stood there motionlessly, its black eyes watching them.

"What do you mean?" said Dario. His voice was slurred.

Cora lifted something with both hands and Dario realized it was the dragon's head key that Leo's friend had given to him. She must have taken it out of his pocket while he was semiconscious. The ruby eyes of the dragon figure were glowing red.

"Hey," he said, but the word came out more as a question than an admonition.

Cora's head lolled back down, but the face that now stared down at him was not hers. Instead, it was the face of a hideous reptilian monster with scaly greenish-gray skin, bony spikes and terrifying leathery snake eyes that glowed red, the pupils like narrow vertical slits. The monster growled at him. A long forked snake's tongue slid out of its mouth.

Dario screamed and threw Cora off him, getting to his feet as quickly as he could while buttoning his trousers. He briefly mused how decency should be his top priority even under the most disturbing of circumstances.

The scales had rapidly spread all over Cora's body; she was now all reptile. Her hands were lethal claws that would not look out of place on a velociraptor. The dragon's head key now looked like a weapon. She lashed at him, tearing at his face with the jagged edge of the key. Dario felt a sharp stab of pain, like a paper cut to the power of ten thousand, as warm blood rushed down his cheek.

She lashed at him again, but he fended off her blow. Then he remembered the banishing book in his pocket and whipped it out.

Even though he had opened it as dramatically as Leo had done at the black metal gig, the book looked and acted like an ordinary book. Dario gave it a shake. It obstinately continued being just an ordinary book.

Cora took one look at Dario's book and burst out laughing. It was a horrible gargling sound.

Dario shook the book some more. At first it was a half-hearted shake, like someone shaking a wet umbrella before entering a building, but as Cora leaped at him, he lashed it energetically, as if it were a whip.

Suddenly the book started vibrating in his hand, like a hair dryer on a high-speed setting.

Cora did not look pleased at this development, but she was not deterred either. She snarled and pounced at him like an enraged bear, her claws poised to tear out his throat. He took a swing with the book at her, but her scaly skin was as hard as armor and the book barely left any mark at all.

Still, it made Cora even angrier. She leaped at him again with a vengeful hiss, making Dario nearly lose his footing.

This lapse in concentration cost him dearly. Cora knocked the book out of his hand, took a swing with her rock-hard fist at his bleeding cheek, and then threw him roughly at the side of the well.

He collided with it painfully, dropping to his knees and leaning heavily over the edge. Blood ran like tears off his face, dripping into the black abyss of the well. Dario's vision blackened.

Before he passed out, he thought he could see red light coming out of the depths.

41

THE BATTLE OF THE CHESTNUTS

T in ran so fast that his fake moustache fell off. It was just as well—the thing had been annoyingly itchy anyway. He didn't stop to think how it could have been possible that he had somehow managed to smack Stunned Ox in the mouth with the spanner. His hand had done it independently, on its own initiative, and for that he was grateful. Because if it had been up to him, he would have been dead by now.

There had been a look of almost comic befuddlement on the hooligan's face as Tin's spanner connected with his jaw, which would have been hard to miss, since it was the size (and shape) of a toilet bowl. Stunned Ox had let him go more out of surprised shock than pain. It must have been unthinkable for his pea-sized brain that someone like Tin should fight back.

As soon as Tin crossed the road, he noticed that there was something wrong with the school. For one thing, there were more people assembled outside than there had ever been before. The other thing that struck him was how strange the school itself appeared to be. For a brief moment, it looked as if the building had somehow transformed into a Gothic castle with gargoyles and battlements. But then a cloud sailed over the Moon and the building looked normal again. Either way, Tin didn't have time to stop and look, since he had told Stella he would meet her and she was probably waiting impatiently for him.

Feeling little enthusiasm for going through the crowd, he went past the southern tower, slipped into the playground through a hole in the fence, and then entered the school through the back entrance.

As he ran up the stairs to the primary school level, he realized two things—first, all the lights were out, and second, it didn't feel as if there were anyone else in the building besides himself. But he had to check whether Stella was there, waiting for him outside the cellar door.

The primary school corridor was a phantasmagoric patchwork of deep shadows and touches of silver moonlight. Tin felt a sense of rising dread as he paced down the deserted corridor toward the dark tunnellike end that led to the Forbidden Cellar. It wasn't just the dark either. The cork panels on the walls were covered in seasonal red leaves, and the cupboards were filled with rows upon rows of bizarre autumn fruit figurines that stood in neat lines like a miniature army.

Sat in their midst, there was one figurine that was at least twice the size of the others. This strange manikin had a yellow squash body, a bulky quince head, ice-lolly stick arms and legs, crab apple feet and star anise hands, one of which held a sharpened pencil like a spear. Its quince head had two black beans for eyes, a green grape for a nose and a bizarre mouth made of two rows of dried corn seeds. It looked like the skull of someone who had died of acute tooth-yellowing.

Suddenly he saw movement with the corner of his eye.

One of the autumn-themed figurines was coming to life. First, there was just a twitch of an apple, which could have been dismissed as a trick of the moonlight, but then the thing sprang to its chestnut feet and hopped down onto the floor before him.

Tin tried to walk around it, but the homunculus wouldn't let him pass, and when he attempted to run, the thing stung his ankle with one of its toothpick arms. Tin let out a startled cry that resonated loudly through the corridor.

He barely had time to notice that more of the fruit figurines were awakening and jumping off the shelves. When he finally turned his attention away from his injured ankle back to the path ahead of him, he saw that a whole army of autumn fruit homunculi had assembled before him like a miniature lynch mob. The manikins held up their toothpicks like weapons, staring up at him with their beady eyes made of corn or, in some cases, barley.

Tin quickly did some calculations in his head. If he turned and ran for the main entrance, he could probably outrun them. But he wanted to go the other way because Stella might be there waiting for him outside the cellar. He would simply have to find a way to go past the strange crowd.

He took a resolute step forward. At the same moment, the chestnut army started marching. The hundreds of tiny feet made rhythmic stomping noises, while the multitude of tiny soulless eyes stared with single-minded focus at him.

With their matching mummy costumes made of gauze bandages, Rea and Ida looked like a couple of recent emergency room discharges. This didn't stop them from plowing their way out of the auditorium through the confused mob that was the rest of their class. But when they got down the stairs to the ground floor, they realized they were suddenly alone. The many dozens of retreating primary school pupils were gone, and the only moving presence in the dark corridor was the brilliant moonlight that poured in through the windows in great shimmering translucent fans. The earthquake had stopped, and the noise of the commotion had been replaced by a cryptic silence.

"Where did the rest of them go?" asked Rea. She sounded more annoyed than frightened. Ida felt too stunned to answer.

Rea growled with frustration. "What is going on?" she shouted. Her voice echoed down the deserted corridor. She looked at Ida, who was still standing there wordlessly. She was staring at something farther down the corridor. Rea followed her gaze.

The red leaves pinned onto the large cork displays were dripping with blood. Small trickles of red were coming out of their pointy ends and then spreading around the walls like spilled red ink. The blood was spreading fast. It dripped onto the floor and even ran up to the ceiling until all of the walls were covered in red. Rea screamed and ran for the exit. In a moment, Ida followed.

42

THE RITUAL

A dome of pulsating red light hovered over the center of the inner courtyard, directly above the Queen's Well. The dome's vertical axis—a pillar of even brighter red—extended from the Queen's Well all the way up to the ceiling of the mountain, beyond which, aboveground, lay the ruins of the old fortress.

Inside the pillar, bright specks of red light were shooting up like blood cells inside a vein. The Black Queen hovered suspended inside it a few feet above the well. Gazing up in a trance, she was being slowly pulled upward by the force of the whirling particles. Her destination was clear; the tunnel of light that held her was linked to the old Queen's Well that sat directly above its newer counterpart. Through the black round opening of the old well that was just about visible on the ceiling of the mountain, it was possible to catch a glimpse of the full Moon as it cast its silver light over the outside world.

The Black Queen's bear guards stood in a circle around the well, watching her breakout ritual in solemn silence. Two of them held Leo by either forearm. The Black Queen had made good on her promise—she had made sure Leo was dragged out of the dungeon before she had commenced the ritual.

But now that he was there in the center of the action, Leo didn't know what to do. He had placed the last of his chips on the Archers, but they had failed to turn up. The red-tinted view of the rest of the inner courtyard that he could glimpse through the dome showed only the Black Queen's forces—legions of wolves and bears waiting for her to break the blue-tinged barrier of Nestis's spell so that they could all storm out into the city.

The only option he was left with was the suicidal one. Leo didn't like the idea of being blown to pieces, but the Black Queen had nearly gone halfway up, and if he didn't act right away, she was bound to burst out into the outside world in less than a minute. And the temporary inconvenience of dying and having to regenerate himself from scratch was still better than the sort of jabbing criticism, harsh disciplinary repercussions and, worst of all, passive-aggressive sense of disappointment that he was bound to be subjected to by the Star Council were he to fail in his mission. And he didn't even dare dwell on what the Star Queen herself might say.

So he summoned his last reserves of strength and slowly reached for his Stick of Sylvicolus.

43

RUKBAT BENDS THE RULES

When Rukbat and his team of Archers, aka Star Force Five, landed at the Underworld fortress in a brilliant beam of blue-white light, they were surprised to see large multitudes of wolflike and bearlike beings armed with heavy weaponry assembled in the central courtyard. The creatures, however, were so intent on staring at a huge glowing red dome in the center that they didn't even notice the arrival of the star daimons. The Archers were equally surprised to see all six members of the Hunters lingering on the outer edge of the circle. The two groups exchanged friendly, albeit perplexed, greetings as the two leaders, Rukbat and Betelgeuse, shook hands.

"What are you lot doing here?" said Rukbat.

Betelgeuse told him about their mission to find the dragon key. "Strangely enough," he added, "we still haven't found it—either down here or in the city above. So we came back to check whether there's anything here we might have missed. And to check on Leo. He seemed to be in some sort of tight spot the last time we saw him. May I ask you the same question? What in Jupiter's Red Spot are you doing here?"

"Same reason," said Rukbat. "Looks like Leo called Nunki some time ago to ask for help. Nunki, what was it exactly that he said?"

"I couldn't hear everything properly," said Nunki, holding in his hand a sparkling silver bow that was almost bigger than him. "I wasn't really there, if you know what I mean. But he definitely said he needed backup at the Bear Fortress."

"But that's against the rules!" cried Alnilam of the Hunters.

"Us Archers are always happy to bend the rules for Leo," said Rukbat. When he saw Betelgeuse giving him a questioning look, he quickly added, "Within reason, of course."

"And it's not as if we do this sort of thing very often," said Ascella, an Archer with long silver hair and a blue bow. "Bend the rules, that is."

The other two Archers, Alnasl and Arkab, promptly offered their own two cents, assuring Betelgeuse that they did this sort of thing very rarely indeed. But their conversation had drawn the attention of the wolves lingering around the outer edge of the courtyard. There was some snarling and barking until some bow-happy wolfling shot a glowing arrow that flew just by Bellatrix's ear.

"Who did that?" she cried. As soon as she spotted the offending wolf, she fired a powerful ice-blue ray out of a special metal band around her wrist, blasting the wolf to pieces.

"Now, Bellatrix," said Betelgeuse, "remember what we said to Leo? We haven't been sent here to fight."

"No mortal shoots at me and lives." She uttered this line in a way that left no doubt as to its literal meaning.

The comrades of the fallen wolf had joined the fray, shooting fiery arrows at Bellatrix with their bows. She fended off the arrows with her left forearm, which was enclosed in an ice-blue metal gauntlet, while firing blue rays out of the metal band on her right hand.

The skirmish soon exploded into a full-fledged battle. The Archers were quick to pick up their magnificent bows, firing deadly arrows filled with the essence of exploding stars.

All Hunters apart from Bellatrix were initially reluctant to take part, but eventually one by one they joined in, until each one of them, including Alnilam, was fighting the Black Queen's forces.

"We'll have some explaining to do if the Star Queen ever finds out," cried Betelgeuse.

"Let's hope she never does!" answered Rukbat.

The battle was fairly predictable until, all of a sudden, in a showy burst of red flames, the Star Warriors materialized at the head of the Black Queen's ranks.

"Well, look at what we've got here," hooted Antares.

"The council's errand runners," said Shargaz contemptuously.

"The barnacle botherers," said Lesath.

When both the Archers and the Hunters failed to look offended, Sharur offered his own contribution.

"The horse whisperers."

"That doesn't even make sense," said Betelgeuse.

"Unbelievable!" said Alnilam to no one in particular. "Why are they here?"

"We are here," said Antares, "because we felt like coming. The Star Warriors need no permission from the council to go from one end of the universe to another. The Star Warriors do as they please."

"Get out of here, Antares," shouted Bellatrix, "and take your hooligans with you."

"Make me," said Antares.

Bellatrix promptly shot Antares's plumed helmet off his head. The exposed locks, packed almost solid with unventilated scalp sweat, had the unmistakable look of Lego hair.

"That's it!" cried Antares indignantly. He turned to his gang. "Fire at will!" he yelled.

The Star Warriors fired an angry volley of red-hot blasts in the general direction of the Hunters and Archers. Their formidable heavy-duty blasters and ray guns made the wolves' fiery swords and arrows look like novelty toys from an amusement park. The Archers and Hunters fired back. The wolves and bears, looking overwhelmed by the sudden appearance of so many outside actors and unable to decide who, if anyone, was on their side, fired at anything that moved.

44

HOT, PULSATING LUMP OF EXQUISITE PAIN

When Dario regained his muddled consciousness, he was kneeling against the well with his head hanging limply over the edge. The whole left side of his face was a hot, pulsating lump of exquisite pain. He lifted his head slowly, achingly. The vertebrae in his neck creaked like ungreased hinges.

Slowly and with great effort, he opened his swollen eyes and was treated to the sight of the real Black Queen—for it had to be her—rising out of the well in a pillar of red light. The wispy thing that had climbed down from the sky stood in front of the well on the opposite side from Dario, its arms reaching out to the rising form. As for the latter, there was no doubt that this was the real deal: whereas the thin spidery form was just an expressionless husk, the real Black Queen was all icy majesty and unyielding determination.

Cora, no longer a reptilian monster but back to being her more attractive self, stood a few steps behind the two figures, observing the spectacle with eager eyes. She clearly no longer had any interest in Dario.

Despite the Black Queen's imposing presence, her form was shimmery and transparent, lacking substance, as if she were not really there. She might have been just a trick of the light. But as she emerged, her essence seemed to pour itself into the spidery shell standing silently by the well, like ink being injected into a vessel of clear water.

As the two forms merged, the resulting figure of the resurrected Black Queen looked solid and very much there indeed.

45

QUINCE HEAD

The army of chestnut figurines advanced toward Tin with an ominous rhythmic stamping of many tiny feet. Within seconds, the manikins let out a collective high-pitched war cry and launched an attack on his ankles. Tin yelped and started stomping his feet. He took out quite a few of them, crushing them to a pulp, but new ones kept jumping off the shelves and coming at him.

All of a sudden, the chestnut army froze.

Something big moved on the top shelf of a cupboard, and Tin saw that it was the big figurine he had noticed before—the one that had a quince for a head, a squash for a body and crab apples for feet, as well as being armed with a threateningly sharp pencil held like a lance in one of its star-shaped hands. This thing was now coming to life.

Quince Head threw itself off the shelf and landed on the floor a few paces away from Tin. The army of smaller figurines parted in the middle with a deferential air. The oversize manikin marched purposefully toward him, its yellow corn-tooth grin turning into something more like a leer.

It raised its pencil lance, aiming it at Tin's leg, but Tin had had enough of mindless pseudomilitaristic fruit homunculi or any other mindless pseudomilitaristic things for one night.

"Arrrgh, to hell with all of you!" he growled.

Driven by a sudden surge of fury, he kicked Quince Head in the face. But Quince Head's quince head remained in place. Its bean eyes narrowed into dangerous slits. Then it drove its pencil into Tin's shoe, piercing his big toe.

Tin howled with pain and then reflexively kicked Quince Head in its gourd belly with his uninjured foot. This sent the figurine flying through the air, whereupon it crashed into the wall. "Take that!" he yelled victoriously.

The manikin's head tumbled off its neck and rolled unceremoniously down the corridor, while the crab apple feet and other fruity pieces fell off their respective sticks and bounced onto the floor.

This made all the smaller figurines charge at Tin with a vengeance. Gone was any pretense of orderly military formation. It was now "fire at will" all around, and Tin's ankles found themselves on the receiving end of many painful toothpick pokes. Bloodstains bloomed around the cuffs of his trouser legs.

His only defense was the tried-and-tested foot-stomping, but given the sheer number of the manikins, this was not going to be effective for long. He stomped his feet faster and faster, like a frenzied tap dancer. Crushed figurines lay in messy heaps all around him, but however many he destroyed, more of them kept coming. So many had sprung up that they were now starting to pile on top of one another, and some were even swinging off the cupboards like monkeys.

Meanwhile, farther down the corridor, Quince Head was slowly rising back to its feet. Its scattered parts had somehow found their way back to the rest of its body, and the homunculus now rose above the rest of the army fully formed. This time there was a distinctly vicious expression on its yellow face. Its mouth was turned down into an evil corn-toothed snarl. Quince Head gripped its spear with both star anise hands and marched toward Tin, treading over the parts of the fallen figurines standing in its way. There was a look of diabolical determination on its face.

Then there came a bloodcurdling inhuman shriek from somewhere below, and all the chestnut creatures froze. Even Quince Head froze. Tin didn't freeze, but he welcomed the break.

The surviving seasonal fruit figurines observed the latest developments with anxiety in their beady eyes. It looked as if some of them were ready to bail. It was no use, however, because they all suddenly started getting wobbly, then mushy, and finally runny. It was as if they were all turning to water or at least some sticky watery substance. Soon the whole corridor was covered in puddles of messy fruit ichor with random bits of fruit and broken sticks floating in it.

The cleaner is going to have a fit, thought Tin.

46

THE STARRY DONGLE

I t all happened so fast that if he had involuntarily blinked to get a piece of dust out of his eye, he would have missed it. Just as Leo was about to take drastic measures, the Archers appeared on the other side of the courtyard, and they must have had reinforcements with them too (Leo couldn't see all the details from behind the curtain of red light), because within a few seconds a major shoot-out began, and soon all the wolves and bears were engaged in fighting an explosive battle against the newly arrived Celestial Realm force.

Those bears that had been guarding the Queen's Well had lost their stance of solemn anticipation and now looked uncertain as to whether to remain by the well or join their comrades in battle. The Black Queen, who had almost reached the top of the red pillar where the tunnel of light joined the other well aboveground, was not much help. She was fully immersed in the ritual, apparently oblivious to what was happening below.

The two guards holding Leo were losing their grip. When he jerked out of their grasp, pulling out his Stick of Sylvicolus, they barely had time to look surprised before he reduced them both to a heap of ashes. He incinerated the rest of the guards with one sweeping fiery stroke.

Then, just as the Black Queen was about to disappear out of sight, he pointed the burning tip of his wand at the well before him and, dragging all the power that was left in his primitive weapon, fired a blinding blast that leveled it into a heap of rubble.

Two things happened then. First, the glittering specks that had been shooting up the red pillar of light changed course and started flowing downward. Second, the Black Queen was pulled down the pillar.

As she got dragged back down, she finally snapped out of her trance. There was a look of mute outrage on her face. When her gaze landed on Leo, her expression immediately morphed into that of pure hatred.

Leo raised his hands, palms out, in a conciliatory manner.

"I can explain."

Before he could add anything else, the extracting force of the shaft finished pulling the Black Queen all the way down, throwing her to the ground about ten feet from him.

For a few moments, the Black Queen lay on her side where she had fallen. Then she picked something up off the ground and, clutching the thing tightly in her fist, slowly got to her feet.

"Now, Barbara," said Leo, "I know you're angry. But I urge you not to do something rash."

The Black Queen stood facing him, her fist raised like a weapon. When she opened it and tossed something at him, Leo was relieved to see that it was nothing more than a tiny black insect. But as the insect flew toward him, it expanded, morphing into something hideous with thick scaly wings, giant mandibles and a long, sharp proboscis. By the time it reached Leo, it was huge—almost man-sized—and deadly.

Leo took a swing with his fiery stick, but the insect dodged it deftly and went straight for Leo's face, mandibles snapping. Leo thrust out his forearm to deflect the attack and felt two rows of fangs bite into his flesh just below the elbow.

Growling with pain, Leo bashed the insect's face with the handle of the stick, taking out one of its slimy, bulbous eyes. The insect shrieked and immediately released Leo's arm, but the next moment, it attacked again. Leo whacked it with the stick, this time the fiery part of it, pouring a barrage of blows on the monster that first broke its proboscis, then cracked its wings, and finally rendered it unconscious. The insect crashed onto the ground in a hideous heap of broken tentacles.

The Black Queen was seething with fury.

"Was this really necessary?" said Leo. "Can't we just talk?"

"I am done talking with you, demon," said the Black Queen, and raised her hand again. A big raven that had been perching on the battlements soared into the air.

Meanwhile, the red light of the dome started fading, the vertical shaft losing force.

The raven flew in through the side of the fading dome and swept down toward the Black Queen, landing on the index finger of her extended hand. It was just an ordinary raven, but even an ordinary bird could be deadly in the Black Queen's hands.

"What are you going to do with that thing?" asked Leo. He had used the Black Queen's raven-charming time to inch discretely toward the remains of the well. His frenzied mind told him that he would have to quickly figure out both how to find an alternative route out of Bear Town, since he couldn't go back the way he had arrived from, and how to finish the job he had been sent to do. Because as long as there existed any sort of link between the aboveground fortress and the Underworld, the Black Queen remained a threat.

In lieu of an answer, the Black Queen released the raven, sending it flying toward Leo. The bird was arrow-fast, its thornlike claws and beak aimed at his head.

My hair! shrieked a panicked voice inside his head. *It's heading for my hair!* Leo silenced the voice for the time being. He would have a hair-related panic attack later.

Then he remembered the starry dongle that Algol had given him.

Taking the pendant out of his pocket, Leo leaped into the waning red shaft that still extended from the remains of the underground well. The red light specks started moving again, and he felt himself being pulled up by a strong magnetic force. He muffled a shout of pain as the tip of the raven's claw tore at his scalp. Then he crushed the tiny glass sphere in his hand.

A surge of power shot through him, sending golden fire out of his pores, and for a moment, he felt like his true self again. The force propelled him up to the edge of the top well—the same aboveground twin of the Black Queen's infernal version below. Leo practically whooped with joy. But the feeling didn't last long, because the next instant the star-shaped beacon on his belt lit up, buzzing with an urgency that could be neither resisted nor postponed. The self-important frequency of the buzzing immediately told Leo who was summoning him—Alnair, no doubt following the orders of the Star Queen. The all-knowing queen of the Celestial Realm had a way of seeing what was happening in every corner of the universe in real time, something that Leo had always considered a nifty albeit potentially exhausting trick. And if anything required the urgent intervention of the Celestial Realm, the Star Queen had no qualms about immediately dispatching a suitable star daimon to that end, usually through the agency of her favorite dogsbody Alnair. The coordinates shown on the display embedded within the circular center of the buckle (small, but tastefully done) told Leo that this might be a particularly dingy, neglected corner of the universe. But before he even had time to utter a single curse, he was sucked out of the very space he was presently occupying and flung into some ill-defined dark pit.

47

THE MAN WITH THE
GRAVITY-DEFYING HAIR

When Stella came to in the cellar, she had a strange sensation of being both physically there and not there at the same time, as if her poison-stunned body were still out cold, lying insensate out of sight somewhere on the dark floor while her spiritual essence roamed free on some less material level. The cellar itself suddenly looked numinous and ethereal, resembling the kind of place where such borderline experiences were an everyday occurrence. This paradox, however, was not something she chose to devote her full attention to since standing a few yards before her was the most extraordinary-looking person imaginable, one that looked like a peculiar combination of ancient Sun god and front man of a mid-1980s progressive hair metal band. This person was patting his head hectically, as if wishing to check whether his hair was still there. Apparently satisfied with what he found, he dropped his hands with obvious relief.

The last vestiges of the blue glow were fading, and yet she was able to see the strange man perfectly in brilliant Technicolor. Presently she realized why—it was because he was himself the source of the illumination. The light was literally radiating from inside of him.

The strange man finally noticed Stella's presence and immediately came to attention, suddenly looking perfectly turned out. His flustered expression had been replaced by a look of alertness in the blink of an eye.

"Are you all right, mister?" asked Stella.

"Of course I'm all right," snapped the glowing man. "What are you suggesting?"

"Nothing, mister. I was just worried because you looked a bit distressed for a moment."

"I'm pleased to inform you that the distress was unfounded, so don't be worried." The man paused for a beat. "And don't call me mister."

"What would you like me to call you, m—uh, sir?"

"You can call me…" The stranger appeared to perform a quick assessment of Stella's age. "…Uncle Leo."

"Nice to meet you, er…Uncle Leo. My name is Stella."

The man swept her introductory remarks aside with a dismissive flick of one hand. Whatever spark of interest he might have shown upon becoming aware of Stella's presence was now gone. His eyes darted around the darkness of the cellar. He was clearly not interested in small talk with school-age children and didn't look particularly happy to be there.

"Anyway, it is not my well-being that should be the object of anyone's concern, but yours. What is a helpless child such as yourself doing all by herself in this foul-smelling pit?"

"I am not helpless," said Stella with a tinge of sharpness in her voice. "And this is the basement of my school, so I have every right to be here. Well, sort of. We aren't really supposed to go down here. But, anyway…what about you, Uncle Leo? What are *you* doing here?"

The man who wished to be called Uncle Leo looked slightly taken aback. "Oh, I…" He cleared his throat. "I am the janitor."

Stella was so taken aback by the sheer absurdity of this statement that she momentarily forgot all about the spider bite, the Black Queen and even the bizarre feeling of not quite being physically there. "No you're not. Our janitor is called Rudi and he looks nothing like you."

"Well, obviously I am not *that* janitor. I am the assistant janitor."

"Assistant janitor?"

"Yes, assistant janitor, or rather janitorial apprentice, if you prefer the less commonplace term. I am here to learn the art and science of janitoring so that one day I may take the current janitor's place."

The more "Uncle Leo" rambled on, the more obvious it became to Stella that he had nothing to do with being a janitor or an assistant janitor and that he was overall not who he claimed to be. For one thing, no assistant janitor ever wore something that looked like a leotard belonging to a futuristic Pilates instructor from outer space. And no assistant janitor's hair ever looked that perfect and yet at the same time out of place, or rather out of *space*. The volume was simply too lush, the arrangement of each individual hair too perfect. Such unearthly perfection could only have one logical explanation—the hairdo was generating its own gravity field. Stella wasn't personally acquainted with any assistant janitors, but she was pretty sure that none of them had access to the sort of advanced hairstyling technology needed to reach such a high level of coiffureal sophistication. Uncle Leo noticed Stella eyeing his curls critically and made a self-conscious hair-smoothing gesture.

"If you're the janitor's assistant," said Stella, "then how come I've never seen you before? We see Rudi the janitor all the time."

Uncle Leo looked hesitant for only the briefest of moments. "Being a janitor's assistant is different, much different, from being the head janitor."

"How so?"

Uncle Leo huffed impatiently. "The assistant janitor's position is less prominent than the head janitor's. There is a lesser degree of visibility involved in the role. Us assistant janitors prefer to work in the background."

"That is strange. You make it sound as if janitors' assistants have more autonomy than real janitors."

Uncle Leo now looked thoroughly fed up and obviously eager to bring this entire conversational thread to a quick conclusion. "It is not strange at all. You're just too young to appreciate the complexities of janitorial work. One day when you are older, you will understand my words."

Stella was about to say more on the topic of janitoring, but the man interrupted her before she could say another word. "Anyway, there are more pressing issues at hand. Such as, you don't happen to know the way out of this place?" He was starting to look like a nicotine addict who had been given permission to leave his workplace for a two-minute cigarette break only to realize upon leaving the office that he had forgotten to bring his lighter.

"Shouldn't you know that, Uncle Leo? You're the assistant janitor."

Uncle Leo faltered in his pacing and came to an uncertain halt. "That's a fair point. But, you see, the thing is—"

"It's all right, Uncle Leo," interjected Stella in order to put the bristly yet oddly likable man out of his misery. "I don't mind if you're not really an assistant janitor."

This seemed to put Uncle Leo at ease. "Well, I'm happy to know I'm talking to a sensible person. Jupiter knows those are in short supply on this planet." Having uttered this puzzling statement, he made as if to take a step forward but then tripped, barely managing to keep his balance. They both looked down and saw one of the giant spider's hideously contorted legs lying motionlessly on the floor.

"Be careful, Uncle Leo," said Stella. "That was one nasty spider."

The strange man first looked stunned, then relieved, then appreciative, and finally chastised. The whole carousel of emotions had played itself out within less than two seconds.

"Is this your work?" said Uncle Leo with something approaching low-key awe in his voice. "Did you kill that thing?"

"Well, sort of." Stella wasn't sure why Uncle Leo was more perplexed by the possibility that she might have killed the giant spider monster than by the fact that such a thing as a giant spider monster existed. "But only because I had to, Uncle Leo. This isn't the sort of thing I normally do."

"How did you do it then?"

"I'm not sure I really did anything. I had a sort of magic bottle and a special whip and those things did most of the work. I was just holding them."

"Drop the unnecessary modesty, child. The whip and the magic bottle might have done most of the work, but those things are not for everyone. In fact, there are very few people who can wield them. Anyway, where did you get the weapons?"

"A friend of mine gave them to me. Or rather an acquaintance. I mean, he's a grown-up, but still a very nice person."

"Let me guess—little fat man, baroque manners, DIY glasses, ludicrous moustache."

"Yes, that's the one!" exclaimed Stella enthusiastically, but then immediately felt bad for taking part in a conversation in which a friend of hers was called fat. The feeling didn't last long, however, because it was obvious that Uncle Leo didn't mean anything bad by it. He was not mean; it was just the way he talked. Stella's mood was further uplifted by the funny feeling that she and the strange man were "talking shop" in some way. "Do you know him, Uncle Leo?"

"I wish I didn't."

"May I ask you something, Uncle Leo?"

"If you must."

"It's just that you don't come across as the least bit surprised by any of this stuff. I mean the dead arachnid monster, the magic weapons and all that. Could it really be that you've seen a giant killer spider before?"

"Oh, yes. Giant killer spider, giant killer fox, giant killer barnacle, you name it." As he expounded his giant creatures list, Uncle Leo sounded like a seasoned car mechanic rattling off the main points of a typical car maintenance checkup. "Even a giant killer bacterium or two, although those technically cease to be bacteria the moment they increase their total cell count beyond one."

"But what does a person have to do in order to see such things, Uncle Leo?"

"You know what? Drop the 'Uncle.' That whole thing was a bad idea. My mistake. Let's just forget about it, okay?"

"Okay."

"And to answer your question, it's not so much a matter of doing as it is of being."

The cryptic remark uttered by the man formerly known as Uncle Leo brought up a recollection in Stella's mind of Otto saying that they (Stella still wasn't sure who exactly "they" were—presumably Otto and his magical associates) had been compelled to ask a powerful external entity to help them fight the Black Queen's creatures. If Stella had to venture a guess, she would have said that the man standing before her was precisely this external entity. In his case, however, "external" clearly meant *very* external. The man looked as if he were not merely from out of town, but out of galaxy.

"Oh," she said. "I know you're probably not allowed to tell me who you are, but can you at least drop a hint?"

"All right." Leo knitted his brow in concentration. "You know how stars are said to be made of cheese?"

"Cheese? I've heard silly stories about the Moon being made of cheese, but not stars."

"Never mind." Another dismissive hand gesture. "It's all nonsense anyway. My point is that stars are said to be made of something inanimate."

"Yes. Hydrogen, helium and things."

"Well, that is not entirely true. Stars are living things."

"So that means you're a…"

"Star daimon."

"What does that mean? That you're some sort of demon that haunts a particular star?"

"No." Leo made a theatrical pause. "I *am* the star."

As soon as Leo had uttered this particular one-liner, Stella knew it to be true. But before she had a chance to ask him what being an actual star meant in practical terms, something stirred in the darkness below. Incredibly, the broken spider's leg was moving.

It can't be, thought Stella. *It's dead—it must be dead.* But her incredulity was to no avail. The presumed-dead Spider of Illusion had indeed come back to life and was unfurling its previously crumpled-up legs with a menacing slowness. Its sagging body began to prop itself up on its still-wobbly legs like some gruesome self-assembling tent. But the laborious recovery must have been some sort of charade, because the next instant, the spider was charging at the two of them with renewed force.

Leo's lightning-quick response foiled the spider's assault. The star daimon launched himself at the approaching monster, bolting through the darkness like a gold-and-electric-blue comet, and met the Spider of Illusion halfway in a fierce clinch. The ethereal golden glow emanating from Leo became more intense. The spider let out a piercing shriek. The light continued to pour out of Leo and into the Spider of Illusion. Wherever the supernatural light touched the monster, that part sizzled, burned, and fell off, melting into a lump of muddy ooze on the floor. As the light poured into the monster, Leo's glow steadily dimmed. The creature's wails became feebler the more incinerated it got. Within a minute, its final shrieks faded into silence and whatever was left of it melted to black gunk.

By the time the spider was finally dead, the last of Leo's supernatural glow had faded away. He staggered away from the liquefied mortal remains of the Black Queen's spider looking disheveled and weary. Even his previously perfect hair was now slightly out of place, although Stella was wise enough to refrain from expressing this particular observation aloud.

"It's fine," said Leo in anticipation of Stella's next question, sounding short of breath. "It really was you who killed the spider. It was an evil, unnatural force that made it come back to life, a force that really wants a piece of me. But don't worry, it's really gone now."

"But are you all right, Un...Leo?"

"I'll be fine," said Leo breathlessly. "I just need some herbal tea and to be as far away from this planet as possible."

"Are you sure?"

Leo didn't look sure, but he nodded.

"There's something I really don't get," said Stella. "Why should a powerful being such as yourself, an actual star, have to come down to Earth to fight some ugly eight-legged monster?"

"With great power comes great responsibility," replied Leo with as much sarcasm as he could muster between husky gulps of air. After he had more or less regained his composure, or a semblance of it, he continued. "Also sometimes star daimons do really stupid, criminally stupid, things, and then they get sent to backward planets to do the dirty work that no one else wants to do. This serves as a punishment for their crimes because there are no prisons in space." Stella must have look confused, because he quickly added, "But you needn't concern yourself with such issues at this point."

"But will I ever get a chance to? I mean concern myself with space and such issues." The everyday world of ordinary people no longer had any appeal to Stella, not that it ever had much in the first place.

Leo gave Stella an assessing look. "You just might." He looked as if he wanted to say more, but then visibly checked himself. "I must stop talking now. We're not allowed to talk about things of a prophetic nature to ordinary humans. In fact, we're not allowed to talk to them at all." The beautiful eight-pointed star on Leo's belt flashed, and he immediately started fading from view amidst a vortex of blue light.

"Wait! You're going to just disappear now?" There were so many questions left that Stella wanted to ask.

"Yes. That's what star daimons do." The disappointment must have been written all over Stella's face, because Leo's demeanor quickly softened. He rolled his eyes. "If you really insist on chatting again, you can try summoning me. But make sure you have a very good reason, such as questions of utmost profundity or matters of life or death, because star daimons don't like time wasters. And if you're ever in any sort of trouble, and I mean real trouble, give me a call and I'll beam down promptly. My summoning name is Regulus."

"Thank you." Stella felt appreciative to the point of bursting into tears but checked herself the way she had seen Leo do only moments before. "Are you sure you want me to call you if I have to, Leo?"

At that precise moment, Leo's star buckle flashed again even more brightly, this time with the addition of a deep, urgent hum. "Well, why not?" The acerbic tone was back in his voice. "Everyone else is doing it." Then he disintegrated, merging with the vortex, and disappeared as if sucked into the ether.

48

THE SUBSTANCE OF PURE NIGHTMARE

The Black Queen stood fully formed and triumphant on her pedestal of red light. Cora walked up to her reverently and went down on her knees, her head bowed.

This was what Leo had been trying to avoid, Dario thought as his mind finally became clearer. This was what he had implicitly expected Dario to prevent in his absence. The worst thing that could have happened to the city, the substance of pure nightmare, the starting point of inevitable doom, was about to happen, and Dario had done nothing to forestall it.

He had failed abjectly. Not only had he failed to actively avert disaster, but he had also inadvertently exacerbated it by allowing himself to be used as a sacrificial lamb by a reptilian succubus.

Dario would no doubt have continued wallowing in the mire of his many failures had he not been startled out of his self-rebuke by the sight of the Black Queen plunging into the well. This happened just as she was about to ceremoniously climb down to the ground. As she was dragged back into the well, the ethereal form of the real Black Queen literally peeled itself off its receiving spidery husk.

The hastily vacated shell reeled like a drunken figure skater performing a pirouette, its spindly arms flailing disorientedly while its empty eyes stared without comprehension. Then it collapsed as if struck, crumbling into a heap of dust.

Cora let out a yelp and sprang to her feet. For a moment, she looked like a cornered animal.

Her gaze landed on Dario and her expression changed to fury. She hissed and seemed to be on the verge of turning into a reptilian monster with super-human strength once again but then gasped and jerked her head back, suddenly writhing as if in great pain.

"Cora?" said Dario and took a step in her direction even though he knew it was an ill-advised move. She was probably playing weak in order to lure him to her so that she might kill him with the least amount of effort.

He never got a chance to find out whether his skepticism was justified or not because before he had managed to reach her, there was a terrible sound of crunching bone and Cora doubled over, collapsing to the ground with a hideous guttural growl. She shrank to the size of a withered mummy right before his eyes and continued to shrink even further, accompanied by an even louder sound of grinding bones.

By the time he reached Cora, there was nothing left of her.

Something moved in the grass by his foot. Dario took a reflexive step back when he realized that it was a black asp. But the snake only flicked out its forked tongue and slithered away into the shadows, disappearing out of sight.

49

THE RUINS

The Black Queen stood in the midst of the ruins of what used to be her underground fortress.

The mountain ceiling above her had been shattered to pieces by the explosion, but instead of opening the way out for her and her army, it had half collapsed and then settled heavily back down in a way that made her feel as if she were buried alive under a mound. What had previously been a high ceiling was now the roof of a narrow tunnel that kept her sealed below. And her only link to the outside world—the Queen's Well above—had caved in, its opening obliterated by collapsing rocks.

Directly below it, there was only a crater where the other well used to be, the multitudes of soldiers who had gone after Leo lying dead among the rubble.

The raven was also there among the dead, lying motionless on its side. One of its wings was broken and the other had been torn off. Its eyes were lifeless black beads.

All around her, the blue light of Nestis's spell glowed undiminished.

The Black Queen threw back her head and let loose a terrifying howl.

50

THE BLUE COAT

Rudi lay on the floor in a pool of crimson blood that was spreading around his head like a halo. As his life faded, so did the terrible memories of the crash. He welcomed the soothing absence of thought. But in his final moments, a forgotten memory resurfaced in his mind.

He had been on his way back from one of his rare ventures into the outside world. He was waiting at the tramway crossing on the main road along with a group of passers-by. Among them there had been a small girl who stood impatiently ahead of them all, clearly eager to get to the other side. A tram was approaching at full speed from the left, but she didn't see it. She looked neither left nor right to see if it was safe to cross. Instead, she took a step forward. Her tiny foot was about to land on the tram tracks just as the whirling hot air of the charging tram blew against his face. Without thinking, Rudi reached out and pulled the girl back by the collar. The tram sped past like a whirlwind. The girl looked back shyly for just a second and then went on her way. The whole event had happened so fast that he barely registered it at the time. He had never thought of it again. But looking back on it now, he was almost certain the girl had been wearing a blue coat.

Rudi smiled.

51

MANDA'S WELL

The next time Stella awoke in the cellar, the sensation of being physically there but not there was gone. This time, there was no doubt that she was physically present in her body, and it felt awful. She was sprawled on the sticky stone floor, her limbs stiff and the spider bite wound throbbing. The silver bottle lay empty beside her. Its purpose had been served, and it was now nothing more than a trinket. The blue glow was gone, leaving the cellar as dark as before. The poison had spread throughout her whole body and she felt as inert as a paperweight. Her breathing was shallow; every breath was a struggle.

Nevertheless, she couldn't just remain lying there on the floor. If she was about to die, she didn't want it to happen in the spider's lair. She had to at least make an effort of getting away from it, even if that meant crawling up the stairs.

With a tremendous effort that felt like pulling the roots of Bear Mountain out of the ground, she slowly got back on her feet. For a moment, she stood swaying from side to side, unable to keep her balance. Her head was spinning. She clutched it with both hands, covering her eyes to push off a surge of nausea.

But when she uncovered her eyes again, it was no longer dark. To be sure, it was still fairly gloomy, but that was only because this place always was. Its ancient walls were soaked in darkness, its polished stones reflecting only subtle candlelight. But from beyond its sweeping archway, a sliver of sunlight was coming through. She was inside the Stone Gate.

"Ah, there you are!" said Otto Goldsmith, springing up to his feet. He had been perched on one of the pews, fiddling with a large mechanical watch. He tucked it into his pocket.

"How did I get here?"

"Ah!" Otto blinked excitedly. "As I might have mentioned, the Stone Gate is not exactly a fixed point." He paused and stared at Stella attentively for a few moments, as if trying to gauge whether he was getting through to her or not. "It's a movable point," he added.

"What?" Stella's voice sounded distant to her own ears.

"Never mind, it's complicated." The goldsmith waved the whole thought away. Then he looked down at Stella's wound. "Is this what that fiend did to you? Oh dear, oh dear." He tsked, shaking his head. "We'd better have it looked at, and the sooner the better."

He led her out of the Stone Gate into the bright sunlight of Upper Town, then into what would normally have been Radić Street but for the fact that the road was now nothing more than a country footpath going down a hill.

"Come on," said Otto, offering Stella his arm, "it's not far."

What isn't far? thought Stella, but her mouth felt too numb to give voice to the idea. The inertia had returned with a vengeance, locking her joints and deadening her limbs. She didn't think she could take another step, but Otto somehow managed to patiently lead her all the way down the hill.

At the end of the path, they found themselves in a green valley dotted with charming groves. A round spring filled with cerulean-blue water glistened in the sun. One side of the spring was semi-enclosed in a low curved wall of rough stone, while a bubbling stream flowed out from the other side.

Stella's eyes followed the stream, which extended in the direction they had come from, disappearing between two ancient burgs, each sitting atop its own hill—Grič on the left and Kaptol on the right.

"Here she is," chirped Otto in an enthusiastic voice behind her. He sounded miles away.

When Stella groggily turned to the spring once again, there was an unknown female figure standing by the water. She was very tall, wore a long white dress and held a silver cup in her hands. The sun was very bright above her head, obscuring most of her features and creating the impression that her hair was made of light.

"Who are you?" asked Stella, but the figure offered no reply.

Otto cleared his throat discreetly. "Trust me," he said in a half whisper, "you wouldn't want her to speak."

Stella took an involuntary step toward the spring, but then lost her balance and fell to one knee. Her vision was blacking out again.

"Oh dear," said the goldsmith and grabbed her elbow for support. "I think we'd better hurry up."

The next thing she knew, there was a sensation of something cool and steely touching her lower lip, and then ice-cold water gushed down her throat. At first, she gagged and coughed but then began to drink with the urgency of someone who had only just realized they were dying of thirst. The water was so shockingly cold that it gave her a stab of brain freeze, but under the circumstances, she didn't mind. Any sensation was better than the terrible leaden inertia.

As the water ran through her, it seemed to wash the poison away, and she felt herself becoming lighter by the second. Soon she felt fresh and reinvigorated. When she opened her eyes, she saw that the cut on her thigh had healed completely. She could also see that the figure in white was gone, as was the cup.

The goldsmith was beaming at her. "You look wonderful, my dear," he said. "As good as new."

"What was that?" she asked, meaning the whole thing with the lady by the spring, but Otto was already busy staring at his complicated pocket watch again. He looked up expectantly.

"Ah, just in time," he said, gazing at something on the west horizon.

Unbelievably, there was a tram in the distance. It moved steadily in the direction of the city, running smoothly over the grass despite the complete absence of either tram tracks or electrical cables. As it got nearer, she could see that it was one of the familiar old trams with two carriages and a single headlight, the same type as "her" number seventeen. And, indeed, there was a square black plate with a yellow "17" sign displayed at the front. She noted that there was no driver in the cabin, but given the improbability of the tram's very existence in a field outside of medieval Zagreb, this was the least surprising part.

The tram stopped a few yards from the spring. Its doors opened with a familiar smacking noise.

"You'd better be off now," said the goldsmith, "because there won't be another tram for a very long time."

"Can I come back sometime?"

"Possibly." The goldsmith looked uncertain for a moment. "If you catch the right tram."

They said farewell, and then Stella hopped on the number seventeen through the first door on the driver's side with three practiced strides. The doors closed. She waved. Otto waved back. The tram glided down the valley. It was heading toward a big black patch that looked as if it had been cut into the sky directly above the east horizon, where it loomed like a monolithic portal of night.

52

ALL TOGETHER NOW

Dario felt confused. He had been leaning against the well when Leo suddenly appeared at the edge of it, let out a very uncharacteristic little whoop, and then disappeared inexplicably a moment later, only to reappear promptly in no less mysterious a manner. All this was followed by the tremor of a powerful blast. The Leo that appeared for the second time looked a bit worse for wear than the first iteration, and he looked a bit drained too, but his mood seemed to improve when he saw Dario.

"Dario!" said Leo cheerfully, as if they were two hikers bumping into one another in the woods. "What on earth happened to you?"

"Um…"

"And what are you doing here? You didn't follow me, did you?"

"No, but I wish I had." He briefly told Leo what had happened, leaving out the most embarrassing parts, mainly those having to do with his falling head over heels for a nymph-shaped snake monster. Instead, he made it sound more like a one-night stand gone horribly wrong.

"That sounds terrible," said Leo afterward. "And I'm sorry that you had to end up getting so…intimately embroiled in this whole Black Queen business."

Suddenly about a dozen star daimons came out of the well. Dario could tell right away that they were star daimons rather than ordinary people who just happened to look like star daimons because they didn't merely jump out of the well—instead, they *beamed* out. The beaming was a dead giveaway.

Leo looked glad to see them all, and he greeted them warmly.

"Thanks again, Nunki," said Leo. "Thanks, Rukbat. I owe you one."

"See you around, Leo," said the one called Rukbat and then disappeared along with the other members of his team.

"Thanks for sticking around, guys," said Leo to the remaining group, who looked like futuristic space hunters.

"Don't worry about it, Leo," said their leader. "What we really came back for is the key. But we still haven't been able to…" The leader paused when he saw something lying in the grass. "Ah! There we are." He crouched and picked something up off the ground. It was the dragon key Cora had dropped.

"Well, looks like we've finally got what we came here for," said the leader as he and the rest of his group started fading. "Better be off now."

"Thanks, Betelgeuse," said Leo. "Thanks, everyone. See you later."

Before Dario was able to utter a single confused question, yet another group of star daimons appeared before them. These were all warriors and, unlike the others, they did not look friendly. Their leader had a helmet with a preposterously big red plume on it. Both the helmet and its owner seemed to have taken a battering of some sort recently.

"There you are," said the leader, cracking his knuckles. "It's payback time."

"Antares," said Leo coolly. "What do you want?"

"You know what I want."

"How did you even know where to find me?"

"I told them," said another star daimon that had just materialized on top of a collapsed wall in the background. Dario immediately recognized him as Leo's friend from the Hidden Tower.

"Algol!" said Leo in an injured tone. "How could you?"

"Oh, come on, Leo," said Algol apathetically, "you already know I can't be trusted. I'm a demon star. It's my job to sow the seeds of chaos and confusion wherever I go."

"Fair enough," said Leo.

"Was it you who sent me that text about meeting up near Illyrian Square?" asked Dario.

"Why, sure," said Algol. "I always like to get as many people involved as possible. It makes the action more interesting."

"Enough with the chatter!" cried Antares. "We are here to wreak vengeance, not to attend a kaffeeklatsch. Go get him, boys!"

The warriors began to advance upon Leo.

"And what do you intend to do?"

"I intend to shave off your hair."

Leo suddenly went pale, but he stood his ground. "You wouldn't do that."

"Oh, yes I would." Antares unsheathed his big iron broadsword and held it up awkwardly, like a razor.

"Now, listen, Antares," said Leo, his voice sounding uncharacteristically nervous. "Surely you already know that what I did was nothing more than an innocent joke? I never thought anything would come of it. I mean, who would have thought that the Star Council is full of such paranoid bores that they'd actually believe that you of all star daimons would indecently expose yourself during an interdimensional summoning? I mean, if it had been Jupiter, sure. But *you*, Antares, indecently expose yourself? What a preposterous thought. And besides, I never meant it to be you. I actually wanted to say 'Aldebaran,' but I got the names mixed up."

"Enough!" snapped Antares. "I won't hear another word from you."

"Hold it!" cried a stern voice from above. Dario looked up and saw three more star daimons—two female warriors and one fairly ordinary-looking youth. Unlike the others, these three hadn't even bothered coming all the way down to Earth. Instead, they floated in the air steadily about twenty feet above the ground, as if standing on an invisible platform.

"Ara," said Antares to the more ill-tempered-looking of the female warriors, "what the hell do you want?"

"Antares, you and the rest of the Star Warriors have committed two serious breaches of the Star Daimon Code."

"What?" Antares cried, outraged.

"First," said Ara, holding up a finger, "threatening another star daimon is a serious offense."

"We didn't threaten him! We are only seeking justice for—"

"Second," cut in Ara, holding up another finger, "taking up arms against other star daimons is an even more serious offense."

"We didn't!"

"Stand back!" shouted the other female warrior.

The Star Warriors stood back.

"I will not be bossed around by anyone!" cried an indignant Antares. "I don't care if you're the Star Force Seven."

"Take them away, Ret," said Ara.

The youth, Ret, produced from his pocket something that looked like a tiny fishing net, which he then cast down in the direction of the Star Warriors. As it fell to the ground, the net expanded to the size of an enormous cage, landing in a way that got all of the Star Warriors entrapped within it. The warriors yelled and snarled like captured beasts, but they could not break out of the cage.

"Haul them off to the council," said Ara.

Navigating remotely with the motions of his hands, Ret made the giant net take off from the ground with its cargo of loudly remonstrating Star Warriors ("I'll get you for this!" shouted Antares at Leo in passing) and then ferried it high up into the night sky until both he and the cage had disappeared from view. The two female warriors followed.

"That was entertaining," said Algol. "Thanks for the show, everyone." Then he, too, started disappearing.

"Where are you going?" asked Leo.

But the demon star had already vanished.

"Wh-what—" began Dario, but there was a bright flash, and a magnificent star daimon made entirely of white light appeared before Leo.

"Leo," said the magnificent being.

"Alnair," said Leo.

"I don't want to take too much of your time," said Alnair. "I know you must be exhausted. This is just to say you've now got the all-clear and you're free to leave the White City whenever you wish to." The luminous being immediately started to disappear.

"Thank you," said Leo, visibly relieved.

"Oh," said Alnair before he had completely vanished, "and of course all your powers have been restored." He pointed his hand at Leo, and a bright white spark shot out of his index finger, making the golden threads and buckles on Leo's outfit light up with a golden glow. The gold star on his belt lit up last.

"Well, Dario," said Leo once Alnair was gone, "it's been nice meeting you, but now it's time that I, too, made my exit." He was starting to glow gold all over. "I realize you must be very confused by what you've just seen, but trust me when I say that if I tried to explain any of it, your confusion would only increase a hundredfold."

"Um, probably."

Leo stopped glowing all of a sudden. "Dario, are you all right?"

Dario assured him, as coherently as he could, that he was.

"Are you going to be all right going home on your own? Are you going to take the bus?"

"Um, I don't think there are any buses this time of night."

"Are you going to take the tram?"

"Probably."

For a moment, Leo seemed to have some sort of internal struggle, but then he gave in.

"All right, let me walk with you to the station."

They plodded down a winding road through the woods, the same road that schoolkids used when going on day trips to Bear Town. The path glowed silver in the moonlight before them, as did the barks of the trees and the dew-covered caps of the mushroom that had sprouted out of the various mossy patches on the ground. Glinting eyes of small animals occasionally peeked out of the bushes. Every once in a while, an owl hooted.

Soon they came into a little clearing that provided them with a spectacular view.

The city sprawled below them all the way from the foot of the mountain to the horizon. Its buildings were mysterious silhouettes against the radiant glow of the streetlights. Traffic crawled like lazy, viscous treacle down the streets.

The two hills of Grič and Kaptol in the old center were like mounds from an ancient civilization. The towers of the city's many churches rose up to the sky, illuminated by their own yellow-white light from below and the persistent silver glow of the full Moon from above.

When they came down to the tram stop at the foot of the mountain, there was a number fourteen, or something like it, already there, waiting to take Dario back to normalcy and civilization, where evil shape-shifting beings wouldn't be luring him to dark abandoned places in order to use him as a blood sacrifice to bring back dead witch-queens.

"So, will you ever come back?" asked Dario as they stood by the blue hull of the tram.

"I wish I could say no, but when it comes to the White City, this is something I am unfortunately never able to do with absolute certainty."

"What about the Black Queen?"

"We needn't worry about her anymore," said Leo. As if remembering something, he took the now-battered Stick of Sylvicolus out of his pocket. "But I might as well give you this, just in case."

Dario accepted the wand gratefully with the air of someone taking on a grave responsibility.

"Just be careful how you handle it lest you burn your face off."

"I will. I mean, I won't…burn my face off."

They said farewell and Leo disappeared into the night. Dario got on board the tram and collapsed exhaustedly onto an overheated seat. As the tram set out on its city-bound route, Dario looked out of the window just in time to see a gold star shoot up into the sky.

53

A NIGHT TO REMEMBER

Many strange things happened at the East Central Primary School that night, none stranger than the earthquake that made people imagine all kinds of fantastical things. The majority of these things were later subject to wildly inconsistent interpretations, and no general consensus as to what exactly had happened was ever reached.

There was one thing, however, that everyone agreed on: a tram stopped outside the school that night.

The tram, a boxy old number seventeen, went all the way to the front side of the school despite there being no tram tracks on that particular road and stopped right outside the main gate. When the tram opened its doors, it revealed the sight of a girl standing at the first door of the first carriage. She stood there for a moment, hands on hips, surveying the scene before her. She looked grimy, exhausted and as if she had recently escaped being eaten by a giant pig (which was what had in fact happened, although most eyewitnesses were not aware of this at the time). But in spite of all this, she was beaming.

The girl hopped down the tram's steps with the zest of an intergalactic explorer descending the gangway of a faster-than-light spaceship in order to stake a claim to an unexplored planet after an epic, perilous journey. Well, perhaps she didn't do it with *that* much zest, but she certainly did look rather excited.

The number seventeen's blue doors flapped closed. The girl turned to the tram and, as if it were a trusty steed, gave it one hearty slap on the rump.

The tram immediately stirred into motion and glided effortlessly down to the end of the street. It made a slow, sweeping turn at the point where the street widened before the intersection with the Village until it had gone full circle and faced the opposite direction.

It sat there for a few moments, its engine resonating with an electric thrum that made everyone's hair stand on end. Then it charged, bolting down the street with mind-boggling speed. It swooshed past the girl, who watched the tram gleefully from the sidewalk, going so fast that the gust of air released in its wake blew her hair back. She stood looking at the receding tram and waved until the tram's back plate with the glowing yellow-against-black number seventeen had disappeared into the distance.

Where the tram had gone, no one knew. But then again, no one knew where it had come from.

Soon the girl was surrounded by an avid crowd of classmates, including a boy dressed in a car mechanic's overalls. Everyone wanted to know where she had been and what she had been up to, and the girl looked happy to share her experiences. And thus many new school legends were born.

Yes, it really was a night to remember, the kind that doesn't happen very often. Of course, people's memories being what they are, the details of the events soon became fuzzy until they almost completely faded from the minds of everyone over twelve years of age. And once that had happened, it was easy for the many wild fables that circulated fervently among the primary school pupils in the following months to be attributed to nothing more than overactive childish fancy.

Indeed, very few adults had been present on-site in the aftermath of the mysterious earthquake. Emergency services were occupied elsewhere in the city, and the few that eventually made it to the school got there once the otherworldly number seventeen had departed.

In fact, one of the few adults present at the scene during the most contested moments was the owner and CEO of the BBP, who had been driven to the site by what he liked to think of as his professional hunch. This was the kind of story he had been waiting for since the time he got his first journalism job. His feature, entitled "The Night of the Witch," was subsequently published in the *White City Chronicle*, but due to the questionable reputation of that publication, it failed to get the attention it deserved. It did, however, get more than the average number of online comments (fourteen, instead of the typical two).

There were also strange rumors about the sudden disappearance of one of the school's senior faculty members, Professor Anka Radovan. Some say that Professor Radovan had an impulsive change of heart about her overdue retirement and that on that night, in an unexpected display of altruism, she had spontaneously resigned in order to give the younger members of the staff a chance to put their teaching skills to use. This, at least, was the official explanation.

But others say that during the fateful Night of the Witches, Professor Radovan had some sort of nervous breakdown that turned her into a raving lunatic, and that she was subsequently carted off to the Vrapče madhouse on the outskirts of the city.

They say that if you happen to walk past Vrapče on certain nights of the full Moon, you can still hear the grunting of the great werepig.

54

THE STAR QUEEN

I t was not often that the Star Queen requested a private audience with anyone. This was why, as he sat on a plush sofa in the waiting room of the resplendent Star Palace on Sirius, Leo felt understandably jittery. As he was ushered into the vast throne room by two silver-clad attendants, he felt positively weak at the knees.

The last time he had spoken to her in this room, she had unleashed a storm of fury upon him for abusing the secrets of the Celestial Realm, sentencing him to eternal bondage of obligation to the White City combined with compulsory earthing upon entering the city as a sign of just how displeased she was with him. There was no way of guessing what she might do to him this time.

The Star Queen sat on a high throne at the far end of the hall. Her gown was a peculiar shade of quantum blue, its long skirts cascading down the throne stairs in a way that would have made anyone looking at the folds long enough lose his mind. On her head, there was a crown of stars.

"Leo," she thundered.

Leo's knees nearly gave way. "Your Highness."

"I have summoned you here today to express my gratitude for the excellent work you have done at the White City. It is my understanding that you have successfully prevented a great catastrophe."

"Oh." Leo relaxed a bit. This didn't sound as bad as he had feared. "Thank you, Your Highness."

"This is all the more admirable when taken in the context of the severe limitations imposed on you by your sentence." She paused. Leo tensed once again.

"I do realize," she continued, "that the sentence has been a harsh one, but I will not suffer having my secrets wasted on the unworthy."

"That is understandable, Your Highness."

"But your recent conduct has shown me that you have outgrown the immaturity that led you to cause misdeeds in the city on your first visit and that you are now willing to take responsibility for your actions."

Leo nodded, thinking that silence was the best policy in this case, especially since he was not really sure what the Star Queen was trying to say. The pressure was starting to make him feel light-headed, and he could barely concentrate on hearing her words, let alone comprehending them.

"This is why I have decided to revoke your sentence."

Leo's heart skipped a beat.

"You are no longer bound to the White City."

"YESSS!" Leo did an enthusiastic fist pump. Then he remembered where he was and promptly put his hands behind his back.

He cleared his throat. "Thank you, Your Highness."

"I trust you will never do anything of that order of foolishness again."

"No, Your Highness." Leo was grinning from ear to ear; he couldn't help it.

The Star Queen waited for a few moments for Leo to compose himself. Leo couldn't do it though. His whole being was buzzing with joy. The best he could do was make his euphoria look like mere giddiness.

"You really did have a tough time down there," she said.

"It was…challenging," said Leo, "but I am always happy to help."

"I'm glad to hear it." The Star Queen smiled. Leo smiled back. "Because right now," she added, "I need you to go and fight me some barnacles."

Leo's face fell. "Fine."

ABOUT THE AUTHOR

Sonya Kudei is a displaced Renaissance person, an informal student of various branches of knowledge that are of absolutely no practical use in the modern world, and an admirer of all things fifteenth century (except maybe the Black Death). She lived in London for over twelve years, where she spent most of her time on commuter trains shuttling from workplace to workplace and now lives in Zagreb, Croatia. *The City Beneath the Hidden Stars* is her debut novel.